UNNATURAL SECRETS

Marvin made a sweeping gesture toward the fenced, vacant area around the lake to the east and then to the north along the shoreline. "The Grahams have bought it all," he said in disgust. "It's almost like they want to get rid of everybody else so they can keep whatever they're doing out here a secret."

"And just what kind of secrets do people keep around a dairy?" Alec asked skeptically.

"I think they've got more than just a dairy going on over there. There're trucks and vans going in and out at all hours, and there're always strange noises coming from the place—especially at night. Strange animal noises that come drifting across the lake when the sky's clear and the air's still . . .

". . . and there were even a couple of times when I thought I heard a baby crying. And I know for sure there aren't any babies over there. Something strange is going on, and it don't have nothing to do with no dairy . . ."

PROJECT GOD

V. M. THOMPSON

ZEBRA BOOKS
KENSINGTON PUBLISHING CORP.

ZEBRA BOOKS

are published by

Kensington Publishing Corp.
475 Park Avenue South
New York, NY 10016

First printing: April, 1989

Printed in the United States of America

*To Martha J. Keller
for believing in me and
urging me to follow my dream.*

Prologue

Paula Matheson closed the gate quietly and turned away; she didn't pause to look back toward the playground. Head lowered, eyes fixed on the flagstone ahead, she walked quickly along the path leading to the parking lot. Not until she stepped down from the curb and turned toward her car did she venture a glance back at the chain-link fence.

Her vision was blurred by tears she could no longer restrain, and for an instant, all she could distinguish was the vague outline of a white-clad nurse standing just beyond the fence. Blinking repeatedly, attempting to focus on her surroundings, Paula shifted her gaze from the nurse to the little girl beside her, the little girl who sat strapped in a wheelchair.

Paula forced a smile and lifted her hand to wave good-bye, but she knew both actions were useless. The little girl, Jill, her seven-year-old daughter, had been born blind. But Jill's lack of sight had proven to be the least worrisome of the child's handicaps; she had also been born with cerebral palsy and epilepsy, and she was severely mentally retarded. Had Jill been able to see Paula, she would not have recognized her as her mother, and she wouldn't have understood the gesture of farewell.

Jill began to convulse violently, the nature of her affliction overriding the strong medication she received several times a

7

day. The nurse immediately began to follow the established procedure for grand mal seizures and called for assistance from a nearby attendant. Working together, they wheeled the child away from the fence and headed in the direction of the home's infirmary.

Paula closed her eyes tightly and bit at her lower lip in frustration and anger. Why did her only child have to suffer such a cruel fate? Why? Why!

Tears streamed down Paula's cheeks. Out of a nervous habit, she began to rub the three small moles on the webbing of her right hand—three small moles that, had they been connected, would have formed a perfect triangle.

Tulsa, Oklahoma

"I believe you'll find everything in here that will finalize the agreement between your company and my clients," Jason Giddons said as he handed a large envelope to the young woman who stood just inside the door to his office.

"I'm sure I'll find everything in order." She glanced inside the envelope, ignoring the biographical-information forms describing the applicants, and the signed adoption papers. Neither was of importance to her; both would be destroyed once the transaction was completed. Her attention was directed to the balance of payment enclosed: $35,000 cash. "Everything appears to be in compliance with our agreement."

"When may we have our baby?" Clarissa Wiseman asked anxiously.

The woman looked across the lawyer's office at the middle-aged couple seated on a sofa in front of a wall full of books. Both were well-dressed, attractive and educated, successful in their chosen fields, but like all of the applicants she had dealt with in the past, they were unable to have children of their own. And like all of the applicants she had dealt with in the past, they were unwilling to have their names placed at the bottom of some adoption agency's

8

waiting list and then still not be assured of receiving a healthy, white infant within a reasonable length of time. They weren't willing to wait, but they were willing to pay. Fifty thousand dollars was the current rate for a healthy white infant, but no one who wanted a baby ever complained about the cost.

"Do you have a name selected for your son?" the woman countered with her own question.

"You were able to find us a boy?" Kevin Wiseman asked, excitement evident in his words.

"I believe you requested a blond, blue-eyed boy," she stated matter-of-factly.

"Yes, we did. But we didn't know if you could—"

"What name have you selected for your son?" she asked again, interrupting him.

"Nick," Kevin answered immediately, smiling at his wife and then taking her hand in his own. "Nicholas Sean," he confirmed, looking back at the woman.

Nodding with a smile, she walked to the door behind her and opened it. There, standing in the doorway to Jason Giddons's secretary's office, was another young woman. She was cradling a blue-blanketed bundle close to her chest.

"Nicholas Sean," the first woman said as she stepped aside.

"Mr. and Mrs. Wiseman," the second woman said with a smile as she walked across the room toward them, "I would like to introduce you to your son, Nicholas Sean." She carefully transferred the baby into Clarissa's outstretched arms, then turned and walked back into the secretary's office.

"Mr. Giddons," the first woman said, touching his arm lightly, "why don't we leave them alone so they can become acquainted."

Giddons followed the woman into his secretary's office and closed the door behind them. He expected her to stop to talk with him, but she continued on across the small office toward the door leading into the hall. Only after she had opened the door and the other woman had exited ahead of

9

her did she turn back toward him.

"If your other clients want the baby they requested, the down payment must be paid by this Friday," she stated firmly.

"They're having a little trouble coming up with that much cash all at once."

"If they can't come up with fifteen thousand now, how do they expect to pay the balance on delivery?"

"A little more time, perhaps. They want a baby quite badly, and they would make excellent parents. They're kind, loving peo—"

"Mr. Giddons, our business operates on a cash basis, not on emotional goodwill. If your clients cannot make the down payment by Friday, I'm sure it will be quite easy to find another couple who would want their baby." She turned abruptly and walked out into the hall.

Hartford, Connecticut

Jay Donoho stood at the hospital window, staring out over the city, but he saw nothing beyond the windowpane. He was no longer able to recognize the scent of the cut flowers sitting on the sill beside him, nor was he able to hear any of the sounds in the room behind him; he'd even succeeded in blocking out the pitiful cries of his sobbing wife.

He was in a state of emotional shock. He'd been in that condition for over an hour, since seeing his newborn son for the first time. Jay and Cherie Donoho had brought a second grotesquely deformed infant into the world.

"Jay," Cherie said as she inhaled between sobs. He didn't hear her, or if he did, he pretended not to. "Jay," she repeated a little louder, trying to control the break in her voice, "what are we going to do?" Still, he didn't respond. "Jay?"

"I don't know," he finally said, turning toward her— turning on her. "Why didn't you have the tests for this one?"

"You know it wouldn't have made any difference. I'd

never have consented to an abortion even if I'd known he wasn't going to be normal. I may have strayed a few times from the straight and narrow, but I'd never go against my religion to do that."

"Then it's *your* fault we have a . . . a monster for a son," he stated flatly, turning away from her. "Two monsters for sons," he mumbled beneath his breath. Jay stared out the window unseeingly, continuing to speak in his own self-defense. "Nothing like this has ever happened on *my* side of the family."

"Or mine either," Cherie countered in her own defense.

"You don't know that!" Jay shouted, turning back to face her. "You were adopted . . ." His anger melted when he looked into her eyes and saw how deeply his words had hurt her. "Oh, God, Cherie, I'm sorry." He sat down on the bed beside her, took her right hand in his and kissed the back of it. "I didn't mean it; it's not your fault any more than it's mine. Forgive me for what I just said."

"I know you didn't mean it. We're both upset now, and we're both saying things we don't mean." She squeezed his hand lovingly before continuing. "What are we going to do?"

"I don't know. It's costing us every spare cent we can squeeze out of the budget now to keep Danny in that home." As Jay aired his concerns, his thumb unconsciously circled the three small moles on the webbing between Cherie's thumb and forefinger—three small moles that, had they been connected, would have formed a perfect triangle. "I don't know where we can squeeze out any more to have someone care for this one."

"Maybe I can find another job."

"You're already working full time the way it is."

"You have two jobs, why can't I?"

"I wish you didn't have to work at all."

"I wish neither one of us had to work as hard as we do, but until we hit the lottery," she added with a forced laugh, "we're going to have to." Cherie was silent for a moment. "Normal or not, I want our sons to have as happy lives as they can for as long as they can, and I won't mind working a little harder to give it to them. After all, they're gifts from

11

God, even if they were damaged a little bit during their transportation from Heaven."

Tacoma, Washington

"Brad, look out!" Toni Stevenson said with an exaggerated note of warning in her voice.

Brad, too, had seen the dogs romping along the side of the road, and he responded quickly when one bounded onto the edge of the pavement several yards ahead of them. Reacting instinctively, he turned the steering wheel to the left. The car swerved in a wide arc, just missing the 75-pound canine that would have left a sizable dent in the Porsche's fender had they collided. Once the dogs were behind them, Brad eased the car back into the right lane of the four-lane highway.

"That was close."

"Close, but not as close as it looked," he said, glancing at his wife. "Don't tell me you're going to be one of those mothers who overreact to everything," he prodded with a chuckle.

"I just don't want anything to happen to Jessica."

"I don't want anything to happen to her either, but you've got to understand that she's going to have her share of bumps and bruises along the way."

"Not if I can help it." Toni looked down at the sleeping infant on her lap, the infant she had first held in her arms less than two hours before. Carefully, she shifted the edge of the pink blanket away from the baby's face. Toni smiled, happy at last to be a mother.

"Adopted or not, Jessica deserves no more protection during childhood than any other kid. She'll need to experience those bumps and bruises to prepare her for adult life, and she needs to know what it means to fall down and then pick herself up again. We both grew up under that philosophy, and I think we turned out to be pretty damn good people."

"You sound gruff now, but I'll lay odds your tough-skinned philosophy will melt in an instant when she comes

12

crying to you because she fell down and scraped her knee."

Brad looked at Toni out of the corner of his eye and couldn't control the grin that crept slowly across his face. "I know you're right," he finally conceded. "I'll probably become an old softy where she's concerned, but I just don't want a spoiled, prissy-sissy kid for a daughter."

"Spoiled she may be, but I don't think she'll ever be a *prissy-sissy*. You won't let her be. You'll probably have her out riding the horses before she can even walk," she added with a laugh. Toni was silent for several moments as she continued to gaze thoughtfully at her new daughter. "Do you think we did the right thing?" she finally ventured to ask.

"About what?"

"About paying fifty thousand dollars for her."

"We can afford it."

"It's not the money, but what if she asks us someday about where she came from? We can't just tell her we bought her like she was a high-priced sale item."

"Why would we ever have to tell her she's adopted?"

"We've already talked about that and agreed it was the right thing to do."

"True, but we don't have to worry about that this very instant. Right now we need to be thinking about how well she's going to adjust to her new home, and how well *we're* going to adjust to having a new baby in the house after all of those years of peace and quiet."

Jacksonville, Florida

Monica Barrett paused at the entrance to the women's lounge to look out across the bus terminal. Activity was heavy; people were hurrying from one desk to another, desperately seeking transportation to all parts of the country. Clerks were showing the stress of a harrowing day, biting their tongues to keep from spouting harsh replies, hoping they could make it to the end of their shift without telling someone to go to hell. Not since the last pilot's strike, when the airport had been closed, had the bus terminal seen

13

so much activity and rudeness on the part of the customers.

With furtive glances, Monica constantly searched the crowd in the terminal. She knew no one was following her, but her feelings of guilt and fear of discovery prompted her to check her surroundings for anyone who might be watching her or even casually glancing in her direction. What would she do if she saw someone she knew?

Not wanting to take the chance of being recognized and then questioned about her presence in the terminal, Monica clutched the basket she carried close to her side as she pushed open the door to the women's lounge. When she entered, the two women standing at the mirrors at the opposite end of the room glanced in her direction. She averted her eyes from their reflected stares and continued on toward the door marked Rest Room. Once inside the long narrow room, she checked the stalls, found only two occupied near the door and continued on toward the last stall snuggled into a niche in the far wall.

Monica closed the door behind her and locked it, sat down on the stool and placed the basket on the floor at her feet. Hesitantly, she removed the towel she had draped over the basket to hide its contents and glanced down at her infant son. During the instant she forced herself to look at his grotesquely deformed face, she found that he was still sleeping. The whiskey she'd put in his milk less than an hour before had worked faster than she'd expected.

Tears clouded her eyes as she slipped her hand down the side of the basket to grasp a utility knife and green garbage bag she had placed in the bottom. "He'll be sorry he deserted us," she whispered bitterly as she laid the knife on the floor beside her feet and began opening the garbage bag. "He'll have to live with this for the rest of his life."

Monica lifted her son from the basket and gently slid him inside the garbage bag. She laid him on her lap while she squeezed the bag tightly around his small body to force out any extra air. When she thought the bag was as devoid of air as she could make it, she twisted the top closed and secured it with a wire tie.

"It won't take long," she whispered, cuddling the bundle

14

close to her and rocking it slowly back and forth. "It won't take long." She felt movement inside the bag and clutched it tighter against her chest. "Don't fight it, little one, let it come easily. Soon you'll be the pretty baby you were supposed to be, and no one will ever stare at you again."

Monica lost track of time as she continued to rock her son. When she finally realized there was no movement coming from inside the bag, and that there had been no movement for a long time, she laid him back in the basket and again covered him with the towel.

"I'm coming to be with you, my pretty baby. Momma's coming to be with you."

Monica picked up the knife as she stood and turned to face the stool. Holding the handle firmly in her left hand, she drove the tip of the sharply honed blade deep into her right wrist and then pulled it up the inside of her forearm toward the bend of her elbow. She was successful in slicing through several of the small arteries supplying blood to her arm.

Bright crimson blood spurted like a miniature fountain with each beat of her heart, splattering the yellow-tiled wall above the stool and the metal partition beside her. The pain was intense—almost overpowering—but she forced her mind to focus beyond it to the eternal peace that lay ahead, and only a small gasp escaped her lips. Soon, all of her suffering would be over.

Monica nodded in approval of her accomplishment as she pulled the knife from her arm and watched a rivulet of bright red blood flow steadily from the deep gash. She lifted her arm slightly and held her palm upward, letting the blood pool in her hand before overflowing its bounds to ooze between her fingers. Then she turned her hand over, letting the blood drip almost artistically into the stool's standing water.

She felt light-headed; her legs began to wobble unsteadily beneath her. Monica knew she didn't have much time left to complete her task.

Transferring the knife to her right hand, she rammed its point into her left wrist, then pulled the blade up the inside of her forearm to the bend of her elbow. Again she succeeded in

15

opening the main arteries, and again, blood spurted with each beat of her heart.

Losing strength, she dropped the knife as she slumped down to her knees. Monica leaned against the stool for support and lifted her head slowly, trying to focus on the workings of the toilet directly in front of her. A weak smile came to her pale face as she reached to flush the toilet.

A rapid exchange of water rushed through the bowl in front of her. In her last act of consciousness, Monica plunged both of her bleeding arms into the swirling liquid. The force of the retreating water pulled the blood from her arteries and carried it down the pipe to the sewer line.

As the stool began to refill, the action of the incoming water washed away the blood from the three small moles on the webbing of her right hand between her thumb and forefinger—three small moles that, had they been connected, would have formed a perfect triangle.

One

"... and if you have a problem no one else seems to be able to solve, give me a call at 555-ALEC, and I'll see what I can do. This is Alec Crispen with WBDC. Have a good evening, Louisville." Alec continued to smile into the camera until the red light went off. Then, as he had done at the close of his troubleshooter news segment for the past three years, he pulled the jack for his microphone from the console, gathered his papers and returned them to their folder, slid his chair back noiselessly from the broadcasting desk and walked off the set.

"Glad you finally nailed those bastards," Hank Kelsey, the station's electronics expert, said in a loud whisper as Alec walked past him. "Wish you'd been around about ten years ago." Alec paused to listen to Hank, showing the same interest he presented to everyone who contacted him with a problem they had been unable to rectify through their own efforts. "Some fly-by-night contractor took my mom for close to fifteen thousand dollars. He said he'd build her a family room on the back of her house in less than two weeks, and he did, all right," he added, interjecting a sarcastic laugh, "but the damn roof caved in with the first big snow. She was just lucky she wasn't sitting in front of the fireplace when it happened, or it would've killed her."

"And I'll lay odds the company was long gone when you tried to find them," Alec responded confidently, speaking from the experience he'd gained through investigating several similar situations.

"Long gone and not even a cold trail to follow. We tried everything, state and local, without getting even an inch of satisfaction, and back then, none of the TV stations had anybody like you to turn to."

"Wish I could have been here to help her."

"Wish you would've been here, too. If anybody would've been able to set those son-of-a-bitches in their place, you would have."

"Thanks for your confidence." Alec placed his hand lightly on Hank's shoulder, then continued on toward the door at the back of the studio.

"Gonna miss you while you're away. Enjoy yourself."

"I plan on it." Alec stepped out into the hallway that gave access to all of the newscasters' offices and closed the studio door behind him. That was his last official act of the day; as of that moment, he was on vacation.

"Got your fishin' gear all polished and sorted?" someone asked as he approached the open double doors to the research department. Alec nodded his head, smiled and kept on walking.

"I know where there's a good sale on lures," someone else added.

"I've got a pair of hip boots you can borrow."

"By the sound of things, I think I need them more in here than I would up at the lake," Alec retorted good-naturedly. A sense of humor regularly dominated his personality when he wasn't at work being a hard-nosed investigative reporter.

Everyone at the station knew Alec wasn't too enthused by his wife's choice of vacation spots, and since he'd made the mistake of voicing his discontent several weeks earlier, no one at the station had let the subject die. The older members of the staff were the ones who hounded him the most. Almost all of them envied his position of being able to spend the next two weeks relaxing at an isolated lake fishing, but they were also the same people who questioned why he would be spending the next two weeks fishing when he didn't even enjoy fishing. They were from the old school; they had always made the decisions for their families' vacations without consulting the others involved. Even though Alec had explained, several times, that this summer would be the last opportunity they would have to spend time at his wife's grandparents' cabin before the property was sold, they still couldn't understand why he had consented to a vacation he wouldn't enjoy.

Sometimes, Alec couldn't understand it himself, but he knew exactly why he had done it. During the nine years he and Krista had been married, they had alternated selecting summer vacation sites. Twice before, he had talked her out of spending their vacation at the cabin where she had spent her summers as a child and teenager, and now, since the property was contracted to be sold in August, he felt guilty for depriving her of something she'd wanted to do and, after this summer, would never be able to do again.

Alec had tried to convince himself that if he put forth an honest effort, he would be able to withstand two weeks of fishing, but just in case he couldn't, he'd already invested in almost a dozen paperback novels to take with him. One way or another, he would relax and enjoy his vacation, and Krista would be happy.

"Remember the worm . . ."

Alec waved off any further comments and continued on toward his office. Even though he enjoyed bantering with his colleagues and delivering a few jabs of his own, he was anxious to put his office in some semblance of order and go home.

Stepping into his office, Alec followed a routine that had become an unconscious habit. He crossed the spacious room and stopped in front of the second of three filing cabinets sitting against the wall behind his desk. Opening the drawer identified as Closed Files—Success, he inserted the Matlock Landfill folder into its alphabetical location between the other folders and closed the drawer.

A smile of accomplishment came to his round face as he looked up at a framed document hanging on the wall above the middle filing cabinet: *Rienhart Investigative Journalism Award*. The regional citation of excellence would have been a prestigious honor for anyone, but it was especially meaningful to Alec. At age thirty-one, he was the youngest journalist in the five-state area ever to have received the award. He felt privileged that his fellow newscasters, veterans from Ohio, Indiana, Illinois, Tennessee and Kentucky, had nominated him in the first place and had then voted that he be last year's recipient. During the short time he had been with WBDC, he'd been able to establish himself as a reliable investigative reporter who wasn't afraid to tackle any challenge, no matter how large or small. That, too, was an aspect of Alec Crispen that impressed his colleagues; he put forth as much effort to help a child find her missing cat as he did to uncover the illegal storage of toxic chemicals at the Matlock Landfill.

"Stop patting yourself on the back," Alec chided himself with an easy laugh, turning away from the filing cabinets and slipping off his suit coat. He hung the coat over the back of his chair, then walked toward the small bathroom adjacent to his office.

After removing his tie and loosening his collar, he reached for a jar of cold cream sitting on the shelf beneath the mirror and began applying a light layer to his face and throat to loosen the makeup he had to wear whenever he was on camera. Most of the other television personalities were fortunate; they only needed spot makeup to camouflage facial imperfections or a light dusting of powder to keep their foreheads and noses from shining beneath the lights, but Alec required a full application of makeup from just below his eyes to the base of his throat. His beard was dark and heavy, extending over his cheeks almost to the sides of his nose, and even though he shaved immediately before each broadcast, the camera would still pick up an unsightly, distracting dark shadow if he failed to wear makeup. The whole process was an annoyance to Alec, but for him to succeed in his chosen career, he knew he had to make people watching his broadcast feel comfortable with his appearance.

When he'd removed all the cold cream and makeup, Alec lathered his face and neck with soap and began rinsing it off. Above the muffling sound of running water, he thought he heard someone calling to him from his office.

"Just a minute," he answered, splashing his face a few more times before reaching for a towel.

"And here we are behind the scenes with the vigilante of the evening news," a voice said.

Alec jerked his head around. When he saw who was standing in the doorway, a smile spread across his face. "Brice! This is an unexpected surprise." Alec exchanged a warm hug with his younger brother, then stepped back to arm's length for a quick survey.

At six feet four inches, Brice was a good six inches taller than Alec. Brice's hair was blond, his eyes blue, in direct contrast with Alec's brown and brown. Both carried muscular, athletic builds, but that was the only aspect of their physical characteristics that might have linked them as being related, which, genetically, they were not. Alec had been adopted. When the pressure to conceive had finally been lifted from his parents, the unexpected happened; thirteen months later, Brice had been born.

"I didn't expect to see you until Thanksgiving," Alec said, ushering Brice back into his office. "What brings you to Louisville?"

"A very quick layover," Brice answered, glancing at his watch. "I knew I would have about two hours to spend here before I had to catch a plane to Atlanta, and I thought I'd bring you something that might be of interest." He walked to Alec's desk and laid his hand on the brown, tattered, water-spotted, partially burnt cardboard box he'd placed there a few minutes earlier. "When you were working up in Rickdon, do you remember hearing anything about a man by the name of Edgar Schmidt?"

Alec thought back to the two years he'd spent on his first job in Rickdon, Illinois. His recollection was cloudy as to any immediate details of the assignments he'd worked on while there, but the name Edgar Schmidt did sound familiar. He'd heard it somewhere, and Alec never forgot anything he heard.

Alec had an audiographic memory. He couldn't always remember everything he read or saw, but he never forgot anything he heard unless he worked to forget it.

"Are you going to give me any hints as to why I might have heard about him?" Alec asked, not wanting to take the time to search his memory for something he might have heard

21

over seven or eight years before.

"I don't have any hints," Brice answered, "but Jerry Wade sure had some interesting stories about the guy."

"Who's Jerry Wade?"

"He's the area foreman on the project I'm heading up near Lashbrook. He grew up just outside of town, and I guess when he was a kid, he and his buddies used to sneak around Schmidt's house like we used to sneak around the 'house of blue lights' when we were kids back in Rapid City."

"Another ghost house," Alec commented with a chuckle. "Every town has one: some old house that gets overgrown with weeds, and then some kid with an overactive imagination starts making up horror stories about it to impress his friends."

"Jerry's stories impressed me, and I'm not a kid anymore," Brice persisted. "According to him, Schmidt actually did some experiments there."

"Possibly, but evidently nothing ever came of them or we'd both recognize the man's name."

"Or maybe his experiments were too much of a secret to be publicized," Brice said slyly, knowing his next sentence would definitely grab his brother's attention. "Maybe nobody but the inside wheels of the government knew about them."

"The government?" Alec arched an eyebrow, a definite sign that his interest had been sparked. "How was Schmidt connected with the government?"

"I don't know, Jerry just mentioned it."

"I see. This Jerry guy again," Alec said skeptically. "Sounds to me like he just threw in the government to keep you interested in his stories. And it worked," he added with a laugh. "You were always so gullible. That's one reason we liked to take you along with us to the 'house of blue lights'; we could make you believe anything. And it sounds like you're *still* willing to believe anything."

"Maybe, maybe not. But Jerry's stories weren't the only things that made me think you might be interested in this." Brice's smile was almost secretive as he carefully removed the box's fragile, deteriorating lid, uncovering a collection of notebooks, journals, letters and photographs.

"What are those?" Alec asked with renewed interest.

"Don't know."

"Where did you get them?"

"We found them in an old safe hidden behind a bricked-up wall in Schmidt's basement." Alec raised his eyebrow again but didn't comment; he continued to look at Brice, waiting for an explanation. "Our company's building a shopping center/condo complex up by the Wisconsin border just north of Lashbrook. We're in the process of clearing and leveling the land right now, and Schmidt's old estate is right smack dab in the middle of it. When we got to tearing down the house and pulling out the foundation, we found a little room in the basement behind a sealed wall that contained a lot of old-fashioned science equipment and a safe."

"And you got nosy and blew the safe to see what was inside."

"We didn't have to; the door was open about an inch. It almost looked like he might have been in a hurry the last time he tried to close it and didn't get it shut."

Alec glanced at the box and then back at his brother. "I thought anything valuable you found during a demolition went back to the previous owner."

"It does unless they sign over salvage rights, which is what Schmidt's nephew did."

"Then I doubt if there's anything in that box of any value or the nephew wouldn't have signed away his rights."

"Unless he didn't think there was anything left in the house; he'd already picked the place clean before he signed the papers. I'll lay odds he didn't even know about the bricked-up room *or* the safe."

Alec walked around his desk, picked up a couple of the letters from the box and glanced at their addresses briefly. "They're probably just some old love letters Schmidt didn't have the heart to throw away."

"You sure don't sound like an award-winning investigative reporter to me. I thought you'd jump at the chance to find out what an old, half-crazed scientist had locked away behind a sealed wall."

"Why would you think I'd be interested in something like that?"

Brice hesitated and smiled slyly. "Because somebody else sure wanted to know what we found." Again, Alec looked at his brother without comment, waiting for an explanation. "Somebody ransacked my motel room the night after we found the safe."

"How do you know they were looking for these?" Alec asked, gesturing with the letters he still held in his hand.

"I don't know for sure, but I'd make a pretty good educated guess that that's what they were after. Jerry and I were walking back from a little restaurant about a half a block up from the motel when we saw a dark blue late-model sedan come barreling out of the motel's parking lot. I wouldn't have made anything out of it, but Jerry said he'd seen that same car around the construction site ever since we started working at tearing down the Schmidt house. He said he thought there was something fishy with them hanging around the way they did, and then when we got back to the motel, we found that both our rooms had been ransacked."

"So? If you're so sure they were after these documents, how come they didn't take them?"

"Luckily, they weren't in either of our rooms. I'd forgotten about them and had left them under the seat in one of the trucks we'd locked up and left at the site." Brice again paused, smiling slyly.

"And?" Alec prodded. "By the looks of that shit-eatin' grin on your face, I know there's got to be more."

"There is." Brice toyed with the box lid for several moments before continuing, knowing Alec liked quick answers and that his hesitation might further ignite the spark of interest Alec had already expressed. "When I got to the site the next morning, Earl and Matt, our two night watchmen, told me there had been a suspicious-looking dark blue late-model sedan driving slowly around the fence most of the night. They said it stopped once, and when they started walking toward it to see what they wanted, it drove away in a hurry."

Brice nonchalantly picked up an old black-and-white Polaroid photograph that was sticking out from beneath the edge of several more letters remaining in the box. "Cute kid," he said, halfheartedly trying to distinguish the faded features of the infant's picture. "It looks like it could be a brand new baby not more than a few hours old." Looking back at Alec, he asked the obvious question that his story had been leading up to. "Are you interested yet?"

"I'm getting there," Alec replied. "But I don't understand why you didn't tell all of this to the police. If somebody ransacked your room—"

"I can live with a ransacked room, and if all of this turns out to be nothing important, who cares. But if it turns out to be something exciting—something worth telling people about—I can always say I was a part of it." Brice handed Alec the photograph. "Cute kid," he repeated. "I wonder if it was Schmidt's?"

"Thanks to you, I guess I'll be finding out." Alec glanced at the photograph briefly, then turned it over. Something had been written on the back, but the ink was faded, and it took him several moments before he thought he had it figured out: PG Delta. 2F-7-12-58. Epsilon 8-13-A. He read it aloud.

"What's that?" Brice questioned.

"I'm not sure. It could be some sort of identification. Are there any other pictures?"

Brice removed a few more letters and some postcards from the box, uncovering five additional black-and-white photographs lying atop the notebooks and journals. He handed them to Alec, and by the time he'd joined his brother behind the desk, Alec had spread the pictures out across the blotter and turned them all facedown. "Have you found something?"

"Maybe," he said as he scanned the faded writing on the back of each photograph. "Wouldn't you think that someone taking pictures of their children would label them with their names and maybe their ages or the dates?"

"Sounds logical."

"But look," Alec directed, pointing to the writing on the photographs' backs. "They look like some kind of serial numbers."

Brice focused his attention on the numbers Alec was referring to and read:

PG Delta
1B-7-12-58
Beta 3-27-A

PG Delta
1F-7-12-58
Gamma 5-18-A

PG Delta
2F-7-12-58
Epsilon 8-13-A

PG Delta
3F-7-12-58
Zeta 11-52-A   .

PG Delta
2B-7-12-58
Eta 2-07-P

PG Delta
4F-7-12-58
Theta 4-11-P

"It looks Greek to me," Brice said, chuckling at his own joke.

"Greek?"

"Yep. The Beta, Gamma, Delta stuff is Greek, the beginning of the alphabet to be exact, but he left out the first letter. Alpha is missing."

"Why would—"

"If you're gonna hang around this place, I'll cancel your two weeks of vacation and give it to somebody else." Alec looked up to see David Trubest, WBDC's station manager, standing in the doorway to his office. "And if you think that's an idle threat, if you're still here in ten minutes when I come back, I'm gonna put you to work. Now get out of here." Trubest was gone as quickly as he'd appeared.

"What time is it?" Brice asked as he glanced at his wristwatch. "Shit! My plane takes off in about thirty minutes, and it's a good twenty-minute drive back to the airport. I've got to be going, or I'm gonna have more than just a short layover in this town." He continued to talk rapidly as he walked toward the door. "Give my love to Krista. I'll call you in a couple of weeks to see if you've found out anything about this Schmidt guy. Take care." Alec barely had time to say goodbye before his brother was gone.

Alec looked back at the photographs on his desk, and a tingling rippled through the pit of his stomach. His gut instinct was making its presence known—and his gut instinct was rarely wrong.

Could there be something important related to the mysteriously labeled pictures? Alec looked at the tattered brown box Brice had left behind. *Had* Schmidt been working on a secret government project? And if Schmidt had been working on a project, what was its connection to the pictured infants?

Knowing his investigative curiosity wouldn't allow him to leave behind something that had sparked his interest, Alec picked up his briefcase off the floor from beside the filing cabinets and set it on his desk. He transferred its contents to one of the desk's drawers, then set the old cardboard box inside. He then gathered the letters and photographs into a neat stack and placed them on top of the notebooks and journals. As he started to replace the box's lid, he glanced at the writing on the topmost photo: *2B-7-12-58.*

The numbers hadn't made an impression on him before, but now they looked strikingly familiar. 7-12-58. July 12, 1958. *That* was Alec's birthday.

"You're grabbing at straws, Crispen," Alec reprimanded himself. "You're tired, and you're trying to find things that aren't really there."

Alec closed the briefcase and picked it up with his left hand. He took his suit coat off the back of his chair, slung it across his right shoulder and began walking toward the door of his office. As he flipped off the light with his right hand, he caught a glimpse of his birthmark: three small moles on the webbing between his thumb and forefinger—three small moles that, had they been connected, would have formed a perfect triangle.

Two

Alec peered in through the back door's window as he slipped his key into the lock. He saw no shadows or movement to indicate anyone was waiting for him, hiding in preparation for a surprise attack. All he could see was the blue and beige striped sofa sitting in the family room in front of the fireplace. He couldn't see anyone, but that didn't mean no one was there. She could be hiding, waiting in ambush, just beyond the sightline of the utility room's café doors.

He turned the key slowly. The mechanism rotated easily, releasing the tumblers, and the entire knob turned in his hand. Quietly, he pushed the door open and stepped into the utility room. So far, everything was going well. So far, he was still ahead of the game.

As Alec turned to quietly shut the door behind him, his briefcase swung out away from his side and hit the front of the washing machine. The sound that echoed from the utility room was like that of a gong struck by a large padded hammer.

Alec cursed silently under his breath, hung his head and released a disappointed sigh. For the third time that week, he'd been unable to enter the house undetected.

He closed the door behind him, no longer attempting to keep his entrance a secret. It didn't matter now if he made any noise or not. The game was over, and he had lost.

Alec started toward the family room, but before he had taken even a half-dozen steps, he heard the clicking of claws against the kitchen's tiled floor. "Who is it?" he asked in a low voice. His words were immediately answered by a series of deep barks. "There's my good girl," he said, smiling broadly. Alec laid his briefcase and suit coat on the carpeted woodbox beside the fireplace and sat down on the hearth to accept Thumper's exuberant greeting.

The black-and-white dog was a mixed breed he'd rescued almost three years ago; Alec called her his authentic Pound Puppy, even though she hadn't been fortunate enough to have come from a reputable animal shelter. "Have you been a good girl today?" he asked as he scratched behind the dog's long ears. Thumper barked in response to his words, and immediately, her tail began to wag, thumping against the sofa with a rapid, muffled beat. "Where's Mom?" he asked, after bending over to accept a wet kiss on his cheek and a sniff to his ear, which was Thumper's routine greeting.

"Welcome home, Alec," a high-pitched, cartoonlike voice said. "We've been waiting for you." Alec looked toward the counter separating the kitchen from the family room and saw one of Krista's handmade, furry stuffed animals waving a stubby paw at him.

"Thanks . . . uh, what's your name?" Alec asked as he walked across the room and leaned against the counter, pretending to carry on an intelligent conversation with the plush toy.

"Grumpy George," the cartoon voice answered in a much deeper tone. "Me and my buddies are gonna be famous."

"Is that so, Grumpy George?"

"Yes it is," Krista said in an excited but near-normal voice as she stood up from behind the counter. "Grumpy George, Pouting Priscilla, Frowning Freddie, Gloomy Gertie . . . my whole line of Crabby Critters is going to be famous!"

"How's that?"

"You'll never believe what happened today."

"Well, why don't you come down here and tell me all about it." Alec took hold of Krista's free hand, guided her around the end of the counter and led her to the sofa. "Sit right down here beside me and tell me about whatever it is that's gotten you all excited."

Not wanting to be left out, Thumper jumped up on the sofa between them and proceeded to give each a sloppy kiss. Both Alec and Krista laughed as they accepted the affection Thumper had been storing up throughout the day, and they returned it with several loving strokes along her sleek back.

Most of their friends couldn't understand their attachment to Thumper; after all, she was *just* a dog, and several were appalled by the fact that they let her up on the furniture and allowed her to sleep in their bed with them. But their friends who commented the most had other outlets for their own affection; most of their friends had children.

Alec and Krista had no children with which to share their love. For the time being, Thumper was their only child.

After their exchange of pats, strokes and kisses was completed, Alec shifted Thumper to his opposite side. He then looked at Krista, waiting for her to continue with the explanation behind her excitement.

"Do you remember me telling you about a representative from the Joy Toy toy company who stopped by the shop a couple of months ago?"

"Vaguely. Hadn't you sent them some pictures of your Crabby Critters?"

"Exactly. Well, when she was here a couple of months ago, she seemed rather standoffish, 'browsing through various small businesses, looking for new ideas to put on the market,' as she put it. I didn't really think she was too impressed with my work, but evidently she was. I got a phone call at the shop today from Erica Lavin, one of the vice presidents at Joy Toy in charge of stuffed animals. She said the company was interested in my line of Crabby Critters. They want to buy the rights to use the patterns for all my stuffed toys and sell them all over the world!"

Alec picked up Grumpy George from Krista's lap and looked at the stuffed animal's surly felt face. "So you're gonna be famous, uh? Guess you're not going to turn out too bad after all for being such an ugly-looking cuss. Congratulations, George ol' boy." Alec shook George's stuffed paw in a mock gesture then slipped his arm around Krista, pulling her closer to him. "And congratulations to you, too,

Mom." He hugged her close and kissed her on the temple.

Seeing their embrace, Thumper lifted her head, whined and then barked. Were they about to start the protection game she loved to play? Were they about to start wrestling playfully so she could come to Krista's defense and gently bite Alec on the arm to pull him away?

Thumper stood and barked again, her tail thumping vigorously against the sofa's back. After a long day of being by herself, she was ready to play.

"It's not playtime, you silly dog," Alec said with a laugh, reaching to rub beneath her chin. "This is people talk now. We'll play later." Seeming to understand, Thumper jumped down from the sofa and lay down beside Alec's feet.

"When is all of this going to take place?" Alec asked as he returned his attention to Krista.

"They're wanting the line to go into production as soon as possible so they can start an advertising campaign for the Christmas season. Just think," she said whimsically, taking Grumpy George from Alec and holding him up in front of her so the television's blank screen could serve as a backdrop. "In a few months, you won't be the only Crispen on television. In a few months, the whole Crabby Critter Crispen clan will be seen from coast to coast." She hugged Grumpy George close to her heart. "I can hardly wait until Wednesday."

"What's going to happen Wednesday?"

"I have to fly out to New York to sign the contracts."

"Wednesday? We're supposed to be up at the lake Wednesday."

"It won't interfere with our vacation that much; in fact, it'll add something a little special. We can drive up to the cabin tomorrow just like we planned and spend a couple of days fishing. Then we can take a plane out of Madison on Tuesday evening and spend a romantic night in New York. I can sign the contracts Wednesday afternoon, and we can fly back Wednesday night. And if you don't think that'll fit into our budget, I'll borrow some money from our savings account and pay it back when I get my advance check." It was quite obvious that Krista had already thought every-

31

thing through—almost everything.

"The money's not what's bothering me."

"What then?"

Alec pointed down toward the floor in front of the sofa. A pair of dark brown eyes looked up at him. The instant Thumper thought she was the object of their attention, her tail began to wag, striking the leg of the coffee table with repeated thumps. "Who's gonna look after Thumper while we're on our two-day junket to New York?"

"I guess in all the excitement, I forgot we were taking her with us." Krista slumped back in the sofa, hugging Grumpy George close to her chest. She was silent for several moments, deep in thought. "Maybe Marvin would watch her for us while we're gone," she finally suggested.

"I wouldn't feel right about leaving her with somebody she doesn't know and who doesn't know her. I've felt bad enough the few times we've left her with Sarah."

"But Sarah knows her and loves her almost as much as we do, and she fits right in with their two dogs."

"But Sarah's not gonna be up at the cabin to look after her."

"We . . . we could always board her," Krista said hesitantly, and then she added quickly, "We won't be gone that long." She focused on Alec, knowing what his reaction to her suggestion was going to be, and she knew she could almost quote him verbatim even before he opened his mouth to speak.

"I'm not putting Thumper back in a cage, not even for a couple of days," he said with unreproachable conviction. "I took her away from that kind of life, and I don't want her to think she's going back to it."

"She was just a puppy then; she doesn't even remember it."

"I'm not going to give her a chance to remember."

Alec leaned forward on the sofa to stroke Thumper's sleek head. When he touched her, her tail immediately began to beat out a steady rhythm against the carpet. As he looked down into her trusting dark brown eyes, the events leading up to her joining their family returned vividly to his mind.

One of his first investigative assignments in Louisville had been to follow up on a barrage of phone calls from people living on the lower west side of town. He talked with each of the callers personally, enduring tears shed by eighty-year-old widows as well as by eight-year-old children; all of their pets had suddenly disappeared.

None of the callers could give any clues as to what might have happened to their dogs and cats; they had searched their neighborhood, checked with both the Humane Society and the police, but none of their pets had been found. Alec rechecked the Humane Society and police, confirming all inquiries and negative responses; then he asked for their assistance in looking for the animals. The Humane Society was too understaffed to help search, and the police had more important human-related matters to tend to, but both departments told him that if he discovered anything where their official services were needed, not to hesitate to call.

Enthusiastic in his new job and wanting to prove himself to his peers, Alec staked out the streets of the lower west side of Louisville for several long evenings and sometimes stayed to well into the morning. Nothing came to him. Days passed, weeks passed, two months slipped from the calendar, and then, early one Saturday morning, he received a call at the station from a little girl living on the lower east side who said her cat had mysteriously disappeared and asked if he could help her find it. By the end of the day, he'd received eight similar phone calls from people living in the area, and Alec had a hunch that whatever had caused the animals to disappear from the west side of town was now preying on the east side.

Relocating his stakeout to the residential area of the latest callers, Alec drove through the streets for three unsuccessful evenings. On the fourth night, something suspicious attracted his attention: he saw a man carrying the limp body of a dog.

Leaving his car, Alec followed the man into an alley and hid behind a dumpster, watching while the man placed the dog in the back of a panel van. Then another man appeared . . . and another, each carrying sedated animals they too placed in the back of the van. Then Alec overheard

33

them talking about delivering their night's catch. After the three men got into the van, he returned to his car and followed them across town to an old warehouse in the center of an abandoned industrial complex.

Alec parked his car in the shadows around the corner from the warehouse, stealthily worked his way across the vacant parking lot and climbed onto a stack of old crates so he could look in one of the windows. What he'd seen had repulsed him. At least fifty caged animals, in various stages of consciousness, were crowded together on the far side of the building, and the animals being unloaded from the van were adding to the number.

Knowing something was amiss, Alec ran to the closest phone booth and called the police. In less than fifteen minutes, three squad cars and the van from the Humane Society arrived. Alec's persistence in finding the missing animals had led to uncovering a ring of kidnappers who had been selling the family pets to black-market companies for uncontrolled experiments. It had also led him to Thumper.

After the police took the men away and while members of the Humane Society worked to revive the sedated animals and transfer them to the shelter, Alec walked around the warehouse, looking at the caged, poorly treated animals. The stench was overpowering. Animals that had been hidden in the warehouse for several days lay semiconscious in their own waste. Their coats, once shiny and silky, were dull and matted; oozing sores had begun to rupture through their once healthy skins. Some were suffering from malnutrition; all were dehydrated. A few had died a slow, unmerciful death.

Man's inhumanity to man had always affected Alec, but now, as he looked at the results of man's inhumanity to helpless animals, a hatred for the culprits tore deep into the core of his soul. The hard shell he had developed as a child—and had always lived behind—was broken. Firsthand, he learned the true meaning of compassion.

Unable to contain the tears misting his eyes, he turned away quickly from the heart of the warehouse and walked hurriedly toward the door. Just as he was about to step out

34

into the fresh air, he heard a weak whimper. Alec glanced down at the cage sitting on the floor beside the door and saw a black-and-white dog lying motionless, her eyes glazed in death. Beside her lay five puppies—all but one as motionless as she.

Alec knelt down beside the cage and spoke softly to her only surviving offspring. The puppy looked up at him with matted, watery brown eyes. It stretched its nose in his direction and tried to stand, but it was too weak. The only response the puppy had strength enough to make was a few wags of its tail. Pitifully, its tail struck with a muffled thump against a dead littermate's side.

Alec had never had an opportunity to grow fond of an animal; he'd never had a pet of his own and often wondered what bonded people so closely to their pets, but now he felt as if he knew. It was a simple thing called love. Gently, he'd removed the puppy from the cage, slipped it inside his shirt and taken it home with him. . . .

"Alec," Krista said softly, laying a hand on his shoulder. Alec broke from his haunted memory and looked at her. His eyes were glistening with a light mist of tears he didn't attempt to hide. Immediately, Krista knew what he'd been thinking about.

"That's just one of the many reasons I love you so much," she said, lifting a finger to trap a single tear that was creeping down his cheek.

"What's that?"

"You're never afraid or ashamed to let people know how you feel." Krista slipped her arms around his neck and hugged him. She held him close to her for several moments, trying to contain her own tears of love and compassion, then released him and settled back against the sofa. After exhaling a long breath, she said, "I've decided I don't want you to go to New York with me after all."

"You're not going by yourself."

"I don't intend to." Krista rose from the sofa and started toward the phone hanging on the wall at the far end of the counter. "The way Sarah was acting today, I bet she'd jump at the chance to go with me. Gordon's going to be home next week, so he can look after their dogs, and you and Thumper can have a few days by yourself at the cabin." She lifted the receiver from its cradle but glanced back at Alec before dialing. "Does that sound all right with you?"

"That sounds fine with me. In fact, I think it's only fitting that Sarah go with you instead of me. Business partners should be together to celebrate their first major success."

"You're sure you don't care?"

"Go on and call her. I'm sure Thumper and I can find plenty of things to keep us occupied while you're gone. Who knows," he added with a laugh as he slid down on the floor beside Thumper and began teasing her with a well-used pull toy, "we might find all sorts of trouble to get ourselves into while you're away."

Three

Heavy fog . . . swirling . . . swirling.
Soft music . . . soothing music.
A strange odor rising to saturate the air.
Sounds . . . muffled sounds.
  A screech . . .
    a laugh . . .
      a cry . . .
        a wail . . .
Dim light . . . fading light.
A hair-covered hand reaching for him . . .
  reaching . . .
    touching . . .
     caressing . . .
      holding him . . . rocking him.
A voice: "Get away! Don't touch him!
    Get out of here!"
Run . . . run . . . run!
Bounce . . . tumble . . . fall . . .
  fall . . .
    fall . . .
     crying . . .
A voice: "Is he all right?"
Crying . . . crying . . .
  crying . . .
    crying . . .
      cr—

Alec's eyes shot open. His heart pounded savagely in his ears. His breaths came short and quick, his muscles twitched spastically. Fear-induced perspiration seeped from his pores, covering his body with a layer of moisture.

He lay motionless, his eyes darting around the room, pausing momentarily to focus on objects that were familiar to him. Alec finally released an extended breath of relief. He was safe. He was in his own bed in his own home.

After over three years, why had that horrid dream come back to him? He stared up at the swirls in the ceiling over his bed that were highlighted by the dim nightlight on the far wall. His eyes focused on the swirls, but in his mind, he was trying to rationalize the dream's recurrence.

He knew he wasn't worried about anything, he wasn't under any pressure, he wasn't overjoyed for any reason, and he definitely wasn't adjusting to the changes his body had had to accept during puberty. The psychiatrist his parents had taken him to see when he was twelve years old had stated that any of those possibilities could cause recurring nightmares. Looking back over his life, Alec could readily accept that explanation. Every time the dream had occurred, its presence had been easily justified: when he'd been changing from a boy into a man, when he'd asked a girl for his first date, when he'd played in the football game for the state high school championship, when he'd graduated from high school and college, when he'd asked Krista to marry him, when he'd accepted jobs in Rickdon, Grand Island, Nebraska, and finally in Louisville. Every time the dream had invaded his sleep, he'd been able to rationalize its presence—every time except now.

Alec felt the water bed move. He lifted his head and glanced toward his feet. Thumper must have sensed that he was awake, because she was in the process of working her way toward the head of the bed in an army-type crawl.

When her nose touched his hand, he slipped it over her head and began to pet her. Immediately, Thumper's tail began to wag, producing a ripple of tiny waves with each rhythmic beat.

"Do you need to go out?" he asked in a whisper. Thumper sat up quickly on her haunches and barked. "Shhhh," he hushed, sitting up and laying a hand lightly on her nose.

Alec glanced at Krista, lying on the bed beside him. She stirred briefly in her sleep but didn't awaken.

"Okay, let's go."

Alec followed Thumper down the hall and through the kitchen, but not until they reached the family room did he pause to turn on a light. He hesitated a moment to allow his eyes to adjust, then followed her toward the back door and let her out. Knowing she would romp for a few minutes in the large fenced lot before doing her duty, Alec returned to the family room and sat down on the carpeted woodbox to wait.

He leaned back against the wall, took a sweeping glance around the family room and smiled with self-satisfaction. Even though they were barely past thirty, he and Krista had done well for themselves. They were in the process of buying their own home, they had furnished it with modern yet modest accessories, and they had been able to buy a few luxury items they'd both wanted. In spite of the unstable stock market, their investments were doing well, and they'd even been able to build their savings account to a comfortable level. There was only one thing missing in their lives: a family—children.

The test results they'd received over two and a half years ago had been disheartening. Krista had tested healthy and normal, but Alec's sperm count had been almost too low to be worth counting. The pain of reality had hit him hard when he learned he'd been classified as being sterile.

After several months of counseling and discussion, they decided to follow the course both of their parents had taken; they decided to adopt. But that decision had brought them no closer to having a family than had their own efforts. For almost sixteen months, their names had been on several adoption agencies' waiting lists; both of them continued to pray they wouldn't have to wait the predicted three to four years before they would receive a child. Alec wanted a family as much as—if not more than—Krista; he wanted a chance to be as good a father as his own had been.

Alec glanced at the face of the digital clock on the television; it was 2:17 A.M. He leaned forward and looked toward the back door, but Thumper had yet to return from

39

her outing.

Why was he feeling so anxious to let her back in? He knew from experience that he wouldn't be able to go back to sleep; anytime he was awakened in the middle of the night, he could expect to remain awake until well into the morning. Sometimes, though not often, Alec had even welcomed in the dawn.

Again he glanced around the room wondering what he was going to do to occupy his waking hours. He couldn't finish packing and take the chance of disturbing Krista, and the books he'd bought to take with him to the cabin were already in the suitcase on the floor at the foot of their bed. The television would make too much noise, the stereo was in the shop for cleaning, and the magazines lying on the coffee table were a month old and had already been read. His gaze finally settled on the briefcase beside him.

Alec contemplated the contents of the box he'd placed inside. He wasn't anxious to become involved in a case he might have to delay pursuing for the next two weeks, and since the area involved was outside the station's broadcasting radius, he wasn't sure if he wanted to become intrigued by a case David Trubest might not let him pursue at all. Yet, his interest had been sparked in his office that afternoon, and he was curious. Even if he found nothing worth investigating, looking over the contents of the box would give him something to do for the rest of the night.

He carried the briefcase to the table in the eating area of the family room, opened it and removed the box's lid. Alec began sorting through the contents, dividing it into four stacks. One stack contained the baby pictures, one the letters, another was for postcards, and the last stack was composed of the notebooks and journals that had been in the bottom of the box. Once everything was organized in front of him, he pulled out a blank sheet of paper from the lid pocket of his briefcase and wrote *Edgar Schmidt???* across the top of it. He didn't really expect to find anything of importance, but just in case he did, he was ready to make notations.

Alec began with the stack of letters. Checking the address on each envelope, he found that they had all been sent to

Schmidt via a post office box in Prairie Dells, Wisconsin, and that the return address was the same on each: 807 North Spencer Boulevard, Lashbrook, Illinois. These two items of information were the first notations he made on the sheet of paper beneath Schmidt's name, and he made a note to himself to check their location on a map.

The first clues to unraveling the puzzle, which he wasn't even sure existed, were written down in front of him. No matter how small or unimportant something appeared to be, Alec always scrutinized the details as closely as he did any major occurrence. Anything, no matter how large or small, could be the essential element that could break a case wide open. Alec was a stickler for details, and very few ever got past him.

Beneath the two addresses, Alec wrote the dates of the faded postmarks he was able to read. All of the letters had been mailed during the middle and late 1950s.

Finding nothing else on the exteriors of the envelopes, Alec carefully removed each fragile piece of lavender stationery and read its communication. As he'd suspected, the bulk of the letters focused on how much Edgar was missed; the need for him to return was of foremost importance to the writer.

The writer: Eleanor. Who was she? A wife? A sister? A mistress? Whoever she was, her letters freely expressed her displeasure with Edgar's absence and urged him repeatedly to return home before he became even more deeply involved in something that was wrong in both the eyes of God and the eyes of man.

. . . *something that was wrong in both the eyes of God and the eyes of man.* That fearful plea was scripted in the letter with the latest date; there were no others to give further explanation as to what was meant.

Alec returned the letters to their envelopes and replaced them in the box. He then turned his attention to the stack of postcards. Looking at the face of each, he noted that they had all been sent to Schmidt at 807 North Spencer Boulevard, Lashbrook, Illinois.

A thin smile of accomplishment tightened Alec's lips; he had made his first connection, no matter how small. The mailing address on the postcards was the same as the return address on the letters, but the connection was obvious and almost meaningless; Brice had already told him they were tearing down Schmidt's house in Lashbrook.

Now, the most obvious questions stood out boldly in Alec's mind. Where had Schmidt been staying when he'd received the letters? And who had then sent the postcards with the Prairie Dells postmark? He hoped he could find the answers to *those* questions before any additional questions began to arise.

Turning the postcards over, Alec immediately noticed they were all dated. He arranged them in chronological order, then began to read:

3/17/52

Ed,
Remember the project we discussed when we were in India? I think JA and I are progressing toward a formula that will make it possible, but we could use your help. Stop by at your convenience, and we'll discuss it.

HG

7/23/53

Ed,
We're working on a new procedure that looks promising. Plan to spend a few extra days the next time you visit, and I'll show you the latest results.

HG

2/27/54

Ed,
Your suggestion proved to be invaluable. Rejection rate is now down to 67%. If they'll just hold on, we could have our first in a couple of months.

HG

5/3/54

Ed,
We've had a major setback. We've lost them all.

Everything was progressing so well, and we don't know what happened. We need your help. Please reconsider joining us at the farm.

HG

8/21/54

Ed,

We've tried everything you suggested, but still cannot maintain an ex. imp. PLEASE reconsider joining us at the farm.

HG

11/9/54

Ed,

Things have been holding their own since you left. They're still with us—and they're growing! We're anxious to continue on with Phase III. Wish you would return so we could continue to work together.

HG

4/8/55

Ed,

Another breakthrough! Rejection is down to 32% in Phase IV. PG—as you have so aptly named it—is coming closer to being reality. You should be here with us to share in the glory.

HG

"PG . . ." Alec glanced at the photographs, then picked one up and turned it over to check and see if his memory was serving him correctly. "PG . . . PG Delta. What could it mean?" He turned the picture back over and studied the faded photograph. He could see nothing unusual; it looked like any other picture of a newborn infant that might have been taken over thirty years ago. "But there *has* to be some connection with all of this, or why else would Schmidt have put the pictures in the box with the rest of these things?" he said to himself as he made a sweeping glance across the cluttered tabletop. "The answer's got to be in here somewhere. All I have to do is find it." Alec laid the pict back on the table and returned to reading the postcards.

12/18/55

Ed,

Phase V is a success! Come join us at the farm. Let's begin the REAL PG together—SOON! JA is anxious to donate whenever the time is right.

HG

9/12/56

Ed,

The numbers are dwindling. Of the 6, only 3 remain. The calendar moves by too slowly. God! How I pray for Xmas—and at least one success—for JA's sake.

HG

12/11/56

Ed,

One remains. For lack of any better identification, we call it Alpha—the first. Any day now, we'll be able to hold the fruits of our labor in our hands. You must be here with us to witness the outcome—to share in the glory. I'll send a car for you at noon on Sunday. We did it!

HG

Alec focused on the final words of the postcard: *We did it!* "Did what?" he asked of no one. "And what's an Alpha?"

Alec thought of Brice's comment that afternoon that had pertained to the photograph's labeling. He'd said the first letter of the Greek alphabet had been missing; there had been no Alpha.

Alec glanced at the pictures and shook his head, unable to make any connections, then continued to read the remaining postcards:

3/27/57

Ed,

Please believe the fault was not yours alone. We've come too far to let a setback like this stop us. We need your help in correcting the error. I'm sure the answer is just waiting to be found. "There's a formula for everything."

I also need your help in convincing JA to let me get rid of it.

HG

7/19/57

Ed,

JA believes in you and in your most recent findings. She is ready to try again whenever you feel the time is right. Please be sure. Remember, her next chance will be her last.

Please change your mind and help me convince her to get rid of it.

HG

5/6/58

Ed,

We've lost 2, but the remaining 6 continue to develop. We've run tests, and things are going well— there will be no repeat of the last disaster. The next 2 months will crawl by as we wait.

Hope E is feeling better by then so you can join us. This time we REALLY did it!

HG

2/14/61

Ed,

I still grieve over the loss of JA. In honor of her memory, and in honor of everything she tried to do for mankind, I have decided to continue with PG for as long as I live. She would have wanted it that way. Maybe someday, I can make her dream come true.

For her sake, I'm even learning to tolerate Alpha— because she loved him.

HG

Alec looked up from the last postcard, shaking his head. Still, nothing had come together; still, nothing had begun to gel in his mind.

He glanced at the baby pictures, then looked at the stack of notebooks and journals. "Just what in the world were you up to over thirty years ago, Edgar Schmidt?" he asked of the deceased man, who had planted a growing seed of curiosity in Alec's mind. "And who—or what—was Alpha? Will I find the answers in one of these?" he questioned as he reached for the top notebook.

Alec laid it on top of the postcards in front of him. When he opened the front cover, he knew at a glance that he wouldn't be able to discover the answers to his questions as easily as he'd hoped. The yellowed pages were filled with scientific-looking formulas, and any notes that had been scribbled in the margins were written in a language foreign to him. He guessed it might have been Latin or maybe even some sort of code.

"This looks like a job for Raymond," he said to himself, referring to the foreign-language specialist at the University of Louisville whom the station kept on retainer.

Alec pulled the rest of the notebooks and journals over in front of him and leafed through them briefly. Each followed a format identical to the first; nothing made any sense to him. Disheartened, he restacked them and was about to return them to the box when he noticed the edge of a yellowed envelope sticking out ever so slightly from between the pages of the bottom journal.

Smiling hopefully, he slipped it out onto the table. Carefully, he lifted the back flap that had stuck to the body, removed a folded piece of paper and opened it. Alec's smile broadened. The short notation of Edgar Schmidt's random thoughts had been written in English.

7/10/58

Tomorrow, I go to be with Hue and JA to wait for the final outcome of Project GOD.

"Project GOD," Alec interjected with a whisper. "Is that what PG stands for?" He continued reading.

I am torn between hoping for success and hoping for

failure. Either could produce as much heartache as happiness. I hope we have done the right thing in trying—I wonder.

People have labeled me crazy . . . mad . . . insane, and I cannot find evidence enough to prove them wrong. But I have never tried to play God—at least not until now.

God forgive me if I have stepped unwittingly on ground that was never meant to be trod by mortal man. Do not hold my immortal soul as hostage for my deeds. I hope we have done the right thing in trying, but still, I wonder. I think I shall always wonder . . .

Alec turned the paper over and read an additional notation on the back:

7/21/58

Six Survive.

Hue is ecstatic, but I now question his motives. He's talking money—money and secrecy. I do not understand him, now.

The premise was good. The time was right, but I fear we have overstepped our bounds. How can he conceive of placing a price on something that was created to fill a void?

I fear he's become deranged with his success, and I wonder if there is any way to stop him before the project becomes totally out of hand. I shall try to reason with him, but alas, Hue was never one to be reckoned with when his mind was set.

God help me. Please don't condemn my soul to an eternity in hell if I fail.

There was a blank space on the page and then an additional few lines near the bottom. It looked as if Schmidt had added them as an afterthought.

I believe all creatures have the right to live, but . . . God forgive me for my evil thoughts. After seeing Alpha at 18 months of age, I strongly believe it would have been better for everyone if he would have been one of those that died.

Alec reread the back page of the letter, then looked again at the photographs lying on the table in front of him. He had a feeling—his gut instinct told him—that somehow, the two were connected. But how? And why? And who was Al—

"What's going on out here?" Alec turned in his chair with a start. Krista stood beside the dividing counter, leaning groggily against it for support. Her light auburn hair was disheveled from turning in her sleep, and the skin beneath her blue-green eyes was puffy. She was not yet fully awake.

"I didn't think I was doing anything that would wake you."

"You're not," she said, nodding toward the back door, "she is."

Alec glanced across the family room to see Thumper, her nose and front paws pressed against the storm door, staring in at him. She barked when he made eye contact, and he could see her upper body wiggle back and forth, responding to the vigorous wagging of her tail.

"She's been jumping up on the door, wanting in, for about the past ten minutes. Didn't you hear her?"

"I guess I had my mind on something else. Sorry."

"What are you doing?" Krista asked, walking to the table while Alec went to let Thumper inside. She glanced at the photographs and immediately questioned, "Whose kids are these?"

"I don't know."

"Where did you get the pictures?"

"They were in the box Brice left. I told you about it."

"Sounds like work to me," she said, gathering together the pictures, letters, notebooks and journals and placing them in the box, "and you're on vacation," she added, scolding him. "I'm not going to watch you spend a well-deserved vacation wasting your time working on something that probably doesn't mean anything anyway."

"Then you don't have to watch me," Alec said jokingly as he returned the box's lid and closed his briefcase. He carried it to the counter and set it down beside the maps and trip diary they'd planned to take with them. "While you and

Sarah are off gallivanting in New York, it might just give me something to occupy my time."

Houston, Texas

Richard Stanton and Evan Baker conferred over Lucas Cromwell's latest test results. As lawyers, they'd worked opposite sides of a case before; within the past three years, they'd faced each other five times in reference to Cromwell.

"It doesn't look like anything's changed since the last test," Stanton said as he looked at Baker. "Lucas is still as sterile as he ever was. There's no way he could be the father of your clients' daughter's child. Just as it's been proven in the past, it's quite evident she's lying just like the others were. There's no possible way she can collect on a paternity suit."

As the senior partner of Stanton, Hughes, Clark & Jenson, Richard Stanton rarely became involved in cases dealing with the Cromwell's multimillion-dollar business corporation, but when it came to cases involving the immediate family, he never entrusted the legalities to anyone else in the firm. He'd been friends with Elias Cromwell, and his wife Nora, for almost thirty years. When they'd all been young, just beginning to make their way in the world, they'd helped each other whenever an opportunity presented itself.

As time passed, the Cromwell Corporation grew at a much faster rate than Stanton's law firm; there was more demand for computer technology than there was for lawyers. But Elias Cromwell never forgot the friend who had helped him in the beginning with legal matters. Twenty years ago, when the Cromwell Building had been built in downtown Houston, he'd hired Stanton's firm to be the sole legal representative for his corporation and had given Stanton the entire seventh floor of the building to house his offices.

Even though the law firm was now a prestigious corporation in its own right, Richard Stanton still felt he owed a debt to Elias Cromwell. The only way he knew to repay that debt was to give personal attention to Cromwell's legal matters. He'd made himself the watchdog over

Cromwell's private fortune.

Over the years he'd protected Cromwell's money, never letting so much as a penny slip through his hands that shouldn't be paid out rightfully. He'd broken scams, he'd uncovered frauds, and during the past few years, he'd defended Cromwell's son in over a dozen paternity suits. Stanton hadn't lost a single paternity case. He couldn't. Elias Cromwell's only son was sterile.

"Janine claims that Lucas is the only man she's had relations with in the past six months."

"Evan, I don't care what she claims," Stanton said as he laid his hand down on top of the file, "these test results prove she's lying. And you know they're correct because they came from Dr. McDonald. *He's* the doctor *your* clients requested run the tests." He leaned back in his chair. "Let's face the facts here. Maybe your clients' daughter did have relations with Lucas, but I can guarantee you, he wasn't the one who impregnated her. The test results, there, prove that's impossible." He shook his head. "It's quite evident she became pregnant by someone else and is just wanting Lucas to pay for her mistake. But that's not going to happen." Stanton leaned forward and slammed his hand down on the desk. "Not a single cent of Cromwell money is going to be paid out to cover that little hussie's mistake."

The buzzer of the interoffice intercom interrupted them. "What is it, Patsy?" Stanton asked after depressing the lever on his small desk speaker.

"Lucas Cromwell is here to see you, sir."

"Send him in." Both Stanton and Baker turned in their chairs to look toward the door.

It opened, and in strutted a tall, lean man with light brown hair and crisp blue eyes. A cocky grin dominated his face as he walked toward Stanton and Baker to sit in a vacant chair beside the desk.

"Afternoon, Richard . . . Evan," he said, expressing no respect for his elders.

"Mr. Cromwell," Baker responded politely with a nod.

Stanton only nodded—not politely or otherwise. In truth, he didn't like Lucas Cromwell; he hadn't liked him since the boy—now a man—had been old enough to show his true

50

nature. Of all the favors Stanton had done for Elias and Nora over the years, he felt he'd made only one grave error. He wished he had never arranged for Lucas's adoption twenty-three years ago.

"I thought I'd just stop by to see how things are going," Lucas said as he leaned back in the chair and propped his elbows on the wooden arms. "Am I gonna get off scot-free on this one, too?"

"The test results confirm the same thing as all the others."

Lucas chuckled self-confidently. "Well, I hope that's the last one of those damn tests I'll ever have to take. It's not real satisfying to have to jack off into a little glass bottle." Stanton and Baker both lowered their eyes in response to the distasteful comment. "Well, since it appears I don't have to stay around to go to court, I think I might just hop in the old family jet and scoot on up to Vegas." Lucas stood and walked toward the door. As he grasped the knob and turned it, he looked back toward the two lawyers. "Maybe I'll be lucky and can find me a pretty showgirl that'll be a lot softer than some old glass bottle." He laughed mockingly. "Oh, and Evan, tell Janine for me . . . tell her it was nice, but sorry, no payoff." He exited, closing the door behind him.

"Arrogant bastard," Baker said only partially under his breath.

"People like him make me believe it's due to the genes and not the environment." Baker looked at Stanton in question. "I thought you knew he was adopted."

"I imagine you told me at one time. But adopted or not, I still think he's one arrogant bastard."

"You're not going to get an argument out of me."

Baker glanced at the folder on Stanton's desk, and then he stared at it for a few moments. "You know," he said, looking up at Stanton, "I hope, someday, he *wants* a child of his own. It'll serve him right not being able to have one. I hope it cuts him clear to the core." He hesitated, and a sadness darkened his face. "We found out a few months back that my boy's sterile. It's really hurt him deeply, knowing he'll never be able to father a child."

At that moment, Evan Baker didn't consider the fact that his son had been adopted as well.

Four

The setting sun was obscured by the not-too-distant hills and by the thick stand of trees bordering the two-lane blacktop road for as far as the eye could see. Ever since they had turned south off the interstate some twenty minutes earlier, the well-kept country road had been surrounded by the dappled shades of early evening.

"We're almost to the turnoff," Krista said anxiously when they came to the bottom of a gently sloping hill and the trees to the east of the road began to thin. For the first time, she was able to catch a brief glimpse of the Dell Creek River, which now ran almost parallel to the road. "It's only another couple of miles or so."

Her eyes sparkled almost as brilliantly as the sun's reflection coming off the rippling water as she leaned forward in her seat. She hadn't been to the cabin on the lake, where she'd spent many happy childhood summers, since she and Alec had lived in Rickdon, Illinois, some seven years before. The distance involved for travel had been the main reason for her long absence, but she also knew Alec didn't enjoy fishing even one tenth as much as she; therefore, even when it had been her turn to pick the activity for their summer vacation, she usually put her own desires aside and opted for a vacation she knew Alec would enjoy.

But this summer was different; this summer, Krista had decided they would come to the cabin on the lake one last time. This was the last summer the cabin would belong to her. After years of refusing to sell the lakeside property, she had finally submitted to the pressure. Besides, since they rarely used the cabin and the property taxes kept rising above a reasonable rate, keeping the secluded hideaway for purely sentimental reasons wasn't in the least way financially prudent. They could always use the money to pay off a big chunk on their home, and there could be a new car coming in the future. Then, there was always the possibility of adopting.

"There's the dairy!" Krista said in excitement, pointing past Alec toward the white colonial house on the far side of the river that was all but hidden by the trees. Thumper barked in response to Krista's enthusiasm. "You're going to love it here," she said, glancing back at the dog. "There's acres of woods where you can chase rabbits and squirrels, and if Amble's still around, you'll have someone to play with."

As soon as Krista directed her attention to Thumper, she knew she had made a mistake. The dog had been fairly quiet throughout the long trip, lying on the blanket that had been spread on the floor between packed boxes and only whining at widely spaced intervals as an indication that she needed to relieve herself. Now, since she had been brought into the conversation, Thumper's tail began to wag vigorously, striking the cardboard boxes on either side of her, beating out a definite rhythm. She tried to stand and worm her way toward Krista, hoping to be accepted on her lap, but the makeshift harness Alec had rigged as a doggie seat belt prevented her from advancing.

"Stay there, girl." Krista patted Thumper's head a few times in consolation, then turned back around in her seat to keep from tempting the dog any further. "There!" Krista said abruptly, pointing at an angle toward a bridge ahead of them and to their left that spanned the river and gave access to the road on the opposite side. "There's where we turn."

Alec slowed the van to a near stop and waited for a stainless steel milk tanker truck to vacate the entrance before turning onto the bridge. He'd expected the old wooden-planked bridge they had crossed the last time they'd come to the lake, but that bridge was a part of history; it had been replaced by one crafted of concrete and steel. Once across the bridge, Alec turned the van right onto another blacktop road then started around the south edge of the lake. They drove for only a few yards, and then he stopped—at the end of the blacktop.

"What's the matter?" Krista asked, looking at him with a frown. "Why did you stop?"

"Why did the road crews stop paving here?" Looking in the van's side mirror, Alec visually followed the blacktop road behind them all the way from the bridge into the trees blocking the view of the colonial house.

"Private money," Krista explained. "The Grahams always kept their drive paved. Everybody on this side of the lake used to chip in once or twice a year to have our lane graded and to have a couple of loads of crushed stone brought in, but since Marvin and I are the only ones left, I know I sure didn't think to have it done, and I doubt if he could afford it on his own."

Alec looked at the unpaved road ahead of them and shook his head. The old lane was deeply rutted and was desperately in need of some major attention. By the looks of the adjacent terrain, he guessed runoff water from rains and melting snow had worked its way down the steep slopes of the bordering hills, accumulating into mini-rivers that had washed out gullies where the cracked and crumbled red-tile culverts had ceased to serve their purpose. In addition to the sorry state of the road itself, dense underbrush had grown close to its edge, hiding any further potential hazards that might entrap the van if it accidentally ventured off the narrow lane. One other aspect of the road's condition bothered Alec: century-old trees, towering high above them, leaned toward the road, appearing to be waiting for just the right moment to fall.

"We can walk," Krista suggested, guessing at the thoughts behind the deepening frown on Alec's face. "It probably isn't much more than a quarter mile or so."

Alec looked at her with a teasing smile. "Where's your spirit of adventure?" He reached for the lever on the floor between their seats and pulled it up. "I didn't pay extra for

54

four-wheel drive for nothing. I haven't had a chance to see if it works, but this looks to be as good a time as any to try it out. Hold on." Alec eased his foot onto the gas pedal, and the van began to advance.

Krista leaned forward in her seat, trying to help Alec watch for the biggest chuckholes and give suggestions for maneuvering around them. "I remember it being bumpy in spots, but I don't remember it being *this* bad," she said, grabbing the arm of her captain's chair for stability. "It's— Look out!"

Her warning came an instant too late. The front wheels of the van dropped abruptly into a deep hole that had been hidden in the twilight's shadows. Both she and Alec pitched forward, and they heard Thumper fall against the boxes in the back.

"Is she all right?" Alec asked, glancing back over his shoulder. He caught the look of uncertainty in Thumper's big brown eyes, the look that always reminded him of the night he'd found her. Even after being loved and pampered—spoiled—for almost three years, Thumper still showed signs of intense fear whenever she was startled or was unsure of the events taking place around her. Alec had often wondered how long it would take for her to get over the trauma of her puppyhood, but then again, he wondered if she ever would. Perhaps every living creature possessed an inner instinct that wouldn't let it totally forget its past.

"She's okay." Krista reached back to ruffle Thumper's ears. Her hand moved to the dog's firm shoulders, and she could feel the muscles trembling beneath. "It's okay, girl. We're almost there."

Alec again applied pressure to the gas pedal. The engine strained to pull the front wheels free, and an instant later, the back wheels dropped into the same hollow; they too rolled up the chuckhole's steep side, conquering the same obstacle the front wheels had just overcome. Hoping to avoid any more "basements," the term Krista always used to describe some of the bigger potholes in the downtown Louisville streets, Alec turned on the headlights to brighten the area directly ahead of them and continued.

The road that led almost halfway around the southern edge of the man-made lake hadn't always been so rough and uninviting. When the area had first been developed back in the late thirties, the lane had been as smooth and the roadside foliage as manicured as the technology of the era could provide; the road had led to a showplace of recreational homes owned by financial survivors of the Depression. At its birth, the area had been revered and envied by those who hadn't been able to afford the luxury of a second home, but as time passed and the novelty wore off, the attention that had once been given to the lakeside property faded as well. Now, little or no attention was given to the area except by the H&J Corporation, the owner of the dairy that operated on the opposite side of the lake.

The H&J Corporation paid a lot of attention to the area. It had already purchased all the land around the lake with the exception of the half-acre lot and cabin Krista had inherited from her grandparents and the property west of hers, belonging to Marvin Horton. But as of August, when Krista had agreed to sign the closing papers on the sale, Marvin's property would be the last on the lake that would be privately owned. Krista still hadn't figured out where she would find the courage to tell Marvin she'd finally sold out.

"There's a light on in Marvin's cabin," Krista said with excitement as they passed a graveled drive. "And look," she added, pointing toward a dim light shining through the trees in the distance. "It looks like he's got that cantankerous generator started, bless his heart. He said he'd have everything ready for us when we got here, and it looks like he has."

Alec continued to struggle to keep the van on the road and within his control as they continued on. He kept glancing toward the distant light, watching it grow nearer, and he knew he would be happy when they finally reached the cabin. The last five minutes of driving had been more exhausting, both physically and mentally, than the rest of the day combined; Alec was ready to sit down, put his feet up and enjoy a good stiff drink.

"Doesn't it look homey?" Krista asked, watching the cabin

as they approached it and then drove on by, heading for the drive several yards beyond.

Something across the road directly in front of them reflected the van's headlights. Even though he was going slow, when Alec jammed his foot on the brake pedal, the jolt of the stop sent them forward in their seats. "What in the world is that?"

A slatted steel barrier, some four feet high, marked an abrupt end to the road. After studying the barrier and the adjacent area for a few moments, Alec readily understood the reason behind its presence. Located some eight to ten feet beyond the barrier was a twelve-foot-high chain-link fence topped with rolled strands of barbed wire. Since the road had at one time continued on into the fenced area, the barrier had obviously been erected to prevent anyone from unknowingly driving into the fence.

"The H&J Corporation," Krista speculated with a note of distaste as her eyes focused on one of the many *No Trespassing* signs mounted at equally spaced intervals along the fence. "They've bought up all the property as far as the fence, and I suppose," she added with a sigh, "the fenceline will be moved to the other side of *my* cabin after I sign the closing papers. Then, it'll all be gone."

"Don't think about it," Alec said, laying an understanding hand on her arm. "Try to enjoy the two weeks we have to spend here, and you'll have some happy memories you can look back on for the rest of your life." Krista nodded and acknowledged his words with a thin smile.

Alec guided the van into the wide lane between the fence and the cabin that had at one time been shared by the fishermen who came to launch their boats at the dock down by the lake's edge. Angling the van toward the cabin, into the pulloff that had once been a firm bed of crushed stone but was now nothing more than an area of overgrown dirt, he immediately noticed that the area surrounding the cabin had been mowed.

"It looks like Marvin's been busy."

"He's such a sweetheart." Alec was barely able to understand her reply. Krista had already unbuckled her seat belt and was sliding off her seat.

Krista hurried across the yard to the front edge, where it began to slope gently down toward the thirty-acre lake. She stopped, looked out across the water, scanned the area in all directions, took in a deep breath and let it out slowly. All of her senses seemed to come alive: the fragrant hint of blooming wildflowers touched her nose; the calls of crickets, frogs and distant birds sang like a romantic ballad to her ears; the lights shining from across the lake and the rising moon and stars against the fading twilight sky were as striking and impressive as any priceless painting. She thought she could almost feel the freshness of her untainted surroundings tingling against her skin.

Thumper barked as she ran past Krista, heading down the grassy incline toward the lake. When she reached the water's edge, Thumper stopped, nosed at the rippling surface, then lifted a paw to touch it, looking and acting more like a curious, cautious cat than a stout-hearted canine.

"That's bigger than any bathtub you've ever seen," Krista called after her with a laugh.

Having walked up behind her, Alec slipped his arms around Krista's waist and gently hugged her back against him. "Happy?" he whispered as he nuzzled his nose against her ear.

"I can't think of anyone who could be much happier than I am right now." She turned to face Alec, slipped her arms around his neck and kissed him. "I've got the most loving and understanding husband that anyone could ever want, my Crabby Critters are on their way to becoming nationally recognized stars, and I have almost two full weeks where I can sit back, relax and do practically nothing with the ones I love most. Now just tell me," she said after kissing the end of his nose, "how could anybody be happier?"

Their conversation was interrupted when Thumper began barking. Alec and Krista turned to see what had attracted the dog's attention, but whatever it was wasn't readily obvious. Neither could see anything other than Thumper, and they both now watched her with undivided attention.

Even though her bark was deep and menacing and the hair

58

along the back of her neck and spine stood rigidly on end, there was a humorous air about Thumper's alert. Each time the dog barked, she took a step or two backward, angling up the sloping yard toward the cabin, Alec and Krista. Eventually, Thumper made her way behind Alec and peeked around his legs, still barking at whatever was hidden by the twilight.

"Some guard dog you are," Alec laughed as he knelt beside Thumper and patted her on the side. A low growl continued to rumble from deep within Thumper's throat; she was still uncertain of whatever was out there.

"Amble," Krista said with a laugh. Alec looked up to see a brown and white cocker spaniel meandering toward them. "Come here, Amble," Krista called as she knelt and extended her hand in the dog's direction. "Do you remember me, boy?" Amble took his time familiarizing himself with her scent, his cold wet nose nudging her hand several times, and then he licked her. "You do remember me. It sure has been a long time, hasn't it, fella?" The dog barked in response to her words and moved closer to Krista to accept a few gentle pats on his side.

"Yes, child, it has been a long time. Too long."

Krista looked up to see a portly man in his mid-sixties walking toward her. The dim lighting barely accented the thick white beard covering his lower face, and his features were hidden further by the shadow cast by the brim of one of his many hats. Even though he was difficult to recognize visually, the sound of his voice identified him immediately to Krista.

"Marvin!" A few quick strides of her long, slender legs eliminated the distance between them. Krista hugged the older man as closely as if he'd been her own father. "Yes, too long," she said, giving him an additional squeeze.

"And even longer for me."

Krista looked past Marvin toward a shadowy figure standing a few feet behind him. Again, the lack of light prevented her from making an immediate visual identification, but again, recognition was confirmed by the sound of the speaker's voice.

"Rebecca?" Krista questioned in a startled tone. "Becky!" Krista sidestepped around Marvin and almost ran to embrace the woman with whom she'd shared countless enjoyable summers at the lake. Following a lingering hug, Krista stepped back to arm's length and gazed with fond remembrance on the face she hadn't seen since Becky had been her matron of honor. "It sure doesn't seem like it's been nine years." Her eyes quickly surveyed the medium frame of her childhood companion, which had always carried an extra twenty to thirty pounds of weight. "You haven't changed a bit."

"Yes, I have," Becky said with a laugh, patting her own round abdomen. "I've added another twenty pounds' worth." Both women laughed, each remembering one of their teenage escapades when Becky's size had been a factor in their being caught while sneaking over to see the mini-zoo across the lake. In an attempt to crawl under a board beneath the fence that crossed a shallow gully, Becky had become stuck, and they were both caught in the act of trespassing by the night watchman.

"Combat," they said in unison, and then they both giggled as if they were teenagers again.

"We told the watchman we were playing Combat," Becky explained to Alec, referring to the wartime television series that had been popular during the era.

"And he believed us and let us go," Krista added with a laugh.

"Good thing. We'd've both been skinned alive if he'd've brought us home under armed guard."

"Becky, the time."

Becky looked at her husband, who stood impatiently behind her, pointing at his watch. "You remember Tom," Becky said matter-of-factly, redirecting her attention back to Krista, "but I don't think . . . I know you've never seen our son. Where is he?" she asked, scanning the immediate area. "Robbie? Robert Thomas, where are you?" When Becky heard no reply to her call, she glanced at Tom, who only shrugged his shoulders. She then looked toward her father.

60

Marvin nodded toward the lake, and everyone turned to look in the direction of the dock. Once their eyes adjusted to the lack of light and the distance, they could distinguish the silhouette of a boy sitting on the far edge, his legs dangling down toward the water.

"He's going through a trying time right now," Becky said in confidence. "One of the neighbor boys was teasing him right before we left home and viciously blurted out about how he's adopted."

"You had told him before, hadn't you?" Krista questioned with concern.

"Yes, he's known since he was old enough to understand, but this is the first time anyone has been mean to him about it. I think he's still too young not to let it bother him."

"He'll get over it," Tom stated flatly, impatiently taking Becky by the arm and guiding her away from the small gathering. "I'll sit down with him after we get back and have a long talk with him about it. But if we don't get moving now, we're going to miss our connection in Madison, and then we won't have to worry about leaving at all."

"Where are you going?" Krista asked, walking with Becky and Tom toward their car.

"Tom won ten glorious days in Hawaii for being the top salesman of the year. This time tomorrow, we'll be lying on the white sandy beaches, basking in the fantastic Pacific sun. I'll tell you all about it when we get back. Maybe I can even drop Grumpy here for an afternoon, and we can take a solitary boat ride out to the middle of the lake and loll the afternoon away sipping coolers and reliving some of the good old days."

"I'll be looking forward to it."

"Keep an eye on Dad for me." Krista nodded. "And don't tell my kid too many lies about his mother. I've had to work pretty hard so far to convince him I'm a saint."

"I won't undo any of your hard work," Krista replied with a laugh.

"And if you want to see Dad blush, ask him about the Widow Blessing."

"Does he have a girlfriend?"

61

"He won't say much one way or the other, but I think he's kind of partial to her."

"Becky," Tom said impatiently.

"Okay, I'm coming."

After Becky slid onto the passenger seat, Krista closed the door and leaned down for a quick farewell. "Have fun, and don't worry about anything while you're gone. I think between Amble, Thumper and me, we'll be able to keep everything well under control."

Tom began backing the car down the drive even as Krista and Becky continued to exchange last-minute bits of information. When the car finally passed a bush at the drive's end, Krista had to stop walking with it; all she could do now was stand and wave.

"Be careful driving down to Madison," Marvin called after them, stepping up beside Krista and joining her in waving good-bye. "Don't worry about anything here. Robbie, Amble and I'll get along just fine."

Krista and Marvin followed the car visually as it made its way along the bumpy road. Finally, it turned and disappeared behind the trees.

"After that long drive up from Lou'ville, I imagine you're ready to put your feet up and relax for a while," Marvin said as he turned and began walking back toward the front of the cabin with Krista.

"I've learned never to argue with a man when he's right," Krista replied. "But before I sit down and put my feet up, I want to get everything emptied out of the van; then that chore won't be facing us in the morning. I swear," she added with an easy laugh, "with everything we brought, somebody'd think we were moving in permanently instead of just coming up to spend a couple of weeks."

As they walked along the cabin and past the front porch, Krista told Marvin about her upcoming trip to New York and of the potential success for her Crabby Critters. When they reached the van, she walked to the sliding door Alec had left open and pulled one of the packed cardboard boxes toward her.

"Alec," she called over her shoulder, "the sooner we get

62

the van unloaded, the sooner we can put the steaks on the grill for supper." She received no response to her request for help. "Alec?" she questioned, turning away from the van. "Will you please—" Krista cut her words short when she saw Marvin standing near the front of the van looking down toward the lake, his hand held up beside him as a gesture for her to be silent. "What's the matter?" she whispered. Marvin nodded toward the dock, and Krista saw what had captured his attention: Alec, Thumper and Amble were walking out onto the dock toward Robbie.

"Why don't you let me help you unload the van so they can talk," Marvin suggested. "Maybe if Robbie talks with someone else who's been adopted, he'll feel better."

"And if Alec can't convince him it's a good thing, then I'll give it my best shot. You know, if Mom and Dad hadn't adopted me, I'd have never had the chance to know you and Becky, and Becky and I would have never become best friends."

"And if you two would've never met, neither one of you would've gotten into near as much trouble when you were kids," Marvin countered with a laugh.

"Speaking of trouble," Krista said in a tease, "what's this I hear about you and the Widow Blessing?"

"Humph" was the only answer Marvin gave in reply. He picked up the cardboard box and started walking toward the cabin.

Alec stopped on the dock a few feet behind Robbie. During his short walk down to the lake, he'd wondered how he could initiate a conversation with the youngster, but nothing imaginative had come to mind.

He'd had only brief contact with preadolescents in his line of work, and the ones he'd had an opportunity to speak with had been of the talkative nature, barely leaving enough time between their quick breaths for him to make a response. He'd never come face-to-face with a child who didn't talk freely, and he was now at a loss as to how to encourage Robbie to begin.

Attempting to recall one of his broadcasting classes in college that had contained a unit on dealing with children, Alec tried to remember the major points his professor had stressed: treat children as separate individuals and not as a sub-unit of their parents; be honest and straightforward with them, communicating in terminology they can readily understand; and yet, never talk down to a child. Once they begin to feel as if you're patronizing them, they'll turn you off forever and treat you as if you'd never been there.

But what was the terminology used by a seven-year-old in this day and age? How big a word would be beyond his vocabulary? How small a word would appear as an insult to his intelligence? What was the fine line Alec would have to walk in order to communicate? He had no answers to any of the questions; all he could hope was that his instincts would lead him in the right direction.

"Mind if I join you?" Robbie's only response was a quick shrug of his shoulders.

Alec sat down on the dock's roughly hewn planks and turned to sit with his legs dangling over the end. He cocked his head to one side and studied Robbie briefly, and in an instant, he was reminded of his younger brother, Brice, when he had been Robbie's age. Both were tall and slender, both had a thick head of sun-yellow blond hair, and Alec surmised that if he could see Robbie's eyes, they too would be a brilliant blue.

"I guess we're going to be neighbors for the next couple of weeks."

"I guess," Robbie responded halfheartedly.

"What's your name?"

"Robbie," he finally answered after a prolonged hesitation.

"Glad to meet you, Robbie." Alec extended his hand, but the boy ignored the gesture. "I'm Alec, my wife is Krista, and we call this authentic pound puppy here Thumper."

"Dumb name for a dog," Robbie retorted. "Thumper was a rabbit."

"Are you going to let him talk about you that way, Thumper?" Alec turned slightly and ran his hand the length

64

of Thumper's back. Once the dog sensed she had become an integral part of the intimate group, her tail began to wag. Just as Alec had expected, it beat against the dock with an audible thump. "Now do you see why we call her Thumper?"

Robbie's head turned slightly, and he looked at Thumper out of the corner of his eye. A hint of a smile crossed his lips, and then it was gone.

"What's the spaniel's name?" Alec asked as he reached to stroke the dog's wavy fur.

"Amble," Robbie replied after another extended hesitation.

"That's an interesting name."

"It's dumb."

Alec straightened around on the dock and looked out across the lake toward the lights on the opposite shore. Biding his time, he counted eight carriage lamps spaced widely apart, their subtle circles of light barely touching at their circumference.

"You don't like the name Amble?" he asked.

"It's dumb."

Alec started to turn his head to look at Robbie, and as he did, he thought he saw a dark figure move—slink—through the shadows along the opposite shore. He returned his attention to the area where he thought he'd seen movement and studied it briefly, but if someone—or something—had been there, it was now gone.

"Why do you think it's a dumb name?" Alec asked.

"It's . . . it's just dumb, that's all."

Alec knew he wasn't making much progress in encouraging Robbie to communicate, but he was beginning to learn the extent of the seven-year-old's vocabulary: *dumb*. "Do you like to fish?" he asked, hoping that a change in the subject would bring about a change in Robbie's sparse conversation.

"Sometimes."

"Are you any good?"

"Sometimes."

Sometimes, Alec thought to himself with a restrained chuckle. *Dumb* and now *sometimes*.

"Are you always this talkative?"

Robbie shot him a sideways glance that could have been interpreted as meaning only *leave me alone;* then he quickly looked away.

Alec again looked out over the water. In all the years he had been an investigative reporter, he'd never skirted the issue; he'd always come directly to the point. Why then was he attempting to take a different approach now? In reality, how much difference could there be in talking with a seven-year-old boy or a seventy-year-old man?

"I understand you ran into a little problem before you left home today," Alec stated directly, looking back at Robbie.

Robbie turned his head sharply toward Alec. The *leave me alone* look had been replaced by an even nastier one that could have easily been interpreted as *go to hell.*

It was Alec's turn now to break eye contact and look away. "I bet that boy told you you were no good . . . worthless . . . and that your real mom and dad gave you away because they didn't want you . . . because they didn't love you." Alec paused, but when he didn't hear a response from Robbie, he continued. "And I bet he might have even told you the mom and dad you have now don't love you either, but that they're only taking care of you because they feel sorry for you."

"How do you know what he said?" Robbie asked, the words escaping around the lump in his throat.

Robbie's question jolted Alec's memory, bringing back to him a part of his childhood he'd tried desperately to forget. He'd been about Robbie's age when the taunting had begun, vicious, painful taunting about his being adopted. The harsh remarks had led to fights on the playground—fights where he could gain no advantage. He'd never been confronted by a single adversary; the fights had always been two against one . . . three against one . . . four against one. But no matter what the odds, Alec had always been able to stand his own ground. That was the time in his life when he learned to be tough.

"Because . . . because someone who didn't know any different said those same things to me a long time ago," Alec finally answered, looking back at Robbie.

"You're adopted?"

"That's right," Alec responded in a more cheerful tone, "and so is my wife. And we both think that makes us extra special."

"Special?"

"You better believe it."

"How can being adopted make you special?"

"Because we were chosen. The moms and dads we have now had so much love to give that they wanted to share it with someone, so they *chose* us to be that special someone. What's the kid's name that was giving you such a hard time?"

"Don."

"Is he adopted?"

"No."

"Ah-ha. Then Don's the one people should feel sorry for. Or better yet, people should feel sorry for his parents. They got stuck with a kid like him without being able to make a choice."

"Yeah. Nobody'd ever chose a brat like Don." Robbie laughed, and a smile brightened his face. Then it faded. He looked at Alec, and his eyes asked the same sad question that came from his lips. "But why did my real mom and dad give me up? Didn't they love me? Was it because they couldn't choose me and felt like they were stuck with me?"

Alec suddenly felt backed into a corner from which there was no escape. Ever since he'd been old enough to ask that very same question, he'd never come up with an answer with which he felt totally at ease. During his adolescence, one of his high school counselors shared an explanation with him that she said she'd been given upon learning of her own adoption. It was the only one that had at any time brought him comfort; it was the only one he could think to use to help Robbie.

"Our natural parents loved us more than anyone," he began. Robbie looked at Alec, not saying anything, but the questioning expression on his young face asked for a further explanation. "You see, for some reason, whether they were too young or too poor or for some other reason, they felt

67

they couldn't give us the kind of life they wanted us to have." Alec paused, feeling somewhat awkward in his explanation, but he knew he had to continue for Robbie . . . and for himself. "They knew they couldn't give us the kind of life they wanted us to have," he repeated, "so they loved us enough to trust our care to someone else who could do what they couldn't." Alec took in a deep breath and released it slowly. "So you see, being adopted means you've been loved twice as much as someone who hasn't been adopted."

"Are you two as hungry as I am?"

Alec and Robbie turned to see Krista standing on the dock behind them.

"I am," Alec answered immediately, thankful an interruption had come to their little talk. "How about you, Robbie?"

"I guess." His attitude seemed a little brighter than before their conversation, but Alec could tell Robbie was not totally convinced, and like Alec, perhaps he never would be.

"Why don't you run ahead and tell your grandpa we're on our way," Alec said as he stood. He then hooked his hands beneath Robbie's arms and lifted him to his feet. "And I want you always to remember that you're someone special."

Robbie looked up at Alec and smiled thinly. "Thanks for trying to help." He turned sharply, ran down the dock and then angled across the grassy slope in the direction of his grandfather's cabin.

"I was eavesdropping," Krista confessed, slipping her arm around Alec's waist as they began walking along the dock. "And you know what?"

"No. What?"

"It reminded me just how much of a very special person you really are."

"We're all special," Alec said as he hugged Krista close to him. "Especially you and me," he added with an arrogant whisper, but at the moment, he didn't know just how special he and Krista really were.

Five

Over the course of the next few days, Alec soon learned Robbie liked to fish more than just *sometimes*. The boy was up early every morning, fishing from the dock by himself, biding his time until Marvin or Krista offered to go out on the lake with him in the boat. Alec had even spent an afternoon on the lake with Robbie.

That particular day, the fish weren't biting, but the time they spent together was enjoyable for both of them. They talked about school and sports and about what Robbie wanted to do when he grew up. They discussed the milk trucks that arrived and left the dairy twice a day like clockwork. They even speculated on what might be causing the bushes to rustle just beyond the fence at the shoreline; perhaps a curious cow was watching them, following them around the lake's perimeter. They had no reason to suspect it could be anything else—there was no way for them to know that it *was* something else.

They talked about a lot of different things, and they talked quite a bit about being adopted. By the end of the afternoon, Robbie appeared to be gradually accepting the idea that he could just possibly be "someone special." Alec was already convinced of that fact, and spending time with Robbie reminded him how much he and Krista longed for "someone special" of their very own.

To add variety to their activities, all four participated in a daily round-robin checker tournament. Marvin won the first day, Krista the second and Robbie the third. Alec teased them all, insisting the games were rigged against him somehow.

Alec also spent at least a half hour each day running Thumper through her paces, reviewing the skills that had earned a first-place ribbon in her dog obedience class the previous winter. Robbie became fascinated with the dog's movements and asked Alec to help him teach Amble. The spaniel had thoughts of his own. "Heel" became an immediate signal for the dog to sit; "stay" would prompt a loping run; and the command "come" was answered by an obstinate bark, after which Amble would lie down on the ground and roll over on his side. Neither Alec nor Robbie thought Amble would ever become an obedient dog.

The few days the foursome spent together by the lake seemed to pass by all too quickly. Before any of them realized, it was Wednesday morning, the day Krista planned to leave for her trip to New York.

"You're sure you don't mind taking care of her?" Alec asked, giving Thumper a farewell pat before getting into the van.

"She won't be any trouble at all," Marvin assured him. "Having two dogs around will be twice the pleasure of having one, and besides," he added, placing a hand on Robbie's shoulder, "I've got a partner here who'll probably do most o' the chores for me."

"I'm not sure what time I'll be back. I thought I'd head on down to Rickdon, since I'm this close, and drop in to see my old boss."

"Don't worry about it. We'll be here when you get back." Marvin looked past Alec at Krista. "You got all them Crabby Critters packed up to take with you?"

"You bet." Krista glanced back at the two suitcases on the floor behind her. One contained the clothes she planned to wear for the next few days, and the other was jam-packed with a sample of each of her Crabby Critters. "If the airline doesn't send them to Alaska, we should all be in New York by this afternoon."

"Have a safe trip," Marvin said as he stepped back from the van, "and you be careful driving down to Rickdon and back."

"We will," Alec and Krista responded almost in unison.

"You be a good girl," Alec called from the window, directing his comment to Thumper, as he began backing the van out of the drive. Thumper barked in response and wagged her tail, but she made no attempt to follow.

After the van disappeared behind the trees at the far end of the lane, Marvin and Robbie turned from the drive and started walking across the yard toward their own cabin. "Thumper, heel," Robbie said, patting the side of his thigh lightly as an indication for her to heed his command. The dog immediately fell into step beside him, and Amble did the same on his opposite side.

Alec had waited at the airport until Krista's plane departed. Standing with her in the terminal, he'd repeatedly reassured her the suitcase containing the Crabby Critters would not end up in Alaska. The joke she'd made with Marvin had remained as vividly in her mind as if it had been reality, and nothing Alec could say would convince her that her furry friends would arrive in Detroit with her to meet Sarah and then that all three of them would be correctly routed to New York on schedule. He was somewhat relieved when she finally boarded the plane, even though she left looking like a child who was afraid she was about to lose her most cherished treasure.

He had waved good-bye to her through the terminal window, and the plane had taxied out onto the runway right on schedule. That had been almost two hours ago. Now, as he approached the Rickdon city limits, he was looking forward to seeing his old boss again.

Alec had begun his broadcasting career at WQXM in Rickdon, the summer following his spring graduation from Indiana University. Enthusiastic, willing to do any job assigned to him, he'd started at the bottom of the televising ladder and begun to work his way up. He had done background research for major reporters, had covered the less publicized sporting events and then written them up and handed them to the sportscaster to read on the air, and he'd followed any lead that focused on a story that might possibly turn into a major news item, even though few rarely did. Anyone else who had expectations of someday being in front of the camera, instead of doing the legwork for those who actually were, might have become discouraged by the hard road he had to follow, but Alec persevered.

During the two years Alec spent in Rickdon, Todd Tyson, WQXM's station manager, had been impressed by his dedication and had offered encouragement at every available opportunity. He had also been instrumental in helping Alec secure his next job at WKWP in Grand Island, Nebraska, which in turn had led to the position he now held at WBDC in Louisville. Todd Tyson had been almost as much of an influence on Alec's career as Alec had been himself, and he was looking forward to seeing Todd again for the first time in almost seven years.

Alec parked the van in one of the visitors' spaces in the lot adjacent to the multilevel building housing the WQXM television station. Several fond memories rolled across his mind as he walked along the sidewalk and then paused in front of the double glass doors leading to the foyer. Looking in, he noticed immediately that the receptionist's area had been redecorated, but sitting behind the unfamiliar desk was a very familiar face—Cookie.

Cookie Franklin was almost as broad as she was tall, and she had the jolly disposition everyone associated with overweight people; she was rarely seen without a friendly smile beaming across her face. From the first day Alec had gone to work at WQXM, she had been like a sister to him, sharing secrets of the trade she'd picked up from conversations she'd overheard throughout the years, giving advice as to where he might find a good lead on a bad story and sharing an occasional off-color joke that reddened her plump cheeks more than anyone else's. Cookie had been a good friend during his short two-year stay at the station, and she was one of a few in Rickdon who still exchanged Christmas cards with Alec and Krista.

"What's the scoop of the day?" Alec asked as he pushed open the doors and walked toward Cookie's desk.

"Vice Governor Mallorey has proved that 'vice' means

72

more than just assistant," Cookie answered before she looked up from her work. When she did glance up, she saw Alec, and a broad smile spread instantly across her pudgy face. "Alec Crispen!" She rose from her chair quickly, waddled around the desk and embraced Alec in a semi-controlled bear hug. "Let me have a look at you," she said, stepping back. After a quick survey, Cookie shook her head. "When is that wife of yours ever gonna start feeding you? I bet you haven't put on a single pound since you left here."

"I have to keep a trim figure now that I'm on the other side of the camera," Alec responded with a chuckle. "You know what they say about it making you look heavier."

"Good thing I'm not a TV personality then," Cookie countered with a laugh. "If the camera would make me look any bigger, there wouldn't be a set in the state that could pull all of me into focus." After laughing at her own joke for a few moments, she asked, "What are you doing here, anyway?"

"I was in the neighborhood, so I thought I'd stop by and see how everyone was getting along."

"Did Todd know you were coming?"

"I didn't tell anyone, just in case something came up and I couldn't make it."

"Well, I'll tell you what, I won't buzz him and tell him you're here. You just head right on up to his office and give him a big surprise."

"Is his office still in the same place?"

"Nothing's changed around here except for this place," she said, glancing at the remodeling around her. "I guess since they couldn't find a pretty receptionist to dress up the place, they tried to camouflage me by putting all this fancy stuff around me. You go on, now. I know you wanted to see me when you came here, but I bet you'll find a lot more interesting things to talk about with Todd. Stop by and see me again on your way out." Cookie gave Alec another quick hug, then returned to her desk to answer the phone.

Alec rode the elevator to the third floor and stepped out into a long hall that divided the floor in half. Along both walls, doors were spaced fifteen to twenty feet apart, marking the entrances to the various offices.

"Second door on the right," Alec whispered to himself as

he began walking in that direction.

When he got to the door, it was closed. He reached for the knob and paused a moment to read *T. Tyson, Station Manager,* engraved on a large bronze plaque at eye level. Alec smiled fondly as he turned the knob and pushed the door open. Todd had received that plaque for twenty years of service to the station; Alec had had the privilege of presenting it to him during a recognition dinner eight years ago.

Alec peeked around the edge of the door and saw Todd sitting in front of his word processor, his back to the door. "Have you got any exciting assignments for me, boss?" he asked as he stepped into the office.

Todd sat up straight in his chair, then turned the swivel seat slowly. He cocked his head down and to the side, looking at Alec over the top of his reading glasses. A warm smile began to spread across his face. "I thought I recognized that voice," he said, standing and walking toward Alec with an extended hand. "How have things been going?"

"I can't complain," Alec answered, taking Todd's hand in a firm shake.

"Sit down. Sit down and tell me how my most enthusiastic apprentice has been doing over the past several years."

For the next hour Alec and Todd traded stories and experiences that had been major focal points in their careers since they had last seen each other. After they covered the highlights of their jobs, the conversation turned to their families. Todd now had three grandchildren; Alec told him that he and Krista were on the waiting list to adopt.

"And how is that younger brother of yours?" Todd asked. "What was his name? Bruce?"

"Brice," Alec corrected with a chuckle. Hardly anyone remembered his brother's unusual name.

"I remember one day when he and your folks came to visit the station." Todd laughed. "I'll never forget him. He was like a wide-eyed kid set loose in a candy store. What's he doing now?"

"He's going to be your neighbor of sorts for a while. He's over in Lashbrook, heading the development of a new shopping center and condo complex." With the mention of

74

Brice and Lashbrook, Alec remembered the old box in his briefcase he'd taken to the lake with him. He'd been too occupied, up until now, to even think about it, but with Krista gone for a few days, maybe he could do a little investigating. He was still curious about the letters, postcards and photographs that had sparked his interest the night before they'd left Louisville.

"Lashbrook? I'll be darned. To coin a phrase, 'Isn't it a small world.' I started out in a little TV station up there doing the same neck-breaking work you started out doing here."

"Did you ever have an opportunity to get to know any of the locals?"

"Several of them. Like I said, I did the not-so-important local stories over there just like you did here."

"Did you ever happen to come across a man by the name of Schmidt?"

"Edgar Schmidt?" Alec nodded. Todd laughed. "Most of the people in Lashbrook called him the Frankenstein of the twenty-first century."

"Why's that?"

"At one time, he was a biochemist for the government. He did a lot of work overseas before he got sick and had to come back to the States. He used to work with some other scientist named Granger . . . or Grand . . . or something like that," he stammered, trying to think of the name. "Anyway, I guess they made a pretty good team together. Between the two of them, they developed several strains of crops that were resistant to the bleak weather in southeast Asia and Africa, and they did a lot of work cross-breeding animals until they came up with some that were pretty good milk and meat producers even when their own food supply was thin. One report I remember seeing on them years ago credited them with keeping the famine deaths in those areas to a minimum. I remember the reporter said if it hadn't been for Schmidt and what's-his-name, the death toll would have probably been doubled or tripled."

"That sounds pretty impressive; it doesn't sound like a reason to label him a Frankenstein."

"The Frankenstein thing came when he got back to the

States. He'd picked up some kind of disease when he was in India or some other backward country like that, and by everything I can remember, it supposedly affected him mentally. The government shipped him back to his place in Lashbrook and provided a caretaker for him, but the guy evidently didn't always do his job," Todd added with a chuckle. "There were several fires in the house people say started in Schmidt's basement lab, and I even remember covering a couple of explosions at the place."

"That still doesn't sound to me like it relates directly to any sort of Frankenstein-type activity," Alec prodded, trying to wring as much information out of Todd's memory as possible.

"No, you're right. It doesn't." Todd thought for several more moments; then he straightened in his chair and smiled. Alec could almost see the proverbial light bulb brighten over his head. "The animals. I remember talking to someone who talked about seeing animal carcasses in the dumpster behind his house. I guess I kind of took it with a grain of salt; you know where people's imaginations can lead them. If there were any animals to speak of, they were probably just some of his experimental subjects that didn't make it. I doubt if it was anything really important, or the ASPCA would have been on his case—and on the government's case—since they were the ones supposedly responsible for looking after him."

Alec's audiographic memory had kicked into high gear; he took in every word Todd said, even though Todd sluffed off some of the information as being unimportant. Later, when his thoughts were more organized concerning Schmidt, Alec would filter through today's conversation, write down the parts he thought might be of importance and try to forget the information that was of no value. That was the hardest part about having an audiographic memory; sometimes, Alec wasn't able to forget.

"Did you ever have a chance to talk with Schmidt personally?" Alec asked.

"A couple of times."

"And?"

"And what?"

"You always told me to follow my gut instincts about

76

people I interviewed. Did you have any gut feelings about Schmidt?"

Todd thought for a few moments, picked up the phone and pushed a two-number sequence. "Sam, look through the old files and bring up the folder on Edgar Schmidt for me. Thanks. Sam Drexler," he explained, returning the phone. "We have a permanent research department now—not just some rookie apprentice we break in the hard way," he added with a laugh. "Gut feeling," Todd said, returning to the previous topic. "Yes, I remember I had a gut feeling about Schmidt. The few times I talked to him, I got the feeling he wasn't as crazy as everybody thought he was. He talked coherently and didn't ramble, his memory seemed clear, and he didn't fit the 'crazy scientist' mold people normally think of. Granted, some of the things he talked about then seemed like bizarre science fiction, but that was over thirty years ago. If some guy would say some of the same things today, people would nod their heads and say they were possible. In fact, some of the things he talked about have probably already become reality."

"Things like what?"

"Where's Sam with that file?" he asked, glancing at the phone. "Everything's in the file. You have been keeping files on all of your stories, haven't you?"

Alec nodded. "You taught me well."

"It may not seem important now, but someday, like now, you'll be glad you kept your files. After over thirty-five years in the business, you can't be expected to remember the details of every story you ever covered, especially the ones from over thirty years ago."

Alec nodded in acceptance of that explanation for Todd's lack of memory. "Is there anything else you can remember about Schmidt?"

Todd again thought for several moments. "Acronyms!" he blurted with a broad smile. "Schmidt liked to label everything with acronyms. There was Project this and Project that; when Sam gets that file up here, I'll show you the names of some of them and tell you what they stood for."

"Acronyms . . ." Alec said to himself aloud. "GOD."

"What's that?"

"GOD," Alec said, repeating the word for Todd. "Does the name Project GOD ring a bell?"

"Project GOD . . . Project GOD . . . no, and it seems like something with a label like that would hang onto some of the gray matter in the back of the old brain somewhere. Project GOD—" The phone rang. "Yes," Todd answered, picking it up quickly. He listened for a few moments in silence, and then responded curtly. "It's got to be there somewhere. Did you check my own personal filing cabinets in the back?" He paused. "And you cross-checked all the other files?" Another pause. "All right, I'll be down to look into it later." Todd returned the phone to its cradle and turned to face Alec, a frown of confusion lining his brow. "Sam said he couldn't find the file on Schmidt, but I'm positive it's down there somewhere. I know I pulled it out six or seven years ago when he died and made the notation. No matter, I'll find it somewhere, and when I do, I'll make a copy of it and send it to you." Todd looked at Alec out of the corner of his eye. "What's gotten you interested in Schmidt, anyway?"

"Brice gave me a box of documents they found in Schmidt's basement when they tore down his house, and they just caught my interest."

"Project GOD?" Alec nodded. "It definitely sounds like something that would attract your curiosity."

"Todd." Cheryl Williams, WQXM's local program promoter, stepped into his office. "Mayor Brownstein is waiting in Studio B, and Stu isn't back yet to do the interview. The mayor's a bit put out, and he said if Stu isn't here to interview him, he won't talk to anyone else but you."

"Geez. If it's not one thing, it's another. Tell Marlene I'm on my way down for makeup, and get Stu's script ready to put on the screen for me." Todd grabbed his suit coat from the back of his chair. "Politicians," he grumbled, shaking his head. "Sorry Alec."

"No problem. I've been there."

"It was good seeing you again, keep in touch. Oh, and let me know if you find out anything interesting on Project GOD."

Six

Alec glanced at his watch. It was after three o'clock; no wonder his stomach had been growling since he'd turned off the interstate. He hadn't eaten anything since seven-thirty that morning, when he and Krista had stopped for a light breakfast in one of the restaurants at the Madison airport.

Passing the city-limits sign for Prairie Dells, the town nearest to the lake and cabin, he smiled inwardly as he noted the population count boldly displayed beneath the town's name: 1,015. That total could have easily been met in just one of Louisville's city blocks that housed high-rise apartments. It had been a long time since he'd stayed in such a small community, and he wondered if the small-town friendliness he used to know in Iowa and Nebraska existed in Wisconsin as well. Locating a mom-and-pop diner, he pulled off into the parking lot and stopped. With any luck, he would be able to enjoy some friendly conversation, acquire a current map of the area and satisfy the growl in his stomach.

"Afternoon," the waitress said in greeting as he slid onto a seat in a booth. "Passing through?" she asked as she placed a glass of water and a menu on the table in front of him.

"We're vacationing at the lake," he answered, returning her friendly smile.

"Which one? There're a dozen lakes within fifty miles of here."

"The one off the Dell Creek River," Alec answered, not recalling the name of the lake itself. Either Krista had never identified it specifically, or it was one of those things he'd labeled as insignificant and had purposely tried to forget. Whatever the case, the lake's name didn't register in his mind.

"That could be one of three, but I guess it doesn't really matter." She took an order pad from her apron pocket, pulled a pencil out from behind her ear and stood poised, ready to take Alec's order. "We've still got homemade chicken and noodles left from our lunch special. It's pretty good and not too greasy."

"That sounds fine," he replied, sliding the menu back toward her. "And I'll have a glass of milk."

"Be back with you in a jiffy." Alec watched her until she disappeared into the kitchen; then he turned his attention to the diner's interior.

The arrangement was much as he'd expected. Eight backless, vinyl-covered stools bordered the counter opposite the serving window from the kitchen. Another counter, running below the window, held the coffeepots, a glass display case for homemade cakes and pies, narrow shelves filled with boxed breakfast cereals, and an assortment of clean dishes and glasses still in their dishwasher racks. Seven booths lined two of the diner's outside walls, four metal-legged tables with unmatched chairs filled in the space between the booths and the counter, and yellow-and-black-speckled square tiles covered the floor. Sitting against the vacant wall opposite the end of the counter was a brightly lighted jukebox, which was silent at the moment, and on the wall beside it hung a standard black pay telephone.

Alec nodded his head in acceptance. The decor of the diner would have provided a perfect setting for any of several of the dime-store paperback novels he enjoyed reading when he found the time to escape from the mental demands of his job.

Alec turned to look out the window beside him. Directly across the street, he saw a large plate glass window with the insignia of the U.S. Post Office. Taking note of the landmark, his thoughts again returned to the box Brice had brought to his office a few days before; the letters written to

80

Schmidt had been addressed to a Prairie Dells post office box number. He made a mental note to check the number on the letters when he returned to the cabin, and the next time he came into town, he planned to stop by the post office and see if that number and same box owner still existed after thirty years.

"I knew it would rain today since I washed my car yesterday," the waitress said with disgust as she set a steaming plate of chicken, noodles and mashed potatoes on the table in front of Alec.

Engrossed in his own thoughts, Alec hadn't noticed the large raindrops beginning to fall on the sidewalk or the gradual accumulation of moisture on the window. "The luck of the Irish," he said in jest, surmising from her bright red hair and smooth freckled skin that her ancestors had most likely come from the distant island noted for its shamrocks and leprechauns.

"Yep. Maybe one of these days it'll turn into good luck." She left and returned immediately with an empty glass and a pint carton of milk. "Will there be anything else for you? There's still a piece of pineapple upside-down cake left that Hazel baked fresh this morning."

"I'll have to think on that," Alec said, glancing down at the enormous helping of the luncheon special on his plate. "I'll have to wait and see how much room I have left after I eat all of this."

"Okay. Enjoy. If you want anything, just call me."

Alec watched her walk back to the counter, and as he did, he saw a cardboard display containing maps of Wisconsin and several of the surrounding states. Remembering that he wanted to find a direct route to Lashbrook so he could go visit Brice next week without having to drive over a hundred miles out of his way by following the interstate, he walked over to the display, picked up a Wisconsin map and brought it back to the table with him. Unfolding the bottom of the map to expose the Wisconsin-Illinois border, he laid it on the table in front of him and began scanning as he ate.

Several of the small-town names labeled on the detailed map were familiar to him. He'd gotten to know the general

81

area during the two years he'd worked in Rickdon, but an additional curiosity had prompted both him and Krista to make a trip to northern Illinois together not long after they'd first met. His eyes shifted along the map toward Dubuque, Iowa, but they stopped just short of the Illinois boundary, focusing on the name of a small town on the east side of the Mississippi River: Fairmont.

Alec and Krista had met during their junior year of college at a meeting sponsored by the local chapter of LAP—Locating Anonymous Parents. Both loved their adoptive parents dearly, and yet, both were curious to locate their birth parents, which in turn had led them to the meeting.

In reviewing their adoption papers, they'd discovered they'd both been adopted through the same agency in Fairmont, Illinois. A spur-of-the-moment decision had sent them to Fairmont, seeking further information, but their trip had produced only discouraging results. The old courthouse and an adjacent building that had housed the adoption agency had burned several years before, destroying any possible documents that might have led them to the identity of their birth parents. Their search had come to an abrupt end, but in the process, they'd met each other.

A blinding flash of white lightning filled the diner. A near-deafening clap of thunder followed immediately, rattling the windows, jiggling the salt and pepper shakers on the table and sending a tingle through the booth in which Alec sat. The overhead lights flickered and dimmed but returned to their normal brightness.

"Yipes!" the waitress said in exaggerated surprise. "That sure sounded like it was close."

In response to her words, Alec glanced toward her. He started to add a comment of his own but saw she was busy at the cash register, making change for two men he hadn't noticed being in the diner until now. He surmised that they'd been sitting in one of the booths on the other side of the door and that the booth's high back had hidden their presence during his brief survey of the diner.

"I'll bring the car around to the front door," Alec heard the younger of the two men say as he returned his attention to his late lunch and the map.

Alec reached for his milk and noticed he had yet to empty the contents of the carton into the glass. Picking up the waxed cardboard container, he couldn't help but notice the words *Prairie Dells Dairy* printed in bright blue letters in contrast to the stark white background. Curious, he looked for an address on the carton, and just as he'd suspected, the milk had been processed in and distributed from Prairie Dells, Wisconsin. As he turned the milk carton around and started to open one corner of the overlapping lip, he noticed an additional line of printing near the bottom of the otherwise white field.

"A subsidiary of the H&J Corporation," he said to himself and then chuckled cynically. "Well, H&J, whatever kind of conglomerate you are, it looks like you're slowly but surely taking over this part of Wisconsin."

"Are you okay?" The concerned tone of the waitress's voice prompted Alec to look back toward the counter. She had moved from behind the cash register and was now standing beside the older man, who had remained inside the diner while his younger companion had gone after their car. "Are you okay?" she asked again. The man shook his head desperately and lifted a hand to his throat. Frantically, she began hitting him on the back with her open hand. "Chuck! Hazel! Come out here! I think this man's choking!"

Panicking, the man pulled away from her. Both of his hands were now clutching at his throat, and then he began tearing at the skin on his neck as if his fingers could break through and dislodge whatever had caught there and cut off his air supply. His lips were beginning to turn blue, and a look of sheer terror filled his bulging eyes.

"Call nine-one-one!" Alec shouted as he slid from the booth's seat. He ran around behind the choking man, slipped his arms around the man's lower chest, balled one hand into a fist and grabbed it with his other hand. With an exhale of exertion, Alec pulled his fist up and back just below the man's rib cage. Nothing. Quickly, he repositioned his fist and tried the maneuver again. This time, the air that had been trapped in the man's lungs was forced out through his mouth, expelling the piece of peppermint candy that had lodged in his windpipe.

Alec felt the man's weight grow heavy in his arms and tried to lower him gently to the floor to keep him from falling. "Did someone call for an ambulance?" Alec asked, looking up at the diner's three workers, who were standing numbly beside him, mesmerized by the man on the floor. "Did any of you call for an ambulance?" Alec persisted. The portly woman in a white uniform and food-stained apron vaguely nodded her head.

Alec returned his attention to the man on the floor. He felt for a pulse along the man's neck and found one. He leaned over and placed his ear close to the man's mouth and nose. He heard an exchange of air and felt the warm breath touch his skin. Feeling that the man's life was no longer in immediate danger, Alec began to loosen the man's tie, then unbuttoned the top few buttons of his crisply starched white shirt.

"How long will it take for them to get here?" Alec asked, again looking up at the trio who still stood beside him.

"The fire station's at the other end of town," the waitress finally answered. "It's not that far. They should be here any time now."

A horn sounded just outside the front door. "That's probably this man's companion," Alec said, glancing at the doorway and then back at the waitress. "Go tell him what happened." He watched her leave, and a few moments later, the front door flew open as the younger man came running back in.

"Dad?" the man questioned as he knelt down on the floor opposite Alec. "Is he going to be all right?" he asked, looking into Alec's eyes.

Alec's eyes locked with his. For an instant, he sensed the man's question wasn't one of deep concern.

"I . . . I don't know," Alec answered, a little jittery now that the brunt of what had just happened was hitting him with full force. "I'm not a doctor or anything. I just did something I learned from watching a TV special."

The faint sound of sirens grew in the distance. "They're

coming," the waitress said, looking out the window. "They'll be here in a few more minutes."

"J . . . or . . . dy." The man on the floor rolled his head slowly from side to side. His eyelids fluttered and gradually opened. "Jor . . . dy."

"It's okay, Dad. I'm here," he responded, almost without emotion.

Alec looked at him in puzzlement and immediately sensed that things were not at all well between father and son. The man across from him showed very few signs of true emotion; it was almost as if he were merely acting out a role he thought the people watching him would expect him to play.

The man on the floor looked at his son and blinked his eyes; then he turned his head slowly toward Alec. A weak smile came to his lips as he whispered, "Thank you."

"Here they are," the waitress said, moving to the side of the door and holding it open for the emergency technicians to enter.

Two men in rain-spotted white shirts hurried into the diner; each carried a medium-size black case containing emergency equipment. Working quickly, they knelt on either side of the man and went into the routine procedures of their profession.

Alec moved out of their way without being asked, but the younger man—the man referred to as Jordy—had to be asked to step aside. "Mr. Graham," the man who had come from the kitchen said, "why don't you have a seat here while they tend to your father." He pulled a chair back from one of the tables and nodded toward it.

"I don't need to sit down," Jordy replied, still looking at his father as if hypnotized.

"Then at least stand back to give them room to work." Jordy finally stepped back, and everyone watched with intense interest as one of the technicians timed the man's pulse while his partner wrapped a cuff around the man's arm to check his blood pressure.

"I'm all right now," the man on the floor said, attempting to sit up.

"We're not going to take any chances, Mr. Graham," one

of the technicians responded, gently laying his hand on the man's shoulder, encouraging him to remain quiet. "I think you're in for a nice little ride down to the hospital in Madison so the doctors can check you out."

"I'm not going to any hospital," the man objected adamantly.

"Dad, don't give them a hard time," Jordy stated, almost as an order. "You've been talking about taking a little time off from work anyway, and this looks like a good time to start." The older man reluctantly agreed to the idea, and he was even cooperative with the technicians when they brought in a collapsible stretcher and helped him onto it.

As they rolled the stretcher toward the door and the ambulance waiting outside, Jordy followed after them but stopped just short of leaving. He turned, looked back at Alec, then walked toward him. "Thank you," he said, extending his hand. "The words don't seem to say enough for saving my father's life, but they're the only ones I can think of." He glanced at Alec's hand as he reached for it.

Alec felt the soft leather of Jordy's driving glove as he exchanged the gesture. "I was just glad I was here to help."

"If there's ever any . . ." The words trailed off as Jordy's glance at Alec's right hand intensified into a stare.

Presuming Jordy's reaction had been brought on by the stress of the past few minutes—and that all of his words and actions had been caused by the sudden shock of the situation—Alec felt guilty for his false appraisal of Jordy's seeming lack of emotion in regards to his father. He attempted to comfort him with a few additional words. "Your father appears to be in good health otherwise. I'm sure he'll come through this all right."

Jordy didn't respond. He continued to stare at Alec's hand without releasing it.

"Your name!" Jordy blurted out. "What is your name?" His eyes darted toward Alec's in accompaniment to his question.

"Alec Crispen."

"Alec Crispen," Jordy repeated. "And where can I reach you? I'm . . . I'm sure my father will want to see you after he

comes home . . . dinner perhaps," he suggested in a somewhat calmer voice.

"There's no need—"

"But I'm sure he'll insist," Jordy interrupted. "Please, how
can I reach you?"

Alec thought for a moment. He didn't know the name of
the lake where the cabin was located, and since they would
only be spending two weeks there, they had decided against
installing a phone. There was only one local point of
reference Alec could think of that would enable Jordy to
contact him. "I'm sure Marvin Horton would take a phone
message for us."

"Marvin Horton?" Jordy questioned with a quick intake
of breath.

"He's our neighbor at the lake. Do you know him?"

"Not personally," he answered with hesitation, "but I do
know the name." A siren whooped outside the diner, and
Jordy turned to see the ambulance pulling out of the parking
lot. "I must be going now to be with my father," he said,
looking back at Alec, "but I'm sure we'll see each other again
very soon. And again, thank you." He squeezed Alec's hand
one last time, glanced at it again, then turned and hurried
toward the door.

Alec followed after him as far as the end booth, where he
paused to look out the rain-streaked window to watch him
leave. He sensed that something other than the shock of his
father's situation had stirred a true emotional response from
Jordy. There was something about Jordy's reaction when
he'd grasped Alec's hand—and then stared at it—that had
pricked Alec's curiosity; there was something about Jordy's
reaction that had stirred Alec's gut instinct.

Alec looked from the window to his right hand, which still
bore a faint imprint from the stitching on Jordy's driving
glove. To him, his hand looked like anyone else's hand: there
were four fingers and a thumb, nails, skin and knuckles. The
only thing about his hand that could distinguish it from a
million others was his birthmark: the three small moles on
the webbing between his thumb and forefinger—three small
moles that, had they been connected, would have formed a

perfect triangle.

"Are you sure?" Hubert Graham asked with excitement as he sat up in his hospital bed. "Are you absolutely sure?"

"I saw it with my own eyes," Jordy assured him. "After living with it for over thirty years, I should know what it looks like better than anyone else."

"How did you react when you saw it? Did you do anything stupid?" Graham asked in a deprecating tone. "Did you do anything to make him suspicious?"

"No." Jordy turned from the bed and walked toward the window. "Anything I might have done could have easily been interpreted as a . . . as a reaction to what happened with you."

For several silent moments, Jordy looked out over the early evening lights that were beginning to outline the downtown area of Madison. His thoughts drifted back . . . back . . . far back into his past to when he had been a child.

"What are you thinking about now?"

Jordy focused on the blue neon lights of the First National Bank in the distance and exhaled a long breath. "I was just thinking about what it might have been like to have grown up with a . . . a brother," he finally answered.

"You had Al," his father said with a muffled scoff.

"Yes." Jordy exhaled a heavy, pitiful sigh. "Al, poor ol' Al." He paused. "But I've always wondered what it would have been like if you would have kept . . . one of the others." Jordy held his right hand up in front of his eyes and looked at the three small dots on the webbing between his thumb and forefinger: three small dots, resembling moles—three small dots that, had they been connected, would have formed a perfect triangle.

Seven

Alec eased the van into a narrow parking space in front of Prairie Dells's only major grocery store. He hadn't been back to the small town since Wednesday and the incident with the choking man at the mom-and-pop diner. The main reason he'd returned today was to stock up on the perishables he'd consumed while Krista had been gone. He needed to replenish their supplies today; it was Friday, and Krista would be back tomorrow.

"Did you bring a shopping list?" Robbie asked, twisting the small catalogue he held tightly in his hands and trying to control the excitement in his voice. Alec looked over at the boy, smiled and nodded his head.

Robbie was with him for two reasons. Today was his birthday, and Alec had brought him into town to pick out a present. When Alec had asked what he might want, Robbie answered without even having to think about it; he wanted a new fishing pole. The other reason Robbie had accompanied him was to give Marvin a chance to pick up the cake he'd ordered and an opportunity to check out all of his gear for night fishing. Robbie had been hounding his grandfather to take him night fishing since the day he'd arrived, and Marvin had repeatedly declined to take him, knowing he would use the excursion as a surprise for his grandson's birthday.

"Do you have one picked out?" Alec asked, nodding at the catalogue. He knew nothing about fishing equipment and had relied on Marvin's expertise in the area to suggest three or four poles from the brochure that had been mailed by the local sporting goods store at the start of the fishing season.

"The red one Grandpa liked," Robbie answered, opening the catalogue to the exact page and showing Alec the picture.

"Then the red one it'll be," he responded with a laugh, reaching toward Robbie to ruffle his blond hair.

Fortunately the red fishing pole Robbie wanted was in stock. It didn't take long for the salesman to complete the transaction and wrap the pole in brown paper, to which he attached a handle made from string. Even though the fishing pole was separated at each of its sections, it presented quite an obstacle to carry through the narrow aisles of the grocery store. But Robbie managed without causing too many problems; he only poked one lady in front of them and stabbed Alec twice.

"Are we going back now?" Robbie asked anxiously as he slid onto the passenger seat of the van and began tearing the brown paper off the fishing pole.

"There's one other place I want to stop," Alec answered as he slid the last sack of groceries into the back. A look of disappointment spread across Robbie's face. "It won't take me too long, and if you want," he added after a moment's thought, "you can move into the back here and start putting your fishing pole together." Robbie didn't need any further encouragement. He moved into the back of the van and began sorting through the items that had come with his new pole. "I'll be back in a jiffy."

Alec walked down the street for about a half a block, then stopped and looked at the emblem on the plate glass window beside him. It identified the building as a U.S. Post Office.

He had thought to look for the post office box number on Edgar Schmidt's letters the night before when he'd again gone through the contents of the box Brice had brought him. He'd sorted through the postcards, letters, journals and photographs, dividing them into neat stacks that now sat on the kitchen table. As he recalled his conversation with Todd Tyson, he'd made notes on the sheet of paper he'd started back in Louisville, trying to make some connection, but nothing had begun to gel in his mind. The only aspect that might in any way be of help to him was the address on the letters, and that would only be of assistance if he could find out who owned the box. It was a slim lead, but it was the only one he had; it was the only thing that might help to satisfy his curiosity about Project GOD.

Alec pulled a slip of paper from his shirt pocket as he walked into the building's small foyer. He looked at the number he'd written down the night before, then walked toward a wall to his right that contained a hundred or more pigeonhole partitions just large enough for a few letters and a tightly rolled newspaper. Each box was fronted with a small wooden door that bore a number and a key-operated lock, and near the top of each door was a small glass window measuring about one inch by two. Scanning over the numbers, his eyes stopped on box number seven.

Who paid the monthly rent on box seven? Who had paid the rent on it over thirty years ago?

Alec stepped closer to the wall of small doors and bent over in front of box number seven. Tilting his head and trying to stay out of the light cast by the single fixture overhead, he attempted to look in through the small window. Maybe there would be a letter inside with a name he could associate with the address.

"Can I help you with something, sir?"

Even though Alec couldn't think of any law he'd broken, he felt somewhat guilty about his actions and turned self-consciously from the wall. He immediately saw an elderly man standing a few feet away from him who was as spindly and thin as his spoken words had been. Alec presumed the man worked there since he wore a matching shirt and pants of post-office blue.

"Are you looking for something?" the man asked, taking a step toward Alec.

During his years as an investigative reporter, Alec had never approached any subject with anything less than total honesty, and he couldn't think of any reason to do otherwise now. "I have a box number, and I was trying to find out who it belongs to."

The old man cocked his head to one side and looked at

Alec suspiciously. "Why do you want to know?"

"I received a box of old letters, and I've become interested in the man they were written to. I was hoping I might be able to find somebody who might have known him."

"What's the name?"

"Edgar Schmidt."

The old man thought for a moment. "Don't know 'im. He from around here?"

"He was up here for a while during the middle and late fifties."

"I'da known him if he was here. I've been postmaster here since fifty-one." He thought again for a few more moments. "Come to think of it, the name seems kinda familiar, but I never knew 'im."

"Maybe he stayed with someone while he was here and had his mail sent to their box number."

"What's the number?"

"Seven."

The old man looked at the rows of boxes that were numbered vertically from left to right.

"Do you know who it belongs to?" Alec asked.

"Yep." He turned his head so he could look Alec directly in the eyes. "But I can't give out that information."

"Why not?"

"Privacy."

Alec had known what the old man's answer was going to be. He had run into a similar situation in Louisville not too long ago and had contacted the police to get a court order to obtain the information. In that situation, the extra effort had been worth it; the bogus mail-order scam had been uncovered, and his investigation had led to the participants' prosecution. But nothing as pressing confronted him now, and he wondered how he was going to obtain the box holder's identity.

"Could you answer a question for me?"

"Maybe."

"Does the same person have box number seven who had it thirty years ago?"

The old man thought for a few moments, and when he

couldn't think of any laws of privacy he might be breaking by answering the question, he answered, "Yep."

"Would you do me a favor then and put a note in the box for me?"

"I could do that."

Alec took one of his business cards from his wallet and wrote on the back: *I'm interested in information on Edgar Schmidt. Please contact me through Marvin Horton.*

"Would you put this in box number seven for me?" he asked as he handed the old man the card.

The man nodded his head as he took the card, then extended his other hand palm up. Alec looked at him questioningly. "That'll be twenty-five cents."

"Twenty-five cents? What for?"

"To mail your card."

"To mail the card? All you have to do is walk around the corner and put it in the box."

"This is an official U.S. Post Office, and if you want to do business here, you're going to have to pay for the transaction."

"Okay, okay," Alec shook his head and chuckled as he reached into the front pocket of his jeans. He pulled out a quarter and placed it in the man's hand. "It's been a pleasure doing business with you," he said as he turned and started toward the door. "I just hope it doesn't get lost in the shuffle," he added under his breath.

"Isn't it about the neatest fishing pole you've ever seen, Grandpa?"

Marvin smiled and nodded in response to Robbie's enthusiasm. "It's about the purtiest pole I've seen in a long time. Why don't you head on over to the cabin and get my tool box and take it out on the porch. I'll be over in a few minutes to help you put on the reel and run the line."

"Okay." Robbie took off running but stopped after a few steps and turned back around. "Thanks for the pole, Alec. You can have all the fish I catch the next time Grandpa and I go out on the lake fishing." He turned and continued toward his grandfather's cabin.

"Did you get your errands run while we were gone?" Alec asked as he reached for the bag of groceries in the back of the van.

"The cake's in a box on your kitchen counter, and all three lamps are full of fuel and set to go for tonight. You sure you don't want to come with us?"

"I'll pass. Besides, it's Robbie's birthday, and you need to spend some time with him alone."

As they started walking toward the cabin, a jeep pulled into the drive behind them. The driver honked the horn. "Who's that?" Alec asked in surprise.

Marvin took one look at the man now walking toward them and answered with a note of disgust. "Jordy Graham." Alec caught the tone in Marvin's voice but didn't have time to question.

"Mr. Crispen," Jordy said as he approached them, "in all the confusion the other day, I failed to introduce myself. Jordy Graham."

Alec again felt the soft leather of Jordy's driving glove against his skin as they exchanged a firm handshake. And he again saw Jordy glance at his right hand, even though the gesture was much more subtle than it had been a few days before.

"This is my neighbor Marvin Horton," Alec said in introduction.

Jordy nodded his head in recognition; Marvin replied with a very unfriendly, "Humph! I'll take that inside for you." Marvin took the sack from Alec's arm. Without a word of farewell, the old man turned and walked away.

"Won't you come up to the porch and sit down?"

"I can't stay. I was on my way into town when I saw your van and thought I'd drop by."

"How's your father?"

"He's doing fine. He came home from the hospital yesterday, and after being in the house for less than a full day, he's already driving everyone crazy."

"I'm glad to hear everything turned out all right with him. I must admit, he had me scared for a little while the

94

other day."

"He had us all scared. Anyway, he's all right and he wanted me to ask you to dinner tonight. I was going to call later on this morning, but since I saw you, I thought I might as well make it a personal invitation."

"I'm afraid I can't make it tonight. I already have plans to help a very special friend celebrate his birthday."

Jordy looked disappointed, but then he asked, "If you're busy this evening, maybe you could come over for a little while this afternoon. My father's very anxious to see you."

"I—"

"It's just across the lake, so it wouldn't be out of your way or take up too much of your time. He's really anxious to see you," Jordy stressed.

"Just across the lake?" Alec reacted with a note of surprise. "You're *those* Grahams?" he asked, turning slightly and glancing at the house on the opposite shore.

"Yes. Small world, isn't it? We're neighbors as well. Will you be able to come over sometime this afternoon?"

"I suppose I could come for a little while," Alec said, turning back to face Jordy. "But I'll tell you now, I'll have to be home by five. The birthday party's for a very special friend."

"Shall we say around three," Jordy suggested with a smile.

"Three's fine."

"I'll send a car over for you."

"That won't be necessary. As close as you are, I know I'd enjoy the walk."

"We'll expect you at three then." Alec reconfirmed the time with a nod. "Well, I'd better be going. I still have to go into town and then get back to make arrangements for this afternoon."

"Don't do anything special on my account."

"And why not, Mr. Crispen? To my father, you're one very special person."

Alec walked across the porch and sat down on a wicker chair beside Marvin. Marvin was staring out across the

95

water in the direction of the colonial house, and his face was set in a hostile expression. His fingers tapped out a fast rhythm on the arm of his chair; his leg bounced up and down nervously. It didn't take a psychiatrist to tell that something was on Marvin's mind.

"I take it you don't care for Jordy Graham."

"I don't hold much worth for any of 'em. If I'da known it was Graham's life you saved the other day, I'da told you I'da just as soon you let him die."

"You don't mean that." Granted, Marvin was a cantankerous, opinionated old man, but Alec knew he was a good man at heart and didn't really mean what he'd just said.

"Nah. I guess even vultures deserve to have an existence." He laughed cynically. "If we didn't have the bad ones around, we wouldn't have anything to compare the good ones to." Marvin's fingers gradually ceased their drumming, and his leg eventually came to rest on the cushion of his chair. "Makes you wonder though sometimes why some people do the things they do."

"Things like what?"

"Like this." Marvin made a sweeping gesture with his hand toward the fenced, vacant area around the lake to the east and then to the north along the shoreline. "Used to be seven more cabins on the other side of Krista's, spaced out clear over to that little peninsula yonder where the Grahams have their dock. Most o' them were owned by older folks like me who lucked out during the twenties and thirties playing the stock market with money they really couldn't afford. But when their money ran out or the taxes started going up and they couldn't afford to hang on to their places here any more, Graham bought them out—every last one of 'em, except for Krista and me."

"Doesn't sound like anything underhanded was going on," Alec commented, intentionally playing the devil's advocate to encourage Marvin to continue.

He glanced down at the birthmark on his right hand. Because of his obvious interest in the unique mark, Jordy Graham was beginning to attract Alec's interest almost as much as Edgar Schmidt. Perhaps Marvin could enlighten him on a few aspects of the Grahams' lives he might not think to ask about on his own.

"In fact," Alec continued, "I'd say it sounds like a pretty prudent move on his part. Buying up the property around here would let him expand his business without having to set up another base of operation elsewhere."

"May sound prudent, but I'll guarantee there's been a lot of underhanded stuff going on. Property taxes don't normally go up as high and as fast as they have been around here for the past twenty-five years without a little scheming somewhere. And since Jordy and a half dozen other of Graham's associates are on the city council, I'd almost bet they're the ones doing the scheming. They vote to keep upping our taxes, but they can take theirs off their business."

"You can take yours off your income taxes too."

Again, Marvin came out with his characteristic, "Humph. It still don't seem right. I could see taxes going up if this was a big industrial complex area, but the Grahams have the only big business for twenty to thirty miles in any direction. It's almost . . . almost like they want to get rid of everybody else so they can keep whatever they're doing out here a secret."

"And just what kind of secrets do people keep around a dairy?" Alec asked.

"I think they've got more than just a dairy going over there." Alec said nothing; he just looked at Marvin, waiting for him to continue. "There're trucks and vans going in and out of that place at all hours of the day and night, and there're always strange noises coming from the place—especially at night." Alec continued to listen without interruption. "There are strange sorta animal noises that come drifting across the lake when the sky's clear and the air's still . . ."

Animals. A thread of Todd Tyson's conversation flickered across the back of Alec's mind.

". . . and there were even a couple of times when I was sitting out on the porch by myself just enjoying the night when I thought I heard what sounded like a baby crying . . ."

Babies . . . photographs . . .

". . . and I know for sure there aren't any babies over

97

there. Jordy's the youngest one living over there that I know of, and he's not married. Something strange is going on over there, and it don't have nothing to do with no dairy."

Alec hadn't heard the last of Marvin's comments; his mind was at work thinking . . . wondering. He wondered why the animals Todd had mentioned and the photographs of the babies that were in the box Brice brought him had surfaced in his mind at almost the same instant. He also wondered why his gut instinct was gnawing at a possible connection. Could the house across the lake have something to do with the photographed babies . . . with Edgar Schmidt . . . with Project GOD? He doubted it. It was such a long shot that it sounded ridiculous even to him, but yet, what harm would it cause to pursue the possibility?

"Have you ever heard of a man by the name of Edgar Schmidt?"

"He supposed to be from around here?"

"I think he visited Prairie Dells sometime back in the late fifties."

Marvin shook his head. "Don't recall the name, but then I was never very good at names. If you had a picture of 'im, I could tell you right off the bat if I'da seen 'im or not. Can't remember names too well, but I never forget a face. Do you have a picture?"

"No, but maybe I can get one," Alec answered, thinking Todd might have a photograph in his file.

"So what did Jordy Graham want?" Marvin asked, the tone in his voice turning sour again.

"He invited me over for a little while this afternoon. His father wants to see me."

"You going?"

"For a little while, but I told him I'd have to be back for Robbie's birthday party," he added quickly to prevent Marvin from developing any further hard feelings. Alec looked across the lake and studied the house for a few brief moments. "Have you ever been over there?"

"I've never been invited, and I've never had any reason to go. Like I said, it's almost like they want to keep the place a secret."

98

"Grandpa," Robbie called from the porch of Marvin's cabin, "I can't find your tool box anywhere."

"It's out in the—" Marvin called back, but then his words stopped abruptly. "I had it out in the shed with me when I was working on the lamps," he said to Alec in a lower volume. "I'm coming," he called back to Robbie as he got up from the chair and began walking across the porch. Marvin descended the steps, then stopped and looked back at Alec. "I'm planning on lighting the candles on Robbie's birthday cake at five-thirty sharp."

"I'll be back," Alec assured him with a nod of his head. "I'll be back."

Eight

Hubert Graham reread the short message on the back of Alec's business card, then looked out through the French doors opening from the den. His gaze passed the bricked patio, cushioned wrought-iron lawn furniture and blossom-filled flower boxes to rest on a cluster of white buildings in the distance.

The card Jordy had discovered in one of their post office boxes had taken him by surprise; he'd brought it to his father in a state of concern. Unlike his son, Hubert Graham was rarely taken by surprise, but when he was, he was at a loss for an immediate response. He had to think in silence. This particular surprise had affected him far more deeply than any other he could remember.

"What do you think it means?" Jordy asked, watching his father intently as he shifted his own weight nervously from one foot to the other. "Do you think he knows something? Do you think he found out about—" Graham held up his hand as an indication for his son to be silent. Jordy complied for a few moments but couldn't contain his questions for any greater length of time. "How did he find out? How . . . how did he know to contact *you?*"

"He doesn't know anything," Graham answered calmly. "He's only guessing."

"But how—"

"Think!" Graham interrupted. He turned sharply to face his son. "Think," he demanded. "What were the names of the men Snider said he thought might have found the journals Ed could have hidden away in his house?"

Jordy thought for a few moments. "Wade . . . Jerry Wade."

"And who else?"

Jordy shook his head, unable to come up with an immediate answer.

"Think! You know the name as well as I do—and you overlooked the connection as readily as I did."

"Crispen!" Jordy finally answered. "Bruce Crispen. Do you think he's Alec's brother?"

"Brother, cousin, whatever, if you'd come across something you didn't understand but thought might be important, where would you take it?"

Jordy looked at his father and nodded in comprehension. "To an investigative reporter." His smile broadened, and he began to chuckle. "Who would have ever thought that all those times we watched him on TV, when we were in Louisville for the races, that our own operation would someday become an object of his investigation."

"We don't know that to be a fact . . . as of yet. Like I said, I don't think he knows anything for sure, but if he does have Ed's notes we may be in for a touchy time. This afternoon should tell us a lot about just how much he knows or doesn't know. Both of us will need to be ready for any questions he might ask." Graham turned again to look out the French doors toward the buildings in the distance. "Is anything on the schedule for today?"

"Three or four are due at any time, but since there haven't been any foreseeable complications, the staff should be able to handle the arrival of the new units."

"We can only hope nothing unexpected happens while he's here."

"I just had an idea," Jordy said, walking across the room to join his father. "While Alec's here this afternoon, why not send Jameson over to have a look around his cabin. If he does have Schmidt's journals, that would be a good time to get them."

"One step at a time. It wouldn't be an intelligent move on

our part to send someone over there in the daytime, and besides, there's no use in being paranoid if there's nothing to be paranoid about. We're just going to have to play it by ear this afternoon and try to learn as much as we can about what he knows." He paused. "If we find out he knows—or suspects—too much, then we can always look for the journals later."

"And if he knows too much?"

"Don't even consider that possibility at the moment."

"But if he does?" Jordy persisted.

Graham pondered the question for several moments before he answered. "If worse comes to worst, then I doubt if there will be any alternative but to . . . to terminate one of the units from the Delta series," he said with a note of regret. "There's too much at stake here to even consider anything else."

"You wouldn't. You *couldn't*. Surely you couldn't—"

"No, I wouldn't want to, but in the end, there may be no other choice." Graham's attention was drawn to a figure he saw leave one of the outbuildings.

Even in the light of midday, the figure appeared dark. The man's shoulders were rounded forward, and his long arms hung freely, swaying like rhythmic pendulums at his side. His gait emphasized a side-to-side movement of his entire body that alternated from one turned in foot to the other, but in spite of his physical handicap, his pace was somewhat quick.

"Have you talked with Al about our visitor who's coming this afternoon?"

"I haven't had a chance. I came directly to you with the card as soon as I got back from town."

"Make sure you talk to him. And make sure he understands he's not to be anywhere where he might be seen. He'd prompt too many questions there wouldn't be any answers for except the truth . . . and I'm not ready to give Alec Crispen all of the answers—not just yet, anyway. After all of these years, I'm not sure how he'd take it . . . or what he might try to do."

*   *   *

The sun peeked out from behind billowy white clouds as Alec followed the road from their cabin toward the Graham estate. Walking became much easier for him once he reached the blacktop on the near side of the bridge, and the entire lake and its surrounding countryside took on a new perspective the closer he came to Graham property. Krista's and Marvin's cabins with their half-acres lots looked dwarfed in comparison to the fenced property that bordered them on every side and even fingered its way between the road and the river. It appeared that everything had been planned for the ultimate takeover. Once the property was acquired all the way around the lake, a simple section of fence would connect the open end by the river's bridge to the corner at the edge of the lake beside their dock. With less than a half mile of fencing, the lake and everything around it would be the sole property of the H&J Corporation.

As he continued along the blacktop road, Alec took in the beauty of his surroundings. Wild violets and daisies bloomed in thick beds along the road's shoulder; water lilies floated at the lake's edge, their white and orange blossoms so large and numerous they all but obliterated the round green leaves beneath. A few feet from the lilies, a mother duck swam unafraid with an orderly line of six hatchlings paddling along behind her.

After he'd walked several yards into the immense stand of densely leaved oak and maple that all but hid the colonial mansion beyond, Alec stopped. A large steel gate spanned the road ahead of him, and rising above it, over twenty feet into the air, was a stark white arc painted with the recognizable blue words *Prairie Dells Dairy*.

"You've already been away from your job too long, Crispen, you're slipping," Alec said to himself. "You knew there was a dairy over here, but you didn't make the connection. And the H&J Corporation . . . that has to be the Grahams. And I'll bet Jordy's father is the *H* and Jordy is the *J*." He chuckled to himself and shook his head. "How many other things have you been missing?"

As Alec approached the gate, he saw another sign, a much smaller one—one he hadn't been expecting or would ever have rationalized to exist there. The small brass plaque attached to the side of the gate was imprinted with the words *The Graham Foundation of Zoological Research*.

"May I help you, sir?" A deep male voice seemed to rise from out of nowhere to fill the trees around him.

Alec stopped abruptly and surveyed the immediate area. Within a few moments, he located a small speaker and camera mounted high atop one of the gate's concrete support posts. The camera was aimed directly toward him.

"I'm Alec Crispen," he said, looking up at the camera. "Jordy Graham invited me over this afternoon."

"Do you have a vehicle?"

"No, I walked over from the other side of the lake."

A few seconds passed, and then a section of the main gate, only large enough for a man to pass through, swung open. "Please come in, Mr. Crispen. Mr. Graham is expecting you."

Alec nodded in response and proceeded through the opening. He'd never liked talking with someone via the impersonal mechanics of electronics and didn't feel comfortable doing so now. He was the type of individual who enjoyed talking to people face-to-face; he liked to see their eyes. He'd learned through experience that eyes could very rarely support a lie—unless the liar was extremely good.

When Alec heard the near-silent hum of the electronic gate closing behind him, he stopped and looked back at it. He wondered why Graham needed such an elaborate front gate, and he began to wonder just how elaborate of a security system had been installed throughout the rest of Graham's property. Then, he began to wonder why. Were there secrets in the dairy business that needed to be protected from theft? Was there some area of their zoological research—whatever that might be—that needed additional security? Or could Marvin have been right? Could there be something going on inside Graham's fenced property they wanted to keep secret from the rest of the world?

"Mr. Graham is expecting you, Mr. Crispen. Follow the lane to your right to the house."

Alec looked up at the camera and noticed it had rotated to

104

focus on him. He nodded again, and a thin smile tightened his lips as he raised his hand and waved. "I'm on my way." He turned from the gate and continued walking along the blacktop road.

By the time he reached the oval drive that curved gently in front of the stately home, Alec had passed the front gate's small guardhouse and had detected three additional cameras partially hidden in the neatly trimmed bushes bordering the road. For each camera he'd discovered, he imagined there had been at least one or two more he hadn't seen. Again, he questioned Graham's need for such elaborate security, and as with so many similar questions that had crossed Alec's mind, he began to wonder if whatever Graham was protecting was illegal.

As Alec walked on toward the house, he took in its majestic beauty. Eight white pillars adorned the front porch and supported a railed balcony of equal length. Decorative black shutters emphasized the six large upstairs windows and set of French doors leading onto the balcony; all this was repeated on the ground level and around the front door. A black window box at each window was filled with blooming red geraniums, and draping gold chains accented the artistic chandelier hanging above the front entrance. Had he not known the house was located in Wisconsin, Alec might have guessed he'd been transported to the Deep South. With all of the other questions he had developed concerning the Grahams, he now added one more: Why had such an elaborate southern-style mansion been built so far north of the Ohio River?

Stepping from the drive onto the brick walk leading to the front porch, Alec stopped to admire two statues of large cats that flanked the walk. One statue depicted the king of beasts sitting upright, licking a paw; the other statue captured the patience of a lioness nursing her three cubs. Both statues had been cast in bronze and shimmered in the dappled sunlight filtering through the trees, giving credit to the diligence of whoever had taken the time to polish them.

As Alec turned back toward the porch, a brief movement from above caught his attention. He looked up at the second-story window on the end. The lace curtains hanging there still fluttered from being disturbed, but whoever had been standing there, looking out at him, was gone.

He shook his head as his eyes quickly surveyed the remaining windows across the second story. He didn't feel comfortable being there, and he laughed uneasily at a thought that skipped across his mind. If he believed in horror stories, this was one house he'd definitely refuse to enter.

Despite his curious nature, for some reason, Alec felt uneasy about being there. He was thankful he could use Robbie's birthday party as an excuse for not having to stay very long.

The front door opened. A tall, white-haired black man dressed in black slacks, a short-sleeved white shirt and a gray-and-black pin-striped vest stepped onto the porch. "Mr. Crispen?"

"Yes."

A smile slowly spread across the man's face as he made a quick visual survey of Alec. "I'm Lewis, Mr. Graham's butler. Mr. Graham has been detained for a few minutes and asked that I show you to the den. Won't you come with me, please."

Alec followed Lewis through a spacious foyer that gave access to four doorways, an impressive winding staircase and a long hall that presumably led to the back of the house. A giant crystal chandelier hung directly overhead; other than that, the decor was simple and uncluttered. Two blue-cushioned, straight-back antique chairs sat on either side of the front door, providing the only furnishings.

"This way, Mr. Crispen." Lewis led him to the second door on the right, opened it and stepped aside for Alec to enter. "Would you care for a beverage while you're waiting?"

"No, thank you."

"Mr. Graham shouldn't be detained much longer." With that brief explanation, Lewis made another quick survey of Alec, then turned and closed the door behind him.

Alec felt somewhat self-conscious standing in the unfamiliar room alone. In an attempt to overcome his uneasiness, he began looking at the displays arranged in a large, lighted, glass-fronted cabinet built into the wall to his right. Just as the two bronze cats at the entrance of the house indicated someone's love for animals, so did the figures stored in the case. Ceramic reproductions of all the great cats were precisely spaced on one shelf; another shelf contained replicas of antelope, elephants, giraffes, deer and bison; and still another shelf contained figures of apes, gorillas, orangutans and chimpanzees. Alec's eyes were drawn to a particular figurine on that shelf. He chuckled. It appeared that someone in the household had a sense of humor; someone had placed a ceramic likeness of a human infant next to the most ferocious-looking gorilla.

After he had looked at all the figures in the cabinet, his attention shifted to the pictures on the wall beside it. Again the animal theme was prevalent, and again, the variety of animals pictured showed no favorites.

As he worked his way on around the room, Alec continued to admire the colorful paintings and stopped momentarily to study an elaborate collection of African spears and shields hanging on the wall in the corner. Passing by the French doors, he approached the fireplace on the wall across the room from the display case. When he finally stopped and looked up at the lighted portrait hanging above the mantel, his breath caught in his throat. He stared unblinking; he stood as if he were frozen—as if he were a statue himself. The portrait hanging above the fireplace was of . . . *could* have been of . . . Krista.

"I understand my mother was a wonderful woman."

Alec turned with a start. He hadn't heard Jordy enter the room, and until he'd spoken, he hadn't been aware of his presence.

"I never really knew her long enough to be able to remember her very well. She died in a plane crash when I was just two and a half years old." Jordy crossed the room and, as he drew nearer to Alec, noticed the stunned expression on his guest's face. "Is something wrong?"

"The portrait . . . it took me by surprise," Alec answered, looking back at it.

"Oh? How's that?" Jordy asked, turning beside Alec to look up at the portrait of his mother.

"If I didn't know any better, I'd say it was a picture of my wife."

"I'm a great believer in possibilities. My mother was from Atlanta, Georgia. Is it possible your wife might have come from there as well? The hands of fate might have brought us together because we're relatives."

"I doubt that." Alec looked at Jordy briefly before returning his attention to the portrait, but for that brief instant, he thought he saw a sparkle of undeniable truth in Jordy's eyes. "We don't know anything about Krista's family. She was adopted, and all of her records were destroyed in a fire. But since the agency that handled her adoption was in Fairmont, Illinois, I doubt if she has roots as far south as Georgia."

"Never consider anything an impossibility, Mr. Crispen."

"Please, call me Alec."

"Only if you will call me Jordy."

Alec and Jordy exchanged a handshake, but instead of feeling the soft leather of Jordy's driving glove as he had felt on two previous occasions, Alec felt something scratchy touch his skin. He glanced down and saw a Band-Aid adhered to the webbing between the thumb and forefinger of Jordy's right hand.

The door to the den opened. Alec and Jordy both turned to see Hubert Graham standing in the opening.

Graham was an inch short of being six feet tall and looked to weigh close to 200 pounds. Even though his stocky build filled out the slacks and sport shirt he wore, there didn't appear to be an excess of fat on his frame. He was muscular for his age, which Alec guessed to be mid-sixties, and he walked with the ease of a much younger man as he approached them.

Alec's quick visual survey surprised him; he didn't remember Graham appearing as he did now, and yet, he knew why. The emergency of the situation surrounding their previous meeting had been so intense, his mind had evidently bypassed his usual diligence of observation to concentrate

108

on saving the man's life.

"Mr. Crispen," Graham said as he stopped opposite Alec, "it's such a pleasure to meet you face-to-face." He grasped Alec's hand in a firm shake, then continued to hold it with a touch of affection.

Now that Graham was closer, Alec continued with his visual survey of the man. Graham was heavily haired; he had bushy eyebrows and a full head of graying hair. The hair on his arms was thick, and Alec could see where Graham had shaved his neck down to the collar line; a dense patch of chest hair was visible through his open collar. He had high cheekbones, fleshy cheeks, a pug nose and a small cleft in the middle of his chin. Upon completing his quick assessment, Alec had a strange sense of familiarity, and his gut instinct began to gnaw at him.

While Alec had made his quick study of Graham, Graham had been making an assessment of his own. When their eyes again met, Graham surprised Alec by pulling him into his arms with a tender hug.

"Thank you," Graham whispered. "And thank you for coming. It's so good to see you again after . . ." Graham's words trailed off.

Alec was at a loss for words of his own, but he returned the hug in kind. When Graham finally released him and stepped back, Alec noticed a glimmer of tears in the older man's eyes. He presumed that such a close call with death would have brought tears to anyone's eyes.

"I've been enjoying looking around your den," Alec commented to relieve the oppressive silence that had suddenly surrounded them. "It appears that someone in this house is very fond of wild animals."

"Julia Ann was," Graham answered. "My wife," he added in explanation. He looked up at the portrait over the fireplace and a fond smile brightened his face. "She was one of the first in her field, a female veterinarian. There are a lot of women in the profession today, but thirty-some years ago, they were a rarity."

"Mother worked with some of the larger zoos across the country," Jordy added. He glanced at his father before continuing. "I've been told she had a special knack with animals, and her scientific curiosity led to some important breakthroughs that helped rebuild the population of several of the species on the endangered list." Alec looked at him with interest. "Working in a lab here on the farm, she was successful in accomplishing in vitro fertilization for many of the species, and she developed a formula that cut the embryo implantation rejection factor almost in half."

"She was way ahead of her time," Graham commented with pride, again glancing at the portrait. "If an untimely plane accident hadn't taken her life at such a young age, perhaps the implantation of embryos in the Homo sapiens species might be further advanced than it is today."

Alec's eyes moved to the portrait as well. "It sounds like she was a remarkable woman."

"Do you like animals, Alec?" Jordy asked.

"Somewhat. We have a dog."

"Would you be interested in seeing some of our latest arrivals?"

"Jordy inherited his mother's love of animals," Graham explained, "and is continuing with Julia Ann's work here at the farm."

"What kind of work do you do?" Alec asked. "Are you trying to develop a better strain of dairy cattle?"

"Hardly," Jordy answered with a light laugh. "Like my mother, I'm interested in the preservation of endangered species. I'm in charge of the zoological research complex we have here on the estate. Would you be interested in a tour?"

"It sounds interesting," Alec said, surmising now the reason for the elaborate security surrounding the Graham estate; it was for the protection of the animals on the verge of extinction. "But you'll have to help me make sure I don't become too involved and forget about the time. I have a birthday party to attend this evening, and I need to leave by a little after five."

Nine

The next hour and a half passed by much too quickly. Alec had become intrigued with his brief introduction to the research taking place in regards to artificial animal husbandry, and the tour he'd been given through the working labs had impressed him beyond a point he ever thought possible. Near the end of their tour, the Grahams had taken him through the nursery complex, where he had seen the results of their scientific endeavors. He was only able to recognize a few species being nurtured there because most were either still on the endangered-species list or had only recently been taken off, limiting their exposure to the general public. But once Jordy stated their common names for him, Alec knew he would never forget them. He also knew he would look for them the next time he visited a zoo, and perhaps, someday, he'd see the same ones he'd seen today after they'd matured into healthy adults.

"It's all been so very fascinating," Alec commented when they stepped from the muted light of the large animal nursery out into the fading light of late afternoon.

Glancing to his left, Alec saw the main house at the distant end of the paved drive that ran beside the building they'd just exited. Shifting his eyes to focus on the area across from the house and adjacent to the research complex, he noticed an older brick building with connecting exterior cages that was almost hidden by a dense stand of blue spruce pine.

"What is that building used for, if I might ask?" he said,

returning his attention to Jordy.

Alec saw Jordy and Graham exchange a subtle glance before Jordy answered. "It used to be the main primate house. My mother was especially fond of primates, and she kept several here as pets. There are only two or three remaining now, and since they're no longer on the endangered-species list, we've been focusing our attention on other animals and haven't been devoting any research time in their area."

"I always enjoy spending some time with the great apes whenever I visit a zoo. They fascinate me; I'm a true believer in Darwin's theory. Who's to say all of our great uncles might not have been monkeys at one time."

"Everyone has his own opinion of the theory." Jordy glanced at his watch. "I don't think we have time today, or I could take you through the building. Besides," he added with hesitation, "we're trying to keep the area as quiet as possible." Alec looked at him questioningly. "We have an old female . . ." Jordy looked to his father for assistance.

"Reka's dying," Graham said in a somber tone. "She was one of my wife's favorite gorillas. She's been with us from the beginning and seems like a part of the family. I can't bear the thought of putting her to sleep, so we're keeping her as comfortable as we know how and are just waiting for nature to take its course."

"I'm sorry," Alec said, identifying with the relationship he knew could develop between a man and an animal. He knew that he would be equally upset whenever the end came for Thumper.

Alec turned from the primate house, hoping to find another topic of conversation that would direct Graham's thoughts away from the dying gorilla. "Those buildings out there," he asked upon locating a cluster of white buildings beyond a closed gate at the opposite end of the lane, "is that the dairy?"

"Yes," Jordy answered immediately. "The actual milking barn in on the left. We have offices just to the right of the loading docks, and across the road is an equipment barn where we keep most of the farm machinery."

112

Alec was barely able to distinguish between the various buildings at that distance, but he could make out the green dome of a water tower, rising high above the black roofs. He guessed the dairy to be a good half to three quarters of a mile north of the rest of the estate and wondered why it had been located so far away. He wondered, but he didn't have an opportunity to ask.

"I don't want you to think I want you to leave," Jordy said as he again glanced at his watch, "but you did say your visit this afternoon would rest on the condition that you would leave by five."

Alec looked at his watch; it was a few minutes before five. "So I did," he responded, giving Jordy an appreciative nod.

The three of them turned and began walking toward the house. "Perhaps we'll have a chance to show you through the dairy on your next visit," Graham invited.

"I'm sure I'd find that quite interesting," Alec replied. "I still love milk, even at my age. What kind of cows do you use?"

"Holsteins," Graham answered with a hint of pride. "In my opinion, they're the best producers."

"They're the black-and-white ones, aren't they?"

"Yes," Graham answered with a chuckle.

"Is it true a cow has to be pregnant to give milk?" Alec asked after a few moments of thought.

"Bred." Jordy corrected Alec's terminology with a laugh. "That used to be the case, but with some recent developments over the past few years, there are a few lines of cows now that can produce milk without producing offspring at the same time."

"That seems like it would take some of the fun out of it," Alec retorted lightly, accepting the humor that had come to the Grahams over his ignorance.

"Our cows still enjoy the pleasures of motherhood," Graham informed him. "I don't care what anyone says, I think there's a definite difference in the taste of the milk, and I want only the best product going out of here with our name on it."

"How many cows do you have?"

113

"We have a little over six hundred head here, but we have almost a thousand more at each of our farms in Utah and Montana."

"That would make for some pretty contented bulls," Alec interjected with another chuckle.

"Unfortunately not," Graham informed him. "It's much less troublesome using artificial insemination."

"Mr. Graham."

All three turned to see a man in a blood-splattered lab coat coming toward them in an electric cart. Alec was shocked by the man's appearance; Jordy and Graham looked equally disconcerted.

"Can't you see we have a guest, Donald?"

"I'm sorry for the interruption Mr. Graham," the man replied as he drew nearer, "but there's been a major problem develop." He stopped the cart directly in front of them. The expression on his face was one of extreme urgency.

"I'll look into it," Jordy said without any prompting from his father. "I hope you can come for a longer visit the next time, Alec. And the next time, do bring your wife. Excuse me." Jordy slid onto the bench seat beside the man and quickly maneuvered the cart around, heading for the dairy's open gate that had been closed just a few minutes before.

"A day never goes by when Donald doesn't think there's some kind of an emergency." In an almost fatherly gesture, Graham placed his hand on Alec's shoulder and guided him toward the house. "How long are you planning to stay up here?"

"Through the end of next week."

"Since your visit today was so short, I would like for you and your wife, as Jordy mentioned, to join us some evening for dinner before you leave."

"I'll discuss the possibility with Krista. Since this is her vacation, I've decided to let her make all of the decisions." He hesitated, then added, "It's her last trip up here before she sells the cabin, and I want to make sure she enjoys her stay."

Graham ignored the implication in Alec's words. "Please try to convince her to humor an old man and accept my invitation."

"I'll talk with her."

They stopped at the edge of the patio beside the house. "Let me have Lewis bring a car around and take you home."

"That's not necessary." Alec glanced at his watch. "I still have plenty of time to make it back before the party, and I kind of enjoyed the walk over. You don't come across this much beautiful countryside in downtown Louisville."

Graham looked at Alec for a few silent moments, then stepped toward him and hugged him with another lingering embrace. "Thank you again, Alec," he said when he finally stepped back. "And it's been so very good to see you." He paused. "Your parents must be so very proud." Graham turned away and walked toward the house.

Alec watched Graham until he entered the French doors opening into the den; then he turned and began following the drive toward the front of the house. A warm smile stretched across his lips. He felt really good about himself, and he felt good about his short visit with the Grahams. The uneasiness that had plagued him when he'd first approached the house had vanished; it had been replaced by a feeling of comfort and acceptance. He now felt at ease; in fact, he felt so much at ease, it was as if he'd just spent the past two hours with his own family.

Hubert Graham stepped from the electric cart he'd driven down to the dairy complex from the house. His arrival hadn't been as immediate as he would have liked, but he'd felt a need to stay with Alec until he was gone. Even after he'd left Alec and gone into the house, Graham had waited and watched through the window until Alec disappeared within the trees at the distant end of the drive. Only then, after glancing at his watch to assure the time would not allow Alec to return, did he leave the house and head for the cluster of white buildings at the far end of the paved drive.

"What happened?" Graham asked one of the white-coated staff members as he stepped up to the observation window to Production Room One. Inside, he saw Jordy dressed in surgical greens, working alongside four other members of

115

the production team.

"Number three-seventeen broke through one of the gates, and the end of a broken board punctured her abdomen."

"How extensive is the damage?"

The staff member looked at Graham and shook his head. "It doesn't look good. By what little I've overheard, it appears the unit has been damaged as well."

"Number three-seventeen?" The staff member nodded. "Has it been paid for?" Again he nodded. Graham watched the activity in the production room for a few silent moments, and then he asked, "Has anyone checked on a replacement?"

"Not yet. We've been waiting to see how things turned out in there."

"I'll go see about it. Anything would be better than standing here waiting. Tell Jordy to come up when he's finished."

Graham turned from the window and began walking down the hall. When he reached the end of the corridor, he stopped in front of an elevator. The doors answered the press of the button almost immediately, and Graham stepped inside.

During the past twenty-five years, since the operation had turned profitable, there had been very few mishaps. Their techniques had continued to improve and only a freak accident, such as had occurred today, prompted any need for concern. Everything always seemed to run smoothly, but just in case it didn't, there was always a limited supply of backups that could be substituted for the original order. And even though the backups might not be needed, there was never an excess; someone was always in a position to buy.

Graham stepped from the elevator. He didn't turn on any additional lights but used the dim illumination from the exit sign to find his way to his office. Once inside the spacious room, he turned on the overhead lights and walked directly toward the eight four-drawer filing cabinets lining the wall to the right of his desk. He scanned over the cabinet's fronts, looking for the drawer containing the file on 317. When he found it, he pulled the drawer open, fingered through the files, and located and pulled out the one labeled *317*.

He looked in the file as he walked back to his desk and

spread it open on top of the blotter as he sat down. His eyes quickly took in the requirements of the order, and then he swiveled his chair toward a two-drawer filing cabinet on the opposite side of the desk. Opening the top drawer, Graham looked through the files until he found one labeled *Wt. F. Br. Br.*

He hoped his luck would be with him as he opened the folder on his desk. As Graham read through the enclosed information, a smile slowly began to form on his lips. A backup was available from number 139.

"Checking for a replacement?" Jordy asked as he stepped into the room.

"Do we need one?"

"Unfortunately, yes. The unit was damaged much too severely to even attempt a repair."

"It's been taken care of?"

Jordy nodded as he sat down in a chair opposite his father's desk, his eyes unconsciously checking the dozen television monitors built into the opposite wall. "That's the first one we've lost in a couple of years," he said with regret.

"It's unfortunate when it happens, but I bet we have a better success rate than any other business in the world."

Jordy leaned forward and glanced at the file on Graham's desk. "Is there a replacement available?"

"There's one. It'll run around three weeks behind the scheduled delivery date, but it fits the order qualifications."

"That's good." Jordy leaned back in his chair and laid his head against its back. "How do you think things went with Alec?"

"Extremely well."

"Do you think he suspects anything?" Graham didn't answer. "As you probably noticed, I tried to slip in a few open-ended comments, but they didn't seem to elicit any reaction."

"I caught them," Graham said somewhat cynically, "and his reaction, or should I say lack of it, was something that surprised me. He's too good to let such an obvious opportunity slip through his fingers." He paused. "And I expected to have to answer a lot of questions about Ed, but

117

he never even mentioned him. That has me puzzled—especially because of his background."

"Do you think he's playing some kind of game with us?"

"You can't play the game until you know the rules, and . . . I really don't think Alec Crispen knows the rules." Jordy looked at his father in question. "The card you found in the mailbox." Graham slipped his fingers into his shirt pocket, but the card wasn't there. Then he remembered he'd left it on his dresser when he'd changed clothes. "The message on that card was too vague. I still don't think he knows what he's stumbled across or who we are. He's just grabbing at straws for the moment, and as long as he can't grab onto anything solid, he won't have anywhere to go from there."

"And just how are we supposed to prevent him from doing that?"

"I think you might have had the right idea after all." Again, Jordy looked at his father in question. "We need to find out for sure if he does or doesn't have some of Ed's things. And if he does, we need to retrieve them as soon as possible so he won't have even a straw to work from."

"And if he's already started piecing things together?"

Graham bit at the inside of his lip as he battled with the decision he'd always known he might have to face someday—someday, if someone from the outside ever discovered their operation. He released a heavy sigh. "There may be no other choice but to eliminate him." The words hung as heavily in the air as the decision hung on his heart.

"Then you'd . . . *really* do it?"

"Only if it's our last way out." Graham thought for a few more moments, knowing there might be no other alternative. "When is his wife due back?"

"I never asked."

"Find out. And the next time you see him, extend a dinner invitation for the both of them—and make sure he doesn't refuse. Then while they're over here, I'll send Jameson to check out their cabin."

*   *   *

118

A dark figure hid in the shadows just outside the open door to Graham's office. He'd been standing there for several minutes, listening to the conversation, and when the topic had turned to Alec, his heart had thumped in response to his own fear. Now that he knew what they had planned for Alec, he knew what he had to do.

He looked down at Alec's business card, which he held in the palm of his hand—the card he'd taken from Graham's dresser over an hour before. Even in the dim light, he could read the line that was important to him: "contact me through Marvin Horton."

He'd never called anyone on the telephone; he'd never even spoken to anyone he didn't know. He was afraid to do it now, but he knew it was the only way to help Alec—and he wanted to help Alec. Alec was someone special; Alec was someone from his *good* past.

He turned away from the doorway and exited down a nearby stairwell as quietly as he had entered. Somewhere, he would find the courage to make the phone call; somewhere, he would find the courage to talk to Alec.

Fayetteville, North Carolina

"Alicia? Honey . . . are you awake?" Sharon Blanton stood beside the hospital bed, looking at the back of her daughter's head. She attempted to sound calm and in control, but her efforts were in vain. Her voice trembled; her words were hesitant. Tears still shimmered in her reddened, puffy eyes.

Alicia stared out the window, not wanting to look at her mother. "Did you . . . did you see . . . it?" she finally asked.

Sharon glanced at her husband, Lee, who stood beside the door; then she returned her attention to her seventeen-year-old daughter. "Dr. Milan suggested we . . . we wait until tomorrow to see the . . . the baby."

"Baby?" Alicia questioned. "By the brief glimpse I had of it in the delivery room, I'd call it a *thing* or an *it,* but I sure wouldn't call it a *baby.*" She was silent for a moment.

119

"Babies are soft and sweet and cute and cuddly . . . but it—it wasn't anything I could even recognize. I wouldn't even want to touch it." Alicia continued to stare out the window for several silent moments; then she finally rolled her head across the pillow to look at her mother. "Does Dr. Milan know what caused it?"

"*You're* the only one who can give a clue to that answer," Lee Blanton said harshly, uttering his first words since entering the room. He walked directly to the foot of his daughter's bed and stared at her accusingly. "What kind of drugs have you been taking the last nine months?"

Alicia gasped and looked at him in disbelief before finally finding the words to use in self-defense. "I don't take drugs, Daddy. I never have."

"Don't lie to me."

"I'm not lying. I don't use drugs—"

"You don't use drugs, huh? I suppose you don't use drugs just like you didn't get knocked up in the back of Stan Rhoades's van, either."

"Lee!" Sharon interjected in a futile attempt to intervene for her daughter.

"There's no use to try to protect her any longer. The truth has to come out, and the sooner it does, the better it'll be for all of us."

"But I don't use drugs, Daddy!"

"No? Ha! You can't deny it any longer. That baby—that *it,* as you called it—is proof enough that you're lying. It's bad enough you abuse your own body by putting God only knows what into it, but to destroy a perfectly innocent soul—"

"I've never used drugs!" Alicia cried out, sitting up in bed, trying to convince her father she was telling the truth.

"And after all your mother and I've done for you, you end up repaying us like this." He turned away from her and walked toward the window. "We've loved you. We gave you a nice home to live in. We worked hard to make sure you had the money to buy the things you wanted . . . nice clothes . . . a computer . . . that little sports car for your birthday. We've done everything we could to make you happy, then

120

you end up treating us like this—"

"And you taught me the difference between right and wrong." Alicia looked at her father thoughtfully even though he continued to gaze out the window. "I know what Stan and I did was wrong, and I'm sorry for that. But believe me, Daddy, I've never taken drugs, and I never will." She hesitated. "If you don't believe me—if you don't believe in what you taught me, then maybe it would have been better if you'd adopted someone else."

"Maybe it would have been better if we'd never spent the money to adopt at all."

Ten

Alec had made it back to the cabin with time to spare before going to Robbie's party. He and Thumper arrived at Marvin's threshold at exactly twenty-six minutes past five, carrying the cake and an additional small plastic box containing a variety of fishhooks for Robbie. After everyone consumed the T-bone steaks Marvin prepared on the grill— Thumper and Amble shared a rare steak between them— and helped themselves to generous spoonfuls of his original recipe creek-bank potatoes, eight candles were lit on the four-layer German chocolate cake. Robbie blew the candles out effortlessly. By the time the birthday meal was completed, everyone was drowsy from overeating. After a short catnap that none of them had planned or expected, the three played a lengthy game of Monopoly. When Alec finally looked at his watch, he noticed it was almost nine o'clock. He announced to Thumper it was time for them to leave so Marvin and Robbie could prepare for their excursion of night fishing.

Back at the cabin, Alec relaxed in one of the cushioned wicker chairs on the porch, gazing absently out across the water. A cool breeze caressed his face, and the air was laced with night sounds. Crickets chirped not too far from the steps, bullfrogs croaked romantic serenades from the edges of their lily pads, and from off in the distance, an occasional soothing sound of lowing cattle filtered in his direction.

It was after eleven and Alec's eyelids were growing heavy, but he still attempted to focus on the gas-powered lights reflecting off Marvin's boat far out in the middle of the lake. His efforts not to doze were wasted. His head nodded forward a couple of times, and then his chin came to rest on his chest, soon followed by the rhythmic breathing of sleep.

A sharp, shrill ringing interrupted his slumber. Disoriented, Alec sat up with a start. When the ringing pierced the silence again, he looked toward Marvin's cabin and immediately knew the source. Marvin preferred pursuing his leisure time activities out of doors whenever the weather allowed, and in order to hear the phone when he was outside, he'd devised an outdoor speaker that amplified the sound.

"I wonder who would be calling Marvin at this time of night?" Thumper yipped in reply. "I think you're right, we should go answer it. It could be something important—or it could be Krista, calling to remind us she's coming home tomorrow."

The phone was on its third ring by the time Alec decided to go answer it. He hurdled down the steps—*ring*—and sprinted across their yard to Marvin's—*ring*. He knew he only let a phone ring five or six times whenever he called someone and received no answer—*ring*—and he hoped whoever was calling Marvin didn't give up with any less persistence. He took Marvin's front steps by twos—*ring*—ran across the porch and hurried through the living room toward the phone on the kitchen wall—*ring*.

"Hello," he said between short breaths. "Hello, this is the Marvin Horton residence." No one responded, but Alec didn't hear a dial tone and knew the line was still open. "Hello. Is anyone there? Marvin can't come to the phone right now, but I can take a message." Alec heard a heavy breath, and then the caller spoke.

"I . . . I need to thspeak to . . . to Awec Crithspen, pweathse," the voice said hesitantly.

Alec was surprised the caller asked for him, but his surprise held second place to the sympathy he felt for the caller and his speech impediment. Alec was vaguely familiar with speech problems; he'd taken a class in speech pathology during college, knowing someday he might need to communicate with someone who had a speech difficulty. At the moment, he didn't remember any details from the class,

123

but he knew he was going to have to listen intently so he would be able to understand the man.

"I'm Alec Crispen."

"Weave Prairie Dewwths, Mithster Crithspen." The man's greatest difficulty was in pronouncing an *s* and an *l*, two of the most troublesome letters in the alphabet; his *r* was slurred but understandable.

"Why should I leave Prairie Dells?" Alec repeated the man's words in question form to assure him he had understood.

"Weave now. You're in danger."

"Danger? How am I in danger?"

The caller didn't respond. Having delivered his message, he hung up. Alec listened numbly to the dial tone.

Thumper, who had followed Alec into Marvin's cabin and now sat attentively at her master's feet, whined and broke the semi-trance into which Alec had fallen. Alec looked down at the dog, then realized he still held the phone in his hand.

"That was strange," he said as he replaced the phone on its hook. Responding to his voice, Thumper whined again. "No," he spoke to her as if she had posed a question and could then understand his answer, "it didn't sound like a prank call. I think the man was sincere in his warning. But why would I be in danger here in Prairie Dells? And who would know to call Marvin to contact me . . ." His words trailed off as the answer to the question materialized in his mind. "Post office box number seven!" He leaned over and ruffled Thumper's ears briskly in response to his own exhilaration. "Not even really looking for it, I think I might have stumbled across something that might be worth investigating. Come on, girl, I want to take another look through Schmidt's documents."

Alec hurried back to the cabin and began rereading Schmidt's postcards and letters, scrutinizing each and every word, looking for something he might have overlooked during his last reading. Still, nothing sparked a revelation. Too tired to even attempt to concentrate any longer, he leaned back in his chair and glanced at the clock on the kitchen wall; it was after two o'clock.

"I'm spinning my wheels here," he said, looking down at

Thumper, who had gone to sleep on the floor near his feet. "My only hope is to make another connection with the mystery caller."

The dog slowly opened her eyes and looked up at him. She exhaled a sound that was a cross between a bark and a whimper.

"I think you've got the right idea," he said as he stood and started toward the bedroom. "I'll write our anonymous friend another note in the morning and drop it off on the way to pick up Krista, but right now, I don't have any more energy than it'll take to fall into bed."

Thumper stood and stretched. Her claws clicked rhythmically against the hardwood floor as she followed him.

A dark figure moved stealthily through the trees, his lanky frame outlined only sporadically when the clouds slipped past the moon. Last autumn's leaves still responded with a muffled crunch in answer to his steps; brittle twigs cracked beneath his feet. A rabbit was startled by his presence and scampered toward its den for safety.

The man was almost a stranger to this side of the lake. For most of his life, he'd been forbidden to approach the cabins that were once located on the east and south edges of the lake. Until a few days earlier, when he'd followed the shoreline to have a closer look at the man and boy fishing from a boat, he'd rarely gone into the area that was now only identified by crumbling foundations. Only a few times, when he'd been a child, had he dared to come *this* far around the lake. His memory was cloudy as to his last visit those many, many years ago.

Keeping in the shadows of the towering, ageless trees, he worked his way to the cabin closest to the fence. He paused at the edge of the porch and looked out at the boat on the lake. He knew he had to be careful; the fishermen would be coming in soon.

Grasping the railing in one strong hand, he hoisted himself effortlessly up and over the safety barrier, landing catlike and quiet on the planked floor. The lights had finally gone out in the cabin almost twenty minutes ago, and at this late hour, he hoped everyone inside had fallen asleep quickly. If someone discovered him, his only hope would be for a quick and unidentifiable escape. If someone caught him, there could be no explanation.

Three elongated steps placed him beside the window on the near side of the front door. Squatting, he placed a heavily haired hand on the windowsill for stability and gradually leaned to his right until he could see in through the partially opened window. Even though the room was dark and the clouds cloaked the moon, he could see fairly well; his night vision was far more acute than most.

Alec was asleep in the double bed just a few feet away. He lay on his side, facing the window; Thumper was curled near his legs.

The man studied Alec: his full head of dark brown hair, his dense eyebrows, his chubby cheeks, his subtly upturned nose and the small cleft in the center of his chin. The man's breaths quickened as he continued his observation, and his heartbeat began to accelerate when he focused on the three small marks on Alec's right hand.

A tentative smile began to spread across his bearded face as his long fingers tightened their grip on the windowsill. He was forcing himself to remain where he was; he was forcing himself not to respond to a desire that burned deep inside him. He fought within himself and did not move, preventing his hand from reaching out—from reaching out to touch someone he had not touched in over thirty years. . . .

Heavy fog . . . swirling . . . swirling.
Soft music . . . soothing music.
A strange odor rising to saturate the air.
Sounds . . . muffled sounds.
   A screech . . .
      a laugh . . .
         a cry . . .
            a wail . . .
Dim light . . . fading light.
A hair-covered hand reaching for him . . .
   reaching . . .

  touching . . .
   caressing . . .
    holding him . . . rocking him.
A voice: "Get away! Don't touch him!
   Get out of here!"
Run . . . run . . . run!
Bounce . . . tumble . . . fall . . .
 fall . . .
  fall . . .
   crying . . .
A voice: "Is he all right?"
Crying . . . crying . . .
Barking.
 crying . . .
Barking. Barking.
 crying . . .
Barking. Barking. Barking.
 cr—

Alec woke abruptly from his dream. Thumper was at the window beside the bed, barking in alarm. Her front paws were up on the sill, and her head was turned at an angle as she worked persistently to nose her way through the narrow opening. The window would not budge.

"Who are you? What are you doing up there?" Alec heard Marvin's shouted words, and then he saw a beam of light sweep across the window.

Responding to the urgency in Marvin's voice, Alec rolled off the bed and stepped toward the window. He reached around Thumper and lifted the sash. The dog immediately sprang past him, landed on the porch and turned in a single motion. Continuing to bark, she jumped from beneath the guard rail to the ground and began running toward the fence.

"What's going on?" Alec called, seeing Marvin and Robbie coming toward the cabin, their path illuminated by the flashlight Marvin had used to highlight the cabin's porch. "What happened?" He stepped through the window out onto the porch, unconcerned that he was dressed only in his shorts and T-shirt.

"Somebody was up on your porch," Marvin explained,

stopping beside the steps.

"Did you see who it was?"

"I got a look at him," Robbie boasted, stepping up on the steps in front of his grandfather.

"What did he look like?" Alec asked. He walked down the steps and sat on the one closest to Robbie. "Have you ever seen him before?"

"No."

"How big was he?" Alec automatically began going down the mental list of questions he usually asked whenever he talked to anyone about another's description.

"About your size."

"Could you see his face?"

"No."

"Could you see what he was wearing?"

"Yes," Robbie answered with enthusiasm. "He had on a furry Halloween costume with shorts on over it. He had a mask on, too, and that's why I couldn't see his face."

Alec glanced at Marvin in question. Based upon Robbie's last answer, Alec now wondered whether the boy had actually seen the intruder or whether he was letting his young mind and vivid imagination create an answer he thought might please them.

Marvin shook his head. "I didn't see much more than a figure standing on the porch."

"A furry costume and a mask?" Alec asked. Robbie nodded. "Is there anything else you remember about him?" Alec asked hesitantly.

Robbie continued nodding as he began to talk. "He walked and ran funny."

"What was so funny about the way he walked?"

"It was kinda . . . kinda like sideways and forward at the same time. Kinda like this." Robbie stepped down off the steps and demonstrated the action he didn't seem able to put into words. He bowed his legs out, like someone who'd ridden a horse for far too long for his first time on a mount, and then he swayed from side to side while shifting his weight from one foot to the other and at the same time, angling each foot forward in an advance.

"Robbie," Marvin said with a laugh, "you look just like a

128

mon—" A high-pitched combination of a howl and a bark obliterated the last of Marvin's words. "Sounds like Amble's got something treed. For a spaniel, he's a purty good treeing dog."

He turned in the direction of the sound and began walking, directing the flashlight's beam on the ground ahead of him. Alec and Robbie joined him, falling into step at his side. Alec ooched and ouched when his bare feet came down on bristly pine needles and cones or when a scattered rock that had once been part of the drive bed came in contact with the soles of his tender feet. Fortunately, the walk between the cabin and the fence wasn't that far, and in a few moments, the three of them stood beside the twelve-foot-tall chain link.

Amble was a few feet from them, his paws against the trunk of a sturdy tree. Pointing his snout at the thickly leaved branches overhead, the dog continued to bark, calling for his master's attention.

"You got something, fella?" Marvin walked over to the tree and aimed the beam up through the branches.

"Do you see anything?" Alec asked.

"Nothing up here."

"Thumper? Where are you, girl?" The dog answered Alec's call with a bark. He could see her vaguely at the edge of the flashlight's reflecting rays, digging at the base of the fence. "Thumper, no," Alec commanded as he walked toward her. "I thought we broke you from digging last summer." Thumper looked up at him and whined, then looked toward the fence—looked past it and barked.

"Did you find anything over here?" Marvin asked as he stepped up beside Alec.

"Just a bad dog regressing to some old habits." Thumper looked up at him and whimpered. He bent over and gave her several firm pats on the side. "I know," he said with a note of understanding, "you were excited."

"She might have been more than just excited. She could have been on to something." Marvin was aiming the flashlight onto a good-sized branch that ran from the tree Amble had been leaning against out over the fence. "Never knew Amble to bark up a wrong tree, and maybe he wasn't this time either." Marvin ran the beam along the branch from the trunk to its end. "It's big enough to support a man's weight. Maybe Amble treed him and Thumper saw where he took off to once he got on the other side of the fence."

Alec focused on the branch, and his eyes followed the light beam Marvin moved along its length all of the way back to the trunk. "Awfully high," he commented, noting the branch was some twenty feet above the ground and that there were no others below it. "I don't see how someone could have gotten up there."

"They do it all the time in the islands," Marvin commented. "I've seen some specials on TV where the natives shinny up palm trees fifty and sixty feet tall, and they don't have any lower branches to help boost them up. I guess it's all in knowing how." Alec looked at the tree and accepted Marvin's explanation without any further question. "Do you want me to give Jake a call and have him come out and take a look around?"

"Who's Jake?"

"He's the county sheriff. He's a friend of mine. All I'd have to do would be give him a call and he'd be right out."

"I don't want to bother him at this time of night." Alec looked off into the darkness of the woods. "Whoever it was, I think we scared him away for the time being."

"It's up to you. I'd like to know my tax money goes for more than just paying him to sleep," Marvin added with a chuckle.

"No, don't bother him."

"Well then, I guess there's nothing more to see out here. Robbie and I have to go clean and freeze the fish we caught. Do you want to help?"

"I'll pass," Alec answered as he looked back at Marvin. "I'm going back to bed. Come on, Thumper." The dog hesitated beside the fence, growled again in the direction of the trees, then turned to follow her master.

Alec took a few tender-footed steps toward the cabin, then stopped and turned to look back at the tree. He again surveyed the thick trunk, momentarily highlighted by the moon, and wondered if it was really possible for a man to climb it without any means of assistance.

130

Eleven

Alec stood patiently in line while a small child peeked over the counter to ask for a book of stamps. After the child completed his transaction, an older, blue-haired woman had a parcel weighed for mailing and talked with the postmaster for several minutes about her three grandchildren who lived in Oklahoma. He then waited while another woman purchased several hundred dollars' worth of small-denomination money orders she said she intended to use to pay off her various charge cards.

When it was finally his turn to step up to the window, Alec smiled at the old man he'd talked to a few days before as he laid a quarter on the counter. "Would you please put this in box number seven for me," he said as he placed an envelope on the counter beside the quarter.

The postmaster glanced at the envelope which bore the handwritten address P.O. Box #7, Prairie Dells, Wisconsin. The old man looked up at Alec, and there was a twinkle in his gray eyes when he said, "I can do that."

"Thank you." Alec turned and walked away. It had taken him over fifteen minutes to mail the short note he'd written to the mystery caller just that morning. Now, he was on his way to meet Krista at the airport.

Alec adjusted his position on the hard plastic seat, knowing full well why most people chose the stand-up phone

131

booths at airports instead of squeezing their bodies into the comfortable-looking ones. Their appearance was deceptive; they were far from being comfortable.

Traffic had been light to and through Madison, and his luck at catching green lights had amazed even him. Arriving at the airport a good half hour before Krista's plane was scheduled to land, he thought he'd make good use of the time and call Todd Tyson. He was anxious to learn whether Todd had found the elusive file on Edgar Schmidt, and if he had, Alec was curious about its contents. He hoped there would be a lead to the identity of the holder of post office box number seven.

"Are you still there, Alec?" Cookie asked, breaking into the semiclassical music that always came over the line whenever she put a caller on hold.

"Still here."

"Todd should be with you in just a minute. I had to track him down and finally found him tinkering about in Studio A. You know what he's like, always checking up on things even though there's nothing to check on." Alec nodded unconsciously, remembering Todd's overefficiency. "His light just came on on the panel. Hold on and I'll switch you over. Good talking to you again."

Alec heard a couple of clicks and buzzes before Todd's voice came over the line loud and clear. "Alec, how's your vacation going?"

"Pretty good, but it's going by too quickly as usual."

"All good things do." Todd paused for an instant. "I bet you're calling about that file on Schmidt, aren't you?"

"It sounds like you still have a knack for reading minds."

"It comes with the job, but you already know that." Todd paused again. "Yes, I located the file. Why in God's name I took it home, I don't know, but it was in one of my cabinets in the basement. I guess I put it there since it was one of my own, not really connected in any way to WQXM, and I didn't want to take the chance of misplacing it in the gargantuan bank of files some of the rookie researchers around here seem to enjoy messing up."

Alec's foot began to tap impatiently. When was Todd

going to get to the point? When was Todd going to tell him what was in the file?

"I copied it for you," Todd continued, "over thirty pages." Alec smiled in anticipation and nodded his head. "It should be waiting for you at the station by the time you get back to Louisville." The smile left Alec's face, and he released a disappointed sigh. "I didn't know where you were staying up here, or I could have sent it to you directly."

"That's all right," Alec said without conviction. "I didn't think to leave an address for you, either." It was Alec's turn to pause. After a few moments of thought, he asked, "Did you happen to look over anything in the file you might remember?"

"I skimmed it and tried to look up some of Schmidt's acronyms I was telling you about. I didn't come across a Project GOD, but I found a few others. There was Project EAT that stood for Energizing Animal Tissue. He worked on that during the mid-forties, and it was credited with keeping the southern half of India's population from being wiped out by starvation. There were some others I can't remember right off the bat, but there's one I do remember because it made me think that Schmidt maybe had a slight sense of humor. It was called Project LOST. It stood for Lotsa Oats for the Sambian Tribe." Todd chuckled. "Lotsa Oats. Now doesn't that sound like real scientific lingo. Anyway, scientific-sounding or not, that project saved one of the biggest tribes in Africa from being eliminated from the face of the earth during the famine in the early fifties. It was the last project Schmidt worked on for the government before they sent him back to the States. I guess he got bit by some voodoo-type fly while he was working in the jungle down there that made him start to go a little wacky."

"Can you remember what any of his other projects focused around?"

"I think most of them were on animal and crop production and reproduction."

"I take it most of them were successful," Alec commented after a brief pause.

"I guess they were. Enough people survived in India back

133

in the forties that the poor country's overpopulated again, and they're facing another food shortage."

Alec contemplated Todd's comment, then asked, "If Schmidt's projects worked before to provide food for the people, why isn't someone repeating his work now to solve the present-day problem?"

"A fly in the ointment, my dear colleague." Todd paused. Alec waited impatiently for him to continue. "The first generation of Schmidt's animals were fine, but there wasn't significant production, or should I say *reproduction,* beyond that. The old boy must have messed up a formula or two here and there along the way, because there was a major flaw with his animals. The males were mostly sterile and about half of the females produced deformed offspring. You can read all about it in detail when you get back to Louisville. There's a short article about it at the end of Schmidt's file." He paused again, then added, "I'd say that by the time you get through that whole file, you'll know as much about Edgar Schmidt as I do."

Alec released another disheartened sigh. By the time he got back to Louisville and read through the file, the opportune time to discover the owner of post office box number seven would be gone. "Do you happen to remember reading about who Schmidt might have worked with?" Alec asked; it was his last ray of hope.

"Schmidt was the head man on all the projects, but he did have an assistant who worked with him from almost day one. What was his name? What was his name . . ."

Alec's breaths grew shallow and quick. He was growing more anxious about receiving the information. Unconsciously, he began rubbing the birthmark on the webbing of his right hand.

"Grand . . . no . . . no, it was Graham. Herbert . . . no, it was Hubert. Hubert Graham."

Alec sucked in a quick breath of air, and his heartbeat accelerated. "Would that be the same Hubert Graham of the H&J Corporation?" he asked, a note of excitement touching his voice.

"Now that I can't tell you . . ."

"Can you find out?"

". . . but I can find out." Todd's words almost mirrored Alec's.

"How much time do you think it'll take?"

"I can put Sam Drexler on it today or tomorrow at the latest. Do you want to leave an address for me?"

"No. No, I'll call back sometime tomorrow afternoon."

"Do you think this Graham guy might have some connection with Schmidt's Project GOD?"

"It's a guess, Todd, just a guess."

"As excited as you're sounding about all of this, I've got a feeling you think you're onto something more than just a guess. If I'm remembering correctly, it took quite a bit to get you excited."

"There's nothing to be too excited about when all I'm working with are bits and pieces."

"But you're the kind of guy who can make those pieces fall into place. You will keep me updated, won't you?"

"If I come across anything solid, you'll be the first to know."

"Sky American flight two-eighteen from Detroit is now arriving at gate three."

Alec looked up at the fabric-covered panels decorating the wall just below the ceiling and knew the announcement had come from a speaker hidden there. "I've got to go, Todd, Krista's plane's coming in. Thanks for everything. I'll talk to you sometime tomorrow afternoon."

"Alec, just one more thing before you go."

"What's that?"

"Something just crossed my mind about this Graham fella." Alec listened intently. "He was a publicity hound. Now that I think about it, I think his name was mentioned in every one of the articles I have on Schmidt, and he's in almost every one of the photographs any of the media people were able to snap of Schmidt. I'd venture to say that if Graham is involved with anything you're looking into, his name will be right there on the front page."

*   *   *

"Where's my father?" Jordy demanded after he literally ran into Lewis at the entrance to the kitchen.

"I believe he's out riding."

Jordy didn't thank Lewis for the information, apologize for their abrupt face-to-face meeting or offer to help pick up the magazines he had inadvertently caused Lewis to drop. He continued across the kitchen toward the back door, taking long, deliberate strides. He was a man with something on his mind.

Once outside, Jordy turned directly to his left, away from the paved road that led to the research complex and dairy, and started following a wide cobblestone path toward the trees opposite the drive behind the house. A few hundred yards after the oak, maple and pine trees had surrounded him, they opened up again. Ahead were the stables and an open meadow that spread for as far as the eye could see.

"Dad," Jordy called as he approached the nearest barn. "Dad, are you in here?" He received no reply other than from the three purebred Arabian horses pastured in a spacious fenced enclosure beside the barn.

Turning toward the meadow, he made a sweeping glance across the gently rolling hills. Jordy knew his father liked to ride alone whenever he had something on his mind, and Hubert Graham's mind was plenty full now that Alec Crispen had reentered their lives. Jordy also knew his father was fighting a battle within himself; his father was hoping he wouldn't have to make the ultimate decision.

Jordy looked down at the envelope he held in his hand—the envelope labeled with the simple address P.O. Box #7, Prairie Dells, Wisconsin. He'd read the brief note it contained and now, in the peacefulness of the secluded meadow, wondered if he should add to his father's troubles by giving it to him. He knew what the outcome would be. He knew his father would be angry—would be furious—that anyone had betrayed him. He knew that bitter fact from experience.

"Yeee-haaa!"

Jordy's attention was drawn in the direction of the sound. Cresting the hill some 500 yards away, Graham rode his favorite stallion at a full gallop toward the stable. It was a habit; it was a tradition. It was the way Graham finished every ride he took across the meadow.

Graham brought the horse to a stop a few feet from Jordy, patted the steed's sturdy neck affectionately and dismounted. "Prince Gallishean has a lot of spirit left in him for his age." He hooked the stirrup over the saddle's horn and loosened the cinch. "He's just like me. We'll both keep going at full speed until we drop." He patted the horse's neck again before turning to face Jordy. "What brings you down here?"

Jordy hesitated, and then extended the envelope toward his father. "I thought you would be interested in seeing this."

Graham looked at the address on the envelope, glanced at Jordy with concern, then removed the single page from inside and read:

> Thank you for your call; however, our conversation was much too short. Could we meet somewhere and talk further? I have several things I would like to discuss with you.
>
> Alec Crispen

"Who!" Graham demanded to know. Rage burned in his eyes. The muscles of his jaw tightened, and the veins bulged along his neck. "Who called Crispen!"

"All I know is what you have in your hand."

Graham looked at the note again, then crumpled it into a wad. "Al . . ." The word hissed past his lips in a coarse whisper.

"You don't know that."

"The hell I don't! That son of a bitch has hated me since the day he was born." Graham began walking back toward the house, his anger fueling each step he took.

"What are you going to do?"

"Find him. Find him and make sure he knows there's a grave with his name on it just waiting to be filled if he's even thinking about trying to destroy me."

Jordy walked quickly to keep up with his father's long strides. "Dad . . ." He reached for Graham's arm.

137

When Graham felt Jordy's touch, he jerked his arm away and swung the riding crop he held in his hand in a high arc. If Jordy hadn't reacted quickly and raised his arm to protect himself, the whip would have struck him across the face.

"Go tend to Gallishean. And stay out of this!" Graham commanded as he continued in his determined walk.

When he reached the back door to the kitchen, Graham flung it open, causing it to bang against the side wall as he stepped inside. Lewis and his wife, Marian, both turned with a start and looked at Graham a bit fearfully. Throughout the years they had worked for him they had seen his stability gradually deteriorate, but neither could remember seeing him in such an uncontrollable state of rage.

"Where's Al?" he demanded.

Lewis and Marian glanced at one another; then Marian answered meekly, "I think he's with Reka."

Graham turned on his heels and stormed out of the kitchen as angrily as he'd entered. Stepping from the porch, he started across the yard, directly toward the primate building. With each step, his anger continued to mount; with each step, he questioned why he had ever allowed Al to live. But he knew why. It had been for Julia Ann. Al had been their first, and even though he'd been a disaster who should have been destroyed, for Julia Ann's sake, Graham had consented to let him live.

But when Julia Ann died, Graham knew he should have buried Al along with her. He knew Al was smart enough to cause trouble for him someday; he knew the day of betrayal would eventually come. He knew that day was here.

Graham flung open the door to the primate building. The hall was dimly lit by the small bulbs in the exit signs at opposite ends of the corridor. Other than the startled, screeching sounds of the few inhabiting primates, the only indication of occupancy was the light at the distant end of the hall that shone from an open door.

"Al!" Graham's boots struck heavily against the tiled floor as he walked along the corridor. "Al! Are you in here?"

A tall, dark figure appeared in the open doorway almost immediately. He turned to face Graham and began walking toward him. "Thhhshh," he said in an attempt to verbalize a *shhh* sound. "Thsweeping."

"I don't care if she's sleeping. I'll be glad when she's dead and gone."

Al stopped several feet from Graham. "Why? Thshe'ths never done anything to you."

"She hasn't, huh? What about you? If it wasn't for her, I wouldn't have had to put up with you for all these years." Graham continued walking toward Al, and when he was close enough, he grabbed the front of Al's shirt and threw him up against the wall. "Why did you call Crispen?" Al's eyes grew wide with fear, the whites reflecting clearly around his dark brown irises in the dim lighting. "What have you been telling him?"

"Nothing."

"Don't lie to me!" Still holding onto Al's shirt, Graham shoved him back against the wall again. "What did you tell him?"

"I . . . I towd him to . . . to weave," Al finally answered timidly. Even though he was much stronger and could have easily overpowered Graham and defended himself, Al didn't attempt to fight back. He'd always been afraid of Graham; he'd always shied away from him. Whenever Graham confronted him, Al cowered.

"Why did you tell him to leave?" Graham asked forcefully, again bouncing Al off the wall.

"To . . . to protect him."

"To protect him from what?"

After a moment's hesitation, Al found the courage to answer. "You."

"Me? Me! Why do you think you need to protect him from me?"

"Thso you won't treat him the way you've treated me."

"Treated you? You damn ingrate! I've given you food and clothing and a place to live where people won't laugh at your ugly face and deformed body. If it wasn't for me, the only place you could live and provide for yourself would be by being a sideshow freak in some two-bit honky-tonk circus. I've kept you from that, and now you repay me by betraying me like this!" Graham tightened his grip on Al's shirt and threw him down on the floor. Almost immediately, he began hitting Al with the riding crop he still carried in his hand. "I should have burnt you to a crisp over thirty years ago like I did all the other mistakes!"

Al wrapped his arms around his head and pulled his knees up toward his chest until he lay in a tightly coiled fetal position. That was the only defense he attempted as Graham continued to rain blows down upon him.

"I'll teach you . . ." Graham's breaths were becoming heavy from the exertion of the beating; his fatigue was evident in his words. "I'll teach you to turn against me . . . after all I've done for you."

"Dad! Stop it!" Jordy pulled Graham away from Al, at the same time positioning himself between the two of them. "Leave him alone, Dad. Go in the house and settle down." Graham stared at his son in a silent standoff, then turned sharply and stormed out of the building.

After the door slammed shut behind his father, Jordy knelt down on the floor beside Al. "Are you all right?" he asked as he helped Al sit up. Al nodded. "Are you sure?" he questioned again after seeing the blood on Al's shirt glisten in the dim light.

"I'm aw right." Jordy and Al looked at each other for a few silent moments; then Jordy shook his head, stood up and started for the door. "Jordy." Jordy paused and looked back at Al. "You've got to hewp Awec." Their eyes again met, but Jordy's troubled conscience prevented him from looking at Al any longer, and he turned away. "You've got to hewp him, Jordy. He'ths . . . he'ths our . . . our brother."

Twelve

Krista was so excited about her trip to New York she talked almost nonstop from Madison to Prairie Dells, telling Alec each and every detail she was able to remember. Only after they'd passed through the small town and turned onto the road leading to the lake did she finish with the tale of her adventure and give Alec an opportunity to relate the events that had occupied his past few days. When Graham's name was mentioned, she listened as intently as Alec had when she had spoken.

"You actually went over there and got to go inside the house?" Krista asked with a child's astonished excitement. Alec nodded. "Was it as magnificent on the inside as it looks from the outside?" Alec nodded again, chuckling to himself and smiling broadly in response to her enthusiasm. "And isn't it all sadly romantic," she said in a soft whisper.

"What's that?"

"That Graham built a stately Southern mansion up here in Wisconsin to make his wife feel at home, and then she died."

"Have you been reading some soapy romance novel again?" he asked with a teasing laugh.

"And what if I have?" Krista reached across the space between their seats and laid her hand high on Alec's thigh. "I had to do something to occupy my time the past few nights." Her fingers pressed gently against his inner thigh. Her touch reminded Alec that he had missed her as much as she had obviously missed him.

141

"You won't have to read any books to occupy your time tonight," he said as he took her hand in his and squeezed it gently.

"I was hoping you had the same idea I have," she said playfully, returning his squeeze.

When they reached the turnoff, Alec eased the van into a slow turn and drove across the bridge. Just as he was about to turn right toward the cabin, an ambulance emerged from the trees, coming from the Graham estate.

"I wonder what's happened?" Alec made sure the van was pulled far enough away from the bridge to be out of the ambulance's way, then stopped.

"I doubt if it's an emergency, or they'd have the siren blaring and the lights flashing," Krista responded as she turned in her seat to watch the ambulance leave.

"Unless there's no need."

"What do you mean by that?" As soon as Krista asked the question, she knew the answer. "Do you think somebody died?"

"I don't know, but I'm going to find out if I can."

Alec backed the van up, turned it around and started driving slowly along the blacktop road toward the trees. When he reached the closed gate, he stopped, climbed out of the van and began walking.

"Hello," he said when he stopped a few feet from the steel barrier and looked up at the camera. "Hello. Is anybody there?"

He saw the camera tilt down slightly, and then he heard a familiar deep male voice. "May I help you, sir?"

"I'm Alec Crispen. I visited with the Grahams yesterday."

"Yes, Mr. Crispen, I remember. What can I do for you?"

"I just saw an ambulance leave, and I wondered if something might have happened."

"One moment, Mr. Crispen."

Alec stood impatiently, facing the gate. He looked past the vertical steel bars, trying to see beyond the trees, but he knew his actions were futile. Anything that might be happening closer to the house was hidden by the dense foliage.

He glanced at his watch; the moments he waited

lengthened into minutes. He looked up at the camera, then turned to glance back at Krista, who still remained in the van. He glanced at his watch again. It had been over five minutes since the voice behind the camera had instructed him to wait for a moment.

"Hello," Alec called again, looking back up at the camera. "Are you still there?"

Before the final words of the question crossed his lips, Alec heard the sound of the electronic gate. When he looked back at the gate, he expected to see the smaller man-size section opening, but instead, the entire barrier was moving, swinging away from him like a double door hinged at opposite sides.

Alec turned and started toward the van, prepared to drive onto the estate, but then he heard the sound of an engine echoing within the trees. He turned back around and focused on the distant turn in the lane. A jeep rounded the corner; Jordy was at the wheel.

Jordy waved as he approached and stopped the jeep directly beside Alec. The gate immediately began to close behind him.

"I didn't expect to see you this afternoon," Jordy said with an inquisitive smile.

"We were on our way home when we passed an ambulance leaving here and—"

"We?" Jordy looked from Alec toward the van. "Is that your wife?" he asked as he raised a gloved hand above his eyes to deflect the glare of the midafternoon sun.

"Yes. But—"

"Then you'll be able to join us for dinner soon. Are you free tonight?"

"I imagine Krista is looking forward to an evening of rest."

"Tomorrow night then."

"Maybe—"

"Then tomorrow it is. I'll have Lewis send a car over for you around seven."

"Jordy!"

Jordy looked at Alec with an almost stunned expression. "What is it, Alec?"

143

"The ambulance that just left here. Is . . . is your father all right?"

"My father's fine." He looked at Alec for a few moments and then laughed. "Oh, the ambulance. I'm so used to them, I sometimes forget they may be alarming to other people. We use them to transport some of our more delicate newborns. You saw some of them in the nursery yesterday. Sometimes they're too fragile to trust to the rough ride in a truck, so we use ambulances equipped with air shocks to take them to their destination. I don't know why some of the zoos are so impatient to get them so young, but when they pay for them, they want them, and they want them right now." Jordy shifted the jeep into first gear and slowly released his foot from the clutch. The jeep began to roll. "I've got to go, I'm late for a town meeting. I'll see you and your wife tomorrow evening around seven. I'm looking forward to meeting her." Jordy pressed his foot down on the accelerator and drove away.

Alec watched the jeep as he walked back to the van. While listening to Jordy's explanation, his gut instinct had begun to gnaw at him. And the eyes—Jordy's eyes—they had reflected a partial truth, but they had also betrayed a hint of a lie.

A broad smile beamed across Krista's face when she could finally see the cabin through the trees. She didn't seem to notice the bumpy ride along the rutted lane; she was filled with the exhilaration of finally being back home. When Alec pulled the van into the lane and stopped, Krista remained motionless in her seat, looking out across the lake in all its midsummer beauty, taking in every aspect of her surroundings as if she were seeing it for the first time.

"Everything's so calm and beautiful," she said in a soft voice. "After the hustle and bustle of the past few days, it's so relaxing just to be able to sit here and take it all in."

"Your relaxation is going to be short-lived," Alec said with a laugh. He nodded toward Thumper, who was running up the hill toward the van, barking and wagging her tail so rapidly it was affecting the efficiency of her gait.

"Here, Thumper," Krista called as she stepped from the van and knelt on the ground. She extended her arms openly toward the dog but wasn't totally prepared for Thumper's overzealous greeting.

A few feet from Krista, Thumper barked and then jumped toward her. The force of the dog's spring pushed Krista down on the ground. Almost immediately, Thumper was at her face, nosing her way in between Krista's arms to leave a shower of wet kisses on her cheeks, nose, forehead and neck.

"I've missed you too, girl," Krista said between laughs. She finally managed to pull herself up to a sitting position and wrapped her arms around Thumper's neck and chest in a loving hug. "You're such a good girl." Those brief words were enough to send Thumper's tail into a wagging rampage. "And you're such a wiggle-butt," Krista added with another laugh.

"I think she's been saving all her energy since you left just so she'd be able to do that," Alec said as he helped Krista to her feet. He collected her two suitcases from the back of the van, and together, they began walking toward the front of the cabin.

"How was your trip?" Marvin asked. He and Robbie had been fishing from the dock when the van had pulled into the drive and was only now making his way up the hill toward the cabin.

"Hectic but great."

"Did you see the Statue of Liberty and the Empire State Building?" Robbie asked as he stepped up beside his grandfather.

"Sarah and I did play tourists for an afternoon."

"I want to hear all about it," Robbie said as he sat down on the steps to their porch. "I want to know if you thought it was as neat as I did when I was there last spring vacation."

"You can compare notes some other time." Marvin took hold of Robbie's upper arm and nudged him from the steps toward their own cabin. "I imagine Krista's ready for a rest right about now, and I'm sure she and Alec have a few things to catch up on." A mischievous twinkle sparkled in Marvin's

145

pale blue eyes when he glanced at Alec and winked. "Let's go on home, boy. What say why don't you and me get cleaned up and go into town for supper and a picture show. That way it'll be nice and quiet around here for a purty good while." He again looked at Alec and winked, then turned and followed Robbie toward their own cabin.

"Marvin's a very considerate person," Alec commented as he climbed the porch steps. He glanced at Krista and grinned.

She immediately detected the sly twinkle in Alec's eyes. "It's beginning to look more like both of you are scheming, conniving dirty old men," she countered with a chuckle.

"You'd better believe it," he answered in a mocking, sinister tone. "We've been plotting since the day you left on how I could get you alone . . ." Alec set the suitcases down just inside the door, turned and gathered Krista up in his arms. ". . . then do nasty, wicked things to you."

Krista began to giggle when Alec started biting playfully along her neck. She joined in the game they often played, pretending to fight off his advances while occasionally slipping in a kiss or a tender bite of her own. Thumper, too, joined in the mock scuffle, barking happily as she jumped at Alec and played at protecting Krista from the master she loved equally as well.

Not totally accustomed to his surroundings, Alec stumbled around the corner of an end table and fell onto the sofa. Krista landed sideways across his legs, sprawling onto the cushions beside him. Thumper, still deeply involved in the game, jumped onto the sofa beside them, then bounded onto their laps. No one was injured in the misadventure, and once Alec and Krista regained their senses, both began to laugh and pet Thumper. The dog's tail thumped repeatedly against them.

"I guess that puts an end to that," Alec said as he sat upright on the sofa.

"It doesn't have to." Krista toyed with Alec as she reached around Thumper to unfasten the top few buttons of his shirt. "It's not a bear skin, but there's an awfully soft rug in front of the fireplace."

"Out here? With Miss Cold Nose in attendance? No, thanks." Alec rubbed Thumper's ears. Both he and Krista laughed, remembering the time, a few weeks before, when their bedroom door hadn't been secured and Thumper had joined them in the midst of their lovemaking. "A cold nose on a bare ass is a lot more lethal to good sex than any cold shower I ever took."

"I'm just glad it was your butt and not mine." Krista laughed as she swung her legs around and stood up from the sofa. "What do you think a hot shower might do for you?" she asked, seductively pulling at the tail of the bow on her blouse that was tied at her neck.

"Is there a lock on the bathroom door?" Alec asked as he stood and began helping Krista with her buttons.

"If there's not, I'm sure you can come up with something to keep Miss Cold Nose from disturbing us."

Marian returned the last pot to the cabinet, and after hanging the dish towels on the pantry door rack, she shut it from the view of the world. Adhering to the routine she followed at the end of every day, she checked the sink to make sure it had dried spotless, glanced at the rack beside the stove to assure herself that all of the condiments had been returned to their rightful place, and made a final sweeping inspection of the kitchen, just to make sure nothing had been missed. Marian liked a tidy kitchen; she knew if she left it in that condition each night, it would be ready for her the following morning—that is, if no one raided for a midnight snack and then failed to clean up the evidence of his intrusion.

As her eyes swept across the instruments monitoring the stoves, she noticed that the red light on the warming oven was still lit. She glanced at her watch; it was almost nine o'clock. She then looked in the direction of the small table that was all but hidden in the far, most secluded corner of the spacious room. The place setting she had laid out over two and a half hours before was still unused, and the miniature centerpiece of wild daisies and violets she'd picked as a

147

special decoration had begun to wilt. Al had yet to come in for dinner.

A wave of sadness washed through Marian as her thoughts focused on Al. After everything he'd had to live with all of his life, he now faced the mournful task of sitting by a deathbed . . . alone.

"You ready to head home?" Lewis asked as he came through the swinging doors that partitioned the kitchen from the short hall leading to the formal dining room.

"Ready as usual," she answered, casting another glance at the unused table setting. "Have you seen Al since Mr. Graham was looking for him this afternoon?"

Lewis's eyes followed the direction of his wife's gaze. He, too, stared momentarily at the unused place setting. "No, I haven't seen him since sometime this morning." He looked back at Marian, knowing full well the compassion she held for Al in a special place in her heart.

"Do you think he's all right?" Marian asked, looking at Lewis with concern. "I've never seen Mr. Graham as angry as he was this afternoon when he was looking for him."

"Al's smart, smarter than the both of us put together. And he's strong enough to take care of himself if he has to."

"I know he is, but *would* he? Would he defend himself if Mr. Graham actually went after him? As angry as he was this afternoon, I was afraid he might be thinking about carrying out the threats he's been making all these years."

"We both saw Jordy go into the building after Graham did, and you know Jordy wouldn't let anything happen to Al." Lewis smiled at Marian, understanding her concern. "Do you want to take a tray out to him?" he asked, attempting to ease her thoughts.

"It won't do any good. I took one out for him around eleven this morning and brought it back in a couple of hours later, untouched."

"What do you want to do, then?" Lewis asked, sensing his sentimental wife already had something in mind.

"Let's go sit with him for a while."

Lewis looked at her for several moments before replying, "Do we really have to?" The tone of his voice indicated his reluctance. Even after being with the Graham household for more than thirty years, he still didn't feel comfortable about being around Al.

"It would be a nice gesture."

"I know, but . . ."

It was now Marian's turn to smile at her husband in understanding. "You go on home. I'm going to stop by and see Al."

Lewis accompanied Marian as far as the back entrance to the primate house. After declining another invitation to join her, he continued on down the brick walkway to their modest home located at the back edge of the paved drive circling the residential complex.

Marian paused just inside the back door to collect her thoughts. What was she going to do? What was she going to say?

Normally, she wouldn't have felt awkward approaching Al; Marian had been like a mother to him since Julia Ann had been killed when he was four years old. Almost from the beginning, she had taken Julia Ann's place. She had nurtured him, comforted him, watched him grow. She had been there to teach and guide him; she had been there to praise and encourage him; she had been there to hold his small hand when no one else would. She had tried to help him understand why he was different, and she had been there to help dry his tears . . . all those many, many tears. Marian had always treated Al as if he were her own son, and so in a way, perhaps he was.

At any other time, Marian wouldn't have felt uneasy about being with Al, but this wasn't another time. This was now, and the situation was an awkward one. She would be glad when it was over; she would be glad for Al's sake.

Marian took in a deep breath and let it out slowly, then began walking down the dimly lighted hallway toward the faint light coming from an open doorway some twenty feet away. Her rubber-soled shoes squeaked on the tiled floor; therefore, she began taking shorter steps on her tiptoes to alleviate the annoying sound from the otherwise near-deafening silence. Even though she as in no hurry, each tiny

149

step brought her closer and closer to the open door—each step brought her closer and closer to Al. She hoped she would be able to find the rights words when the time came for her to express her sympathy.

Stopping just outside the door, Marian looked into the room. She saw Al sitting on the edge of a blanket that had been spread over a generous mound of straw. His back was turned toward her; he was unaware of her presence.

Beyond Al, the aged gorilla, Reka, lay on the blanket. Her broad chest rose and fell laboriously with each of her shallow breaths; a rhythmic wheeze escaped her nostrils with the repeated exchange of air. The thin lids covering her eyes fluttered sporadically, and only occasionally was she able to focus on the figure who held her hand. Al held Reka's hand—a hand that differed little from his own.

"How is she?" Marian asked softly, stepping up behind Al and laying a comforting hand on his shoulder. Al shook his head slowly in response. "Has Jordy been in recently to look at her?" Al nodded. "What did he have to say?" Again, Al shook his head slowly. Marian gently squeezed her hand that remained on Al's shoulder. "I'm sorry, Al."

Al laid his free hand on top of Marian's and held it tightly. Slowly, he turned his head toward her. The accumulation of tears that had been pooling in his dark brown eyes brimmed past his lids and ran down onto his cheeks. "I know." His voice trembled in his grief. "You're the onwy one who'ths thsorry."

Now that Marian was able to see Al's face, she gasped at what she saw. The area around his left eye was swollen and bruised, and there was a cut just below the eye that was caked with dried blood. Blood that had once run freely from the wound was now dried along his cheek and matted in his thick beard.

"My God," Marian said in astonishment as she knelt down beside him. "What happened?" Her hand reached to touch him gently, but Al turned away. The only contact he allowed was to let her brush the hair back from his eyes.

"Him." The word spit bitterly from Al's mouth.

"Mr. Graham?" For the first time, Marian saw the rips

150

and blood on the arms and back of Al's shirt. "Did he do this? Did he beat you?" Al nodded. "Why?"

Al ignored Marian's question and looked back at Reka. "Thshe tried to hewp me," he said softly. "Thshe muthst have heard him and tried to come hewp me. After he weft, I came back here and found her on the fwoor near the door." He looked back at Marian, tears now flowing freely from his eyes. "Thshe waths dying, Marian, and thshe thstill tried to hewp me." Al leaned his head against Marian's chest and cried.

Marian laid her hand gently on the back of Al's head and slowly rocked him back and forth, much as she had done when he had been a child. "She loved you, Al. She loved you so very much." The words caught in Marian's throat; tears came to her eyes as well. "Always remember how much she loved you."

"I hate him! I hate him for hurting her!"

"Don't hate, Al. Hate will kill you someday if you let it." She touched his uninjured cheek caringly, making sure she had his attention. "Forget the hate, Al. Always remember the love . . . Julia Ann's love . . . my love . . . Reka's love . . ."

All of a sudden, Al was aware of the silence surrounding them. He jerked his head around sharply in order to concentrate on Reka. In an instant, he knew why it was so quiet. Reka was no longer wheezing; Reka was no longer breathing. Reka had died.

"Forget the hate, Al, and remember the love."

Tears flooded Al's eyes as he released Reka's hand and laid it gently on her chest. He picked up a white sheet that had lain on the blanket beside him, unfolded it and carefully floated it down over the giant primate's lifeless body.

Thirteen

Krista stood at the stove, humming to herself while she stirred a skillet full of scrambled eggs. The exhilaration of the night before still lingered, and she smiled inwardly with satisfaction. She wondered how, and if, anyone could be any more contented than she. She had a loving husband and family, a nice home, and she worked at a job she enjoyed that appeared to have unlimited potential. By all rights, she felt she couldn't ask for anything more.

But there was still a void in her life she wanted to have filled; Krista still longed to have a baby. Almost constantly, she wondered how much longer they were going to have to wait before having their wish fulfilled. The sixteen months that had passed since they'd submitted their applications to several different adoption agencies seemed like a lifetime. How much longer would it be before she could cradle an infant of their own in her arms?

"Good morning." Alec walked up behind Krista, slipped his arms around her waist and pulled her back against him with a hug. "How did you sleep last night?"

"Completely relaxed. How about you?"

"If I'd been any more relaxed, I would have probably slid right out of the bed." He kissed her on the neck but didn't interfere with her breakfast preparations. Alec was hungry—famished—and he wasn't about to do anything that would delay satisfying his basic need for food. "Anything I can do to help?"

"I haven't put the toast down yet, and you can clear all of that stuff off the table," she added, referring to the brown box and a variety of papers and notebooks Alec had left on the table the day before. "What's all of that about, anyway? Haven't you been letting yourself take a vacation while I was gone?" she asked suspiciously.

"I've been taking it easy," Alec tried to assure her. "I haven't been pushing anything, anyway. In fact, a few things have fallen into my lap quite unexpectedly."

"Uh-huh." Krista nodded skeptically, knowing Alec worked very hard for most of the opportunities he said came to him by accident. "The toast," she reminded him, nodding toward the loaf of bread on the counter as she began dividing the eggs onto two plates already containing link sausages. "What kinds of things just *fell* into your lap this time?"

Alec picked up one of the letters that had been sent to Schmidt while he was staying in Prairie Dells and pointed to the address. "Right here, this box number seven. I left my card in it with a short note to contact me, and do you know what happened?"

Krista shook her head as she transferred the two plates to the serving counter and then turned to prepare the toast Alec had already forgotten. "Not, but I have a feeling you're going to tell me," she answered half approvingly.

Krista and Alec had always shared aspects of their work with each other, but Krista took much more interest in the field of investigative reporting than Alec did in the creation of her Crabby Critters. In fact, she was as much of a mystery lover as Alec and had read almost as many books of that type as he. She always enjoyed trying to solve the crime before it was finally revealed near the end of the book, and she was right far more often than she was wrong.

Her interest wasn't limited to mystery literature, however; she also enjoyed discussing Alec's cases with him. On a few occasions, she had even asked some questions no one else had thought to ask before or had pointed out a seemingly unimportant aspect of the case that had helped lead Alec in cornering the culprit. Krista had often thought that if she were to start her career all over again, she would probably choose the field of investigative reporting.

"That very evening, I received a phone call."

Krista looked at him skeptically and then glanced at the vacant hookup on the wall where a phone had once been. "Oh, really?"

"I told him in the note he could contact me through Marvin," Alec explained.

"So what did your caller have to say?"

"He told me to leave Prairie Dells because I was in danger."

"Danger?" Krista's brow wrinkled with her question. "What kind of danger?"

"He didn't say. He just told me to leave and then hung up." Alec glanced at the letter he still held in his hand, then looked back at Krista. "Do you remember ever hearing about someone around here who has a speech impediment?"

"No," she answered after a few moments' thought. She buttered the toast, placed a slice on each plate, then carried them with her as she joined Alec at the table. "What kind of speech impediment?" she asked as she sat down.

"The most common kind."

Krista looked at Alec in question. "Can you give me a better hint than that? I'm not familiar with speech disorders."

"The letters and sounds that are the hardest to coordinate your mouth to make." Krista again looked at him with a frown. "Awec. He called me Awec instead of Alec because he couldn't control his tongue to make an l sound."

"L . . . l . . . l." Krista repeated the letter several times, concentrating on how the tip of her tongue rose to meet the roof of her mouth just behind her front teeth. Then she said "Alec" and "Awec" over and over, noting the difference in the positioning of her tongue. "I've never stopped to think about it before. I always took talking for granted and figured people who couldn't talk right had just never outgrown their baby talk stage. I guess I didn't even consider it might be due to something they couldn't control."

"Unless there's a physical defect that can't be repaired, most people can learn to control at least part of their speech

154

problems with training. It was obvious this man had never been taught . . . or else he has an uncorrectable deformity," he added as an afterthought.

"What else did he have trouble saying?" Krista asked with interest.

Alec took a moment to think back to the conversation, then repeated the man's first few words verbatim. "'I need to thspeak . . .' He couldn't pronounce an *s* clearly. It sounded like his tongue flattened out across the inside of his teeth and prevented the *sss* sound from escaping," Alec explained.

Krista sounded out the letters and noticed how her tongue again flattened across her mouth with the *ths* sound, similar to the way it had moved on the *w* sound.

"'I need to thspeak to Awec Crithspen,'" he continued. "The *r* in Crispen wasn't real clear either, but it was the least noticeable of his difficulties."

"That's sad," Krista sympathized. "Can you imagine what it would be like to go through life without being able to talk plainly? And can you imagine what kind of fun people must have made of him all his life? That would be just awful."

From outside, a sharp, shrill sound invaded their conversation. Alec turned abruptly in his chair and looked toward Marvin's cabin. *Ring.* As he'd suspected, it was Marvin's phone. Alec practically jumped from his chair and started toward the front door.

"What's the matter?" Krista asked in startled confusion. *Ring.* Alec stopped on the porch just outside the door and stared toward Marvin's cabin.

"What's the matter?" Krista repeated. "It's only Marvin's phone. You know that."

"I know." Alec remained on the porch, looking toward Marvin's cabin, hoping to see the old man come out and motion to him that the call was for him.

"Alec, would you please tell me what's going on."

"I left another note in box number seven yesterday morning before I went to pick you up at the airport. I was hoping the phone call might have been the man calling me back."

Krista stretched in her chair to look out the window

155

toward Marvin's porch. After a few moments, when Marvin didn't appear, she assumed the call wasn't the one Alec had been hoping for. "Come on back in here and eat your breakfast before it gets cold." Alec returned to the table and sat down, releasing a disappointed sigh. "If I were you, I don't think I'd even expect another phone call from your mystery man."

"Why not?"

"If he hung up on you the first time he called, what makes you think he'd call back?" Alec just looked at Krista, hoping she wasn't right. "Go on now and finish your breakfast, and when we're through, you can tell me about the rest of the things on the table here that have captured your interest."

Alec did just that. After they cleared away the breakfast dishes, he spread Schmidt's postcards, letters, journals and the photographs across the table and brought out the piece of paper he'd been using to take notes. Krista was very attentive throughout his sketchy analysis of the items and his synopsis of Todd Tyson's information pertaining to Edgar Schmidt. After listening to Alec for almost two hours and looking over the items on the table, Krista was as intrigued about Schmidt and Project GOD as Alec; she was almost as anxious as Alec to hear what Todd had found out about Hubert Graham.

"I've got another one!" Robbie held tightly to his red fishing pole as he began reeling in the line. "We must be right in the middle of a school of them. This is the fourth one I've caught in the last ten minutes."

"It's the skill of the fisherman," Alec said with a laugh as he reached to tap the bill of Robbie's cap. "I've had my line over the other side of the boat as long as we've been out here, and I haven't even gotten a nibble." Even though Alec didn't enjoy fishing, he'd agreed to accompany Krista and Robbie to appease their requests.

The sound of Marvin's phone pierced the air. Alec turned abruptly on his seat to face the cabin, rocking the boat severely. The phone didn't ring a second time.

"Would you relax," Krista said, using her own weight to counterbalance Alec's sharp movement. "You're as jumpy as a mouse in a cat house. Marvin said he'd come out and wave to us if the phone was for you."

Alec didn't respond; his eyes remained fixed on Marvin's front porch. Marvin never appeared.

"Alec, you've got a bite!" Robbie pointed out across the water at the bobber attached to Alec's line. The blue and white plastic ball looked as if it were sitting on top of a pogo stick, bouncing up and down in the water, and then, it went completely under. "Pull it hard to set the hook!" Robbie instructed with a shout.

Alec did as he'd been told and immediately felt a steady pull against his pole. He'd finally made his first catch of the day.

"Pull him in steady. You don't want to lose him now." Robbie continued to coach Alec as he reached for the net on the floor of the boat. "Keep the line tight. Don't give him any slack."

Krista pulled in her own line to keep it from tangling with Alec's in case the fish started to run. She was tempted to make her own suggestions as to how to bring the fish nearer the boat, but she remained silent. She watched as Alec and Robbie interacted—like a father and son—and again wondered how much longer they'd have to wait before they could have a child of their own.

"Bring him in nice and close," Robbie said as he slipped the net into the water. "Closer . . . closer . . . Got him!" Robbie scooped the fish out of the water and held the wiggling, horny-mouthed catfish up for Alec to see. "He's a keeper, Alec. He's a real beauty."

Alec looked at the twelve- to fourteen-inch-long fish and commented somewhat disappointedly, "It felt like he'd be bigger than that." Krista looked at him with a smug grin, but she didn't say anything.

"That's the limit for this time out," Robbie said as he carefully removed the catfish from the net and placed it in the cooler with the others they'd caught.

"What do you mean the limit? That's my first one," Alec

157

said in mock protest.

"I caught seven, Krista caught four and this one makes twelve," Robbie explained. "That's the limit. It's time to quit."

"And just who said twelve was the limit?" Alec asked, pretending to be more upset about quitting fishing than he actually was.

"Grandpa says when you go fishing, the limit's three apiece. He says after you clean 'em and cook 'em and eat 'em, you can always go back for more if you're still hungry, but there isn't any use to catch more than you'll eat. It's wasteful."

Alec looked at Krista and winked, then directed his attention back to Robbie. "Your grandfather has a very good point. If people would only take what they eat, there'd be a lot more for everybody." Unconsciously, Alec's eyes drifted to the opposite side of the lake. "And if people would only take what they could eat, we wouldn't have so many animals on the endangered-species list," he added as an afterthought.

Krista turned her head and followed Alec's gaze toward the Graham estate. She wondered what had initiated his last comment.

"You said you'd row back if Krista and I rowed out," Robbie said as he shifted onto the seat beside Alec to vacate the center one.

"That I did." Alec moved onto the middle seat, positioned the oars for his comfort and began rowing.

As they approached the dock, Robbie pointed past Alec and Krista toward a man standing on shore. "Who's that?" Since they were both riding backward in the boat, Alec and Krista had to turn in their seats to see who Robbie was talking about.

"That's Jordy Graham," Alec answered with a note of surprise. "I wonder what he's doing over here."

When they neared the dock, Jordy walked out to meet them. "Want me to tie that off for you?" he asked, nodding toward the coil of rope Krista had picked up from the bow.

"Thanks," she said with a smile, tossing him the rope.

After Jordy had the boat secured, he extended a hand to assist Krista up onto the deck. "Jordy Graham," he said in introduction as his gloved hand closed around hers.

"Krista Crispen," Krista responded as she stepped up on the dock in front of him.

"I've been looking forward to meeting you." He squeezed her hand gently instead of exchanging a firm shake, and as he did, he glanced down.

The breath caught in Jordy's throat. There, on the webbing between Krista's thumb and forefinger, were two small dots. His eyes quickly searched for a third dot that would make the triangle complete, but he was unable to find it; a thin scar covered the area where the third dot should have been.

Was it possible? Could Krista also be—

"Yes." He cleared his throat and tried to control the expression of shock and surprise he knew had overtaken his face. "Yes, I've been looking forward to meeting you," he repeated rather awkwardly as he released her hand.

"I've been wanting to meet you, too . . . for a very long time. We used to come to the lake every summer until I graduated from high school, and I used to see you occasionally—or at least I presume it was you—on the other side of the lake." As Krista spoke, she removed the scarf she'd worn over her head while they'd been fishing. Using her fingers as a makeshift comb, she fluffed her auburn hair, then shook her head gently. Her hair fell in soft, gentle waves that reached down to touch her shoulders.

Jordy's breath became lodged in his throat, and again, he found himself speechless. Looking at Krista, he now knew why Alec had commented about his mother's picture that hung over their fireplace. Krista could have just as easily posed for the portrait as his mother. Their resemblance was striking. Their high cheekbones were the same, their chins were the same, the blue-green shade of their eyes was the same, the short widow's peaks that marked the boundaries of their foreheads were identical, and the way Krista's hair framed her face was reminiscent of the brush strokes in the painting. Krista was almost an exact replica of Julia Ann, and Jordy knew why. He had just seen the mark—the remnants of the mark—on her hand. There was no way Krista *could* look like anyone other than his mother.

"Jordy," Alec said as he approached, after having taken the time to tie off the back of the boat and help Robbie lift the cooler onto the dock. "I see you've met my wife."

Somehow, Jordy was able to choke out a reply. "Yes. We were just discussing the fact that we were neighbors many years ago and never had the opportunity to meet each other until now."

"Stranger things have happened," Alec said in passing.

"Yes, they have," Jordy agreed, "and stranger things continue to happen all the time." Alec looked at him quizzically but didn't ask for an explanation. "I was a bit rushed yesterday when I talked to you," Jordy continued with a completely different topic, "and I wanted to stop by sometime today to assure you that my invitation for dinner this evening had been quite sincere. You will be able to join us, won't you?"

Alec's face flushed. "I'm afraid we became preoccupied with something else last night, and I forgot to mention it to Krista."

Jordy looked from Alec to Krista and smiled. "My father and I would like for you and Alec to join us for dinner this evening if you don't already have plans."

"They've got plans," Robbie said as he pushed his way in between them and looked up at Jordy. "They're eating fish with Grandpa and me. We just caught the limit, and we can't let them go to waste."

Krista glanced down at Robbie with a thin smile, looked at Alec and then back at Jordy, disappointment clouding her eyes. "Yes, I'm afraid we already have plans for dinner."

Robbie smiled smugly as he crossed his arms across his chest and looked up at Jordy. "Told ya."

"Is this your boy?" Jordy asked with curious interest.

"No, he's our neighbor's grandson," Krista explained. "This is Robbie Burroughs."

Jordy forced a smile to his lips as he looked down at Robbie. He would really have liked to flatten the little brat

160

right then and there—the kid was throwing a wrench into the works of his plan—but he knew the only acceptable response he could give would be to bow out gracefully.

"Looks like you're one step ahead of me, Robbie," he said, reaching to pat the boy on the top of his hat. Robbie turned his head away and stepped back out of Jordy's reach. "Cocktails perhaps," Jordy suggested as he looked back at Alec and Krista. "Say about eight o'clock."

"I think we can arrange that," Krista answered without conferring with Alec. In truth, Krista didn't care whether she had dinner or cocktails or anything else with the Grahams; she really wanted a chance to see inside the beautiful house across the lake that she'd dreamed about ever since she had been a young girl. "Eight o'clock would be fine," she added, finally looking toward Alec. He smiled and nodded, guessing at the thoughts going through her mind.

"Then cocktails at eight it will be." Jordy glanced at Robbie briefly with his own smug smile, then returned his attention to Alec and Krista. "I'll send a car for you. See you this evening." Jordy didn't wait for a response. He nodded his head, turned and began walking away.

As he neared his jeep, Jordy smiled with satisfaction. He'd fulfilled his mission; their cabin would be vacant tonight in order to give Jameson time to look for any of Schmidt's documents that might be there. An additional prize had been handed Jordy on the proverbial silver platter: there were now two instead of only one. He could hardly wait to return home to tell his father of his most recent discovery.

Fourteen

Hubert Graham stood in front of the fireplace, peering up at the lighted portrait of his wife. Even now, after over twenty-five years, he still felt a tingle of excitement as he gazed at her likeness. Julia Ann's auburn hair hung in loose waves at her shoulders; her blue-green eyes were framed by delicately arched brows and high sculptured cheekbones; her slender nose turned up slightly at the end, which enhanced her full lips and contoured chin. She was beautiful, and that was the way he would always remember her; he felt bitter that they'd been robbed of the opportunity to grow old together.

"Jordy says she looks a lot like you," he said in a soft whisper. "How lovely she must be." A mist of tears clouded his dark eyes. "I wish you were here to see them. I wish you were here to see the results of everything you worked for. Your efforts have brought happiness to thousands of people all over the world you never even knew, and now it appears it's come full circle. Two of our own have finally come home." A knock on the door interrupted his reverie.

"Yes." Graham turned his head to see the door open, offering him a full view of the tall, muscular man who had interrupted his solitary conversation with Julia Ann. "What is it, Jameson?"

"It's quarter 'til eight, sir."

Graham glanced at his watch and smiled. "So it is. Is the car ready?"

162

"I have it parked out front."

"And you know what to do after you bring them here?"

"Yes, sir. Jordy's already told me what to look for."

Graham glanced at his watch again. "Time yourself so you'll be at their cabin at eight o'clock and not a second before. I don't want them to think we're too anxious to get them over here. That's all."

After Jameson left the room and closed the door behind him, Graham repeated to himself, "We don't want them to think we're too anxious." He glanced up at Julia Ann's portrait and added, "Even though we are."

"Don't let me forget to call Todd tomorrow," Alec called from the bathroom.

"I'll try to remember." Krista leaned closer to the mirror so she could see to guide the post of her sapphire-and-diamond earring into the tiny hole of her left lobe. Normally, she wouldn't have taken the most expensive pair of earrings she owned on vacation with her, but this trip had been different. She'd brought them with her to wear with her sapphire blue cocktail dress while she had been in New York, and now she had the opportunity to wear them again.

Once she secured the back in place, Krista stood upright and gazed at her reflection. Even though her hair all but hid the precious stones she wore on her ears, she knew they were there, and their presence gave her a feeling of elegance. She also enjoyed wearing them because, combined with the color of her dress, they helped to bring out the blue in her eyes that was often hidden by the dominant green.

"I still think you're overdoing it," Alec said as he walked from the bathroom, adjusting the tie Krista had insisted he wear. "They're just regular people like the rest of us; they put on their pants one leg at a time."

Krista ignored his comment and reached for the gold chain of her matching sapphire-and-diamond necklace, which lay in the velvet-lined box that had also contained her earrings. "Would you fasten this for me, please?" she asked as she draped the chain around her neck and held the loose

163

ends out for Alec.

"I think I can handle that." Once the necklace's clasp was secured, the pendant hung freely just beneath the hollow of Krista's throat, attractively decorating her smooth skin exposed above the dress's V-neckline. Alec looked at her reflection in the mirror. "You look lovely, Mrs. Crispen," he whispered as he kissed her on the curve of her neck.

"Don't start anything we don't have time to finish," she cautioned. Krista's eyes sparkled as she looked at him in the mirror. Her hand reached up to touch the one Alec had placed on her shoulder. For a silent moment, they looked at each other through their combined reflections.

"Maybe it's true what they say," Alec said as he looked at their features.

"What's that?"

"They say the longer people live together, the more they start to look like each other."

"Don't be silly."

"Don't you think we look somewhat alike?"

Krista studied their reflections for a moment. "Not really."

"Look at our noses. They both turn up a little on the end."

"Mine's cuter."

"And our cheekbones. They follow the same basic angle even though mine are camouflaged with a little more flesh."

"You are silly, and besides, I'm never going to eat like you do and end up with chubby cheeks." Krista reached back over her shoulder with her right hand and gently pinched Alec's right cheek.

Alec took hold of her wrist in his own right hand, and as he turned his head away, he caught a glimpse of his birthmark—and of the scar and two moles on the webbing between Krista's thumb and forefinger. For the first time since he'd known of their existence, the scar and moles bothered him; they bothered his gut instinct.

The sound of a knock filtered into the room from the front of the cabin. "I bet that's him," Krista said with excitement as she turned from the mirror and started toward the bedroom door. "Don't forget your jacket," she called back over her shoulder as she disappeared into the living room, "it's hanging in the closet."

Alec remained in front of the mirror, staring at the hand he had yet to lower after releasing Krista's wrist. He'd lived with his birthmark all of his life, never having thought anything about it. But now . . . now, something didn't seem right about it—something didn't seem right in the fact that Krista had a birthmark too similar to his own.

His gaze slowly traveled up the mirror until he stared into the dark brown eyes of his own reflection. What would the webbing on Krista's hand look like if the scar hadn't been there? What would the webbing on Krista's hand look like if she hadn't been injured by a fishhook when she was four years old.

If the scar hadn't been there, would the skin have been unmarked—or could there have been a third mole . . . a third mole that, had all three been connected, would have formed a perfect triangle? And if a third mole had once existed, could it have been a mere coincidence?

Something deep down inside nagged at Alec; he sensed it was trying to tell him their similar birthmarks were much, much more than just a mere coincidence. "You *are* onto something, aren't you?" he asked the image in the mirror. "Your gut instinct hasn't given you *this* much trouble since the Bailey case a few years back. But what—"

"Alec," Krista said as she stepped back into the doorway, "come on. He's here. And don't forget your jacket."

As Alec walked to the closet for his jacket, he shook his head. At the moment, he was unable to match any of the pieces together of his growing puzzle. Maybe tomorrow he would find the time to write down some of his thoughts; maybe tomorrow, he would hear from the mystery caller. The mystery caller. Alec had a feeling that *he* could answer all of his questions.

Sitting behind the driver, nestled into the plush comfort of the limousine's back seat, Krista was like a wide-eyed child. She'd never ridden in such style before and had been totally disillusioned and disappointed when her transportation in New York had been nothing more than a taxicab. Now, enjoying the luxury of her surroundings, she took in every detail from the computer built into a small unit directly in front of them to the silver bud vases mounted beside the windows that contained freshly picked white and red rose buds. She was even impressed by the car's functional design; the ride was fairly smooth—even as they traveled over the rutted road.

When the limousine stopped at the electric gate, Krista turned her attention to her exterior surroundings. She eyed the gate with interest as they passed through, then turned in the seat to peer out the back window to watch it close behind them. "Seems kind of spooky being closed in," she said in a whisper, even though she assumed the driver couldn't hear their conversation through the glass partition behind his seat.

"The Graham's have quite an extensive security system." Alec looked out the window beside him, glancing from one amber-lighted bush to the next. When he spotted one of the poorly hidden cameras along the drive, he pointed it out to her.

"It's not very good security if you can find them," she commented upon seeing the camera.

"I doubt if those even work." Krista looked at him in question. "I got to thinking about them the last time I walked back from here and stopped to have a look at one. It didn't work; it was a fake. The cameras we can see are probably only decoys. I'd almost bet there are several hidden that *do* work that nobody'd ever be able to find."

"Why would they do that?"

"To keep one step ahead of any intruders who might make their way in here. Anybody who got inside the gate and fence and saw the cameras would probably think they were the only ones and try to stay out of their way, which would undoubtedly lead them right into the picture-path of the ones that actually do work."

"Seems kind of complicated."

"Most good security systems are. There can be all kinds of

checks and balances to make sure nothing's missed."

"How do you know so much?"

"The Penrod case three or four years ago. Remember? The phony security people with the big price tags."

Krista vaguely remembered Alec talking about the case and nodded, but she didn't dwell on the past. "But why would the Grahams need such an elaborate security system?"

"I wondered about that myself, and the only answer I could come up with was to protect the animals. With as many different species of endangered animals as they work with at the research complex, there would probably be several people who might want to steal them and sell them on the black market for a sizable profit."

Krista was about to express her disbelief at someone doing such an inhumane act, but she didn't. She'd spent many evenings talking with Alec about his cases and knew that stealing animals to sell for profit would be classified at the lower end of the list of man's inhumanity against man and nature. Instead of saying anything, Krista just shook her head.

"Do you know if Jordy's married?" she asked, purposely redirecting her thoughts.

"I have no idea. If he has a wife, I didn't meet her the last time I was over here."

"It would be kind of nice to have another woman to talk to, but I don't think I'd mind being surrounded by three handsome men." She looked at Alec. "Jordy is handsome, you know. He's almost as handsome as you," she said, reaching for his hand and squeezing it. She studied Alec's face for a moment in the limousine's soft lighting. "Maybe it's just me, but I think the two of you have very similar features."

Once they passed the guardhouse at the fork in the drive, the trees around them gave way to the clearing in which the house had been built. Leaning forward in her seat to see the majestic home through the windshield, then looking out the side window as the limousine followed the curve of the drive, Krista took in every aspect of the impressive mansion she had never before had the opportunity to view this closely. "It's beautiful," she whispered wistfully.

"You'll love the two statues near the front door." Alec was almost as entranced watching Krista look at the house as she was by actually doing so.

"What kind of statues?" she asked anxiously, glancing toward the lighted chandelier hanging over the front door to gain her bearings. Her eyes then traveled along the path leading away from the entrance. Even though the area was well lighted at ground level, the illumination didn't travel very far upward. All Krista was able to distinguish were two vaguely shaped, dark masses on either side of the main walk. "What are they?"

"You'll see."

But Krista didn't have an opportunity to see the bronze statues. Jameson didn't turn the limousine into the oval drive in front of the house but continued to follow the main lane past the turnoff.

"Where is he taking us?" Krista asked, more a note of surprise in her voice than one of concern.

"Your guess is as good as mine."

"No, it's not. You've been here before, and I haven't. What's on around the house this way?"

"Any number of things," Alec answered as he leaned toward her to look out the side window, trying to figure out where the driver was taking them. "The research labs and nursery, the residential complex, the dairy . . ." At that moment, the limousine turned onto the lane leading directly beside the house. Up ahead, Alec saw Jordy and Graham stand from where they had been sitting at a table on the patio. ". . . and our hosts," he said, directing Krista's attention toward the patio.

"Are we going to stay outside?" Krista asked with a note of disappointment. "I was hoping we'd get to see the inside of the house."

"I'm sure with your feminine charm, you'll be able to coax Jordy into a tour before the evening's over."

"And do you think we'll be able to visit the animals in the nursery?"

"More than likely."

168

Jameson stopped the limousine just short of the entrance to the waist-high decorative brick wall surrounding the patio. He was out of his seat quite quickly, for a man of his immense size, and opening the door for Krista even before she had shifted forward on the seat in preparation to exit. Jameson offered her his hand in assistance, which she accepted with a smile and a brief "Thank you" as she stepped out onto the pavement. Alec didn't wait for Jameson to walk around and open his door but slid across the seat and stepped out behind Krista.

"Krista, Alec," Jordy said in greeting as he walked toward them. He exchanged a quick handshake with Alec, then touched Krista on the arm to direct her toward the patio. "My father has been looking forward to meeting you ever since I told him you'd be joining us for cocktails this evening."

"I've been looking forward to meeting him as well, and," her eyes left Jordy's momentarily to linger on the house, "and I've always wanted to see your home. It's fascinated me for as long as I can remember."

Jordy didn't respond to her comment concerning the house but led her onto the patio directly to his father. "Krista, this is my father, Hubert Graham; Dad, Krista Crispen."

"Mr. Graham, it's a pleasure to meet you," Krista said with an open smile.

Graham didn't reply immediately. For a moment, he was caught in a near-hypnotic trance, looking at Krista— looking at a reincarnation of his dead wife, Julia Ann.

"The pleasure is all mine," he finally said, taking Krista's right hand into his own and holding it tenderly. Graham's eyes left Krista's for a brief instant; he glanced quickly at her hand. When he saw the scar and the two small marks on the webbing between her thumb and forefinger, he squeezed her hand in his excitement. Jordy had been correct in his assessment; Krista *was* one of their own. "Yes, indeed," he said, again looking into her blue-green eyes, "the pleasure is entirely mine. And please, call me Hue."

Knowing he couldn't devote any more attention solely to

169

Krista without raising some suspicion, Graham reluctantly released Krista's hand and reached for Alec's. "Alec, it's good to see you again. I'm so happy you could find the time to join us this evening."

Alec returned Graham's handshake with a smile and a nod, and he wasn't surprised when the older man's eyes left his briefly to glance at his hand. The same thing had happened the last time they had shaken hands, and Alec had noticed an identical gesture when Graham had held Krista's hand momentarily. He wondered what intrigued Graham—and Jordy on previous occasions—about the birthmarks on their hands. He wondered. . . .

"What's your pleasure?" Jordy had walked across the patio and was now standing at a portable bar located beside the French doors leading to the den. He'd already begun putting ice in four glasses and now waited for Krista's and Alec's response to his question.

"If you have peach schnapps and orange juice, I'd like a Fuzzy Navel," Krista answered.

"Scotch and water would be fine," Alec added.

"Even though I'm not a certified bartender, I think I can manage those. The usual?" Jordy asked, glancing at his father.

Graham nodded, then returned his attention to Krista and Alec. "Please make yourselves at home," he said, motioning to the cushioned wrought-iron chairs situated around a glass-topped table. Alec and Krista took seats beside each other; Graham sat down on the chair next to Krista. When Jordy delivered the drinks, he positioned himself in the chair that remained between Alec and his father.

Over the course of the next two hours, Krista and Alec did most of the talking, answering questions about their lives. Graham was sometimes overly intense in his questioning, inquiring about their families, schooling and careers and occasionally slipping in a medical or health-related question.

Krista took the question-answer session in stride. She'd answered several of the same questions in casual conversation with some of the executives from Joy Toy during her brief trip to New York.

170

But the intensity with which Graham seemed to be prying into their backgrounds and personal lives bothered Alec. At times, he felt as if he were an innocent man sitting under a bare bulb being interrogated for a heinous crime. That uneasy feeling, combined with Graham's repeated glances at both of their right hands—which were no longer as subtle as they had once been—fueled Alec's suspicions and his determination to find the reason behind Graham's interest. He now knew it had to do with something much more important than just a neighborly gesture.

A hand tentatively pulled back the edge of the sheer curtains at a second-floor window. Standing off to the side, Al peered through the narrow opening down onto the patio. He knew he had to be cautious in his actions. Graham and Jordy sat with their backs to the house; Alec and Krista were situated so that just a slight uplift of their heads would allow them to see any movement at the window. Even if Krista saw movement, he doubted if she would think anything of it, but Alec—Alec might. During his last visit, Alec had almost caught a glimpse of him at another window. If a similar situation occurred again, he was certain Alec would inquire as to who else might be in the house.

Al couldn't chance such an inquiry. Al wasn't supposed to be in the house; in fact, Al wasn't supposed to be anywhere near where the Crispens might be.

Late that afternoon, Jordy had approached him with instructions from Graham. He'd been told to stay away from the house, the primate house, the research lab and the nursery from seven o'clock until after the Crispens had gone. Al was familiar with the instructions; he'd received them hundreds of times over the years whenever outsiders came to visit the estate. In the past, he'd complied without resistance, occupying himself in one of the spare rooms at either the stable or the dairy, whichever provided the most distance between himself and the visitors. But this time it was different. This time, the visitors were people he knew, even though it was in an all but forgotten way. They were people

171

he wanted to see; they were people he loved from a distance. They were people he wanted to protect . . . to protect from Graham.

Al's eyes remained fixed on the foursome seated around the table below him, watching, wishing the window were open so he could hear their voices. He knew Alec had a pleasant voice, since he'd spoken to him briefly over the phone only a few days ago, but what did Krista's voice sound like? She looked almost identical to the picture of the woman who had nurtured him during the first few years of his life. He wondered if Krista's voice was as soft and endearing as Julia Ann's had been. He wondered. . . .

When Al saw all four people stand, he let the curtain slip from his hand. The fabric was sheer, and he was still able to see their moving forms even though he'd lost the clarity of their features.

He wondered where they were going, but his question was immediately answered when he saw them approach the house. He could have guessed without ever questioning. Most first-time visitors requested a tour inside the mansion, and Graham was always happy to oblige. Al knew they would soon be coming upstairs.

He moved away from the window and crossed the luxurious guest room quickly. He stepped out into the hall, closed the door quietly behind him, then turned to walk to the back staircase that led down to the pantry beside the kitchen. Al would wait there on the landing until he heard voices coming from the main staircase that divided the second floor in half; then he would exit the house the way he'd entered. No one would ever know he'd been in the house; no one would ever know he'd used the old tunnel that still connected the basement to the primate house.

Fifteen

"They're all so precious," Krista said as she left the animal nursery and walked to the middle of the drive.

Graham remained close to her; in fact, he'd never really left Krista's side throughout the tour of the house, the research labs and the nursery. Ever since he'd shown her Julia Ann's portrait and commented on their amazing likeness, his subconscious had regressed thirty years into his past. He was aware of the difference between the two women—at least partially aware—but for the time being, he was allowing himself the luxury of a mind game. For the time being, Krista *was* Julia Ann.

Alec lingered at the door to the nursery and turned to look back down the dimly lit hall. Something was bothering him. Something in particular had been bothering him throughout the tour of the nursery, but he hadn't been able to pinpoint what it was.

Slowly, his eyes trailed along the wall from one observation window to the next. Nothing. He made a sweeping glance of the tiled floor; then his eyes turned upward to the ceiling. A porous-looking panel some ten feet from him attracted his attention. He stared at it for a few seconds and then realized the panel was covering a speaker—a speaker that was emitting the barely audible melody of classical music.

"Is something the matter?" Jordy asked. For the past several moments, he'd stood in silence at Alec's side, watching his every action, wondering what was going through his mind.

"Music," Alec finally answered, his eyes never wavering from the ceiling panel. "The music."

"It plays constantly," Jordy explained. "It helps mask the whimpers of the newborns so one doesn't wake up another one and another one and so on and so on."

"I guess I just didn't notice it the last time I was here." Alec looked at Jordy and smiled awkwardly, self-consciously.

"It was there. Music's been playing in the nursery for as long as I can remember . . . and it played in the primate house even before I was born. It was my mother's idea. She always said music could soothe the heart of even the most savage beast, and it does wonders at calming the newborns. Shall we?" Jordy said, gesturing toward the drive. Alec nodded and led the way.

"The zoo?" Alec heard Krista ask as he stepped up beside her. "Do you still have the little zoo? My friend and I once tried to sneak over here and see it when we were kids," she added, a hint of a blush coloring her cheeks.

"The facility's still used to contain several of the animals from the research complex, but we no longer keep any exotic animals just for our own enjoyment."

"The brick building we passed when we walked down here, what is it used for?"

Alec wondered if Krista might not be becoming perhaps a bit too inquisitive about her surroundings. They had discussed Graham that evening while they'd been dressing and speculated on his connection with Project GOD. Near the end of their conversation, Alec had stated it would probably be best to avoid the topic during their visit with the Grahams. Krista had countered, asking what harm a few seemingly unrelated questions might cause.

Was that what she was doing now? Was she asking a few "seemingly unrelated questions" in hopes of finding a few straightforward answers? Alec hoped not. He hoped he was only overreacting to her chain of questions—a chain of questions that had only been a result of her innocent curiosity.

174

"That's the primate house, where we keep the chimpanzees and orangutans," Graham answered.

"I've always enjoyed watching the trained orangutans perform on television," she responded immediately. "Some of their actions and expressions make them look almost human."

"Primates are our closest relatives in the animal kingdom," Jordy informed her. "Many of their actions are quite humanlike, and biologically, we're very similar."

"Sometimes they're *too* similar," Graham added without bothering to conceal his sarcasm.

Jordy knew the reason behind the bitterness of his father's words. To prevent any inquiry, he immediately brought up a different subject. "I'm afraid you're not dressed for a tour of the dairy," he said, nodding at Krista's open-toed shoes. "Even though we try to keep it as clean as possible, occasionally a cow will slip one past us, and we end up with a not-so-inviting deposit on the floor." Krista and Alec both laughed; his diversion had apparently worked.

"How often do you have to milk your cows?" Krista asked as she began walking toward the house.

"Twice a day." Graham had regained the composure he'd momentarily lost and was once again the congenial host. "We start in the morning around five o'clock and run the various herds through in shifts. By the time we get the morning's supply loaded into the tankers and have an early afternoon lunch, it's almost time to start taking them through for the second milking."

"It sounds like a lot of work."

"It's a lot easier than it used to be. Almost everything's computerized now." Graham continued to talk about the dairy's operation as they walked on toward the house. Alec and Jordy followed behind them in attentive silence. When they neared the patio, Graham asked if Krista and Alec would join them for another cocktail.

Krista glanced at her watch, then reacted in wide-eyed surprise. "It's after midnight." She looked at Alec. "I really think we should be going. It's already long past Marvin's bedtime, and we need to get Thumper out of his way." Alec

175

nodded in agreement.

"You're sure I can't coax you into staying just a little while longer?" As Graham spoke, he took Krista's hand into his own as if he were reluctant to let her leave. "It's been such an enjoyable evening for me, meeting you and sharing your company."

"I've enjoyed it tremendously," Krista confirmed. "I've been wanting to visit your home for a very long time, and I'm so happy you gave me the opportunity, but I'm afraid we must be going now."

Graham looked at Krista for a few silent moments, then said, "So be it." He took a small rectangular black box from his jacket pocket, pointed it toward the six-bay garage set back behind the house some 300 feet and pushed the white button in the box's center. "Jameson will bring the car around for you in just a little bit. I do hope you'll be able to come for another visit before you leave. When will that be?"

"Saturday."

"Saturday. Ahhh, how quickly time passes by us. How quickly life passes by us." Graham looked into Krista's blue-green eyes, and his thoughts again traveled back through thirty years of time. For an instant, he felt as if he were holding Julia Ann's hand.

"Thank you," Krista said with a smile as she took Jameson's hand and stepped out onto her own drive.

After Alec slid across the seat and stepped out, Jameson closed the back door then raised his hand to touch the bill of his hat. "Good night." He turned crisply, slid in behind the wheel and backed the limousine out of the drive. Within a matter of moments, he'd driven out of view.

"I'd hate to run into him in a dark alley," Krista said in passing as they started walking toward the cabin. "He's *big,* and he doesn't seem to have a very friendly disposition."

"I doubt if he's being paid to have a friendly disposition, but I imagine he pulls in a pretty hefty salary because of his size." Krista looked at Alec without comprehending, the nearly full moon highlighting her eyes. "I'd lay odds he's not

176

just a chauffeur. If the facts were known, I'd say he's a high-paid bodyguard."

"A bodyguard? Why would the Grahams want a body-guard?"

"Probably for the same reason they have such an elaborate security system. When you've got something you want to protect, you pay for the best protection you can get."

They stopped at the base of the porch steps. Krista had thought to turn on the light before they had left, and the area around them was adequately lit.

"Do you want me to go in with you before I go get Thumper?" Alec asked.

"I don't see any reason to," Krista answered as she started up the steps. "You need to go get Thumper so Marvin can go to bed. He's been such a dear to keep her for us this long." Alec didn't say anything in response but turned and started across the yard.

As Krista walked across the porch, she reached into her handbag and took out a small key ring. Finding the cabin's oversized key was easy, and within a matter of moments, she was inside, turning on the overhead light in the living room.

She glanced around the room absently as she walked toward the counter that divided the kitchen from the dining area. After setting her handbag on the counter, she turned on the kitchen light and started for the refrigerator for the ritual glass of milk she had every night before she went to bed. She took the milk carton from its shelf, and as she turned toward the cabinets for a glass, she felt something scrape lightly against the floor beneath her foot. Glancing down at the tiled floor, she saw the edge of a black-and-white photograph sticking out from beneath her shoe.

"What in the world?" she asked herself as she reached down to retrieve the photograph. She looked at it for a moment, then recognized it as being one of the baby pictures Alec had shown her that morning.

Her eyes immediately sought out the table where she thought Alec had left the pictures and accompanying documents. Everything was gone.

"Here she comes," Alec warned as he opened the cabin's

177

screen door. Thumper barked happily as she bounded into the cabin and ran directly toward Krista.

Krista was used to the dog's overzealous greetings. By the time Thumper was close to her, she'd freed her hands and was reaching down to keep Thumper from jumping up on her dress. "Stay down, girl," she said as she patted the dog. "I don't need you to put a run in my hose, and I'd be awfully upset if you tore this dress, even though it would be my fault for not having taken it off." After Thumper was somewhat appeased by her greeting, the dog settled down, and Krista returned her attention to the photograph. "Did you drop this when you moved the things off the table?" she asked, holding the picture up for Alec to see.

Alec glanced at the baby picture. "I didn't move—" His eyes shot toward the vacant table. "Where is everything? Where are all of Schmidt's papers?"

"I have no idea. Didn't you move them?"

"No."

"Then what happened to them?"

Alec stared at the empty tabletop in numb silence. A dozen possibilities raced across his mind, but only one emerged as the prime suspect.

He turned to look out the screen door—to look out across the lake—to look at the Graham estate. The gut instinct that had been gnawing at him for the past few days finally got his attention with a big bite. "Graham."

"How— What does Mr. Graham have to do with their being missing?"

"I'm not sure, but now I know there *is* some connection between him and Schmidt's Project GOD. And I'm going to find out what it is even if I have to break into that place to have a look around."

"You wouldn't."

"You're damn right I would," Alec said as he turned back to face Krista. "He sent someone over here to break into our house, and I won't hesitate to return the favor."

"But how can you be so sure Graham's behind it?"

"A logical sequence of happenings I've been ignoring because there didn't seem to be a real reason to associate them 'til now, Graham's overfriendliness to us in light of the

178

takeover planned for around the lake and . . ." Alec lifted the first two fingers of his right hand to first contact his lower chest and then the temple beside his right eye. Krista knew the symbolism well; Alec was referring to his inner instinct.

For as long as she'd know him, Alec had relied on what he called his gut instinct. She had never known it to fail him, but she did know of a few times when he thought it was too bizarre to follow—only to find out later that if he had heeded his inner feelings, he would have solved his case in much less time than his drawn-out legwork had taken him. Now there was never any question when that feeling came to him; Alec had come to rely on it like a sixth sense. Krista had come to accept it as well.

"What do you think it means?" Krista asked as she walked past Alec toward the front door. She stopped and looked out across the lake toward the Graham estate.

"I'm not sure." Alec joined her, his eyes also focusing on the lights on the opposite side of the water.

"What are you going to do?"

"I'm not sure about that either."

Several silent moments passed before Krista asked, "Are you going to call in the police?"

"Not yet. I don't have anything solid to go on."

"And if you find something?" An uncertain tremor filtered through Krista's voice.

"You know me; I'm basically a coward. The first sign of anything that looks even halfway dangerous, and I'll call in the troops."

"You promise?" Krista asked, knowing in the past Alec had waited a few times almost too long before asking for help.

"Promise." Alec slipped his arm around Krista's shoulders and guided her toward the bedroom. "There's nothing I can do tonight, so we might as well try to get some sleep. In the morning, I'll try to figure out just how I'm going to go about finding out about Graham and his connection to Project GOD—whatever that is."

Graham waited impatiently for the elevator door to open.

He'd instructed Jameson to deliver Schmidt's documents, if they were indeed at the Crispens' cabin, to his office at the dairy. Now he was anxious to find out if they were there, and if they were there, he was anxious to find out exactly what they contained—he was anxious to find out what Alec might have learned.

Jordy silently studied his father's face. Deep lines creased the elder's forehead and around his eyes and mouth, making him appear much older than his sixty-six years. His shoulders seemed to slump; his entire upper body appeared to be succumbing to the unrelenting pull of gravity. Jordy could tell that the past few days had definitely taken their toll on his father physically as well as mentally and emotionally.

The elevator doors slid open. Graham walked directly to the door of his office and continued on toward his desk.

His eyes were fixed on the desk. Something was there; something was sitting on the highly polished mahogany surface that hadn't been there before. It was a box, a brown cardboard box, sporting faded water spots, frayed edges and torn corners that had been recently mended with a new layer of Scotch tape.

Jordy paused just inside the door and watched as his father slowly removed the box's lid. "Is it—" Graham's hand flew up in the air, an indication for Jordy to remain silent.

Slowly, almost reverently, Graham laid the lid aside and began sorting through the box's contents. He looked at each of the photographs, then laid them aside. He reread each of the postcards he'd written to Schmidt those many years ago and felt an excitement grow within him as his mind filtered back to the passion that had engulfed both him and Julia Ann over thirty years ago. He read the concerned letters from Eleanor, the page of notes Alec had made, and then he reached for the ledger—the journal Edgar Schmidt had kept.

Graham laid the journal on the desk and carefully opened its cover. A smile slowly spread across his face; he felt the project was still safe.

"What prompted that reaction?" Jordy asked, stepping up beside his father to have a closer look at the journal. He glanced down at the first page. Even though it was

180

completely filled with faded script, the only words he could make out were *Project GOD,* printed in bold letters in the wide top margin. "What does it say?" he asked, sweeping his hand in a broad gesture across the entire page.

"I'd have to sit down and study it for a while to be able to translate it word for word, but by what little I can still remember from over the years, I'd say it pretty much parallels the notes I have in the basement that recorded the first stages of the project."

"Is it written in some sort of code?" Jordy asked as he focused on the script.

"I guess you could call it that. It's Ed's code, so to speak. It's part Latin, part African, part Spanish and Portuguese, taken from our stint in South America, and I wouldn't doubt if there's a little southeast Asian thrown in as well. Ed liked dabbling in words. It wouldn't even surprise me if it contained some words he made up on his own."

"Why would he do that?"

"Partly for the challenge," Graham paused as his eyes momentarily settled on the acronym GOD, "and partly because he knew if this journal ever got into the wrong hands, it would have to be written so no one else could figure it out."

Jordy surveyed the items on the desk, and his eyes were drawn to the infants' pictures. He picked up the photographs, turned them over and shuffled through them, reading through their identifications. When he came to the one labeled *Beta 3-27-A,* he turned it over and contemplated the picture of the infant boy.

A chill tingled through Jordy as he studied the faded photograph. He'd never seen it before; he'd never seen any picture that had been taken of him when he'd been so young—when he'd been but a few minutes old.

"Then you were right," Jordy said as he laid the pictures back on the desk and returned his thoughts to the previous topic. "There's no way Alec could have known what all of this was about."

"I had a hunch that anything Ed might have written down would be untranslatable to anyone else, but I had to be sure."

Graham picked up the journal and returned it to the box; then he began placing the rest of the items on top if it.

"Then if Alec doesn't know anything, there'll be no problem in letting them go."

"I thought about that this evening," Graham said as he slid the box lid into place. "Every time I looked at Krista, I was reminded of Julia Ann." He paused. "She would want them to be free to live out their own lives." He paused again. "And unless something happens to endanger the project, I've decided that's exactly what will happen."

Jordy thought for a moment, and then asked, "Do you think we'll get by that easy?" Graham looked at him, the frown on his face asking for an explanation. "Once Alec discovers the documents are missing, don't you think he'll start probing a little deeper to find out who took them and why?"

"For his sake, let's hope he doesn't." Graham picked up the box and turned toward the door. "As long as he doesn't put the project in jeopardy, he's safe, but if it comes down to a choice between Alec Crispen and Project GOD," he said, glancing down at the box, "Alec Crispen will lose. Come on, help me find a place in the basement to store this." Jordy didn't immediately follow. Graham, noticing his son's hesitation, asked, "What's the matter?"

"You know I don't like to go down there."

A somewhat sinister grin slowly crept across Graham's face, and then he laughed, verging on the diabolical. "You don't like visiting your predecessors?" Jordy's eyes left his father's and sought out the floor as a diversion. "I would have thought you would've liked to visit them quite often. I would have thought you would've liked to go down there and gloat. After all, you were the first one to succeed. You were the first one who could walk the streets and be accepted by society."

Music . . . soft music.
Voices . . . soft voices . . .
   a feminine voice . . . a child's voice

182

*"Leave the others alone, Al, this one is ours to keep.
His name is Jordan. Do you like the name?"*
"Yeths."
"Can you say his name? Can you say Jordan?"
"Jow . . . Jow"
*"Maybe Jordy would be easier.
Can you say Jordy?"*
"Jow . . .
Jor . . .
Jor . . . dee"

Jordy!

Alec bolted upright in bed. His breaths came quick and shallow, rivulets of perspiration trickled past his temples. His eyes darted from one darkened corner of the room to another, and then he realized where he was. He was safe in his bed in the cabin on the lake.

He looked down at Krista, lying beside him. His abrupt awakening hadn't disturbed her; she was still asleep.

He turned his head slightly and looked toward his feet. Thumper's dark eyes stared at him quizzically. Alec knew he couldn't acknowledge the dog's presence or her tail would immediately begin to beat against the bed and awaken Krista. He also knew he couldn't just sit there, or that might encourage a response from Thumper as well.

Alec slid his legs over the side of the bed. As he stood and motioned for Thumper to come with him, he glanced at the clock on the nightstand; it was quarter 'til four. He stumbled across the bedroom and managed to close the door behind himself and Thumper without waking Krista.

Sleep hadn't come easily to Alec. Even though his body was tired, his mind had remained active; he continued to think about Hubert Graham and Project GOD. He'd last noted the time a little before three.

When sleep finally came to him, it wasn't restful. He dreamed. He dreamed a familiar dream—a dream that had haunted him since the days of his youth. Only this time, there had been a difference; this time there had been a voice he recognized and a name he knew. But why? What possible

183

connection could there be between the mystery caller, Jordy Graham and the nightmare that had haunted his sleep for almost thirty years?

Alec walked out onto the front porch and sat down on the glider. Thumper jumped up next to him and curled up on the cushion beside him. She laid her head across his leg and whimpered softly to attract his attention. Alec took the hint and absently slid his hand across her head several times before letting it come to rest on her back.

A soft breeze blew in from the lake, carrying with it the solitary croak of a lonely frog. The full moon shone brightly in the cloudless sky, adding its wavy reflection across the water's gently rippling surface to the ones cast by the widely spaced security lights bordering the Graham estate. A gentle illusion of peacefulness encompassed the entire area.

Alec let his eyes wander aimlessly along the distant shore. A barrage of scattered thoughts bombarded his mind, but he was unable to sort them into any logical order . . . into any logical sequence . . . into any logical purpose. He knew his gut instinct was working overtime, for it had happened a few times before, but there was something else that was bothering him now—something he couldn't quite understand.

As he looked at the Graham mansion, a strange feeling came over him. He couldn't readily translate the feeling into meaningful words, but if he had tried to explain it to someone, he would have said it felt like another instinct—an instinct a wild animal might try to follow when it sought to return to the place of its birth.

Sixteen

Krista stood patiently in line, waiting for an older woman to have a parcel weighed for mailing, for a little girl to buy a book of stamps and for a middle-aged man to pick up a package that had been too large to leave in his post office box. When it was her turn to step up to the counter, she eyed the old postmaster Alec had told her about and immediately turned on her feminine charm.

"Good morning," she said with a flirtatious smile.

The old man nodded, and Krista thought she saw the glimmer of a twinkle in his aged eyes. "What can I do for you?" he asked, returning a smile not quite as perky.

"I'm trying to find an address for someone here in Prairie Dells. I looked through the phone book, but I guess he must have an unlisted number because it wasn't in there."

Krista wasn't lying to the postmaster. She and Alec had looked through the local phone directory that morning but had been unable to find a listing for Hubert Graham or for Jordy Graham. They had found a listing for the Graham Foundation of Zoological Research, but the address accompanying the Foundation's phone number hadn't brought a triumphant reaction. The address was P.O. Box #8. Playing a hunch, Alec looked under the heading of Prairie Dells Dairy. Again, the dairy was listed and again the address failed to produce a lead; its mailing address was P.O. Box #9.

They hadn't found what they'd been looking for, but their

185

suspicions had all but been confirmed. Knowing that boxes eight and nine belonged to the Grahams, Krista and Alec had made a logical guess that the Grahams held the key to box number seven as well. Krista had come to the post office in an attempt to find out whether their assumption was right or wrong.

"So then I thought the next best place to look for an address would be at the post office," she continued. "Can you help me?"

"I think maybe I can." The old man took a small book from a cubbyhole shelf on the wall to his left and laid it on the counter. "What's the name?"

"Graham, Hubert Graham. Or it might be listed in his son's name, Jordy Graham." As Krista spoke, she noticed that the postmaster just stood there; he didn't attempt to open as much as the front cover of the book he'd taken from the shelf. "We were at their home last night for a delightful little cocktail party, and since I doubt if I'll ever have the opportunity to see them again, I wanted to send them a thank-you note."

The postmaster continued to look at Krista in silence, and she was beginning to wonder if he believed her. It had been over ten years since she'd last acted in college, and she hadn't thought the task would be too difficult to pull off a little white lie today. Had she been wrong?

"Can you help me?" she asked, relying on her last batch of courage to see her through. "Can you give me his address?" Krista wasn't sure how she would react if the old man said no.

"Box number seven," he answered congenially.

Krista exhaled a silent sigh of relief as she made a note of the address on a small note pad she'd brought with her. "Thank you for your help." She smiled at the old man and nodded, then turned and started to leave. The postmaster called out a series of five numbers. "I beg your pardon," she said, glancing back at him.

"The zip code." He repeated the five numbers.

"Oh," she said, pausing a moment; then she wrote the numbers down on the pad even though she knew she'd never

186

use them. "I didn't think about the zip code."

"Always remember to use the zip code, miss. It'll help your mail get to its destination much quicker."

"Thank you." She nodded again in appreciation, then turned and walked out of the building.

"Our hunch was right," Krista said as she stepped up into the van and slid onto the front passenger seat. Her breaths were short; she had practically run down the half block from the post office and then around the corner to where Alec had parked the van. He wasn't sure the postmaster would remember the van from Alec's last visit to inquire about the owner of box number seven, but he wasn't about to take any chances of the old man recognizing it and then refusing to give Krista the information they were after.

"Box number seven?"

Krista nodded. A smile of accomplishment brightened her face as she handed Alec the small notepad.

"Did he give you any trouble?"

"Not a bit. In fact, he was quite helpful. He even made sure I had the zip code," she said as she pointed to the numbers she'd scribbled near the bottom of the sheet. "There was a moment, though, when I started to wonder if he was going to give me the address or not."

"What happened?"

"He took out a book I presume contains the addresses of everyone in Prairie Dells, and when I asked him for Graham's address, he didn't open it. I thought I was in trouble, but then he told me the address without even having to look it up."

Alec looked at Krista for a few silent moments, but he wasn't actually looking at her, he was thinking back through time. "Then he knew when I asked him last week," he finally said.

"So? You told me he said he couldn't give you the name because of privacy. You even agreed that complies with the law."

"I'm just curious as to whether the old man knows—or is maybe even involved with whatever is going on at the Grahams'."

187

"Are you grabbing at straws?"

"At this point, I'm grabbing for anything I can get."

Krista looked out the windshield, not really seeing the cars pass by on the street, and she didn't notice the fine mist that was beginning to accumulate on the glass. She was thinking; she was trying to come up with anything that could help Alec.

"Let's say he is involved, or at least he knows what's going on," Krista began, looking at Alec. "Then you know Graham got the notes you left for him." Alec nodded. "Then I'm wondering why he didn't say anything to us about them when we were over there. Even if he didn't want to say anything in front of me, he had a chance to talk to you when you went over there by yourself before I got back."

"I've already wondered about that too. That's one of those situations I told you about that didn't fall into place like I thought it should."

Krista thought for a few moments before she asked, "So what about your mystery caller? Where does he fit into all of this?"

"I don't know. He's something else that just doesn't fit at all. I keep wondering why he didn't respond to my letter after he called so quickly after I left my card."

"Maybe he couldn't." Alec looked at Krista, wanting her to continue. "Maybe he never saw the letter." Alec considered the possibility, and his face immediately reflected his concern as he mentally predicted Krista's next words. "There are a lot more people living on the estate besides the Grahams. Maybe one of them learned you were asking about Schmidt and knew if you found out about whatever it was Schmidt and Graham were talking about on those postcards, you could be in danger. You did tell me he warned you to leave because you could be in danger, didn't you?"

Alec nodded, and then his eyes left Krista's to focus on the address written on the notepad. "I wonder . . . if by sending the letter, asking to speak with him again, could I have put *him* in danger?"

During all the years Alec had been an investigator, he'd used extreme caution to maintain his informants' safety and to keep their identities a secret. He now wondered if he'd failed in that area.

"Do you think we should contact the police?" Krista asked, breaking into Alec's pensive thoughts.

"And tell them what? I don't have anything solid to go on. I don't even have Schmidt's documents any more."

"But back home—"

"Back home, Lt. Ratliff was used to me. He'd been through enough cases with me he'd be ready to back me on any of my hunches, but the cops up here don't know me. They'd probably think I'd gone off the deep end if I went in to them claiming to suspect something unlawful about one of their most prominent citizens. And besides, if there's a possibility the postmaster knows what's going on at Graham's place— and he's being paid to keep silent—that same possibility exists for the local police. Corrupt cops aren't limited to just the big cities, you know."

Krista sat silently for several moments, and then she said, "Let's go home. Let's go back to the cabin and pack up our things and go home. Let's just leave and forget about all of this."

Alec reached for her hand and squeezed it gently. "You know I can't do that. It's not in my nature to give up on a case. I've never done that before, and I'm not going to start now." He paused. "I would feel better, though, if you would go back home."

"No way," Krista stated firmly. "I worry about you enough, sometimes, when we're in the same city, and I'm not going to put several hundred miles between us now to make it any worse. I can worry about you right here just as well, if not better, than if I was back home. If you stay, I stay, and that's final."

Alec knew there wasn't any use in arguing with her; Krista had a stubborn streak that was almost as strong as his. Any disagreement now would only produce hard feelings between them, and that was the last thing he wanted to have on his mind.

"All right, you can stay. But I want you to promise me one thing. If anything does start to happen that looks like it

189

could get out of hand, I want you to promise me you'll get Marvin and Robbie and get away from here as fast as you can. Will you promise me that?" Krista nodded her head slightly. "Promise me."

"All right, I promise." Alec squeezed her hand again, leaned across to kiss her on the cheek, then righted himself on his seat and turned the key in the ignition. "What are you going to do now?"

"I'm going to call Todd to see what he's found out about Graham, and then I'm going shopping."

"Shopping?"

"Yep. I've got a list forming in my mind, and I'm going out of town to fill it."

"Why out of town?"

"I don't know who all in Prairie Dells may be associated with Graham's secret project or who all may be keeping an eye on us for him. If I happen to buy something someone might think is a little strange, I don't want to take the chance of the wrong person seeing it and telling Graham. I don't want him to get even the slightest hint that I'm coming to see him."

". . . and that's all Sam was able to put together," Todd said at the end of his report on Hubert Graham.

Todd hadn't been able to give Alec any information he didn't already know. Even the facts Todd thought might have been noteworthy—the development of the H&J Corporation, Graham's involvement in the dairy business and nationwide distribution of dairy products, his wife formerly working in artificial animal husbandry and his son's continuing with her work—none of it had taken Alec by surprise. He knew about all of it, maybe not in the detail Todd had provided, but he knew about it. He knew about everything because Graham or Jordy had told him.

It appeared the Grahams weren't trying to keep any aspect of their corporation a secret; it appeared they had been totally open with Alec—at least as far as common knowledge was concerned. But Alec knew there was something

190

more; his gut feeling told him there was something more. Now he was more determined than before to find out exactly what it was.

"Thanks for your time," Alec said, glancing at the sack of items he'd set on the shelf in the phone booth beside him. "And thank Sam for taking the time to put the information together for me."

"No problem. Business has been kinda slow the past couple of days, and it gave him something to do." Todd paused, and Alec sensed he had something on his mind.

"What is it, Todd?" he asked. "What kind of skeptical thoughts are running through your head?"

Todd hesitated before he spoke. "Something doesn't make sense to me." Alec didn't ask what; he knew Todd was about to tell him. "I've been in this business for a long time, and something just doesn't sit right with me about this Graham fella." Again, Alec didn't question.

"Remember, I told you Graham was always a publicity hound when he worked with the government. Even that file I sent you on Schmidt had a lot of references to Graham, and he appeared in just about every photo any reporter was able to snap of Schmidt. But when he broke with the government and started working on his own, Graham appeared to drop out of the public spotlight. And in my opinion, it looks like he did it by choice. Since the mid-fifties, when he founded the H&J Corporation, about the only references Sam could find on him in print were brief mentions to his being president of the corporation and his involvement with his three dairies.

"Now, it seems to me that someone who had been so involved in research—and publicity—during the early days of his career would take the opportunity to jump on the bandwagon where this research foundation his son's running is concerned. But he hasn't. In fact, in my opinion, it almost looks like he's avoiding the whole thing. My curiosity on the matter got me to looking through the articles and clippings Sam put together, and do you know, when it comes to any reference to the research foundation, there's not one single mention of Hubert Graham. Now wouldn't you think

191

someone with his background for publicity would want to take at least a little credit where the foundation is concerned? And I don't think his conspicuous absence is just to allow his son to take all the credit. That's not in the man's character." Todd paused. "A man like Graham wouldn't be content to keep silent and play nursemaid to a bunch of cows. It looks as if he's made a complete one-eighty turnaround, and I think there's a reason for it. In my opinion, I think Graham's trying to hide something." Alec couldn't think of anything to say in disagreement; therefore, he said nothing.

"This thing you were wondering about with Schmidt . . . this Project GOD. Have you found out anything more about it?"

"Nothing."

"But you do think Graham's involved."

"I found out the letters Schmidt received were addressed to Graham's residence."

"Then there *is* a connection."

Alec paused before answering. "I'm almost sure."

"Has your famed gut instinct been telling you something?"

"It's been practically eating me alive for the past few days."

"I had a hunch something was going on or you wouldn't have been pushing for this information on Graham." Todd paused. "I know I've said this before, but you will keep me posted on anything you find."

"That I will."

"Damn. I've got a call on another line. I'm expecting a response from the mayor, and I imagine that's him. I've got to go. Keep in touch."

"I will, and thanks again for your help." Alec replaced the phone and just stared at it for a few moments, thinking. Even though Todd hadn't been able to provide him with any new information on Graham, his comments pertaining to Graham's avoiding the limelight that would have come easily with his association with the research foundation had sparked his interest.

Alec was familiar with individuals with similar personalities, people who liked to see their names in print, their pictures accompanying articles and their faces and voices broadcast on the evening news. He also knew, as Todd had made reference to, that individuals with that sort of personality rarely changed unless there was a strong reason to do so.

So what had been the reason behind Graham's turn-around? What had prompted him to forgo a life that could have kept him in the public eye for one that was all but cloaked in total privacy . . . total secrecy? There could be only one reason, and Todd had hit upon it as well. Graham was definitely trying to hide something.

A gentle peck sounded on the glass beside him. Alec jumped. Then he turned to see Krista's sparkling eyes looking at him.

"I got them." Her muffled voice reached Alec's ears as she held up a shopping bag to verify her purchase. "Now what?" she asked as Alec stepped from the booth, carrying the sack of supplies he'd bought while she had been on her own shopping trip.

"We're heading back. I want to have a look around the place, and then I want to try to finalize my plan."

"I'm ready," Krista said with a touch of excitement.

Alec looked at her suspiciously. He knew she enjoyed talking with him about his cases, but he didn't remember ever seeing her this enthusiastic. He wondered what was fueling her zest. Alec didn't know Krista was working on a plan of her own.

Al removed the wilted wildflowers from the can he'd buried in the ground up to its rim and replaced them with the fresh ones he'd collected during his walk through the woods. After he arranged the flowers to his liking, he squatted beside the mound of dirt that was not yet three days old. His eyes focused on the flowers then shifted to the makeshift cross behind them. He hadn't known what might have been considered appropriate for the unique situation and had kept the marker simple. It was a plain cross made from two fairly straight sticks that he'd tied together with twine, but

193

it wasn't totally plain; Al had adorned it with something personal.

Even if the marker hadn't been there, he would have been able to find his way to Reka's grave without any difficulty. He'd buried her beneath the outstretched limbs of his favorite maple tree, where he and Jordy had played as children. Al still came there often when he wanted to be alone. The setting was quiet, high on a hill overlooking the lake and the estate.

A gentle breeze rustled the leaves and split the branches sporadically, allowing a dappling of midafternoon light to filter through. Al always felt comfortable whenever he came up on the hill; it was much like a security blanket. That was the reason he had buried Reka there, so she could feel comfortable and secure for the rest of eternity. He'd told Jordy he wanted to be buried there beside her whenever the day came for him to die. Jordy had nodded his head in a simple confirmation.

Al sat down on the ground and untied then removed both his tennis shoes and socks. He then stood, removed his T-shirt and let his jeans slide down his legs. He hooked his thumbs inside his underwear but had second thoughts about exposing himself totally to the world. Looking down, he thought the garment none too obvious, its dark blue coloring not contrasting as starkly with his body as it would if it were white. He decided to leave it on.

Al walked around the foot of Reka's grave and stopped beneath a limb that spread like a giant hand ten to twelve feet above his head. He looked at the trunk some six to eight yards away; then he began to run toward it.

When Al was about four feet from the tree, he leaped—sprang—through the air toward it. One foot contacted the rough bark, pushing him upward. His second foot reached higher up on the trunk, still pushing him upward . . . upward until his hands could reach the limb. Once he secured a firm grip, Al hoisted himself up and over the sturdy branch, straddling it.

Secure in his high perch, Al leaned back against the trunk and surveyed his surroundings. By all rights, he should have been surveying his own land; by all rights, he should have been able to claim half of the property around him as provided by his birthright. But no rights had been given to him. Even as the firstborn son of Hubert Charles Graham, nothing had been given to him—nothing but pain, that is.

Al was an outcast. Al was a mistake. Al was a freak who, by all rights of nature, should have never been born. God, in all of His infinite wisdom, had erred in allowing Al to be created . . . and then to survive.

His eye was attracted by mass movement in the distance. Off to the northeast, he could see a herd of cows—the herd of *special* cows that never ventured from their isolated pasture to roam the woods carefree like the rest of the dairy milkers. Al felt as sorry for them as he did for himself . . . as he had for Reka. All of them were prisoners on the Graham estate, and they would remain prisoners as long as it suited Graham's needs.

Al knew the project would be discovered someday, but he hoped that *someday* was a long way off. If and when that day came, his sanctuary would be destroyed along with everything else. Al didn't want that to happen.

Even though his existence was limited to the twelve hundred acres around him, Al still managed to enjoy life. He enjoyed living and hoped his life would last for a very long time. He would never intentionally do anything to disrupt his home, and he hoped no one else would either.

Al's gaze left the distant herd of cows, and he slowly scanned along the opposite shore. Again, movement caught his eye. He concentrated, trying to focus on the two people entering a boat at the dock at the far corner of the fenceline, but they were too far away to recognize. He continued to study their basic forms and watch their movements. By what little he could distinguish, he didn't think it was the old man and the boy. That left only two other people who would be using the semiprivate dock.

"Awec. Krithsta." A smile came to Al's bearded face as he spoke their names, and then it faded. He wished they would leave. For their own safety, he wished they would go far away from Prairie Dells.

195

After eavesdropping on Graham and Jordy's conversation the night before, Al didn't think Graham would go after them now as he'd once feared. But what if he was wrong? Or what if he was right, but then Alec started asking the wrong questions or became too curious for his own good? How far would Graham go to protect his project?

Al watched their boat disappear behind the trees bordering the shore. He'd expected them to row toward the center of the lake, drop anchor and cast their lines to fish. He didn't expect them to follow so closely to the lake's perimeter, and he wondered why they were. Fishing wouldn't be as good so close to shore. The water was shallow, and there was the chance of snagging their lines on hidden trees and brush and weeds. Why would they want to row so close to shore unless . . . unless—

"No!" Al shouted, but no one was near enough to hear him. "No! Go away! Go away!"

Powered by fear, Al jumped down from the tree. When his feet hit the ground, his knees buckled beneath him, and he rolled, the coarse dark hair covering his body picking up debris off the ground. He started running through the woods toward the lake, and in his haste, regressed to using his arms as well as his legs. Any time Al was in a hurry, he sometimes forgot to walk—or run—upright.

"Are you sure we don't look conspicuous?" Krista asked, keeping her chin down near her chest as her eyes strained to see around the hat blocking her view.

"We'd look a lot less conspicuous if you'd just act normal." Alec hadn't wanted to bring her along in his survey of the fence around the lake, but Krista had insisted, and she had brought up a logical point. It would appear more believable if both of them were out in the boat instead of just one. "You do the fishing, and I'll do the rowing and looking. And for God's sake, keep your head up. You look like somebody who's got a twenty-pound weight tied around her neck."

"So I'm not as good at this espionage thing as you are,"

196

Krista said curtly as she lifted her head up straight and tilted her hat toward the back of her head. "How am I going to get any better if I don't practice?"

"There's no need for you to practice because there's no need for you to get any better. Once we get back to shore, you're finished."

"We'll see about that." Krista turned sideways on the seat and cast her line toward the middle of the lake. She remained quiet for quite a while, while Alec continued to row the boat around the lake about ten to twelve feet out from shore.

As Alec rowed, he scanned the fence that ran parallel to and about a foot in from the waterline. He was looking specifically for surveillance cameras that might be mounted at intervals on the support posts, but so far, he'd located none. In reality, Alec didn't expect to find any cameras. He'd walked the fence beside their cabin and along the rutted road back to the river by the bridge and hadn't found a single camera. What Alec *had* noticed along the newer stretches of fence was a small mound of dirt about three feet in from the fence and running parallel to it. Digging back into his memory, in reference to the Penrod security system case he'd covered a few years before, he speculated the long-running, continuous mound covered a weight-sensitive sensor that had been buried there. With the weight sensor in place, there would be little or no need for additional cameras to monitor the area. Besides, there was little need for Graham to maintain such close surveillance on the outskirts of his property; if he was protecting something, Graham would have it close to him—close enough so that he could keep watch over it almost constantly.

Alec figured he could make it through the woods without too much difficulty. The challenge would come when he reached the high-security area, when he reached the area under the cameras' constant watch. He had a plan to outsmart the cameras—if it worked. Even if his plan did work, he'd have to make sure he didn't miss a single camera, or his entire plan would be a failure. Then, how would he explain his presence on the estate?

"Are you finding what you're looking for?" Krista asked

as she reeled in her line and checked the hook to make sure the bait hadn't been taken as a free meal.

"Yes and no." She looked at him with a frown. "I'm finding what I expected, which is nothing. I told you that's what I thought we'd find even before we left."

"Do you think we might find anything noteworthy up here?" she asked, nodding toward a nearly perpendicular junction in the fence a few yards farther down the shore.

Alec started to turn his head but didn't. At the rate he was rowing, he knew he'd arrive near the area Krista was referring to in just a few more pulls of the oars. If there was something there, a camera for instance, then it wouldn't appear as if he were looking for it if he merely glanced nonchalantly in its direction as they passed.

"I see one!" Krista said in excitement. She lifted her hand and started to point but lowered it quickly, then dropped her chin to her chest to allow the overhanging brim of her hat to shadow her face. "I saw one," she repeated, her voice muffled. "Did you hear me?"

"I heard you." Alec tried to remain calm even though the words left his mouth through clenched teeth. "And I saw you almost give us away." He pulled harder on the oars, trying to divert his anger, trying to control the frustration that was mounting from their so-called leisurely trip around the lake. "Just sit there and don't say another word."

Krista again turned sideways on the seat and cast her line toward the center of the lake. Tears clouded her eyes, and she bit at the inside of her lower lip in an attempt to keep it from quivering. She had made a foolish error, almost pointing at the camera, and any more errors she made now would only lessen her chances of being able to carry out her own plan for that evening. If she wasn't careful, she would have too many strikes against her, and then there would be no way she could talk Alec into letting her go with him.

Al waited for the boat to move past him, then slipped his hands beyond the edge of a bush and cautiously pushed it aside. At the moment, his view of the boat and its passengers

198

was clear. He saw Krista point briefly—quickly—at something, then jerk her hand and arm back.

His eyes followed the direction of her gesture. When he spotted the camera mounted high on a fence post, he began to shake his head, positive now that their unorthodox trip around the lake was not for pleasure at all.

"Don't do it," Al said in a low whisper. "Go home. Pweathse, go home and weave uths awone."

St. Louis, Missouri

"This is *my* ace," Clara Rath said pointedly, glaring across the table at her partner as she laid the ace of diamonds on the king that had been led, "and don't you trump it unless that's all you've got left in your hand. And if it is, use the smallest trump you've got."

Juanetta Goltsman looked across the table at Clara and clenched her teeth, holding in a sarcastic retort. During the three years she'd been attending the card parties, she'd heard Clara make that same comment dozens of times, and she especially didn't like it when the comment was directed toward her. Juanetta knew her ability when it came to playing cards, and she didn't appreciate Clara's implication that she was anything more than a novice. She was happy she only had to be Clara's partner once every seven months.

But playing cards was only a front for the gathering, and everyone in attendance knew it. Playing cards was the explanation they gave to their husbands, but they really congregated together one afternoon a month to share the gossip they'd collected during the previous thirty days and to be informed of anything they might have missed hearing on their own.

"If she can't follow suit, she's going to have to have a bigger trump than this one to take the trick," Irene Owens said as she laid the ace of spades on Clara's ace of diamonds. She winked slyly at her partner, Ruby Hyatt.

"I do." Juanetta laid the jack of clubs on top of the other three cards and pulled the trick across the table toward her.

199

"Did you hear Barry and Stephanie Cordell adopted a little girl?" she asked as she led back a card she knew her partner would be able to trump.

"Bought would be a better way of putting it," Clara said in condemnation as she touched the corner of the card she intended to play. She then leaned closer to the table and lowered her voice as if the information she was about to share was a prized secret. "Esther Berdick told me Goldie DeLaney told her she overheard Hazel Nern and Wilma Summers talking about it at the hairdresser's." When Clara paused, the other three ladies sitting at the table leaned closer to her, giving Clara the undivided attention she wanted. "The Cordells paid fifty thousand dollars for that baby."

"No," Ruby gasped. "You mean they actually *bought* a baby?" Clara nodded and smiled with the satisfaction that she'd brought a new tidbit of gossip to the table.

"Why should that surprise you?" Juanetta asked. "People who can afford it do it all the time."

"Really? I've never known any—"

"Sure you have. Kevin and Marilyn Hickman did it years ago—"

"And you know what happened with that," Clara interrupted all-knowingly.

"No, what happened?" Ruby asked with interest.

"God got even with them for buying that baby."

"What?"

"God got even with them."

"Their grandchild," Juanetta attempted to clarify, "their adopted daughter's baby. The poor little thing was born so horribly deformed that he had to be put away in a home somewhere where nobody would ever have to look at him."

"Not a very good return off their original investment," Clara added cynically. "But they got what they deserved, buying their daughter the way they did."

As soon as she realized where the course of the conversation was leading, Irene Owens scooted back in her chair away from the table. She didn't ask any questions; she didn't want to listen to the proffered explanations; she didn't

200

even want to look at the three people sitting close to her.

Irene knew of a similar situation, and her knowledge of that situation was almost firsthand. Twenty-two years ago, her sister and brother-in-law had adopted—paid a large fee for— an infant girl.

Vicky had been a lovely girl, an intelligent girl, a healthy girl, all of her life. When she married and then became pregnant, Irene shared in her sister's joy and anticipation— but that happiness was short-lived. Vicky delivered a grotesquely deformed infant for whom there was no explanation.

The tragedy of Vicky's baby was a hardship enough in itself for any family to overcome, but it only added to the heartache they'd already had to endure. Larry, Irene's nephew—Irene's *adopted* nephew, who had been obtained through the same lawyer four years before Vicky's adoption—had been tested after five years in a childless marriage. He was found to be sterile.

Two unfortunate incidents within the same family—two unfortunate incidents involving adopted children who had been . . . who had been *purchased* for an astronomical sum.

Irene contemplated Clara's comment as the conversation around her again registered in her mind. Was it possible? Had God really been trying to get even? She hoped not, for if He was, she knew there were probably thousands of other families who would someday suffer the same fate.

Seventeen

Alec held his fork loosely, haphazardly shifting the food on his plate from one side to the other. Occasionally, he lifted a small tidbit to his mouth.

Krista tried not to appear conspicuous as she watched him out of the corner of her eye. She had seen Alec in similar moods several times before. Each day . . . each evening . . . each night before he left the house to go in search of information to support a case, he'd followed a nearly identical pattern. If there was time to think and plan, he'd do so in their study, alone. If there was too much time allotted before his scheduled departure, or if someone was late in arriving to accompany him, he'd pace the floor in front of the fireplace in their family room. And if the hour was right, which would indicate there was time for a meal before he was to leave, Alec would do exactly what he was doing now.

Unconsciously, Alec played with his food. His thoughts were focused on what he considered to be much more important matters. The furthest thing from his mind was the task of supplying his body with the sustenance that would fuel his activity until his next encounter with food.

"Do you have everything figured out?" Krista asked tentatively. "Do you know what you're going to do?"

"No." Alec dropped his fork on the plate and slid it away from him. He leaned back in his chair, lifting the two front legs up in the air. He teetered there for a moment, then returned all four legs of the chair to the floor. "I've got a plan . . . a very sketchy plan, but who's to say whether it'll work or not." He slid the chair back from the table, stood, walked silently across the room and let the screen door slam behind him as he stepped out onto the front porch. Thumper made a tight exit behind him, her tail barely missing being caught by the door.

Krista slid her chair back from the table and followed after him at a respectful distance. She stopped at the door and looked out. Alec was standing at the top edge of the steps, leaning against a support post and looking out across the lake in the direction of the Graham estate. Soft amber lights highlighted the drive and colonial mansion in the onset of late evening twilight.

"Do you want to talk?" Krista asked as she stepped out onto the porch behind him. "We've talked in the past when something was bothering you about one of your cases."

Alec tilted his head to look at her over his shoulder. He smiled thinly; then he turned and reached to run the back of his fingers down her smooth cheek. "I'm sorry I snapped at you this afternoon when we were out in the boat."

"I deserved it," she said, taking his hand in her own. "I could have blown everything for you." Krista glanced down at his hand and then looked back into his eyes. "I guess I'd never make it as an investigative reporter."

"Everybody makes mistakes. God knows I've made my share." Alec slipped his arm around Krista's shoulders and walked with her toward the glider.

"Then you think there's hope for me?" she asked as she sat down beside him.

"Let's put it this way: Don't give up your other job." Alec hugged her close to him, then settled into a comfortable position. His eyes again searched out the lights on the opposite shore. "When you and Rebecca tried to sneak in to see the zoo when you were kids, how did you try to get in?"

Krista also concentrated on the lights of the estate, and then her eyes began to move eastward along the shore into the darkness. Her gaze hesitated when she came to the junction in the fence where she'd seen the camera that afternoon. Leaning forward on the glider, as if the action would help her think, she settled her elbows on her knees and continued to scrutinize the distant area that was cloaked in the shadows of early night.

"There used to be seven more cabins on around the lake between here and the Grahams'. There were the Bucks, the Surfaces, the Rosenbaums . . . ." As Krista recalled the names of her former neighbors, her eyes followed the shoreline. She mentally visualized each of the cabin's former locations. ". . . the Blankenbakers, the Loucks, the Walters and the Garretts. There was a fence on the other side of the Garrett cabin, and there was a little gully that dipped beneath it. That was where Becky got stuck," she added with a chuckle. "That was where the night watchman caught us when we told him we were playing Combat." She sat up straight and turned to look at Alec. "Is that how you're planning on going in?"

"By everything I've seen, the woods seem to have the least security."

"Until you get to the camera on the fence."

"I think I've got that covered." Alec didn't give Krista an opportunity to question. "Do you remember anything from when you were inside?"

"Geez, that was over fifteen years ago. Even if I could remember what it was like before you got to the old zoo, things have probably changed a lot since then." Krista looked back across the lake to the right of the lighted estate. "You know yourself there's a whole new residential complex now where the caretaker's house used to be." Krista was silent for a few moments. "To be quite honest," she finally admitted, "Becky and I didn't get very far. We chickened out and turned back before we got anywhere near the zoo. All I really know about the layout of the place is what I saw yesterday when Mr. Graham took us on his little tour. Sorry I can't be of any more help."

Alec smiled in understanding, then gently pulled her back against him. "You're always good moral support." He kissed her on the temple and squeezed her close to him.

"Maybe I can—"

Ring. The shrill sound of Marvin's telephone pierced the

evening's silence.

"I wonder who that could be?" Krista asked as she leaned forward and looked toward Marvin's cabin.

"There's only one way to find out." Alec stood and started toward the steps. "Marvin and Robbie went to the drive-in tonight, so I guess it's up to me to answer it."

"Is everything ready for transport?" Hubert Graham stood at an observation window, looking into the dimly lit room at four occupied incubators. Two technicians, wearing masks and dressed in white, were attending the monitors that were connected to the sterile cubicles by a half-dozen cables each.

"The units are healthy and stable," Donald answered with a smile of accomplishment. "Jess should be here in a couple of hours for the pickup, and I've notified Elaine to expect delivery sometime early this morning."

Graham nodded in satisfaction. "What about the other one? How soon do you think it'll be?"

"She's being monitored closely, and it's my guess, maybe she'll come sometime late tonight or early in the morning."

"Did you give Elaine the extra one's description?"

"I gave it to her last week. She told me when I talked to her a little while ago that she'd already located a client."

"Was there ever any doubt?" Graham looked at Donald, and a smirk pulled at the corners of his lips. "There'll always be a market for our product." He glanced back at the incubators, then turned and began walking down the hall. "Have you talked to Jordy recently?"

"Not since we finished up. He had a long afternoon and evening with the four of them coming almost all at once, and he said he was going to get some rest. I imagine he's asleep in his room upstairs. You know Jordy, he's wanting to be close by in case this next one decides to surprise us and come in the middle of the night."

"He's a good boy," Graham said, a touch of melancholy invading his voice. He cleared his throat, then patted Donald on the shoulder as he added, "You're all good boys."

205

"Thank you, sir. I enjoy my work, and I enjoy being able to help make other people happy."

"And you can't complain about the salary," Graham said with a laugh.

"No, sir, that I can't."

"I think I'm going to call it a night. I'll check with you in the morning to see if we have another one."

After Graham left the building, he climbed into the electric cart he'd driven down from the house and began his journey home. When he reached the gate that separated the dairy from the rest of the complex, he waved to the guards who had just come on the night shift as they opened the barrier to let him pass through. He smiled to himself as he continued on. He had a profitable operation going on here, and he had a staff of loyal people working for him. There was little else that he could ask for . . . unless, somehow, he could make amends with his son for the unfortunate mishap that had occurred a few years ago.

When he reached the house, Graham parked the cart in the small lot beside the back door and went inside. A twinge of hunger growled inside his stomach, and he decided to check the refrigerator for a snack before going to bed.

Walking into the kitchen, he slid his hand along the wall toward the switch but stopped before turning on the light. Something on the wall to his right attracted his attention; one of the lights on the wall phone was lit, indicating someone was using one of the extensions connected to the residential line.

Who would be making a phone call from his private line? Jordy and Donald were at the dairy, and Lewis and Marian were surely in their own home by now. Other than for the four of them, no one else ever used the residential phone line except for Graham. No one—

"That son of a . . ."

By the location of the light, Graham thought he knew which extension was being used, but to make sure, he walked to the phone and checked the printed label beneath the light. "The stable. I thought so." Turning sharply, he started back toward the door. He was going to the stable to see if his hunch was right. And if it was, maybe he would take care of the problem once and for all.

"Hello," Alec said as he sat down on one of the stools at Marvin's kitchen counter. "This is the Marvin Horton residence, but Marvin isn't home at the moment. May I take a message?" He reached for one of the pencils Marvin kept in a ceramic mug on the counter and pulled a small notepad toward him, ready to write down any message the caller might wish to leave, but the caller didn't speak. "Hello," Alec repeated. Still, the caller failed to respond, but Alec knew someone was there; he could hear breathing.

Immediately, Alec thought of his mystery caller. A slow smile steadily worked its way across his face. Guessing—hoping—he continued with the conversation that had so far been one-sided.

"This is Alec Crispen. I was hoping to hear from you again." The caller didn't reply, but Alec heard a short gasp. He knew he'd taken the caller by surprise. "It is you, isn't it?" Alec nudged verbally.

"Yeths," the caller finally answered in hesitation.

"Are you all right?"

"Yeths."

"I thought something might have happened since I didn't hear from you after I sent you the note." The caller didn't respond.

"Who is it?" Krista asked as she stepped in from the porch. Alec raised his hand abruptly, motioning for her silence, then pointed repeatedly toward the Graham estate. "Is it *him?*" she asked in a whisper. Alec nodded, and again he motioned for her to be silent. "I'm going to listen on the bedroom phone," Krista said in a whisper as she hurried across the room toward the hall.

"You did get the note, didn't you?" Alec asked, returning all of his attention to the caller.

"No."

Alec was silent for a moment, then asked, "Did someone else get it?"

"Yeths," the caller answered after a brief hesitation.

A wave of dread swept over Alec. By sending the second note, had he unknowingly placed the caller in the danger he, himself, had been warned about? "I didn't get you in trouble, did I?" No response. "Did I?"

"It'ths aw right. Juthst don't do anything ewthse. Don't do what you're pwanning. Don't come over here!" The caller paused. "I thsaw you on the wake today. I thsaw you wooking, trying to find a way to get in. Don't do it. Don't do it! Take Krithsta and weave. Take her and weave now before it'ths too wate."

Alec was stunned by the tone of desperation in the man's words. He had to take a few moments to organize his thoughts before he could respond. "What's Graham trying to hide over there?" No answer. "What he's hiding? And how does it affect Krista and me?" His words came out more forcefully than he'd intended. Alec hoped the caller wouldn't take offense and hang up. "What's he hiding?" he repeated in a more controlled voice.

"You don't want to know...." An extended silence passed before the caller spoke again. "Pweathse weave. Weave now. I don't want anything to happen to—"

When Graham reached the end of the cobblestone path, he saw a light coming from the window of the tack room— the room that housed the only phone in the stable. "It's you, isn't it, you son of a bitch." A shadow of madness darkened his words; a shadow of madness darkened his soul.

Silently, Graham worked his way toward the window. When he was close enough to touch the windowsill, he looked inside the room. Through the sheer curtains, he could see Al standing a few feet from him, his back to the window, the phone pressed against his misshapen ear.

"You treacherous freak," Graham whispered coarsely between clenched teeth. "This is the last chance you'll ever have to betray me!"

Pure hatred fueled Graham as he walked around the corner of the building and stopped in front of the tack room door. He looked around quickly, searching for anything with which to arm himself—looking for anything he could use to kill Al. A pitchfork, sticking out of a bale of straw beside the nearest Dutch door, caught his eye. He grabbed it, gripped it firmly in both hands, turned back toward the door and kicked it open.

". . . anything to happen to—" Al spun around toward the door. He saw Graham run toward him, the pitchfork leveled, aimed directly for him. Before he could do anything more to defend himself than take a step to the side, Graham was across the narrow room, ramming the pointed tines into the soft flesh of Al's side.

Al cried out—a cry that wasn't human . . . a cry that wasn't animal. It was a cry combined from the sounds of each; it was a cry that had been born through the evolution of forgotten time.

"You bastard freak!" Graham shouted as he pulled the pitchfork free and lifted it to strike again. "This is the last time you'll ever betray me. The last time!"

As Graham lunged at him again, Al was quicker on his feet to step aside. The tines barely missed catching his shirt and plunged into a support post of the bare wooden wall behind him. Seeing an opening—like a cornered animal taking the opportunity to escape—Al ran for the open door, a hand clutching his wounded side.

"Run, you bastard freak, run!" Graham shouted after him. "But you can't run far enough. Sooner or later I'll find you, and when I do, you'll be dead. You're dead, Al. Dead! Anybody who tries to stop me is dead!"

In his anger, Graham pulled the pitchfork from the wall and threw it. The handle hit the spiral cord of the dangling phone, knocking it against the wall with a bang. He looked at the phone, then grabbed it in his hand. With one firm yank, he pulled the cord from the wall and threw it across the room.

"*Anybody* who tries to stop me is dead. I've done it before, and I won't hesitate to do it again," Graham swore through clenched teeth. He ran from the stable and hurried along the cobblestone path. He knew he had to find Jameson—fast.

*   *   *

Krista ran horror-stricken from the bedroom. "Did you ear that?"

Alec sat numbly at the counter, the phone still at his ear, but he heard nothing. There was nothing for him to hear, no crackle, no dial tone—nothing. The line was dead.

"Alec!" Krista stopped beside him and grabbed his arm in panic. "Alec!"

"I heard." The quaver in his voice revealed that he, too, was unnerved. His hand trembled as he returned the phone to its hook.

"Did you hear that . . . that cry . . . that scream?" Krista's fingers dug into the flesh of Alec's upper arm. She was frightened—nearly hysterical. "It . . . it wasn't human. The man . . . the . . . the *whatever* you were talking to . . . it wasn't human!"

Alec looked into her eyes. His own thoughts about the caller's lineage revealed themselves to her as clearly as if they'd been spoken. He agreed with her. He doubted if the caller was human—at least entirely human, and that thought reinforced his need to know exactly what was going on at the Graham estate.

"You've got to get out of here," Alec said as he stood quickly from the stool.

"Why?"

"You heard Graham's threat."

"But you can't believe he'd actually try to kill someone. He seemed to be too nice of a man to—"

"I'm not going to take the chance to find out *what* kind of a man he is." Alec grabbed Krista's hand and started toward the front door, almost pulling her behind him until she gained the presence of mind to quicken her steps to keep up with him.

"If you think something's wrong, shouldn't you call the police?" Krista questioned as they hurried down the porch steps.

"There's no time. I want you to get out of here before I do anything else."

"But—"

"Don't argue."

"But I won't leave without you." Krista jerked her hand free and stopped abruptly.

"Yes you will," Alec said forcefully, leaving her momentarily to go into their cabin. He returned with her purse, Thumper following close at his heels. Taking hold of her arm firmly, he started toward the van. "Do you remember any of the back roads leading away from here?"

"I think so, but—"

"Use them. Stay off the main roads as long as you can. Go to Rickdon and tell Todd about everything that's happened, and he'll figure out what to do."

"I'm not leaving without you!" Krista said adamantly, digging her heels in the ground to make a stand.

"Krista, you have to." Alec turned her toward him and looked directly into her eyes. His voice became less demanding and the tone more persuasive, expressing concern and understanding. "Krista, I want you to be safe, and my gut instinct is telling me you won't be safe if you stay here."

"Then let's leave together . . . both of us. Right now."

"I can't. You know I can't."

"Why? I *don't* know why." Her lower lip trembled, a film of tears began to cloud her eyes. "Why won't you come with me?"

Alec's head turned slowly, and his eyes drifted across the water to focus on the Graham estate. "I've got to try to help him . . . whoever he is. I've never left an informant . . . I've never left anyone who tried to help me in the lurch before, and I'm not going to begin now."

"Alec—"

"You're wasting time. Get out of here." Alec opened the van's door on the driver's side and practically lifted Krista up and onto the seat. He motioned for Thumper to get inside the van, which the dog readily did, and then closed the door with a firm hand. "Remember, stay off the beaten path. Get to Todd as fast as you can, and he can take it from there."

Resigned to the fact that there was no use in arguing with Alec and that any further verbal debate would only be a waste of precious time, Krista looked down at the handbag

211

Alec had shoved into her hands a few moments before. It was the white, soft-straw clutch she had taken with her the night before. She stared at it for only a moment, remembering the pleasant evening she'd had with the Grahams, then opened the flap and reached inside for her keys.

"What about the police?" she asked as she quickly sorted through the keys on her ring.

"Don't worry about it. Todd will do whatever he thinks needs to be done."

"I can't help but worry." Krista located the van's key. Her hand shook as she inserted it into the ignition. "You will be careful," she said, looking out the window at Alec as she started the engine.

"Careful's my middle name." Alec leaned toward the open window and kissed Krista on the cheek, then stepped back. "Now get out of here. Get out of here and don't come back without your Combat reinforcements." Alec attempted to smile at the touch of humor he tried to bring to the end of their conversation, but deep down inside, he was as scared as he knew Krista must be.

Eighteen

Alec waited impatiently at the edge of the drive until the van turned at the far end of the lane and its taillights disappeared. With Krista safely on her way, his thoughts now turned to Graham and the mystery caller . . . and to the secret that was hidden somewhere on the estate—the secret the caller had said Alec didn't really want to know about.

Was the secret based on Schmidt's mysterious Project GOD? And if it was, what exactly *was* Project GOD?

Turning abruptly toward the cabin, Alec ran to the back steps, hurdled them and walked hurriedly into the utility room just off the stoop. As he walked through the kitchen, his eyes sought out the two paper bags he'd left on the sofa following their shopping trip that morning. He hoped he'd have everything he needed.

At one time, he'd planned to analyze the purchases and chance going into Prairie Dells for any additional equipment he thought he might need, but he didn't have time for any analysis now. He didn't have time to do anything but put his sketchy plan into action. All he had to work with was contained in the two brown paper bags.

Alec picked up the bag containing his purchases from both the sporting goods and hardware stores and dumped its contents on the sofa. He grabbed the black-and-gray camouflage-print backpack, unzipped its compartments and began stuffing everything else into it. When that task was completed, he picked up the sack containing the items Krista had picked up. The second bag was identical to the first; both bore the same bold advertisement of the same sporting goods store.

It had been Krista's idea to appear to shop separately. "To avoid suspicion," she'd told him. Alec didn't see any need to be so cautious since they had driven to a town more than forty miles from Prairie Dells to make their purchases, but he'd consented to her suggestion to satisfy her need to help him.

They had entered the sporting goods store a few minutes apart, appeared to talk like friendly strangers, at which time he told her the exact camouflage outfit he wanted; then they had parted. He had purchased everything available to him there, then left to go to the hardware store for additional supplies. Krista had remained behind to buy the outfit he'd indicated, and then she met him at the telephone booth where he'd called Todd. Now all of Krista's cautious maneuvers didn't seem to matter; Alec wasn't even thinking about them. What he was thinking about was the contents of the second bag; he hoped the suit would fit.

Alec upended the bag and dumped the black-and-gray camouflage-print clothing out onto the sofa. He immediately stripped down to his underwear and reached for the long-sleeve, hooded shirt he intended to wear.

After slipping his arms into the sleeves that clung to him too tightly, he pulled the neck opening over his head and tugged the tail down past his waist. Even though the fabric was a stretchy knit, the shirt was too tight. Alec knew he wouldn't be able to function freely without pulling out the seams, but there was nothing he could do but wear it as is.

When he reached for the matching pants, Alec uncovered an additional camouflage outfit. Curious, he looked at the tags indicating the size. To his surprise, the outfit remaining on the sofa was a large, the size he'd instructed Krista to buy.

He quickly took off the shirt he'd struggled to put on and checked its size. It was a medium, and Alec immediately realized what had happened. Krista had bought two out-fits—one for him and one for her. She had planned to go with him; she had planned to accompany him on his excursion to the Graham estate.

"I'm glad you're gone," he said as if Krista could hear him. "I wouldn't have wanted to fight *that* battle with you."

Alec didn't waste any more time considering what wasn't going to happen. He quickly put on the large-size camouflage outfit, then stuffed both his clothes and the extra outfit back into the bag and jammed it into the small space between the sofa and the wall. It was a precaution. If, for any reason, someone were to come into the cabin while he was gone, there would be no evidence to indicate that either one of them had done anything other than leave in the van.

For the first time, that thought bothered Alec. Had he done the right thing by sending Krista away, or would she have been safer staying there and hiding in the woods?

What if they went after her? Worse yet, what if they caught her? What would Graham do then?

Anybody who tries to stop me is dead. Graham's threatening words echoed across Alec's mind.

But there was nothing Alec could do now to change the course of events. All he could do was pray that Krista would make it to Todd's safely.

Alec grabbed the canvas strap of the backpack and slung it over his shoulder. He glanced around the room as he walked toward the door. Seeing nothing that would be considered unusual, he felt he'd left no clues as to his whereabouts. He was as ready as he would ever be to infiltrate the Graham estate.

Krista applied a steadily increasing pressure to the brake pedal, and the van gradually came to a stop. Directly ahead of her, illuminated by the low beam of the headlights, was a yellow, diamond-shaped sign that bore a boldly printed black *T* in its center.

After crossing the bridge from the lake, she had turned left instead of right, the route they would have normally taken to reach any major highway. She had chosen to go left in compliance with Alec's request that she use the back roads; turning left had brought her to the T in the road.

She looked in both directions down the gravel road, trying to remember where each led. Her memory was cloudy; she

215

couldn't remember having traveled in either direction on the road even though she knew she and Rebecca must have roamed the area extensively during their middle teens.

"Which way, Thumper?" Krista's voice still shook with uncertainty as she looked at the dog on the passenger seat beside her. Thumper looked at Krista and barked, and her tail began to beat repeatedly against the seat's back. "Oh, Thumper . . ." An uncontrolled surge of tears flooded Krista's eyes, and she allowed herself a few moments to give way to her fears.

Ever since she'd pulled out of the cabin's drive, Krista had been functioning on pure adrenaline. Her thoughts had been focused on Alec, his safety and why she had let him convince her to leave. She had given in too easily. But deep inside, she knew why. She had been too scared to think; she had been too scared to do much else than follow the orders Alec had given her.

"He'll be all right," she said with a heavy exhalation of breath in an attempt to ease her tension. "He knows how to take care of himself." She wiped the backs of her hands across her eyes and face and tried to convince herself to have faith in her own words.

Indeed, Alec knew how to take care of himself. Lt. Wayne Ratliff, his friend from the Louisville police force, had instructed him in the basics of self-defense and had even tutored him in the use of a handgun. And Alec was smart. He had a good deal of common sense that warned him when it was time to pull out; he had done just that, several times. No one could even begin to count the number of cases he'd investigated that could have put his life on the line had he waited to call for assistance. He knew when to quit trying to tackle a case alone.

That thought aroused more concern in Krista. Alec wasn't in his own territory now; he wasn't in a position where he could call for assistance. She was his only link to any form of outside help, and she knew she had to succeed—she had to succeed as quickly as possible. Alec could be in danger; his life could be at stake.

"Which way, girl?" Krista asked again, making a final swipe at her tears. As if the dog could understand, Thumper looked at Krista and whined, then turned her head to look out the passenger side window and barked. "To the right?" Thumper barked again and continued to thump her tail against the seat. Krista turned in her seat to look out the back window. "I think maybe you're right. Prairie Dells is way behind us, and I bet this road will angle on southwest and eventually run into the main road way south of town. From there, we'll have a straight shot at Rickdon, and we can get to Todd."

Krista took a firm grip on the wheel and gradually lifted her foot from the brake. She guided the van through an easy turn, and once she was straight on the road, she gave the engine a little more gas.

Ahead of her, the headlights beamed across the old road that was almost as bumpy and rutted as the lane beside the cabin. The going would be slow—she would have to be careful—but she knew she would make it. Krista knew she would make it to the highway . . . and to Todd.

Edging himself forward on his stomach, Alec felt the limb begin to sag noticeably beneath his weight and knew he couldn't advance much farther before testing its breaking point. He glanced back at the chain-link fence some eight feet behind him, eyed the single-wire electric fence three feet closer to him and judged it was safe to return to the security of the solid ground below.

He shifted his position to let his legs dangle beneath him, then pushed himself away from the limb. His knees gave beneath him as his feet touched the ground. His landing wasn't perfect, but he'd succeeded in crossing the fence. He was now on Graham property.

Alec stood, looked up at the limb and followed its line all the way back to the tree trunk on the opposite side of the fence. That was the same tree his uninvited visitor had used a few nights before to gain access to the cabin and then escape. Alec still couldn't figure out how the man had reached the twenty-foot-high limb without any assistance. The only way he'd been successful at climbing onto the limb was by using a makeshift rope-and-pulley system he'd fashioned from some of the supplies he'd had in the backpack.

He continued to look at the tree and limb in wonder as he recoiled the length of nylon rope he'd used to conquer it. "There's no way," he said to himself, shaking his head. "There's no way anybody could get up there on his own." When Alec felt the end of the rope slip past his hand, he took hold of the rope about a foot from its end and wound it around to secure the coil. He then slipped the coil over his head and shoulder and adjusted it to fit comfortably against the backpack.

"Well," he said as he turned his back to the fence and the tree and the cabin, "this is it." He looked out across the lake toward the Graham estate. "Let's hope you're not getting yourself into something more than you can handle," he said to himself hesitantly.

But Alec sensed he was already into something more than he could handle. His curiosity had led him to . . . to what? Project GOD? And whatever Project GOD happened to be was something Hubert Graham apparently felt strongly enough about to kill for. *To kill for.* That was the reason Alec hadn't left with Krista, even though he had had to force himself to keep from jumping in the van and driving away with her. His innocent curiosity had placed another man's life in danger, and he felt responsible. Alec didn't like that feeling of responsibility—responsibility over which he had no control. If there was any way he could shed himself of that responsibility, he planned to do it, and maybe, just maybe, he would be able to find the answers to the questions that had started his gut instinct behaving like a rabid animal.

"There had better be one helluva good story behind all of this," he said in an attempt to control his rampant thoughts and boost his waning courage. "There had—"

Alec cut his monologue short when he saw a set of headlights come up the drive beside Graham's house. He watched them turn to follow the lane and immediately saw a second set appear behind them. He followed their movement until they disappeared behind the trees. Moments later, they reappeared and stopped momentarily beside the electronic gate.

"Are you coming after me?" Alec questioned with an

almost cynical snicker. "I'm pretty good at playing cat and mouse in the dark. That's how I make my living."

He started walking into the woods. Every half-dozen or so steps, Alec glanced back over his shoulder, expecting to see headlights coming up the bumpy lane toward the cabin. Within a matter of minutes, his expectations were fulfilled.

Finding a cover of brush that had grown up around an old cabin's foundation, Alec squatted down behind it. He slipped the backpack off his shoulders and reached inside for the pair of binoculars he'd bought at the sporting goods store. The illumination from the headlights and the security light between the two cabins offered him enough light to focus . . . and to watch.

The first car pulled into the cabin's drive; the second one stopped behind the rear entrance. Alec saw shadowy figures emerge from each vehicle and approach the cabin.

He was surprised when the lights on the porch and inside the cabin—lights he'd purposely turned off to darken his own actions—burst into brightness. Apparently, whoever had invaded the cabin had no intention of keeping their presence a secret.

Alec focused on the lighted windows, and a smirk pulled at the corners of his lips when he saw a shadow move past to momentarily block the light. For the moment, he felt smugly superior. "There's no one in there to find," he whispered under his breath.

His attention returned to the front porch when a tall, muscular figure came out of the cabin. Alec turned the focusing knob on the binoculars ever so slightly and brought the face of the man into clear view. "Jameson," he said with self-satisfaction, "I knew you were more than just a two-bit chauffeur." Jameson remained on the porch for only a few moments, then returned to his vehicle.

"That's my cue to be on the move." Alec returned the binoculars to the backpack and slipped its straps up over his shoulders. "While the troops are away, this is the best time for me to do a little snooping of my own." Alec stood, turned toward the woods and began walking.

*   *   *

"No!" Graham's face reddened with his anger. His jaw tightened; the veins along his neck stood out like pulsing vines clinging to the side of a tree.

"We've searched both cabins and the surrounding area. Since their van's gone, I can come to no other conclusion but that they've left."

Graham stared at the radio speaker that had delivered Jameson's words via the mobile unit mounted on the dash of one of their many vehicles. He couldn't allow Alec and Krista Crispen to get away—not now—not now that he was sure they might have heard his threat to Al. He feared they would bring outsiders in to search the estate. He feared they might bring an end to Project GOD.

"Find them!" he shouted into the microphone mounted on the console.

"Sir?"

"Whatever it takes, find them!"

Jameson hesitated. "Billings and I can't do it alone, sir."

"Then get whoever it takes to find them. Take everybody, but find them. And tell somebody to stop and pick me up. I'm not going to sit around here wondering what's going on when I can be out there helping look for them."

Alec had moved down from the dense growth of the woods and was now following the well-trodden cow path that ran close to the electric fence. He wasn't concerned about being seen. Tall weeds grew between the electric fence and the chain-link; brush, briers and an occasional tree bordered the lake; the moon was shrouded in clouds more often than not, and the dark coloring of his attire worked to conceal him whenever the elements of nature did not.

Periodically, he glanced in the direction of the road. Both cars had left the cabin not long after Jameson had returned to the porch. Alec had watched them leave and had been surprised when he saw the lights appear near the bridge and then stop. He wondered what they were planning, and he felt scared all over again.

Alec continued to watch the parked cars as he followed the path around the lake's edge. "What are you up to?" His

220

question was almost immediately answered when he saw three additional sets of headlights emerge from within the Graham complex. "I was afraid of that."

He looked toward the southern sky and whispered into the still night air. "Krista, my love, I hope you're doing what I told you to do. I hope you're long gone from here by now. Godspeed."

Al remained hidden in the bushes several hundred yards down the lane from the stable, directly across from the massive garage. He'd taken refuge there after fleeing from the stable—after fleeing from Graham's attack. From his secluded position, he'd seen almost everything that had occurred during the past twenty minutes: Graham running from the stable to the garage's office, screaming like a madman; Jameson and Billings leaving in a hurry in two separate jeeps; and then, several minutes later, Malone, Ticen and Darnell leaving in three more vehicles. He had even watched as one of the cars had stopped to pick up Graham at the house.

Now that the area had quieted—now that the majority of the night's security men were gone—Al thought it safe for him to venture out into the open. Standing from the squat he'd maintained since he'd first gone into hiding, Al shook his legs to help speed up the return of normal circulation. Even though he was used to squatting over extended periods of time and didn't mind what most people would classify as an uncomfortable position, his legs were telling him it was time to move. Rarely did his legs tingle from lack of circulation, but on occasion, when he was overly tired, worried or tense, the muscles in his legs seemed to tighten more than usual and inhibit the blood flow. He experienced that feeling now, and he knew why. He was worried, tense—and scared.

Al couldn't remember the last time he had been *really* scared. Even though Graham had taunted him with the threat of death throughout his entire life, Al had never taken it seriously. There was a bond linking the two of them . . . a bond linking both of them to Julia Ann. Al knew that deep down in Graham's heart, he would never be able to destroy anything Julia Ann had helped create.

But tonight, that certainty had been shaken. Tonight, there had been a look in Graham's eyes that had spoken of that bond not only being broken but totally shattered. Tonight, Graham had actually tried to kill him, and Al felt that if he hadn't fled when he had, Graham would have. That was why Al was so scared.

As Al lifted an arm to push a branch out of his way, a dull pain came from his left side. He looked down at the fresh blood obliterating the print of his checkered shirt. He didn't think the wound was serious, he had cried out more from startled surprise than from agony, but he knew it needed to be tended to.

Cautiously, Al stepped out from behind the bushes. He glanced in both directions along the drive and saw nothing. His eyes then lifted to look at the camera mounted high on the garage's corner. The cameras meant nothing to him; he knew he could outmaneuver every one of them.

As a child, he'd played the game of dodging the cameras. By the age of nine, he'd become so adept at avoiding their roaming eyes, he could go anywhere on the estate without being detected. His ability to remain unseen had led to the discovery of his origin. His origin . . . Jordy's origin . . . and the origin of all the others.

"Awec." Al had become so engrossed in his own fear that for a while he'd forgotten what had caused it—the phone call he'd been caught making to Alec. "Not Awec. No. I won't wet you hurt Awec."

Al watched the camera on the corner of the garage until it rotated to the precise angle he wanted; then he ran across the drive and crouched down behind a low shrub to wait for the camera to rotate past him again. He then turned his attention to the camera mounted on the corner of the research building. When that camera rotated past him, Al again made his move. He was working his way toward the primate house. Once there, he would tend to the wound in his side. Then he would try to find out what was going on.

Nineteen

Alec wasn't sure how long he'd been following the cow path, but glancing at his watch, he guessed he'd left the cabin over forty minutes ago. He stopped opposite the lake's intake from the river to gain his bearings.

Silence surrounded him. No breeze rustled the leaves; no night-prowling animals scampered through the brush to disturb the ground cover or crack a branch; even the bullfrogs that normally sang their serenades throughout the night were silent. The stillness seemed odd . . . and disquieting. Alec felt almost suffocated.

The clouds broke sporadically to reveal the moon. Nature's night-light was dimming. Its rotation around the earth had placed it in a position where it was no longer full; its edge was beginning to be shaved off by the earth's shadow.

Alec looked up at the moon and listened to the silence around him. His stomach felt queasy, and an ominous chill was creeping up the length of his spine. Had he been one to believe in omens, he would have taken the signs as a warning. But he didn't believe in omens; he didn't believe in anything associated with the supernatural—anything other than his own gut instinct. That was what had brought him this far, and that was what would keep him going.

Looking around the lake, Alec tried to remember where Krista had seen the camera mounted on the fence post. If his memory served him correctly, he estimated it to be located a few hundred yards ahead. Not wanting to take the chance of being detected, he decided to return to the cover of the woods as he continued toward the heart of the Graham complex.

The van's headlights brightened the gravel road ahead, enabling Krista to spot the rough areas well in advance and maneuver around them. She glanced at her watch, as she had done every few minutes, but this time it marked a milestone. She had been on the road exactly one hour since she had first looked at the time. She didn't know how far she had traveled, for she hadn't thought to check the odometer until sometime after she'd turned onto the gravel road, but she had a feeling she wasn't making very good progress. The old gravel road was indeed as bumpy as the lane beside the cabin, and only on a few semismooth stretches was Krista able to push the van to the speed of 20 mph.

"This is exasperating," she said, exhaling heavily. "We'll never make it to Todd in time at this rate."

As if she understood the plight they were facing, Thumper whined and wagged her tail only slightly.

"Now what?" Krista braked when she saw another yellow, diamond-shaped sign directly ahead of her. Again, the sign informed her she was at a T junction.

"Guess we need to go left this time," she said. "That's the way to Rickdon." But as Krista started to turn, her eyes caught sight of another sign that made her heart drop.

Less than ten feet down the road stood a formidable black-and-white-striped barricade. Positioned in front of the barricade was an oversized black-and-white road sign that bore the words BRIDGE OUT.

"No!" Krista said firmly as if the force behind the word could alter the situation. "I don't have time for this. I don't have time!" Even though she was on the verge of losing control, Krista forced herself to relax. "And I don't have time to be yelling at some damn bridge," she said in a calmer voice, grabbing hold of the steering wheel.

Without even thinking about her actions, Krista cranked

the wheel hard to the right and gently applied pressure to the gas pedal. The van responded beautifully, turning in a somewhat tight circle in spite of its size. Once straightened out on the road, she pushed down on the gas pedal even more and glanced down to see the speedometer approach 40. Unlike the gravel road she had just turned from, this one had been recently paved with a new layer of blacktop; she could still see signs of fresh tar on the grass along the shoulder.

Krista knew she would be able to make better time on the nice smooth road, but the object of speed was not now foremost in her mind. The thought that bothered her—the thought that kept repeating itself over and over in her mind—was the fact that she was heading back toward Prairie Dells.

Alec's trek through the woods presented a much greater challenge than his easy walk along the cow path had. Almost directly behind where the line of old cabins had been, the ground rose sharply, much steeper than the hill behind their own cabin. Climbing that hill was a task in itself, but it was compounded by the fact that the area was dense with briers and tangled underbrush. Evidently, the cows didn't think the foliage was inviting enough to take a chance on the unstable footing of the steep hill to graze. There was no indication that they had ever been there.

Some 400 feet into his climb, the ground leveled off, and Alec was able to stand upright without feeling as if he might fall. He took a few moments to survey the sizable plateau that separated the hill he'd just climbed from another one beyond that rose just as sharply.

A cow path bisected the area, and apparently they had taken time to graze there, since the ground cover was cropped low, barely reaching ankle height. Five massive trees spread their heavily leaved branches over the area, giving it an air of peaceful serenity and—

Alec's breath caught in his throat. He stood motionless, as if frozen, his eyes searching out the source of the brief reflection that had instantly captured his attention.

An ominous shiver traversed the length of his spine. Had he become careless? Had he allowed his image to be captured on the lens of a camera? Had he just informed Graham of his whereabouts?

Alec's eyes strained to see through the darkness, trying to spot the location of the reflection's source. Could it have been the lens of a camera or—God please let it be—something else?

As if in answer to an unspoken prayer, the clouds released the moon, lighting the area dimly. Off to his left, maybe thirty feet or more, Alec could see a large mound of dirt. Atop the mound he saw something that appeared to be a cross, and from somewhere about halfway down the cross's vertical shaft, he could see a glimmer . . . a sparkle . . . a reflection of the moon's soft light.

He exhaled slowly with the release of his tension and began walking toward the mound. What could it be?

As Alec approached the mound, the clouds recaptured the moon. Slipping the backpack off his shoulders and laying it on the ground, he reached inside and retrieved the small flashlight he'd bought that morning.

Being careful to keep the beam close to the ground, Alec walked on toward the mound and then knelt beside it. He tilted the flashlight slightly, until its rays illuminated the object atop the mound. He had been correct in his speculation; it was a cross, a cross made from two small branches and held together by what appeared to be baling twine.

Alec immediately sensed the purpose of the mound. It was a grave—a fresh grave with fresh flowers. He didn't even want to speculate as to who or what might be buried there.

He lifted the flashlight a little higher. His action was immediately answered by a twinkling reflection. Alec could see a heavy silver chain draped across the horizontal bar of the cross, and hanging from the chain was a sturdy silver cross.

Curious, he slid his hand down behind the chain until he cradled the silver cross in the palm of his hand. It was a simple cross, a plain cross, but by its weight and thickness, he could tell it must have been expensive.

Lifting his fingers and creasing his palm slightly, he turned the cross over. Something was engraved down the length of the shaft. Alec moved the flashlight closer, so that it shone directly onto the palm of his hand. He read: *Al, All My Love. Julia Ann.*

"Julia Ann," he whispered to himself. "That was Graham's wife's name."

Alec forgot his caution and lifted the flashlight to follow the outline of the freshly mounded dirt. The area was large enough to bury a full-grown man.

"No," he said, shaking his head. "It can't be her. She died too long ago, and Graham wouldn't have put her up here in an unmarked grave."

He looked back at the cross in his hand. "Al?" He thought for a moment, remembering the name he had heard Graham call out over the telephone. "No, there hasn't been enough time for that." Alec looked back at the grave and spoke compassionately. "I don't know who you might be, but I won't disturb you. I'll leave you to rest in peace." Slowly, reverently, Alec lowered his hand and returned the silver cross and chain to the position where he'd found them.

Alec returned to his backpack and replaced the flashlight. As he straightened up and started to slip the straps over his shoulders, for the first time he noticed the view his location on the hill provided.

Every part of the Graham estate was visible: the house, the stable, the research complex and the dairy. Alec could see the vague outline of everything, highlighted by the vapor security lights.

"What are you hiding down there?" His eyes focused solely on the three-story research building. "What am I going to find if I can get in there?" His eyes then swept across the entire complex. "And, how am I ever going to find . . . Al?"

A moving light attracted Alec's attention. "Visitors?" he questioned as he watched the lights cross the bridge and then turn on the road leading to the electric gate. "Are you a regular returning or someone else?"

227

Alec's curiosity prompted him to grab the binoculars from the backpack, but by the time he had them in focus, the vehicle had disappeared within the trees. He waited impatiently, moving the binoculars along the drive at the rate of speed he thought the vehicle might be traveling. He arrived at an opening in the trees before the vehicle, but he only had to wait a moment before the headlights appeared.

He followed their movement until they disappeared behind the house but was able to pick them up again when they emerged. As the vehicle passed beneath one of the security lights, Alec was finally able to make out its identity. "An ambulance?" Then he remembered Jordy's explanation for the last ambulance Alec had seen. "Why would anyone be coming to pick up animals at this time of night?"

He continued to watch the ambulance as it rounded the curve toward the nursery entrance, but it didn't stop there—it didn't even slow down. The ambulance continued on past the research building and followed the road leading back to the dairy.

"What the?" Alec asked himself as he watched the ambulance stop at the gate across the road then continue on after it opened. "Why is he going back to the—"

The realization of what he was seeing finally came to him. "It's not in the research building," Alec said to himself as he lowered the binoculars. "Whatever Graham's hiding isn't in the research building . . . it's back in the dairy."

Alec returned the binoculars to his eyes and continued to follow the ambulance's movement until it disappeared between two buildings. "What's going on back there that Graham has to keep so secret?"

Alec began to search the area between himself and the dairy. He was hoping he'd be able to find a fast and safe way to get back there.

Al paused on the landing at the top of the basement stairs. He stood motionless for several moments, just listening. Not a word, not a footstep, not even the ticking of a clock rode on a wave to reach his ears. Silence hung heavily in the air

228

around him.

Cautiously, he stepped out into the short hall beside the kitchen. Again he listened . . . and again he heard nothing. As he'd anticipated, the house was empty.

Having no fear of discovery, Al walked boldly down the hall, past the formal dining room, and stopped at the junction of the main hall that led to the front door and the grand staircase. The path he now followed was one he rarely used. To avoid confrontations with Graham, he always took the back stairs to the second floor, but until the past few days, he hadn't even done that on a regular basis.

Even though a room was provided for him upstairs, he hadn't used it in a long, long time. Instead, he'd slept in one of his makeshift rooms in either the stable or primate house and had felt perfectly happy there. This grand mansion wasn't his home—this grand mansion only reminded him of his pain and heartache. Al had taken to living with the animals. They were his true family; they were the only ones with whom he could find peace and solace.

Turning toward the front door, Al walked until he came to the door of the den. He turned the knob slowly, then inched the door open. With the exception of the lights surrounding Julia Ann's picture like a halo, the room was dark. Knowing why he had come to the house, Al walked directly toward the lighted portrait. He had come to talk to Julia Ann.

Al stopped a few feet in front of the fireplace and turned to look up at the portrait. Julia Ann's serene face smiled down at him. For a few brief moments, Al forgot about the rest of the world around him and relished memories of the love she'd given him. The first few years of his life were the happiest he could remember. Until Julia Ann had died, he'd actually understood the meaning of love. Unfortunately, that love had been buried with her.

"It'ths going wrong," he whispered, looking up into her blue-green eyes. "The beauty of your dream iths being tarnithshed. He doethsn't care anymore about fiwwing the emptinethss in peopwe'ths wiveths. Aw he careths about now iths the money and about how he can protect the project and keep peopwe from finding out about it.

229

"You wouldn't wet him do what he'ths pwanning if you were thstill here. You wouldn't wet him hurt Awec and Krithsta juthst to protect the project. Thsomebody'ths got to thstop him." Al focused on Julia Ann's face, and in his mind, he thought he saw her nod. "Jordy won't thstop him even though he hateths him for what he did. He'ths too much a part of it himthself." Al's subconscious saw Julia Ann nod again. "Thso I guethss it'ths up to me to do it." He studied Julia Ann's face a little while longer before finally admitting to the only possible solution. "If there'ths no project to hide, then there wouldn't be any need for him to hurt Awec and Krithsta."

Al turned away from the portrait and started toward the patio's French doors. He knew what he had to do, and he was determined that nothing would stop him from doing it.

Krista had been making good time, the kind of time she wished she could have been making from the very beginning, but the closer she came to town, the more concerned she was becoming about the possibility that someone might be there she didn't want to see—someone that she didn't want to see her. All during the time she had driven on the blacktop road, she had hoped to come to an intersection where she could turn and again head south. The opportunity hadn't presented itself; there had been no crossroads.

Up ahead to her left, Krista saw a faint light. At first she was puzzled, but as she grew nearer, the source of light became obvious. "The drive-in," she whispered barely loud enough for her own ears to hear.

She remembered the landmark. She and Rebecca had spent many evenings at the drive-in during their teen years, gathering together with the friends they'd made from around town, meeting new boys and occasionally even watching a movie.

Now that she had her bearings, Krista knew exactly where she was, and she didn't feel at all comfortable with her location. The road leading past the drive-in was an extension of Main Street; the road she was on led directly into the heart of Prairie Dells.

"We would have been long gone from here an hour ago if we'd only left the lake the way we normally do." Thumper replied with a half-bark–half-whimper and barely moved the white tip of her black tail. Krista glanced at the dog and guessed she too sensed things weren't exactly the way they should be.

Alec felt he'd made good time following the cow path. He was trying to hurry; he wanted to get to the dairy as quickly as possible so he could see where the ambulance had gone. He was looking for as many clues as he could find that would lead him in the right direction.

At the bottom of the hill, the woods gave way to a vast expanse of open pasture. Very few trees interrupted the gently rolling landscape, and even fewer shrubs made their presence known through the darkness. The grass was short; it had been grazed on frequently.

To the left of the pasture, the chain-link fence marked the boundary to the complex. It curved almost gracefully around the residential area, then straightened out to run parallel to the road. Only one obstacle broke the fence's continuous line. There was a gate with a guardhouse at the head of the lane leading to the dairy. Alec knew there were guards stationed there; that was where the ambulance had made its second stop before proceeding on.

Alec knew the quickest way to get to the dairy was to follow a straight line, but he also knew that to follow that direct path would put him out in the open where he could be easily detected. Was the risk worth the time he would save? He pondered the point for only a moment and decided the risk was worth it as long as it didn't outweigh the gain by a ridiculous amount.

He looked up at the sky. The thinner clouds that had periodically released the moon had moved on toward the east. A thicker bank of clouds now hung directly overhead and extended far back toward the west. They were moving slowly, and it appeared the moon would be hidden for a long enough period of time to allow him to cross the pasture without being too obvious. That element of darkness, plus the fact that he was wearing a night-print camouflage outfit, solidified his decision. Alec made sure his backpack was secure, and then he started jogging across the pasture toward the dairy.

Krista left the drive-in behind her. The screen had been visible to the road and reflected the projected images of aliens doing battle, but she really hadn't noticed. Her thoughts were focused on what she was going to do when she reached the edge of town. Would she turn on the first side street available and try to sneak out, or would she try to find a phone and call Todd?

Time kept slipping away from her. The closer she got to Prairie Dells, the more the second option began to appeal to her.

Alec reached the opposite end of the pasture in an amazingly short length of time. He stopped behind the first tree he came to and surveyed his surroundings. A random location of security lights highlighted the area dimly, aiding his vision.

The chain-link fence had continued to follow the drive until it connected to a gate attached to the corner of a large equipment barn. A row of large trees bordered the east side of the dairy, which Alec thought was strange since they failed to offer the type of security that had surrounded the rest of the estate. With that thought came the speculation of more surveillance cameras.

He looked up, searching along the eaves of the equipment barn. His assumption proved to be correct. He saw a camera on each of the three corners of the building; two were rotating across the area, and the third remained stationary. His relatively worry-free entrance onto the Graham estate had come to an end. Alec knew he was going to have to be fully alert from now on in order to escape the cameras' detection.

Staying within the cover of the trees, Alec moved along the back of the equipment barn. Once he passed the building, he came to a fairly open area containing a water tower and four massive silos. Shifting to see beyond the silos, he saw the ambulance parked on a gravel lot nestled within a U formed by the dairy offices, the milking barn and another building for which he was unable to guess a purpose.

The area within the U was dim. Apparently, the security light that was supposed to brighten the lot had either been turned off or was burnt out. Whatever the case, the only lights that offered even a hint of brightness to the secluded area were the yellow lights bordering the ambulance's roofline.

Alec could see two vague forms standing on the steps to the unknown building. He pulled the binoculars from the backpack. Once he had them to his eyes, he slowly turned the focusing knob. There was barely enough light to make his efforts worthwhile.

He could identify one of the men as Donald, the man who had interrupted Alec's first visit with the Grahams. The second man he didn't remember seeing before. Both men stood casually, talking as if to kill time, talking as if waiting for something.

Alec wondered what they might be waiting for. He wondered if whatever it was had anything to do with Project GOD.

Alec scanned the part of the building he was able to see. He was not surprised to see a small red light almost directly above Donald's head, and in a moment he had located the camera a little to the right of the steps to which its power source was attached. He had been correct to guess that the lack of a fence would indicate the presence of more cameras.

He located another camera at the near corner of the fence confining a lone cow, one on the fourth corner of the equipment barn, and one mounted on a brace attached to and spanning the distance between the two silos beside the water tower. The cameras on the equipment barn's corners and the one on the silos' brace were too high, but the camera on the fence and the one beside the door were well within his reach. Alec was finally going to have a chance to try out his plan to outsmart the cameras; his biggest hope was that it would work.

Alec glanced back at the two men then started to put the binoculars away, but the door opened and out stepped a woman carrying what looked like a cardboard box about the size of a laundry basket. He continued to watch as she stopped between the two men and extended the box toward them to show them what she carried. Donald appeared to be unaffected by what he saw, but the unknown man reached in the box, appeared to say something to whatever was inside the box, and then withdrew his hand.

After a few moments of conversation, the woman continued on toward the ambulance. She stepped inside the back door and was only out of sight for perhaps thirty seconds before she reappeared, empty-handed. She stopped again to talk briefly with the two men, then went back inside the building.

Alec's curiosity was pestering him like flies swarming around a bottle of spilled syrup. What had the woman deposited inside the ambulance? What was inside the box? Did it have something to do with Project GOD? He had to find out.

Alec replaced the binoculars in the backpack and removed an aerosol can. Freon. That was how he planned to outsmart the cameras. If his theory proved correct, the freon would crystalize after he sprayed the lens, completely blocking out—or at least distorting—any image the camera might pick up. He wasn't sure how long the effect would last, but he hoped that it would last long enough to allow him to make his way to his destination. The cleverest aspect of his theory was that if anyone eventually came to check out the malfunctioning camera, the freon would have warmed, melted and evaporated, and there would be no remaining evidence to give a hint as to what might have been wrong.

To lighten his load and to assure his mobility, Alec decided to leave the backpack beside the tree. He reached inside, took out a flashlight, a small roll of duct tape and a thin piece of sturdy plastic, and shoved them all into the pockets of his shirt. Armed with only the can of freon, Alec

234

was ready.

Scooting close to the edge of the tree, Alec waited until the camera on the fence rotated away from him, then ran up beside the corner post. When the camera began to rotate back toward him, he reached up with the can of freon and hit the lens squarely in the center with an ample spray. Even in the darkness, Alec could see the lens and dark plastic around it lighten. It appeared the first part of his theory had worked. Now, how long would it last?

Alec wasn't going to wait to find out. He bent over and squatted down low as he ran across a twelve-foot opening toward the first of the silos he planned to use for cover as he made his way closer to the building. Leaning against the cool metal, he glanced back at the camera and held his position until it rotated on past him. Lens crystallized or not, he had come too far to take any foolish chances now.

He continued on to the next silo and eventually made his way to beneath the water tower. Once there, he lay down on the ground and crawled on his belly army-style until he was positioned behind a small storage shed.

He pulled himself to the end of the shed and cautiously peeked around its corner. The two men were less than twenty feet from him. That was as close as Alec dared to go, but at least he was now close enough to hear them.

"How many does this make?" the unknown man asked.

"These four make it a grand total of nine thousand, three hundred and sixty-six," Donald replied without even having to think about the answer.

"Not a bad total when you think what that gives you when you multiply most of them by fifty thousand."

"It's not just for the money, and you know it. It's—"

At that moment, the door opened and the woman came out carrying another cardboard box. As if performing a ritual, she stopped again to show the men what she carried. Each man responded exactly as he had before.

"He's the last one," the woman said as she turned toward the steps. "Let's get going. We've got a long drive ahead of us."

As she stepped down onto the step, the high heel of her

235

shoe twisted beneath her. She lost her balance, teetered . . . stumbled . . . and fell. Even though she tried to hold onto the box during her fall, it slipped from her hands and landed on the gravel lot.

A cry rang out in the night.

Alec had to force himself to keep from going to help her, but much more than just self-control kept him in his place. The cry that had pierced the air when the box had hit the ground—the cry that still continued loud and clear even now that Donald had come to the rescue—was a cry that could be mistaken for no other. It was the cry of a newborn infant— the cry of a newborn *human* infant.

Twenty

Alec scooted away from the corner and slumped against the shed's shadowed wall. The cries he'd just heard had stunned him beyond his wildest belief.

A hundred answerless questions bombarded his brain. What was a human infant doing back at the dairy? And if all of the boxes the woman had placed in the ambulance had contained babies, what were *four* human infants doing back at the dairy? How had they gotten there? Why? Where were they being taken now?

What in God's name was going on? God . . . God . . . *Project GOD!* Was there even the remotest connection between the infants and the undecipherable writing in Schmidt's stolen journal?

. . . *most of them were on animal and crop production and reproduction* . . . Something Todd had told him, concerning Schmidt's former projects, overpowered the rest of the thoughts crowding Alec's mind.

"Reproduction," Alec whispered to himself, "animal reproduction . . ." He contemplated the possibility briefly. Project GOD . . . and the . . . the *pictures of the babies!* "No. There's no way anyone could possibly—"

"I'll contact you as soon as we have another shipment available," Alec heard Donald say. "The way things look, it may be as soon as tonight or tomorrow."

"We'll be ready."

Alec heard the door to the ambulance close, and almost

immediately, he heard the engine start. Out of the corner of his eye, he saw the headlights come to life; then he heard the tires crunch against the gravel drive as they began to roll. He leaned forward to look around the far corner of the shed and saw the taillights pass by as the ambulance made its way along the drive between the equipment barn and the dairy's offices. They were gone; now all he had to do was wait for Donald to leave. Then, he hoped, he could find some answers to his questions.

"Feeling uncomfortable?"

The words reached Alec's ears, taking him by surprise. They came from a source that was close—too close. His heart jumped into his throat. He turned his head sharply, expecting to see someone standing beside him, exposing his presence. But no one was there—at least not immediately there.

Through the semidarkness, Alec could see Donald standing at the fence perhaps fifteen feet away, talking to the lone cow. Alec's first thoughts were to run—to get away—but any movement on his part was bound to attract attention. He knew his best bet was to sit there and remain perfectly still.

"It won't be much longer," Donald said as he rested his arms on the top rail of the fence. The cow didn't respond to his soft words. "But you know what's coming, don't you, girl? You're an old pro at this. How many will this be?" Donald thought for a moment. "Isn't this the sixth one for you?" The cow finally answered him with a guttural moo. "I thought so."

Even in his state of apprehension, Alec felt a grin twitch at his lips. Here was Donald, apparently a highly educated man, carrying on a conversation with, of all things, a cow. The scene seemed idiotic, dumb, stupid—until Alec thought of his own conversations with Thumper. All of a sudden, Donald's seemingly strange camaraderie with the cow took on a whole new light. Really, there wasn't any difference.

"It's been a long night," Donald continued. "I'm going to go up to my room and try to catch a few winks. I'll be back down to check on you in an hour or so." Donald left the cow and walked back toward the building.

Once he felt it was safe to move, Alec inched toward the edge of the shed and cautiously peeked around the corner. He could see Donald climbing the steps and watched as he reached for the door. It opened easily; there had been no fuss with a lock and a key. Alec felt a tingle of exhilaration ripple through him. Would he be able to enter the building as easily?

Alec turned to again sit with his back against the shed. He'd wait a few minutes to give Donald enough time to go upstairs, and then he would chance his own entry.

Moo.

In response to the unexpected sound, Alec jerked his head to the side and looked toward the fence several feet from him. Even in the dim lighting, he could see the cow's dark eyes peering at him.

Looking at her and noting her swollen sides, Alec spoke in a whisper barely audible to his own ears. "Going to be a momma soon?" As if she had heard and understood his words, she emitted another moo. "I thought so." Alec stared at the cow a few moments more. "I bet you could tell me what's going on around here. I bet you could tell me about Project GOD." The cow didn't respond. She turned away from Alec and walked toward a water trough located beside the building and began to drink. "Yes, I just bet you could."

Alec again leaned to look around the corner of the shed. He looked at the steps, at the door, then studied the camera that held both within its range. It was a stationary camera, permanently fixed on the single location it was intended to monitor. There would be no movement to allow Alec time to sneak up from its blind side; any advance toward the camera would have to be planned carefully to avoid being taken in by the lens's convex edges.

He scanned the immediate area. There was nothing close except for the fence . . . the fence. His eyes darted from the top railing of the wooden fence to the camera and back again. The fence . . . He thought the fence would be perfect. By standing on its top rail and using the building beside it for support and cover, Alec thought he would be in a perfect position to reach the camera and spray it with freon.

Alec took in a deep breath and released it slowly. He was ready to go—as ready as he would ever be. Gathering his feet and legs beneath him, crouching, he took in another deep breath to boost his courage, then took off across the open area between himself and the fence.

Al paused beside the end silo, watching the camera mounted at the corner of the fence rotate. He knew the area well; he knew where every camera was mounted and how their cycles ran. Al had visited the secluded building often. Any time there was talk of new deliveries, he followed the course he traveled now to the northeast corner of the building. There, he entered through the massive elevator shaft, made his way through the spacious lab, then stepped out in the hall to stand in plain view of the cameras while he looked at the babies through the observation window.

There was no way he could avoid the cameras inside the building. There were several of them on each floor and they didn't rotate; there was no way he could escape their detection.

In the past, he'd made a game of entering the building, waving to Mike Sellers or Bill Clark, whichever night watchman was in charge of monitoring the cameras from his post on the top floor of the equipment barn. But tonight, it wouldn't be a game.

When the camera moved past him, Al ran across the opening toward the fence. As he ran, he glanced toward the building and thought he saw something—someone—climbing the fence. He stopped when he reached the cover of the corner post, then peeked cautiously around it.

He watched as the man stood upright on the top railing, balancing himself at the corner of the building. The man took something from his pocket, held it up in front of the camera above the door for a few moments, then returned the object to his pocket. He then jumped down from the fence, ran in a crouched position up the stairs and straightened as he opened the door.

240

As the man looked around, the dim light coming from the open door highlighted his features. Al recognized him immediately; it was Alec.

Al opened his mouth as if to shout, but the fear tightening his throat trapped any words of warning he might have wanted to call out. He watched in numb silence as Alec stepped into the building and the door closed behind him.

Krista stopped the van at Glen Drive, the first named street she'd come to on the outskirts of Prairie Dells. She sat there a moment, thinking. She had to make a decision and make it quickly. She could turn left and try to work her way toward the highway, or she could try to find the nearest phone booth and call Todd.

Which should she do? Which should she do! The question was answered when she spotted a lighted telephone sign on the distant corner of the block.

As she accelerated, she steered the van toward the curb under a darkened streetlight halfway down the block. "Stay here, Thumper," Krista said as she switched off the ignition and reached for her purse on the floor between the seats. "I'll be back in just a couple of minutes."

Thumper whimpered when Krista stepped down out of the van and barked after her as she walked toward the sidewalk. The dog leaned her front paws against the dash, pressed her nose against the windshield and began to whine. Thumper didn't like being left alone.

Krista walked down the rest of the block quickly, hugging the shadows of the building beside her. Every time a car passed by on the street ahead of her, her heart pounded and she held her breath. She prayed Todd would be home and that he would answer his phone on the first ring. She didn't want to stand in the phone booth any longer than she had to; she didn't want to have to stand under the block's only working streetlight.

When she reached the end of the block, Krista stopped to peek around the building's corner. She saw two cars stopped at the light a block away; fortunately, they were not coming

241

in her direction.

Krista looked at the phone booth some eight feet away; then she turned her attention to the handbag she clutched close to her side. Opening it, she used the dim light to find the small address/phone book then opened the coin pocket of her wallet to look for change. Three quarters were nestled in the small compartment; she hoped one would be sufficient.

Holding tightly to the coins and book, Krista looked at the phone booth, took in a deep breath and began walking toward it. Once inside, she closed the door and squinted against the bright light that came on automatically above her head. She set the book on the shelf in front of her, opened it with trembling hands to the Ts and located Todd's number.

Her hand shook nervously as she took the phone from the hook and trembled even more as she tried to fit the coin into its thin slot. A dial tone finally came over the wire, and she released the breath she'd been holding as she pushed the button marked O.

It rang once . . . twice . . . three times . . . four—"Operator. May I help you?"

"Yes," Krista answered quickly. "I'd like to place a collect call to Todd Tyson in Rickdon." After she gave Todd's number to the operator, she added, "Please hurry. This is an emergency."

Krista heard clicks and buzzes come across the line as the computer worked to link a cross-state connection. "Hurry," she said under her breath. "Please hurry."

As she waited, she nervously searched both directions of the street. When she saw a car coming toward her, she turned her back against its lights, hoping whoever occupied the vehicle would only notice her with a passing glance. "Oh, please hurry."

The disheartening buzz of a busy signal crossed the wire to reach her ear. "I'm sorry, that number is busy," the operator said in a polite voice. "Would you like to try the number later?" Krista was numb, unable to immediately respond. "Hello?" the operator questioned. "Are you still there?"

"Can't you break in?" Krista blurted out, on the verge of losing control. "I have to talk to him!"

"We're not allowed to do that unless it's for an emergency."

"This is an emergency!" Krista shouted. "It could be a matter of life and death!"

"I'd be more than happy to connect you with the police," the operator offered.

"No!" Krista shouted again. "I can't trust them!" She slammed the phone down, grabbed the book and remaining two quarters and turned toward the door.

A tall, muscular man stood opposite the door, looking in at her. When he had full view of her face, his eyes opened wide in recognition and amazement.

Krista stood as if paralyzed as the man lifted a hand to push open the bifold door. "Krista Crispen?"

Her heartbeat quickened; her throat tightened. Tears came to her eyes as she tried to shake her head from side to side.

"Jameson was right," the man said, reaching for her arm. "You *do* look remarkably like the picture of the former Mrs. Graham." Out of the corner of her eye, Krista saw a hardtop jeep pull to a stop beside the phone booth. "Please come with me, Mrs. Crispen. Mr. Graham is anxious to see you."

When he touched her arm, Krista drew upon her inner strength to ward off his advance. "No!" she screamed at the top of her voice. She drew back a foot and immediately kicked him in the shin. She drew back again with all intentions of kicking him in the crotch, but he had been trained well, and a swift movement of his arm thwarted her action.

He grabbed her by the arm and pulled her toward him, turning her so her back was pressed against his chest. He had her arms held in firm control. "You can make this easy, or you can make this hard. Take your choice."

"It's not going to be easy," she said as she lifted a foot and kicked backward to again connect with his shin.

"Then have it your way." He turned her around sharply and slapped her hard across the face. The force of the blow caused her head to spin, and her knees crumpled beneath her. "It was your choice," the man said as he scooped her up

243

in his arms and carried her toward the jeep.

From her position halfway down the block, Thumper had seen the man attack Krista. She barked viciously—angrily. She jumped from seat to seat and pawed at the closed windows, looking for a way to get out. Her barking changed from anger to frustration, and then she began to whimper. No matter how desperately Thumper tried, there was no way she could go to the aid of her mistress.

Alec stood with his back pressed against the wall. His heart hammered savagely, feeling as if it were ready to burst free from the muscles and ribs confining it. His breath came in quick shallow gasps. Perspiration beaded across his forehead; a rivulet trickled past the corner of his eye and ran down the side of his cheek. His palms were damp and clammy. Alec could never remember being as nervous as he felt at that moment, and he couldn't draw on any of his past experiences to help calm himself. Nothing fit. He'd never done anything before that could actually be classified as being illegal—at least *totally* illegal. He'd never done anything before that might have put his life in this much risk.

. . . *Anybody who tries to stop me is dead* . . . Graham's words echoed inside Alec's head.

He glanced back at the door less than a foot from him, then looked down at the knob. It would be so easy for him to grab it, push the door open and leave the way he'd come in. It would be so easy to turn and walk—run—away from whatever was being guarded with such secrecy in this place, but Alec knew that wasn't the course he would follow. He'd never turned away from anything he thought important enough to investigate. His integrity wouldn't let him; his gut instinct wouldn't let him.

Alec took in a deep breath and let it out slowly, then turned his head to look down the long hall opposite the door. The area was dimly lighted by the exit sign above him and by another soft light coming from beyond a large window at the hall's opposite end. The lack of bright lights didn't relieve his tension because he surmised the high-tech cameras Graham

244

had undoubtedly installed to keep watch over his secret project could deliver a high-quality picture in any sort of light short of total darkness.

He reached into his pocket for the can of freon as his eyes searched out the corners of the ceiling. He saw no camera mounted there and guessed the entrance was guarded by the exterior camera alone. For the time being, his presence had gone undetected.

The absence of a camera inside the door led Alec to wonder where another one might be. He began to speculate and came up with what seemed to be the only logical answer. He guessed there would be another camera at the junction of the halls by the glass window.

"I'll never know if I keep standing here," he said under his breath. Hesitantly, his feet began to move across the tiled floor.

Mike Sellers leaned forward in his cushioned swivel chair and tapped the monitor for the camera outside the entrance door. Something wasn't working right. The picture was distorted—almost completely blanked out—by crystal-like images. It reminded him of looking through a frost-covered window in the dead of winter. He tapped the monitor again, but his actions failed to produce any results.

"Damn," he grumbled to himself as he glanced at his watch. "Howard'll skin me alive if I call him now. He's already been asleep a couple of hours."

A buzzer sounded behind Mike, and he knew that meant someone was at the door to the monitoring station he manned on the second floor of the equipment barn. He looked at the monitor for the camera guarding the door and immediately recognized the figure in focus who was playfully waving at him.

"Come on in, Al," Mike said as he pushed the button on the console beside him that released the lock on the steel door on the opposite side of the room.

"How are thingths going?" Al asked as he crossed the room and sat down in a chair beside Mike.

Al's presence in the monitoring station was nothing unusual. He came there often to see Mike or Bill Clark, the other night watchman. Sometimes they talked, sometimes they played cards, or sometimes they just sat and watched TV. Al liked Mike and Bill because they didn't seem to take into account the fact that he was different. They treated him like a real human being; they didn't seem to mind that his appearance was unique or that he talked in a strange manner. Other than Marian and sometimes Jordy, Mike and Bill were the only people on the estate Al felt comfortable being around.

But his arrival now was not for a social visit. After seeing Alec enter the building, Al's thoughts turned immediately to the cameras inside. They would detect Alec's presence within a matter of moments, relaying their information to one of the two dozen monitors Mike was paid to watch. At the moment Mike saw a stranger inside the building, Al knew he would sound an alarm that would bring the security men out in force to capture the intruder. Al had come to the monitoring station to prevent that from happening.

"Something's wrong with the exterior entrance camera," Mike said as he again tapped the monitor with his fingers.

Al scooted his chair closer to Mike, as if interested in the problem. As he moved, his eyes scanned the other monitors he knew to be connected to cameras on the building's main floor. So far, Alec's image had yet to be transmitted.

"What'ths wrong with it?" Al asked as he leaned closer to Mike, trying to block his view of the other monitors.

"The hell if I know. It's Howard's job to keep these things working right. I don't know anything about them."

At that instant, out of the corner of his eye, Al saw Alec round a corner, his image captured on a monitor. Alec appeared to run toward the monitor—the camera—hold something up in front of it and . . . The image on the monitor crystallized.

"Thiths one'ths doing the thsame thing," Al said. Making a sweeping gesture toward the monitor where he'd just seen Alec, Al purposefully knocked over Mike's large plastic coffee cup, which was almost three-quarters full. A geyser of sparks immediately erupted from the console.

Almost in unison, Mike and Al leaped from their chairs and ran to the opposite side of the room. They turned to face the wall full of monitors and watched as one by one they began to blank out.

"I'm thsorry," Al said after the last sparks and sizzles finally died out. "I waths onwy trying to hewp."

Mike looked at him and shook his head. "Like it or not, Howard's going to have to wake up and come take a look at this now," he said as he walked toward the wall phone opposite the console. After he dialed the number and waited for an answer, Mike looked back at Al. "You know, if I didn't know better, I'd almost say you did that on purpose."

Al looked from Mike to the wall of blank monitors then hung his head as if he were ashamed. Fortunately, his heavy beard hid the smile of satisfaction that spread across his full lips.

Twenty-One

Alec stood with his back pressed against the wall, looking up at the camera directly over his head. The lens was a frosty white, as was the black plastic holding it in place. He shoved the can of freon back into his pocket, wondering how much time he had to explore the area before the icy crystals began to melt. One element was in his favor: the building was air-conditioned. There wouldn't be an excessive amount of heat to speed the melting process.

He checked his watch. Alec would give himself five minutes to look around, then return to check the status of the lens. At that time he would decide whether to chance spraying the camera again, which might prompt the arrival of a maintenance man to investigate the problem, or let it return to normal and move on to another part of the building. He had five minutes, and the seconds were already ticking away.

Alec walked toward the window he had seen while standing just inside the entrance. It was the first of four large windows lining the wall to his right. Beyond the window, directly in front of him, he could see what appeared to be an open-sided elevator. It was a very large elevator, and Alec presumed it was probably used to move large, bulky equipment from one floor to the other.

To the left of the elevator, spanning the rest of the distance in front of the remaining three windows, were three parallel rows of stainless-steel laboratory counters. The counters were fairly clear of equipment now, but each was within easy reach of storage racks containing a countless supply of beakers, flasks, test tubes and dozens of other items of a scientific nature that Alec couldn't even begin to identify. He wondered what all of the equipment was used for; but then, if he knew the answer to that question, he would probably know the nature of Graham's secret project.

Alec glanced back at the camera lens; it was still a frosty white. He then looked at his watch. He had used a little more than a minute surveying the laboratory.

He began walking down the hallway. Since the windows dominated the wall's length on his right, Alec focused his attention to his left. He passed the closed doors of a regular elevator. Next he came to a glass-windowed door and a medium-size window just beyond it. He paused in front of the window to look into the room beyond.

Alec's brow wrinkled in further surprise as he stared at a half-dozen cribs lined up in neat order along the wall bordering the window's casing. Three incubators lined the wall at the far end of the room, and to the left, just beyond the clearance where the door would open, were two infant-changing tables stocked with an ample supply of disposable diapers, tiny nightshirts, socks, caps and blankets. More than likely, this was where the woman had come to pick up the four babies she'd placed in the ambulance. But what had the infants been doing here in the first place? Even more puzzling, he wondered how they had come to be there at all.

". . . Not a bad total when you think what that gives you when you multiply most of them by fifty thousand . . ." The ambulance driver's conversation with Donald came back to Alec, and a new train of thought crossed his mind.

Was Graham associated with . . . the black market? Was he somehow acquiring infants to sell for a profit?

Alec considered the possibility. But if Graham was in the business of selling babies, how and where had he obtained the infants? And why would he be using the dairy as a middleman's holding place? Questions . . . more unanswerable questions.

Alec continued to look at the cribs in the dairy nursery, as he'd labeled it in his mind. They were all empty now, and there was no rational reason for him to stand there staring into an unoccupied room. All he was doing was wasting precious moments he could be using to discover something of greater importance—time he could be using to find proof to either support or nullify his theory. He glanced at his watch; two and a half minutes were gone.

He walked on to the next door. This particular door was solid; it had no window and there was no window beside it to give visual access to what might lie beyond. Alec grasped the knob, turned it and pushed, but the dead-bolt lock was evidently engaged. What was in there? Alec searched around the door's casing and above it, looking for even a small sign that might provide a clue as to the room's contents, but there was nothing. Again, instead of wasting precious moments dwelling on unanswerable questions, Alec moved on.

One glass-windowed door remained for him to investigate. It faced the end of the hallway, and without hesitation, Alec walked directly toward it. As he stopped, he glanced down at his watch; in just a little over a minute and a half his five minutes would be up.

As Alec lifted his head, his eyes took in the scene opposite the door's glass. The room beyond was wide and extended in both directions from the door; it was perhaps as long as the entire width of the building. But it wasn't the room's size that amazed him; it was what he saw within the room that had Alec completely bewildered.

Six cows were hanging in heavy mesh harnesses, suspended in the air just high enough to keep their hooves from touching the floor. Each cow had a series of tubes leading from her body; each tube was connected to a different IV bottle hanging from a rack near the cow's side. There was writing on each of the bottles' labels, but the lighting was dim and Alec was too far away to read the words.

Alec focused his attention on the cow closest to him. Except for the expansion and contraction of her sides as she breathed, her body hung motionless—limp. Had her head and neck not been supported by an extension of the harness, they too would have succumbed to the pull of gravity and would have hung as lifelessly as her legs and tail.

Alec looked at her face and then into her eyes. Her eyelids drooped, covering over half of the glassy, dark brown irises beneath.

"She's drugged," Alec said to himself in a barely audible whisper. But why? What was going on?

He continued to study the cows and their surroundings, wondering . . . wondering. Then he was jolted by an icy shiver that raced the length of his spine. What time was it?

His eyes darted toward his watch. He had overstayed his allotted time by almost forty-five seconds.

Alec turned sharply and started running down the hall, his soft-soled shoes emitting no audible sounds to betray his presence. As he ran, his eyes focused on the camera mounted in the far corner. Was his image still obliterated or was someone watching him?

When Alec saw that the lens was still covered in a frosty white, he slowed his steps and exhaled in relief. The freon was working as well—if not better—than he'd hoped.

He paused at the corner to glance down the entrance hall before crossing to the stairwell that had gaped at him like an open mouth when he'd first stood under the camera. Alec walked onto the landing and paused to look up the stairs to his left and then down the stairs to his right. Which way should he go?

I'm going to go up to my room and try to catch a few winks. Donald's conversation with the lone cow came back to Alec as clearly as if it had just been spoken. *Up to my room. Up.* If Donald had gone up, then his best course was to go down.

Alec pulled the can of freon from his pocket and began to descend the stairs. If the camera locations were standard, he expected to find another one somewhere near the lower floor's landing.

His expectations were fulfilled. Mounted in the corner of the ceiling directly across from the stairs was another camera.

Alec stayed in the shadows of the stairwell for a few

251

moments, refueling his courage to go on. He then took in a deep breath and charged the second camera as he had the first, hoping whoever was watching its monitor had turned his attention elsewhere.

Once the lens was a frosty white, Alec's confidence returned. He turned to face the hallway behind him.

Another row of large windows spanned the wall to his right, but instead of revealing a laboratory setting, it provided a view of several straw-bedded stalls, four of which contained cows, lying on their sides. Alec looked from one cow to the next and noticed that each had a sutured incision on the side of her lower abdomen.

As his eyes retraced the stalls, he saw the large elevator shaft in the near corner. He now presumed the elevator was used to transport the cows from one floor to the next. But why?

Was this part of the building a clinic for sick or injured livestock? Were the cows involved with some sort of experimentation associated with the research complex? Were these four being prepared to be suspended like the ones he'd seen upstairs—or had they already been there?

Who ... what ... why ... ? Alec was becoming frustrated; he was tired of asking himself questions for which he had no ready answers.

Shaking his head in his own bewilderment, Alec continued on down the hall. Once he passed the row of stalls, he came to another window that overlooked what appeared to be an operating room. The door at the end of the hall led to a scrub room and another operating room beyond, and to his left, directly opposite the window to the first operating room, was another window revealing yet another operating room.

As he turned around to retrace his steps, Alec continued to shake his head. None of his past experiences could help tie together all he had just seen. The whole scenario had grown more and more bizarre as each minute ticked by. He was no closer to finding an answer now than he had been before he'd left the cabin.

Alec stopped just short of the regular elevator and glanced

back at the solid door he'd just passed. His eyes were drawn to an engraved plaque affixed to the door. *RECORDS*.

Alec's heart leaped with anticipation. Could the answers to all of his questions be waiting for him beyond that door?

He reached for the knob and tried to turn it, but it was locked. He studied the lock for a moment and discovered that, unlike the dead-bolt lock securing the door upstairs, this lock was an in-knob lock—one that could be opened easily by anyone who had . . . a thin piece of plastic.

Alec reached into his shirt pocket and pulled out the thin piece of plastic he'd brought with him for just this exact purpose. With a practiced touch, he slipped the plastic into the thin space between the door and its casing and began to apply gentle pressure to the spring lock's latch. He jiggled the knob . . . applied firmer pressure . . . jiggled the knob . . . It turned in his hand, and the door opened. A smile of triumph spread across his face, and he nodded his head in self-approval. He'd learned well some of the undercover tricks of the law-enforcement trade that Lt. Ratliff had tried to teach him.

He slipped the piece of plastic back into his pocket, removed the small roll of duct tape, tore off a piece three or four inches long and pressed it over the door's latch to keep it from relocking. After returning the tape to his pocket, Alec pushed the door open slowly and peeked around its edge.

The room beyond was dark—totally dark. There were no windows to offer even a hint of illumination from the outside night nor were there any safety or security lights to brighten the area.

Alec stepped into the room and closed the door behind him. He stood with his back against the door, his eyes searching out the ceiling and its corners, looking for a small telltale red light indicating the presence of a camera. He saw nothing; there was no hint of the camera in the far corner of the room that was hidden behind a louvered panel.

Slipping his hand into his pocket, Alec pulled out the small flashlight he'd thought to bring with him. He aimed the beam toward the floor until his eyes adjusted to the sudden brightness, then slowly lifted the flashlight until its rays rebounded back off the shelving on both sides of him.

He ran the beam along the fronts of the large cardboard boxes stacked on the shelves from floor to ceiling. There was nothing to indicate what might be inside the boxes, but each was labeled with a beginning and ending date. The boxes immediately around him bore dates beginning in the mid-eighties; the box closest to him on his right had a beginning date of two months ago, and at the moment, no ending date had been noted.

Curious, Alec removed the lid from that box and directed the light inside. It contained perhaps forty manila file folders, standing on end so that the numbers written on the identification tabs were readily visible.

Alec removed the folder closest to him; it was marked with the number 9,366. "... *These four make it a grand total of 9,366* ..." Donald's words came back to him to confirm his suspicions about what the files might contain: information on the babies taken from the dairy.

He opened the folder and balanced it against his arm, focusing the light on the single sheet that was its only contents. The number was repeated on the top of the sheet, followed by an arrival date of two days before and today's date indicating the time of delivery. Alec skimmed down the rest of the page but was unable to make any sense of the letters and numbers he assumed represented some sort of code. He still didn't have any solid evidence to support his latest theory; he wasn't any closer to finding out what was actually going on here at the dairy.

After returning the file and box lid, Alec turned and held the flashlight to again survey the contents of the room around him. The shelving on the wall to his right spanned the entire length of the wall; the shelving to his left continued for about twenty feet and stopped to leave about a five-foot clearance in front of the filing cabinets fronting the wall facing him.

Alec walked toward the cabinets, directing the flashlight toward them. Something sitting on top of the second cabinet from the left attracted his attention. As he drew closer, a thin smile of recognition tightened his lips. It was the brown box

Brice had given him containing all of Schmidt's documents pertaining to Project GOD.

He moved the flashlight's beam to the drawer fronts and the small white labels affixed to each. The drawers weren't identified in any more detail than the large boxes had been, but their labeling was categorized with letters of the alphabet instead of by dates. Playing a hunch, Alec looked for the drawer bearing the letter G.

Fortunately, the filing cabinet wasn't locked. When Alec grasped the handle and pulled, the drawer slid open easily.

He didn't have to search for the information he was looking for; it was right there in front of him. The entire contents of the drawer contained only one labeling; everything pertained to Project GOD.

Exhilaration tingled through him. At long last, maybe he had finally found what he'd been looking for. He tucked the end of the flashlight beneath his chin and focused it inside the drawer. Using both hands, he began leafing through the files, pausing when he came to something he could read and understand.

Donald lay on his bed, staring up at the ceiling. He'd tried closing his eyes and coaxing his mind into relaxing enough to allow him a short nap, but he was still wide awake. He reacted in a similar manner every week any of the scheduled deliveries weren't on time. Even though the Grahams were officially in charge of and totally responsible for the entire operation, Donald had taken it upon himself to do the worrying for all of them whenever something didn't fall into place.

He rolled his head across the pillow and looked at the lighted numbers on the digital clock beside him. He'd been lying there less than fifteen minutes, but since his attempt at napping had been unsuccessful, he doubted that he would sleep. His thoughts were focused on the lone cow in the holding pen; he kept wondering how much longer she would be. Timing was crucial. If she went into forced labor and the strong contractions weren't inhibited in time, the unit could be damaged. One of his main jobs was to see that that didn't happen. So far, it never had.

Donald sat up and swung his legs over the edge of the narrow bed. He knew he would feel better if he were down with the cow, waiting where he could keep an eye on her, but he wasn't in the mood to stand by the fence until he was needed. Her time could still be hours away, and he didn't relish the foreseen boredom.

"Guess I can catch up on some reading," Donald said to himself as he stood and picked up a paperback book from the nightstand beside his bed.

He walked down the hall past the small rooms where the on-call staff slept when there was a possibility their services would be needed. Several of the rooms were occupied at the moment. Donald presumed everyone other than himself was asleep and guessed they would probably stay that way for the rest of the night unless he had cause to wake them.

As Donald angled across the hall toward Hubert Graham's office, he glanced toward the door to Jordy's room. Boss or not, like the others sleeping on the second floor, Jordy's length of peaceful slumber rested on Donald's decision. The thought of having even a minute element of power within the Graham organization gave his ego a boost he desperately needed.

Donald walked into Graham's office without hesitation, as he had done on hundreds of nights before when similar situations had arisen. He turned on the overhead light, walked behind Graham's desk to grab the plushly cushioned chair and rolled it toward the wall of monitors on the far side of the spacious room.

He was in the process of situating the chair in front of the monitor for the camera at the corner of the holding pen when he saw movement on an adjacent monitor. "What the . . ." Donald questioned as he focused his attention on the second monitor. Someone was in the records room going through the files. "How in God's name did he get in there?"

Donald hurried from Graham's office and went directly to the door of Jordy's room. He knocked once . . . twice, then reached for the knob, turned it and walked in. "Jordy," he called as he crossed the room. "Jordy, wake up." He placed a hand on Jordy's shoulder and began shaking him. "Jordy, wake up."

"What?" Jordy asked groggily. He rolled over and opened his heavy eyelids. "Is it time?" he asked upon recognizing Donald. "Is she ready?"

"Somebody's in the building. Somebody's down in the records room going through the files."

"God, no." Jordy sat up quickly, the unexpected news rousing him from his sleepy state. "How could anyone have gotten past the guards?" He reached for his slacks draped over a chair beside the bed and yanked them on as he stood.

"What are you going to do?"

"I'm going down there to find out who he is and just how he got in here."

"What do you want me to do?"

"Call Jameson and tell him to get his ass down here." As Jordy spoke, he reached into the drawer of his nightstand and pulled out a 9mm Beretta. "Heads are gonna roll when I find out how this guy got past the guards. Somebody wasn't doing the job he was being paid to do." Jordy checked the revolver's clip, then turned and started toward the door.

Twenty-Two

Alec had progressed almost halfway through the drawer's contents. The wording in the files hadn't been jumbled—coded—as it had been in Schmidt's journal and notebooks, but it was very technical. With the exception of a few medical terms he remembered from a med-news report or from his high school health class years before, he recognized very little of the scientific terminology. He wasn't making much progress, but he thought he had at least a small grasp on what Project GOD might pertain to; he was beginning to think his original, bizarre speculation might have been correct. Project GOD had something to do with repro—

The door flew open and banged against the shelving beside it. Alec turned sharply as the overhead light burst into brightness. His eyes squinted in reaction to the sudden glare, and for a few seconds, for the time it took for his eyes to adjust, he could see nothing more than a blurred figure standing in the doorway.

There was a moment of awkward silence; then the man at the door spoke. "Alec?"

Alec recognized the voice immediately but didn't respond. He couldn't respond. His heart was pounding in his throat, cutting off any possible passage for sound to escape.

"What in the hell—"

"Jameson's not here," Donald interrupted, running up behind Jordy. "Nobody's available. They're all gone."

"It's okay," Jordy replied, glancing at Donald briefly. "I

think I can handle things here. You go on and tend to the other business." Jordy returned his attention to Alec. He stared at him momentarily and then asked, "What in God's name are you doing here?"

His eyes now adjusted to the light, Alec stared at the handgun Jordy had leveled at him, then shifted his gaze to meet Jordy's eyes directly. "That's exactly why I'm here," he answered, trying not to betray his uncertainty and fear. Jordy's brow wrinkled, and he looked at Alec in question. "I'm here to find out about GOD . . . Project GOD to be exact." Knowing the best defense was a good offense, Alec continued on as if he were completely in charge of the entire situation. "Somebody broke into our cabin last night, taking what little information I had on the subject. I was curious in my own right before that happened, but then I figured if it was something worth stealing, it was definitely something I needed to look into."

"But what led you . . . here?"

"My gut instinct." Alec laid his hand on the edge of the file drawer and looked squarely into Jordy's eyes. "And it was right. Everything's right here." Alec and Jordy looked at each other for several silent moments; then Alec asked, "What is Project GOD?"

Jordy lowered his eyes. When he saw the revolver he still held pointed at Alec, he lowered it as well. "It would be better for you if you didn't know," he finally said, again making eye contact. "You could leave right now and forget all about it. You and Krista could go back to Louisville and live out the rest of your lives—"

"Live out the rest of our lives wondering what all of this was about?" Alec interrupted gruffly. "That's not my style. I've gotten myself in this deep, and I'm not about to turn tail and run now. Level with me, Jordy," Alec said after a brief hesitation. "What is Project GOD?"

Jordy's eyes left Alec's to stare at the box fronts on either side of the aisle, box fronts bearing dates that spanned over ten years of time. It was here—all of it was here—if not on this row of shelves, then on the next one or the one after that. Everything that had ever happened pertaining to Project

259

GOD was recorded here; everything that had happened from the very beginning, over thirty-five years ago, up through today. *Everything* could be found right here in the basement floor records room.

"My mother was a brilliant woman," Jordy began hesitantly as he walked toward Alec. "In most respects, she was far ahead of what the times would allow." He closed the file drawer beside Alec and turned the corner toward the aisle between the next two rows of packed shelving. Jordy motioned for Alec to follow. "But I doubt that even if she were alive today she would be able to accomplish any more than what she did over thirty years ago. What with our prudish, moralistic society looking on as watchdogs over other people's business, she would have probably had to keep it all as much of a secret today as she did back then." Jordy shook his head. "Some of the most brilliant breakthroughs in science have been scrapped because they didn't meet with society's Puritanical attitudes and judgments."

Alec felt that Jordy was rambling, but he made no attempt to interrupt the conversation. He was on his way—albeit a roundabout way—to finding out about Project GOD.

He followed Jordy through yet another turn that led them to yet another aisle. Where was the maze leading them? What would they find when they finally reached its end?

Jordy stopped halfway down the aisle. He turned to his left, but instead of facing shelves packed with boxes, he faced the first of two side-by-side wooden cabinets fronted with a dual set of doors. Slipping a hand into the front pocket of his slacks, he pulled out a crowded key ring. After locating a small gold key on the ring, he slipped it into the lock on the door in front of him.

"She became well known in the field of animal husbandry," he continued, looking back at Alec, "but she wanted to do so much more. With a growing number of animals being added to the endangered-species list every day, she wanted to find a way of producing an abundance of offspring to counteract their approach to extinction. Are you familiar with the term surrogate?"

"Just by what I've heard on TV."

Jordy nodded in acceptance of Alec's answer, then reached for the handle of the cabinet he'd unlocked. "All of the animals that leave our research facility aren't always *born* as you might understand the definition of the word. Over thirty-five years ago, my mother discovered a way to override the natural rejection factors of an animal's body so that it would accept and nurture an implanted embryo of a different species."

"By what little I know about science, I didn't think that was possible."

"One of my mother's favorite sayings that my father has quoted to me hundreds of times was 'There's a formula to conquer everything if you'll only look long enough and hard enough to find it.'"

Jordy finally opened the cabinet's door, revealing dozens of large jars containing a variety of small animals. Alec guessed the animals had been preserved in formaldehyde, because most of them were completely whole and appeared as peaceful as if they were merely sleeping.

"She began small, implanting mice embryos into rats, rats into guinea pigs, guinea pigs into cats and so on. Every animal you see here developed inside an animal other than its own species.

"The other day, you even saw some living examples of how well my mother's procedure works." Alec's brow wrinkled in confusion. Jordy continued with an explanation. "The animals in the nursery at the research center, all of them came from surrogate mothers. Remember all of the goats and deer we have at the old zoo facility?" Alec nodded. "We use them as the surrogates for the animals we sell to zoos all across the country."

"Amazing," Alec said as he looked from Jordy back to the preserved animals in front of him. "So this is Project GOD." He was totally fascinated by what he saw, and yet, his gut instinct told him there was more—much more.

"The beginning stages," Jordy answered after a brief hesitation.

Jordy removed the key that still hung in the door's lock

and stepped to his right until he stood facing the closed doors of the second cabinet. He paused, looking at the door, and Alec noticed a tremor in Jordy's hand as he inserted the key into that lock and turned it slowly.

"My mother was barren," Jordy said as he looked back at Alec. "And . . . and I'm *not* adopted." The questioning look that clouded Alec's face didn't surprise Jordy; in fact, he would have been surprised had Alec reacted any differently.

"My mother wanted a child of her own, but her fallopian tubes were blocked with scar tissue from a previous surgery, and she couldn't conceive. She figured if her antirejection formula could work on other animal species, she didn't know why it wouldn't work on the human animal. As you can see," Jordy said as he lifted a tremulous hand to the cabinet's handle, "her first attempts at implanting a human embryo into another animal species didn't turn out as well as she'd planned." He pulled open the door to the second cabinet and immediately turned away from it.

Alec looked inside the second cabinet and was immediately repulsed by the deformed infants contained within the preserving jars, but he didn't turn away—he couldn't. He was mesmerized with incredulity.

Some of the unfortunate creatures were merely heads and trunks without arms and legs; some had recognizable bodies, but their heads were unstructured masses of bone and tissue; others looked as if their bodies had been turned inside out, their internal organs floating freely in the liquid surrounding them. Two preserved forms, in jars on the top shelf, were so unorganized in body composition that they were unrecognizable as ever having come from human origin.

Seeing all that his stomach would allow before rebelling, Alec wrenched himself away and stood facing Jordy. Both men stood in silence for several minutes before Alec found the courage to ask, "Were they all . . . hers?"

"No." Jordy took in a deep breath and released it slowly. "She had several friends in the medical profession and was able to obtain ovaries from women who'd died young or who'd needed to have hysterectomies for reasons that didn't affect the ovaries' ability to produce ova. She was even able to develop a hormone solution that kept the ovaries functioning for several months before they finally quit producing and had to be discarded." Jordy took in another breath and released it. "And during the experimental stages, the sperm didn't come from my father. He wanted to wait for the 'real thing' before donating," Jordy added with a cynical laugh. "Even back then there were technicians working for them who liked to prove their virility . . . even though they knew the seeds of their loins might end up fathering something like that," he said, nodding his head sideways toward the cabinet beside him.

"So how did you?" Alec asked after deliberating the choice of his words.

"How did I come to turn out any different from the likes of them? Schmidt. It was Edgar Schmidt who came to the rescue. My father got tired of seeing my mother cry over her losses, and even working together, they couldn't uncover the flaws in any of her formulas. But Schmidt did. Schmidt spotted the errors almost immediately and set about helping to correct them; he recalculated the formulas based on the ones he'd developed years before. Then, on his guarantee of success, my mother had one of her ovaries removed."

"And that's how you came to be born?"

"No." Jordy again took in a deep breath and let it out slowly. "The surrogate was . . . was wrong, and . . ." his words trailed off. "About eight months later," he continued after a lengthy hesitation, "Schmidt guaranteed all errors had been corrected and tested against a repeat failure. He asked her to trust him one last time—which was all she could do since she had only one ovary left," he said cynically.

"And it worked the second time," Alec prompted when Jordy failed to continue on his own.

"It worked. It worked quite well. Of the initial eight fertilized eggs, six survived. There were two boys and four girls," Jordy added with an almost maniacal laugh. "Project GOD was finally a success. *Graham's Obstetric Development* was finally a success. And *you* were a part of it." Jordy placed his right hand over Alec's right wrist and lifted them both up into the light. "You've carried the mark of Project

263

GOD with you all of your life."

Alec looked at his hand—looked at the three small dots on the webbing between his thumb and forefinger—the three small dots that, had they been connected, would have formed a perfect triangle. Then he looked at Jordy's hand. His fingers were wrapped around Alec's wrist so that an identical mark on his hand was visible directly beneath the one on Alec's.

Alec stared at the marking on Jordy's hand, comparing it to his own. He wondered why he'd never noticed it before, especially after attention had been drawn to the mark on his own hand. Then he rationalized an answer to his question. Jordy had worn driving gloves the first few times they'd exchanged handshakes, and when Alec had visited the estate, the mark on Jordy's hand had been concealed by a Band-aid.

"You've carried the Delta mark all of your life, but you never knew what it meant until now . . . *brother.*"

Brother!

Alec was dumbfounded by the enormity of what he'd just heard. At first he doubted the story Jordy had just told him, but then, why would Jordy lie about something that sounded so ultimately unbelievable? Why . . . how could he make up such a bizarre tale?

Alec finally admitted to himself that Jordy couldn't be lying—Jordy *had* to be telling the truth. Alec's gut instinct didn't attempt to convince him otherwise.

Now that he accepted—believed in—the origin of his heritage, a hundred questions raced through his mind. The first one to leave his lips was, "Why didn't she keep them . . . us? Why didn't she keep all of . . . us?"

"The logic of the times. Healthy, white infants were at a premium in the late fifties and early sixties, as they still are today. My parents could have easily explained to their friends about being able to adopt one infant, but how could they explain the sudden appearance of six?" Jordy looked at Alec, and a note of compassion came to his voice. "Since I was the firstborn, they kept me. The rest of them . . . the rest of you, they made arrangements with a couple of adoption

264

agencies to have adopted.

"That's when my mother conceived the idea to continue with the project. Times were hard for people trying to adopt, and she wanted everyone who ever wanted to have a baby, but couldn't, to have one. She had a dream that someday there would be enough babies in the world so that childless couples wouldn't have to wait very long to adopt. We haven't reached her goal as of yet, but during the past thirty years, the fruits of her labors have made a lot of people happy. The records of our successes are all around you."

Alec looked from Jordy to the packed shelves towering around him. He had expected to find something horrifying—something evil connected with Project GOD. But was it really all that bad? And perhaps Jordy had been right. *If our society weren't so closed-minded in the area of medical research,* he thought, *maybe something like Project GOD could have made thousands—even tens of thousands of childless couples happy over the years. If it were only allowed to operate with the blessing instead of the scorn of our too prudent society, maybe couples like Krista and me wouldn't have to wait three or four years only to be told there are no infants available.*

"How?" Alec asked out of curiosity. "Who . . . *what* was *our* surrogate?"

"The dairy was built back here for a purpose. The project grew too quickly to be contained in the old primate house, and then of course, something had to be developed to disguise the workings of the project." Jordy paused and looked at Alec with a slight grin. "The cows here at the dairy do more than just supply us with milk."

"A cow?"

Jordy nodded. "After the . . . the mishap with the first surrogate, my mother did a lot of research and experimenting with several different animals and found that a cow was the most compatible for the reproduction of our own species."

A cow . . . Had Alec read about it in a book or seen it in a movie, the whole idea of being nurtured by a cow would have seemed absurd, outlandish or maybe even humorous. But it didn't seem absurd or funny at the moment. It was a miracle; his whole life was a scientific miracle. "It's . . . it's all so hard to believe," he said half-knowingly.

"Believe it. We're both proof that there's a formula to conquer everything. I'm just glad my . . . *our* mother was able to find it. And we still use the same formulas today my mother and Dr. Schmidt developed years ago," he added with a note of pride. "The technology has been updated, of course, but the formulas are exactly the same."

"Jordy?" Donald's voice filtered into the room. "Jordy? Are you still in here?"

"We're back here," he answered, turning to quickly close the cabinet's doors without looking at its contents.

"She's just about ready to deliver," Donald said as he stepped into view at the end of the aisle. "The team's already getting things together, and I thought I'd better come find you."

"I'll be right there," Jordy responded as he locked the second cabinet. "Do you have a strong stomach, Alec?"

"It depends."

"Would you like to see number," Jordy thought for a moment, "number nine thousand three hundred and sixty-seven make her entry into the world?"

"There have been that many?" Alec questioned. He was so fascinated by the information he'd received and by everything else going on around him that he'd all but forgotten about the file he'd seen several minutes earlier.

"That many here. I can't give you the exact count on our two other farms in Utah and Montana without looking it up, but I'd guess there've been as many or more produced at each one of them as there have been here." Jordy began walking down the aisle; Alec followed behind him. "Are you interested in joining me in the delivery room?"

"I guess I can try anything once."

Alec followed Jordy back through the maze of shelves and was momentarily puzzled when Jordy stopped in front of the filing cabinet and took down the brown box containing Schmidt's documents. He shuffled through the contents, then handed Alec one of the black-and-white photographs.

"Would you like to have your very first baby picture?" A hesitant smile came to Alec's face as he accepted it. "I'm not sure which one of the girls is Krista, or you could have that one too."

"Krista? She's . . . ?"

"You noticed the resemblance the first time you saw my . . . *our* mother's picture. And then when I saw the mark on her hand—"

"The birthmark," Alec whispered to himself. "The birthmark," he repeated aloud as he looked down at his own.

Krista! Panic unnerved Alec. How was he going to tell Krista . . . his wife . . . his lover . . . that she was also his sister? . . .

Twenty-Three

"Just get out," Howard grumbled, examining the console of the monitoring station and speculating on the length of time it would take for him to repair it.

"I'm thsorry," Al said rather convincingly. "I waths onwy trying to hewp Mike find out what waths wrong."

"Well, you didn't help. You only made things worse. Now get out of here and leave us alone. Go find somebody else to cause trouble for."

Al hung his head as if he were ashamed of his actions, but deep inside, he knew the verbal abuse was worth whatever time his actions had brought Alec. Seemingly overcome with remorse, Al backed out of the room.

The moment he was out of their sight, Al lifted his head and smiled openly, descending the stairs almost gaily. Once outside the equipment barn, he stopped for a moment to survey his surroundings.

With Alec inside the building, Al couldn't continue with what he had set out to do. Following through with his plan at this particular time would only put Alec's life in danger, and the sole purpose behind his plan was to do the exact opposite. If there was no project left to protect, then there would be no need for Graham to fear any repercussions from what Alec might have discovered. And if there were no records left to account for the project's history, then there would be no physical evidence to back any statement Alec might make about it in the future. There was only one simple way to solve all of the problems; Al planned to destroy all evidence of Project GOD.

He glanced at the wing of the dairy housing the project. Should he go find Alec and attempt to persuade him to leave? Should he confront Alec face-to-face? . . . *Face-to-face* . . . The thought of coming face-to-face with someone from the outside sent a shiver of uncertainty down Al's spine. He'd never come *face-to-face* with someone he didn't know . . . or with someone who didn't know about him. He wondered how an outsider would react—

Al's attention was drawn from the project wing to the house off in the distance. He could see a small caravan of lights following the drive around the back, returning to the garage. He wondered what was going on. Why had they left in such a frenzy in the first place, and now, why were they returning in a group?

His curiosity got the better of him. Knowing the cameras in the project wing would be out of commission for quite a while, somewhat assuring Alec's safety, and wanting to prolong any *face-to-face* meeting until it was necessary, Al decided to go investigate. He started toward the primate building and the tunnel that would take him into the main house. He could return to the dairy later to finish what he'd started out to do.

"Where is she?" Graham shouted as he burst into the den. From the moment his foot had touched the ground in front of the house until he now stood panting just inside the den door, he had run all the way.

There was no need for a verbal response. In reaction to his abrupt entry, Krista had turned in her seat on the couch to face him. She now stared at Graham over the sofa's rounded back, a look of growing apprehension, mingled with confusion, consuming her face.

"Krista," Graham said in a much calmer voice when their eyes met. "Krista, my dear, you had me worried." He walked around the end of the sofa and stopped to face her, his right side turned toward the fireplace and the lighted portrait of

269

Julia Ann. "Are you all right?" He took her hands in his, and with a gentle tug, urged her to stand in front of him. "Since we couldn't find you at the cabin, I was afraid something might have happened to you."

A concerned frown replaced the thin smile that had come to Graham's face. Gingerly, he lifted a hand to cup Krista's chin. He turned her head ever so slightly so that the reflected light from the portrait would highlight the left side of her face.

A thin cut followed the line of her high cheekbone. The flesh around the cut was already beginning to darken into a bruise, and the skin beneath her eye was puffed and swollen.

"Who did this?" Graham demanded. His murderous glare pierced the distance between himself and the two men standing beside the door he'd just entered. "Ticen?" he asked in a threatening tone. The man to whom the question had been directed shook his head; then his eyes drifted from Graham to the man standing beside him. "Darnell, did you do this?"

"She tried to put up a fight, sir," Darnell answered defensively.

"A fight? You mean to tell me a two-hundred-and-thirty-pound man can't defend himself against a one-hundred-and-twenty-pound woman without doing this?" he asked angrily, turning Krista's cheek toward Darnell. "Get out!" he commanded. "Go back to your quarters until I decide what's to be done with you." His eyes shifted to the other man. "Ticen, wait in the hall."

After both men had exited, Graham returned his attention to Krista. "I'm so sorry this had to happen, my dear." He finally released her chin and let his fingers trail down the length of her sleek neck toward her shoulder.

Yesterday Krista had found Graham's touch almost paternal; now she felt repulsion. She took a step backward, freeing herself from his touch. "Why did you send them after me?" she finally found the courage to ask. "Why didn't you just let me go?"

Graham ignored her questions. He turned and walked toward a bar built into the corner of the room and slowly—

almost leisurely—fixed himself a drink. "Don't you like it here?" he asked when he finally turned back to face her. "Why, just last night you were telling me how beautiful you thought my home was." He made a sweeping gesture around the room as he spoke, and then his eyes again focused on Krista. "By the way you were talking last night, I thought you might like to live here." He took a sip from his glass and then asked, "Wouldn't you like to live here, Krista? Wouldn't you like to spend the rest of your life living in the house you've admired ever since you were a child?"

"No!" Krista blurted out adamantly. "I wouldn't want to live here now even if it was the last place left standing on the face of the earth."

"Well, you're going to have to," Graham countered as forcefully. "You're going to have to live here . . . if you want to live at all." He stared at her for several moments before the hard lines of his face softened.

"Your mother would have wanted you to live here," he said in a much softer tone as he crossed the room to stand in front of Julia Ann's portrait. He glanced at Krista, then looked up at the picture's smiling face. "No doubt she would have dressed you in ruffles and ribbons—blue ruffles and ribbons that would have brought out the blue in your eyes. You do have her eyes, you know," he said, looking back at Krista. "You have her eyes and her hair . . . and her smile." Graham chuckled. "And if you truly gave Darnell the tussle he claims you did, you inherited her temperament as well."

"Stop it!" Krista shouted, even though she was uncertain as to why she had spoken at all.

"Surely you can see it. Looking at Julia Ann's picture must be like looking at the reflection in your own mirror."

"No! Stop it! You're crazy!" Tears swelled in Krista's eyes and slipped past her long lashes onto her cheeks. But she didn't know for sure why she was crying. Was she so frightened of Hubert Graham that her fear was rushing from her in the form of tears? Or was she actually beginning to believe what he was saying? . . .

"Oh, Alec," she whispered to herself, "where are you? *Please* come take me away from all of this."

271

"No matter how hard you try, my dear, you can't deny the truth of your heritage," Graham continued as he looked back up at the portrait and smiled. "Julia Ann was your mother, and I," he said proudly as he looked back at Krista, "I am your long-lost father."

Krista shrank away from him, stumbling over the corner of the sofa. She almost fell, but caught herself with the aid of its padded arm.

She had to get out of there. Hubert Graham was a madman, and she feared he might soon make her the object of his insanity.

"You carry the mark of GOD," he said as he took a step toward her. "It's been defaced by an unsightly scar, but it's still there. Look on your hand—your right hand—on the webbing between your thumb and forefinger. On either side of the scar, you'll find the two remaining points of Delta that were tattooed there a few days after you were born. That's how we marked the first series of our successes so we could identify you if we ever happened to meet someday."

Krista looked down at her right hand—at the webbing between her thumb and forefinger. The scar . . . the twin moles—

"Do you know how remote the chances were of finding you? The chances of finding just one of you were phenomenal enough in themselves, but to find two of you together—two of you *both* bearing the mark of GOD . . ."

The mark of GOD? What did it all mean?

"God," Graham said as he took another step toward her. "Do you have any idea what it's like to play God? Can you even begin to imagine what it's like to create life from two cells that, in a million years, would have never had the slightest chance of meeting? It gives you the feeling of power," he said, thrusting his arms up in the air toward the ceiling as if in praise of the Almighty. "It gives you the feeling of greatness. It gives you the feeling of . . . *being* God."

"You're crazy!" Krista screamed. Tears now streamed freely from her eyes as she continued to back away from him.

"And no one's going to rob me of that feeling." His voice turned suddenly cold and threatening. "Not you. Not Alec.

272

Not even that bastard freak! No one's going to take away what I've devoted all my life to. No one will ever stop me from being God!"

Krista turned sharply and ran toward the French doors that opened onto the patio. But her escape attempt carried her no farther than a few steps onto the brick.

Jameson had been stationed there, apparently waiting for such an occurrence. He captured her almost immediately, and even though she struggled, fought and kicked, he held her steadfast in steel-muscled arms.

"Lock her upstairs in the guest room," Graham ordered after finishing the contents of his glass. "As soon as we find Alec, I'll have to decide what to do with the two of them."

Al had entered the guest room directly over the den a few minutes before. Peering down through the grate covering the old convection register, he had been able to observe everything that had happened since Graham pointed out Krista's birthmark.

Now, as she struggled with Jameson, Al wished he could help her, but he couldn't—not just yet. There were too many of Graham's men in the house to chance a confrontation. Even though he was strong, Al knew he couldn't overpower all of them . . . and then there were their guns.

Al hated their guns; he was afraid of them. He had seen what they could do to flesh and bone; he had seen what they had done to the cows that had grown too old to be of any use to Project GOD. The huge incinerator behind the dairy had been used for much more than just the burning of refuse.

"No!" Al heard Krista scream as Jameson carried her toward the den's hall door.

He knew he had to leave. In all likelihood, Krista would be brought to the room he now occupied. It was the guest room closest to the main source of activity on the ground floor, and to his knowledge, it was the only room that had a lock.

Quietly, Al hurried across the room. After checking the hall, he stepped out and closed the door behind him. As he walked toward the back stairwell, he heard voices coming from the main staircase halfway down the hall.

Alec stood at the window overlooking the room housing the incubators. He didn't seem to notice the white-clothed technician bustling around the room attending to the routine matters she'd done hundreds of times before. His attention was focused solely on the newborn infant who was wrapped in a pink blanket and sleeping peacefully. Even though he'd seen her birth—had seen her tiny body removed through a ten-inch incision in the side of the cow that had nurtured her development from the day of implantation—it was still hard for him to believe.

Following the infant's delivery, Jordy had taken Alec on a tour of the facility and tried to explain how the procedure worked from beginning to end. Alec was fascinated by the sperm and ovary banks housed in the room on the main floor he'd been unable to enter, and he became totally mesmerized when Jordy explained how they had improved upon his mother's hormonal-rich solution that preserved the ovaries until they harvested the ovum they desired.

With his sketchy knowledge of what was actually taking place at the dairy, Alec had even nodded his head, as if in total understanding, when Jordy explained the workings in the lab. Once the egg and sperm were selected, to comply with the adoptive parents' requirements of race, stature, hair and eye coloring, they were united within one of two hormone-based solutions. The choice of solutions was determined by the sex the adoptive parents had chosen for their forthcoming child. One solution destroyed all Y-carrying sperm, assuring the development of a female; the second solution did likewise to all X-carrying sperm, guaranteeing the production of a male. Once conception was attained, the united cells were watched closely as they developed from a zygote into a recognizable embryo. At that point, it was then ready to be implanted into the surrogate.

Alec also learned the reason behind the suspended cows he'd seen during his own unguided tour of the building. The cows were indeed drugged; the precaution was necessary to insure their immobility while the newly implanted embryos had an opportunity to take a firm hold and begin their growth. Jordy had also explained what had been in the bottles connected to the cows. One bottle controlled the sedative, one contained the antirejection formula, and, Jordy had added, each cow was given a weekly injection of the formula throughout gestation. Another bottle contained concentrated hormones that stabilized the lining of the cow's uterus for implantation, and the remaining bottles were filled with a booster dose of vitamins and minerals to insure the health of both the cow and the implanted embryo.

Alec now knew the reason for the operating rooms and for the stalls. The cows he had seen in the stalls earlier were gone, but the cow that had been the surrogate mother of the baby girl he was peering at through the window was recovering in one of the stalls that very moment. In a couple of days, she would rejoin the rest of the herd, and within six months, she would begin a term of motherhood all over again.

Alec shifted his weight, and by so doing, he inadvertently moved a few inches closer to the partially open door. Something attracted his attention. Something shifted his point of focus away from the infant, but he wasn't exactly sure what it was.

He glanced along both directions of the hall and saw nothing. He looked back into the dairy's nursery, but he couldn't detect anything he hadn't noticed before. Then, from out of the air around him, he knew what had tugged at his mind. The technician was humming—humming to the classical music playing in the nursery that was barely audible to his ears.

The music. Why had the soft mus—

Music . . . his dream—his nightmare.

Jordy's comment concerning the music that had been playing in the research complex's nursery echoed across Alec's mind. *"Music's been playing in the nursery for as long as I can remember . . . and it played in the primate house even before I was born."*

Born . . . And what about after he'd—*they'd*—been born?

Was it possible? Had Alec's audiographic memory been so acute that it had conjured up memories from the first few days of his life?

"Do you have any more questions?" Jordy asked as he stepped up beside Alec.

Startled, Alec turned abruptly and answered almost immediately in a reflex response, "Hundreds, but I'm afraid I'm not smart enough in the field to even know what words to put together in order to be able to ask an intelligent question."

He hesitated, forgetting about the nightmares that had haunted his sleep over the years; he focused on the nightmare that might be yet to come. "I am intelligent enough to ask one question, but I'm not sure if I want to know the answer." Alec paused, looking Jordy directly in the eyes. "What happens now?" he asked in a somber tone. "What happens to me now that I know all about Project GOD?"

Jordy turned his head and looked away. His eyes were directed toward the baby girl in the incubator, but he didn't actually see anything that was taking place in front of him. "That's a question I don't have a ready answer for," he finally said in resignation. "I suppose the answer to that question will hinge on the answers you have for some of my father's questions."

"Questions like what?"

"That I can't predict," Jordy answered, returning his gaze to Alec. "My father is a changeable man. He's getting old, and he has many moods. I guess it'll all depend on how he reacts to your presence here—and to what you've seen—as to what he decides to do."

The elevator door to their left opened, and Donald stepped out. "Everything's all squared away," he said as he approached. "Everybody was glad to go back home to their own beds. I'll be happy to do the same." He glanced at Alec, then looked back at Jordy. "Is there anything else you want me to do before I leave?"

"Go on home," Jordy answered. "It's been a long night, and I know you're looking forward to getting some sleep." Donald nodded, and without hesitation, he turned and

276

walked away.

"Well," Jordy said as he turned to face Alec, "I guess it's time we go have a talk with my father."

Al crouched behind the leg of the water tower closest to the entry door and peeked around the corner of the shed. He'd already seen several of the technicians leave, and he would continue to wait patiently until the rest of them were gone. If tonight's delivery followed the course of hundreds that had gone before it, Donald would leave after the rest of the personnel had cleared the building, and then Jordy would be the very last one to leave.

The building would not be entirely empty, however; one technician would remain throughout the night to watch over the new delivery. But her presence wouldn't hamper Al's plans. He could handle her easily.

Twenty-Four

Marvin glanced across the bench seat of the old pickup truck. Robbie was curled up asleep, leaning against the locked door; Amble was asleep on the seat between them, his head resting on Robbie's legs.

All three of them had fallen asleep halfway through the second feature, and only after the lights came on and cars started moving around them did Marvin happen to wake up. He still wasn't fully awake.

He yawned and shook his head. As sleepy as he was, Marvin wondered how safe it was for him to be driving. But how else would they make it back to the cabin? Unlike the characters they'd just seen in the futuristic science-fiction movies, their bodies couldn't be dematerialized at one location and reassembled at another.

The road ahead lay straight and smooth; there was nothing to break the monotony, and there wouldn't be anything until they reached the edge of town. Marvin wondered if he'd made the right decision by coming this direction. If he'd taken the back road to the lake, maybe he would be more fully awake and in better control of his senses. The back road was rough and bumpy, and if nothing else, the constant jarring would have kept him awake. Right now, he was fighting to stay alert.

Up ahead, he saw a pair of taillights brighten, then turn off to the left. If his memory served him correctly, the upcoming driveway should be the second to the last one before they reached town.

Town. Marvin made a vow right then and there that he would stop at the all-night café for a cup of coffee before he even attempted to drive on home.

Al stayed in hiding until after Jordy and Alec left the building and climbed into an electric cart to ride back to the house. Stepping out from behind the small storage shed at the base of the water tower, he stood at the foot of the steps and looked down the gravel drive until he saw the cart turn and disappear around the corner of the dairy's offices. Time was at a premium; he had to hurry.

After hurdling the steps, he opened the door slowly to prevent any creak and closed it with equal care behind him. He hurried down the hall, made a sharp turn to his right and descended the steps as quickly as his turns on the landings would allow.

Once on the basement floor, Al ran the length of the long hall toward the operating rooms' common scrub room. He knew none of the rooms would be locked—there was no need for an abundance of locks in a building which was meant to be so closely guarded.

When he entered the scrub room and looked up at the camera mounted high in the corner, Al grinned with satisfaction. Its red light shone brightly in the dim lighting around it, indicating it was working, but he wasn't concerned that his image was being transmitted to the monitoring station. On his way back to the dairy, he had thought to check out the progress on the second floor of the equipment barn. Howard was still there, frustrated at his lack of progress in repairing the monitoring console.

Turning away from the camera, Al walked toward the main storage cabinet at the opposite end of the room. He opened the doors to the metal cabinet and began searching the labels on the bottles sitting on the shelves directly in front of him. Everything was neat and orderly, and it didn't take him long to look over the alphabetically arranged bottles before he found what he wanted: chloroform. There were two bottles of chloroform sitting on the shelf; Al grabbed the smaller of the two.

He then opened a nearby drawer and took out two packages of gauze pads and a couple of rolls of adhesive tape. Once he had everything he thought he might need, Al left the scrub room as quickly as he'd entered.

After retracing his route up the stairs, Al walked directly to the door leading into the room containing the incubators. He leaned forward cautiously, peeking in through the window. He saw the infant asleep in the incubator, and he could see the technician sitting in a chair in the far corner of the room, reading a book. So far, everything was falling into place for him.

He stepped back from the door, quietly tore open one of the gauze packages and poured a liberal amount of chloroform onto the pad. After setting the bottle on the floor, he cradled the pad in one large hand and slipped it behind his back. Using his free hand, Al reached for the knob, turned it and opened the door.

The technician looked up with a start. When she recognized him, a scowl came to her face. "What are you doing here?" she snapped rudely as she watched Al walk into the room. "You know you're not supposed to come in here. Now get out."

"I juthst wanted to thsee the baby," Al replied as he sidestepped closer to the incubator.

"Get away from there!" The technician was out of her seat in an instant. She stepped purposefully between Al and the incubator and turned to face him. "I told you to get out. There's no use in taking a chance that you'll contaminate her. Now get out of here before I call security."

The technician was now in a perfect position facing Al, and he took the opportunity to act. In one quick move, he pulled the chloroformed pad out from behind his back and placed it over her mouth and nose. At the same instant, he slipped his other arm around her waist and pulled her close to him, holding her securely. She struggled briefly, but within a matter of moments, the chloroform had taken effect, and she hung limply in his arms.

After easing her gently down to the floor, Al took one of the rolls of adhesive tape from his pocket and began taping her wrists together and then her ankles. Once she was secure, he removed the second gauze pad from his pocket, opened it and taped it securely over her mouth. Now that the technician was in a position where she would cause him no more trouble, Al turned his attention to the infant.

He looked down at the tiny form lying in the incubator beside him, and a tender smile crossed his face. Al had seen hundreds—thousands—of newborns during their brief stay in the unique nursery. Each time he had looked upon their sleeping faces, he'd wondered what their futures would hold in store for them. Would they grow up to be beautiful or handsome? Would they be intelligent? Would their parents love them? . . .

Al felt a special attachment for each newborn that passed through the nursery. He was their predecessor; his creation had led to theirs. The errors made with him had led to their perfection. Every time Al looked upon an infant, he wished it could have been different for him.

"Don't be frightened. I won't hurt you," he whispered. Gently, Al reached into the incubator and picked the tiny girl up in his powerful hands. He cradled her in his arms close to his chest and rocked her back and forth ever so carefully. "Don't be frightened. I'm going to take you thsomewhere where you'wa be thsafe."

Al shifted the little girl to cradle her securely in one arm. He then squatted beside the technician, slipped an arm around her waist and stood, lifting her up off the floor.

With the two of them safely in hand, he left the building, planning to take them into the woods. Once they were a safe distance away, Al would return to the building and complete the job he'd set out to do.

Alec had remained silent throughout their ride, but as they now sat at the dairy's security gate, waiting for it to open, he found the courage to ask, "Who's Al?"

Jordy's head turned with a jerk. The security lights on

either side of the gate illuminated the incredulous expression that totally encompassed his face. "How . . . how do you know about Al?" he asked when he finally found the words to speak.

Alec told him of the phone call Al had made to warn him of the danger he could be facing if he remained in Prairie Dells, then related the essence of the call he'd received that evening. After he described hearing the attack made on Al, he repeated his original question. "Who is Al?"

Jordy watched the gate open in front of him and proceeded through it before attempting to answer Alec's question. "Al's my," he hesitated, finding it difficult to put into words the fact he had known all of his adult life, "my brother . . . my *older* brother."

Jordy fell silent. Alec wanted him to continue, but he didn't. Alec waited patiently.

Experience had taught Alec that oftentimes questioning silence worked far better at persuading someone to continue talking than verbal encouragement. As it had worked in the past, it worked equally well now.

"Al is short for Alpha," Jordy finally continued. "In all reality *he* was the first." He paused, taking in a deep breath. "Al was the first survivor of Project GOD, not me.

"Remember I told you the first implantation made using my mother's ova and my father's sperm hadn't worked because the surrogate had been wrong?" He glanced at Alec, and Alec responded with a nod of his head. "Well, it really *did* work . . . in an unnatural sort of a way." Jordy returned his eyes to the road ahead of them.

"I guess all scientists are anxious to see their theories become reality, and they sometimes make mistakes when they act too soon. Schmidt was anxious . . . too anxious.

"Almost immediately after he viewed the conception take place under the microscope, he implanted the developing zygote into the prepared surrogate. What he hadn't taken into consideration—what he'd overlooked entirely—was the fact that some of my father's sperm were still alive in the solution containing the fertilized egg and that they had been inadvertently deposited into the surrogate's uterus as well.

"Apparently, my father's sperm fertilized one of the surrogate's own natural ova." He paused. "The whole idea goes against every law of nature, one species breeding with another, but with the presence of the antirejection formula overriding the surrogate's own natural forces to expel something that didn't belong, combined with the intensive hormone therapy she had been on in preparation for the implant, the laws of nature were broken . . . shattered." Jordy's voice broke with the last word.

Curiosity led Alec to ask the question he doubted Jordy would answer without encouragement. "What was the surrogate?"

"It came from the family Pongidae. Everyone presumed it would be the most logical choice because of its close association with Homo sapiens. Well, as my father has been noted for saying thousands of times, it was *too* close."

"Pongidae? Would you put that in layman's terms for me?"

"Al's natural mother—Al's *real* mother was . . . was a primate. Reka was a gorilla."

Marvin stopped at the first cross street on the edge of town. He glanced in both directions, then took his foot off the brake. His eyes were focused on the lighted phone booth at the opposite end of the block; it offered a landmark for him. Just around that corner was the café where he planned to stop for a cup of coffee.

As the truck coasted past the intersection, Marvin heard the muffled sound of a barking dog. He tried to ignore it, not giving it much thought; dogs were always barking for meaningless reasons in the middle of the night.

But the tormented sound didn't pass by Amble's ears unnoticed. The old dog lifted his head from Robbie's legs and pricked his ears in attention. In response to another muffled bark, a bark erupted from him as well.

"Amble, be quiet," Marvin said, laying a hand on the dog's bristled back.

But Marvin's touch did little to squelch the old dog's need

283

to reply. Amble barked again as he climbed over Robbie toward the window and barked again as he put his paws up on the door so he could see out.

"What's . . . what's going on?" Robbie asked sleepily as he rubbed his hands over his eyes. "Are we home yet?"

"Not yet. Something's got Amble all stirred up, and he seems to think he has to make as much noise as all the other dogs in town."

"What's the matter, fella?" Robbie asked as he sat up in the seat and rubbed the scruff of the dog's neck. Amble ignored Robbie's attention and continued to bark at the window. "Something interesting going on out there that's got your attention?"

Robbie looked out the side window as Marvin drove past a van parked by the curb. His attention was drawn to movement inside, and then, to his surprise, he thought he recognized the van . . . and the dog inside.

"Grandpa, stop!"

Marvin jammed his foot onto the brake, and they all jolted forward as the truck came to a sudden stop. "What is it?"

"Back there," Robbie said, pointing toward the van they'd just passed. "Isn't that Thumper?"

Marvin craned his neck to look out the truck's back window. It took a moment for his eyes to adjust, but then he too could see the dog inside the van. "It looks like it could be her. And that looks like it could be Alec and Krista's van. If it is, I wonder what it's doing parked out here at this time of night."

"It *is* Thumper," Robbie said with undeniable certainty. "And by the way she's barking, it sounds like something's wrong."

Marvin pulled the truck over to the curb in front of the van and parked. "You stay in here," he said as he reached into the glove compartment for a flashlight.

Reluctantly, Robbie obeyed his grandfather's request. He turned around on the seat and watched through the back window as Marvin approached the van and then directed his light in through the side windows. He wondered what was going on.

284

Satisfied that the van was empty except for the dog, Marvin reached for the handle on the driver's door and opened it. "What are you doing out here all by yourself?"

Once the door was open wide enough to offer an avenue of escape, Thumper bounded past Marvin and started running up the street toward the telephone booth. "Thumper! Come back here," Marvin called after her, but the dog didn't respond to his command; she didn't even slow down.

"Thumper," Robbie called as he stepped down from the truck onto the sidewalk. "Grandpa," he questioned, looking back at Marvin, "what's the matter?"

"I don't know."

"Thumper," Robbie called again, turning to watch the dog run away. "Thumper, come back."

But neither Marvin's nor Robbie's words slowed the dog in her run down the street. Thumper was determined. She was determined to go to the last place she'd seen her mistress and to find out where Krista had gone from there.

As Thumper approached the phone booth, her run slowed to a hurried trot and finally settled into a fast walk. When she neared the booth, she began sniffing the concrete around it, seeking Krista's scent. When she found it, she barked, then followed it along the walk into the booth itself.

Balancing on her hind legs, Thumper placed her paws on the narrow shelf beneath the phone and sniffed at the white straw purse sitting there. A mournful whine escaped her as she nosed the purse. Krista's scent was strong, but Krista was nowhere to be found.

"What have you got there, girl?" Marvin asked, reaching past Thumper to pick up the purse.

Aided by the streetlight over the booth, Marvin opened the purse and then the billfold inside. The first credit card he came to was imprinted with the name Krista Crispen.

"What is it, Grandpa?"

"It's Krista's purse," he answered in a puzzled tone.

"But where is she?"

"I don't know, Robbie."

"If she's like Mom, she wouldn't go off and just leave her purse sitting there."

"Not if she had a choice." Marvin stepped out on the sidewalk, then looked up and down the street in both directions. "Something doesn't seem right. Something doesn't seem right about any of this." He glanced down at Thumper, who looked up at him and whimpered. "Krista thinks too much of Thumper to just go off and leave her in the van like that, and you're right, too," he added, looking at Robbie. "I've never known of a woman who would just take off and leave her purse behind unless there was a good reason for it."

"Do you think something might have happened to her?"

"Anything's possible in this day and age." Marvin glanced quickly along the street one more time, then started walking back toward the truck. "Thumper, heel," he commanded, but the dog only looked at him. "Come on, Robbie. Thumper, heel," he said in a sterner voice as he patted the side of his thigh. Reluctantly, the dog obeyed, falling into step at Marvin's left side.

"What are you gonna do, Grandpa?"

"We're going to see Jake."

Twenty-Five

Al had taken the technician and infant girl as far as the trees on the opposite side of the silos. He figured they would be safe there until he finished with what he had to do inside the building and could return to take them to a more suitable place.

He now stood in the hall on the main floor. Except for the chemicals stored in the lab, he could think of nothing else on that floor which might serve his purpose. He considered taking them with him to the basement; they would add fuel to the fire he planned to start there, but then he wondered why he should take the time. Once the fire began to spread, the chemicals would serve the same purpose right where they were.

Al started to turn toward the steps, but something at the far end of the hall caught his eye. The cows—the suspended cows. He knew if they remained in the building, they would perish. Al couldn't bear to let that happen if he could help it. He knew he had to take the time to set them free.

He ran down the hall and into the implant holding room. Working quickly, he set the cow's hookup monitors on hold to prevent an alarm from sounding, then went from one cow to the next, removing the needles that served as direct links between their bloodstreams and the bottles hanging high above them. After all of the bottles were disconnected, Al ran to the end of the room and opened a large sliding door that led into a hallway. Hurrying across the hall, he opened a

287

second sliding door that gave access to a holding pen outside.

One more barrier still needed to be removed if the cows were going to be able to reach safety. Without even thinking of the precious moments he might be wasting, Al ran to the far corner of the holding pen and opened the sturdy metal gate separating the pen from the acres of rolling pasture beyond. The way was open for them now, if they only had the strength to make it.

Returning to the holding room, Al stopped in front of a wall panel containing six levers. All six levers were in an up position; he immediately pulled all six down.

The whir of electric motors filled the room. Al watched as six sets of pulleys, mounted in the ceiling above the cows, began to rotate and unroll the nylon ropes that had been wound on metal spools. Slowly, all six cows were lowered onto the floor.

The cows made little or no movement when their hooves touched. They were still heavily drugged; their knees buckled beneath them. The pulleys continued to lower the cows until they lay flat on the floor.

Again Al moved from one cow to the next, this time unbuckling the harnesses that had held them suspended in the air. When he finished unfastening the last harness, he returned to the door leading to the hallway. He paused and looked back at the cows that were lying all but motionless on the floor, staring at him through clouded eyes.

"I'm thsorry, but that'ths aw I can do for you. I don't have time to wait." As Al turned away from the cows, he glanced at the camera mounted above the doorway. Time was slipping away from him; the camera could come back on at any time.

Al ran back down the hall and hurried down the stairs. When he stepped out in the basement hall, he immediately saw a cow lying in one of the stalls and knew he had to try to get her out as well. He hoped this one would be easier to save. At least she wasn't drugged.

"Yo!" he shouted as he walked into the room. Startled, the cow worked to get to her feet and mooed fitfully in response to the sharp pain that came from the sutured wound on the lower side of her abdomen. "Thiths way," he said, trying to direct her toward the huge elevator in the corner of the room.

The cow wasn't the most cooperative animal Al had ever been around, but he finally managed to get her in the elevator. After securing the guard rails, he rode with her to the main floor and led her to the outside door he'd opened a few minutes before. Waving his arms and shouting after her, Al was sure she would find the open gate and make her way to the safety of the pasture.

As he turned back toward the hall, a gray metal door on the wall a few feet from him caught his attention. It was the door for the service entrance—the door covering all of the breaker switches controlling power to the project wing. Al smiled to himself as he reached for the door's ring and pulled.

He located the main breaker switch and pushed it to the off position. Immediately, all of the lights went out; the hum of the air-conditioner fans ceased; the incessant drone of the water pump came to an abrupt halt. All was dark and silent around him.

His vision unimpaired, Al turned from the service entrance and began walking down the hall. As he stepped onto the platform elevator in preparation for climbing down, a dim light appeared overhead. He looked up at the cone-shaped fixture mounted in the corner of the ceiling and knew that the backup generator had kicked into operation.

Al didn't care about the light; he could have functioned equally well without it, and he wasn't concerned that the generator had gone into operation. Its only connection was to the emergency lights mounted at widely spaced intervals on every floor. Nothing concerned him at the moment. With the main power source shut off, nothing of any importance to him would work. There would be no cameras; there would be no hookup monitors to override the ten-minute hold mode to send jumbled readings from the disconnected cows; there would be no alarms to give warning of the fire he planned to start.

Once back on the basement floor, Al went about the task

at hand. He raided the storage cabinets, throwing their contents into the stalls, purposefully breaking the bottles of chemicals so they would be soaked up by the straw and therefore provide a good source of fuel for the fire. He emptied the three operating rooms of their gaseous canisters and anything else he thought might burn or explode, adding them to the growing pile of combustible materials inside the stalls.

Still wanting more fuel to ensure an uncontrollable fire, he broke into the records room and began carrying out cardboard boxes. He scattered the files from one end of the room to the other and made sure there were plenty of papers piled around each of the canisters to ensure a high-intensity flame.

Flame . . . heat . . . *boom!* Then, it would all be gone. Everything he had hated from the day he had been old enough to understand—it would all be gone.

Hate . . . hate. Al remembered what he hated most of all—Project GOD. The source of his existence was the source of his hate. He was going to make sure that none of it survived.

After following the maze of shelving through the records room, Al stopped in front of the locked cabinet doors. He found enough room between one of the doors and the framing to wedge in his fingers and pull. Succumbing to the strength of his powerful hands and arms, the wood gave way and split along its grain.

Al picked up a preserving jar, looked at its contents momentarily, then threw it against the basement wall. The glass shattered on contact; formaldehyde splattered and ran down the wall and onto the floor. The long-since dead body of the creature the jar had contained fell to the floor, where it lay staring with unseeing eyes, looking up at the man who had finally freed it from its eternal prison.

Jar after jar was taken from the cabinet and thrown against the wall. When that cabinet was finally empty, Al proceeded on to the second one. Again he found access into the cabinet by way of a mismatched door, and again he threw its contents against the wall. When all but two jars had been destroyed, Al paused in his maddened frenzy.

He looked at the preserved, grotesquely deformed infants, and a pitiful sadness overcame him. They were his predecessors, and even though they had never known life, they had been the fortunate ones. They had never been tormented because of their deformities; they had never had to suffer unending emotional pain because they were different from the rest of the world around them; they had never looked into a mirror and seen a monstrous image reflected back at them.

Tears came to Al's dark eyes. Even though he loved life— loved the isolated world around him—he often wished he had never survived. He often wished the true God had put an end to Project GOD long before he was ever created. Then, none of this would be happening—then none of this would *have* to happen.

Shaking himself from his reverie, Al turned and walked away, leaving the two preserved infants to face their fate from the place on the shelf they had occupied for almost thirty years. Too much time had already slipped away from him, and he didn't want to waste any more.

Stopping at the door to the records room, Al pulled a book of matches from his pocket, lit one and then used it to ignite the rest. He watched it burn for several seconds, then threw it onto a scattered stack of files a few feet from him. It didn't take long for the old papers to burst into flames.

He hurried across the hall, and when he reached the door opening to the stalls, he pulled out another book of matches. Again lighting a single match and then the whole book, he made a sweeping glance around the disheveled room before tossing the burning matchbook toward a mound of straw. The straw ignited much more quickly than the papers had, and the flames multiplied tenfold when they came in contact with the chemicals. Al allowed himself the luxury of a brief smile of accomplishment.

With his first task completed, he turned and started toward the exit. He still had to take the technician and infant to a more reliable place of safety, and once he was finished with that, Al had to find a way to get Alec and Krista out of the estate . . . alive.

Marvin stood on Jake Rasdall's front porch, pounding his fist on the door. He hadn't hesitated in coming straight to Jake's home, and he wasn't about to turn away unsatisfied. Besides being Marvin's longtime friend and poker buddy, Jake was the sheriff of Dells County.

"Jake," Marvin called as he stepped down on the walk and looked up at the second-floor window. "Jake, get up."

A light came on behind the window's shade, and a few seconds later, someone drew the shade and opened the window. "What's going on down there?" a feminine voice asked.

"Roberta, it's me, Marvin Horton. I've got to talk to Jake."

"Marvin? Is that you?"

"Yes," he shouted, presuming Roberta wasn't wearing her hearing aid.

"What in God's name are you doing in town at this time of night?"

"I've got to talk to Jake."

"I can't make out much of what you're saying. I'll be down in a jiffy."

"Just send Jake down," he called to her, but Roberta was already gone from the window.

Marvin looked back at his truck and lifted a hand in an acknowledging wave. Robbie waved back at him through the open window, having had to reach around both dogs in order to do so.

Marvin wished Thumper could talk and tell him what she'd seen. Since he wasn't sure of the facts himself, he had a feeling it was going to be difficult to convince Jake that something shady had actually happened.

A light brightened opposite the ground-floor picture window; then an outside light came to life. By the time Marvin had returned to the porch, Roberta was opening the front door.

"What's the matter?" she asked, attempting to fit the

hearing aid inside her ear while at the same time pulling the belt tight to her lightweight robe.

"I need to talk to Jake," Marvin said, looking past Roberta into the house. "Where is he?"

"He's not here. He went down to Madison yesterday for some kind of sheriff's convention and won't be back 'til tomorrow."

"Damn," Marvin said, and then he looked at Roberta in apology for his language.

"What's the matter? Maybe there's something I can do to help."

"I doubt it. I need Jake . . . I need a cop. How come they're never around when you need them?"

"Did you stop by the station? Maybe somebody down there can do what you need done."

"I doubt it. They're all a bunch of pansy-wipes."

"Marvin," Roberta said, laying a hand on his arm. "Calm down. You're going to have a stroke letting yourself get all worked up like this."

"I can't calm down. Krista's missing and I've got to find her."

"Krista? Your neighbor at the lake you told us about?" Marvin nodded. "She's missing?" Roberta asked with a gasp.

"Yes, and . . ." Marvin's eyes widened as a thought came to his mind. "The Grahams." The name left his lips with a hiss.

"What?"

"The Grahams," he said more forcefully. "Besides me, they're the only other people around here Alec and Krista have talked to."

"So? If that's the case, it seems to me like the Grahams are just trying to be neighborly, what with all of you being out there at the lake the way you are."

"But they're *not* the neighborly type—not unless they want something. I told you and Jake how they treated me a few years back, wining and dining me, taking me to those high-priced restaurants down in Madison, trying to get me to sell them my land. But they were never *neighborly,* not

293

even way back.

"When all of us on our side of the lake would pitch in for a holiday cookout or just get together to swap fishing stories, Graham never joined us. Hell, he never even answered an invitation, so we just quit inviting him. Soon enough, it turned out to be him against us, and now, it's him against just Krista and me." He looked directly into Roberta's eyes. "And I don't like it, the way he's all of a sudden shifted gears—if you want to call it being *neighborly*. He's scheming about something. I know he is." Marvin paused. "And I know Alec and Krista went over to his place last night." He thought for a moment. "Maybe Graham couldn't talk them into selling in a civilized manner, so now he's gone and done something heavy-handed. I sure as hell wouldn't put it past him."

"Marvin, you really don't think—"

"You don't know Graham, Roberta, not really. All you've ever seen of him is what he wants you to see, but I've seen the real man behind his fake front. He's the kind of man who'd stop at nothing to get what he wants."

"Marvin, you're—"

"To hell with it." Marvin turned and started off the porch.

"Where are you going?"

"Since Jake's not here to help me, *I'm* going over to Graham's to see what he's done with Krista and Alec."

"Marvin, don't fly off the handle and go and do something foolish."

"Don't do something foolish, huh," Marvin said to himself as he reached for the truck's door handle. "The only thing I'd be doing foolish is if I'd go over there without my shotgun. The only thing I'd be doing that was foolish is if I don't go over there and blast the hell out of them."

Jordy had driven slowly all the way back from the dairy. Sometimes, Alec thought it felt as if the electric cart was doing little more than coasting; he knew they could have made better time if they had walked.

He wondered what thoughts were going through Jordy's

mind. Was he as apprehensive about their upcoming meeting with Graham as Alec was? And if so, why?

Since Jordy had explained the mishap of Al's creation, neither had spoken another word. The disquieting silence hung over them all the way back to the house as if it were an omen of things to come. Now, as Jordy guided the cart into the small blacktop lot behind the house, Alec felt the need to hear a voice. Maybe a sound—any sound—would help relieve the wrenching tightness in his stomach that felt like a coil ready to snap.

"Al," he said in a surprisingly controlled voice, "I couldn't help but notice he has a speech impediment."

Alec didn't know why his thoughts had turned in that direction. With so many other things he could have questioned, why had he brought up something that seemed to be so insignificant? He didn't know. Maybe subconsciously, he was trying to focus on something that would take his mind off his own dilemma.

"I'm curious." Alec struggled to put together a sequence of words that seemed to make sense. "Is there a reason for it? Possibly a physical reason due to . . . due to the way he . . . he developed?"

"That's exactly the reason," Jordy answered as he brought the cart to a stop and turned it off. Instead of stepping out, he turned and looked at Alec, seeming to enjoy the time they spent talking together and wanting to extend it even more.

In truth, Jordy had taken a liking to his newfound brother. With no past sibling rivalry to stand between them, they had met on equal terms and had begun to solidify their relationship as adults. Since their first meeting, he had often wondered what it might have been like for them to have grown up together; he'd always wanted a true friend and a *real* brother. He wondered now if there might be a future for their relationship—he wondered if there was a future for Alec at all. That thought was unsettling to Jordy, and he had long ago vowed that if the situation materialized, he would try to convince his father to let Alec and Krista go.

"The human side of Al's genetic structure allows him the possibility of mastering speech, but the primate side is what

295

gives him his difficulty. It's totally physical. His vocal cords function properly—humanly—but the structure of his mouth, lips and tongue prevents him from being able to make the finite movements that would enable him to perfect the *l* and *s* sounds and any combinations containing those sounds. I'm truly surprised he pronounces some of the other letter sounds as well as he does, but I guess my mother can take most of the credit for that. She worked with him quite a lot before she died. After she was gone, Marian tried to help him the best she could." That was all Jordy could think to say in answer to Alec's question.

Jordy and Alec looked at each other for a few silent moments, and then, as if they could read each other's thoughts, they stepped from the cart in unison. The uneasiness of the impending confrontation with Graham hung over Jordy as much as it did Alec. If he thought he could get away with it, he would tell Alec to leave now and act as if he'd never been there, but Jordy knew his father would eventually find out. Donald was a good technician and cooperated in every way with Jordy, but like everyone else who had been hired to work in the company, Donald's loyalties were to Hubert Graham. Sooner or later he would tell of Alec's being in the project wing, and depending upon Graham's mood at the time, Jordy could become the target of his wrath. Jordy and Al shared more than just the genes of their father; they both shared a fear of him.

"Has anyone else ever found out about Project GOD?" Alec asked as he walked with Jordy toward the brick patio.

"None that have—" Jordy stopped his sentence short, and they walked on for several more yards before he finally said, "My father doesn't tell me everything."

When they came to the opening of the patio's low wall, both saw Jameson positioned outside the French doors. The chauffeur-bodyguard stood in a wide, defensive stance with his arms crossed over his chest; he made no attempt to hide the revolver in the holster beneath his left arm.

If Jordy had had plans to help Alec escape, he had waited too long to suggest them. If Alec had had plans of his own, his opportunity had long ago passed him by.

296

"Is my father in?" Jordy asked as he and Alec crossed the patio.

"He's waiting in the den."

"Waiting?"

Jameson didn't respond verbally. He stepped to one side, opened the door closest to him and nodded for the two of them to go inside.

Hearing the door open, Graham turned sharply toward it. His attention had been focused on Julia Ann's portrait, but now he glared directly at the two men standing in the doorway. He smiled confidently, and a twinkle of triumph glistened in his dark eyes.

"I see you found the other one," Graham said, glancing from Jordy to Alec.

"Other one?" Alec questioned with a start.

"Alec!"

From somewhere above his head, Alec heard Krista's terrified scream. He started across the den toward the door leading into the front hall, but Jordy grabbed his arm and motioned for him to remain where he was.

"I found your other *son,*" Jordy emphasized as he walked toward his father. He stopped in front of the fireplace and looked up at Julia Ann's portrait. "Mother would be happy to see all of us here together."

"Not if she knew the treachery he intended." The words spit from Graham's mouth like double-edged shards; the twinkle in his eyes darkened to a burning ember.

"Treachery?" Jordy questioned calmly. "What treachery is there in a man wanting to find the origin of his existence?" Jordy was entering into a game of words, as he and his father often did. He wondered which one of them would be the first to break—he wondered which one of them would win.

"The treachery is in the way he went about it, sneaking around like a thief in the night," Graham continued.

"And would you have told him if he'd asked openly?"

"He—"

"He did, you know, in a roundabout way. He sent a card asking about Schmidt. He was open in his question, but you weren't open with the answer."

297

A look of puzzlement—confusion—contorted Graham's face as he looked into Jordy's eyes; then that expression blackened into one of pure hatred. "You! You're siding with him! You're siding with an outsider who wants to destroy everything your mother and I worked for all of our lives. *You're* the traitor!"

Graham lifted his right hand quickly and brought it down forcefully across the side of Jordy's head. Jordy staggered from the impact and took a couple of steps backward, but he refused to fall.

Alec took a step forward, as if to intervene, but he heard a revolver cock and glanced back over his shoulder to see Jameson's .357 Magnum pointed directly toward him. He held up his hands, as if in surrender, and dared not move a muscle.

"No one's trying to betray you," Jordy said after regaining a stable stance. "No one's wanting to destroy the project."

"Liar!" Graham lunged toward Jordy, his hands reaching for his son's throat. Jordy sidestepped his father's advance, and as Graham turned to come at him again, an explosion sounded loudly in the distance.

"Mr. Graham!" Jameson shouted as he stepped out on the patio. "The dairy! Something's happened back at the dairy."

"No!" A look of impending doom shadowed Graham's face as he ran across the room and out onto the patio.

Alec turned to follow—to help if his assistance was needed—but Jordy grabbed his arm. "Go get Krista and get out of here. For God's sake, get out of here while you've got the chance." Jordy left Alec standing in the den as he took off running across the patio.

Twenty-Six

"Krista!" Alec shouted as he paused at the head of the grand staircase, looking down one direction of the second-floor hall and then the other. "Krista, where are you?"

"Alec!" He heard her call from the far end of the corridor to his left. "I'm in here. Here!"

"Where?" he shouted as he ran down the hall. "Where are you? Which room?"

"The end one. Hurry!" Krista beat on the door with her fists, providing Alec with a sound to follow. "Please . . . hurry!" Her voice shook with fear.

"Are you all right?" he asked as he stopped opposite the door.

"Yes . . . yes. Just get me out of here. Get me out!"

Alec quickly surveyed the barrier standing between them. "Give me a minute." He reached into his pocket and pulled out one of the thin pieces of plastic he still carried with him. He slipped it into the narrow slit between the door and the casing and tried to jiggle the lock open, but it wouldn't budge.

"That won't work," a voice said hesitantly. "It'ths a dead-bowt wock."

Alec's heart skipped a beat or two; then he turned toward the voice. He stared uncertainly at the figure across the hall from him. Even in the dim lighting, Alec could make out the features of the man standing there.

He stood close to six feet tall; his arms hung low, his

299

fingers nearly reaching down to his knees. The portions of his body not hidden by his shirt and slacks were covered by a heavy growth of coarse and dark hair; the hair continued up his neck to meet his hairline and spread across his face in a heavy, though neatly trimmed, beard. The color of his skin was a mottled combination of distinct light and dark patches and was marred even further by an abundant dotting of black moles. His forehead angled back toward his hairline and was bordered by heavy brows emphasizing the protruding bone structure above his dark, deep-set eyes. His nose was broad and flat, and his thick lips pulled back from squared teeth in a tentative smile.

Alec knew immediately who the man must be, but his greeting still crossed his lips as a question. "Al?"

The man nodded. He hesitated, then stepped out into the middle of the hall, motioning with a large hair-covered hand for Alec to step aside. "Thstand back."

"Krista," Alec called, seeing what Al intended to do, "move back away from the door." He waited for a moment, then asked, "Are you clear?"

"Yes." Upon hearing Krista's reply, Alec looked at Al and nodded.

Turning his back to the door, Al braced his arms against the opposite wall, then kicked backward with both feet. The creak of straining wood fibers answered the forceful hit, but the solid-core door remained standing. Al kicked again . . . and again. Each time his boots came in contact with the door, the straining wood fibers gave a little more. With the fourth kick, the door flew open, the dead-bolt lock ripped free of the casing's splintered wood.

"Alec!" Krista cried out as she ran from the room. Her exit was so hurried and uncontrolled that she ran directly into Al as he was working to regain his footing. To keep them both from falling, he grabbed her protectively in his arms.

Krista looked up into Al's discolored, deformed face, and a scream of sheer terror tore free from her lips. Not knowing who he was or that he had come to help them, she fought to get away from him, swinging her fists in random roundhouse punches while shouting for Alec to come to her rescue.

300

Al released her immediately, the shock of her reaction to him nullifying the blows of her fists connecting with his chest and head. Tears came to his eyes as he shrank away from her.

All of his life, he'd known he was different; all of his life, he'd known he was what most people would call ugly. But this was the first time he had ever come *face-to-face* with someone who hadn't been prepared for his appearance. This was the first indication from the outside of how really ugly he must actually be. Al lifted his massive hands to cover his face and turned away.

"Krista." Alec grabbed her and pulled her close to him. She buried her face against his chest and cried. "Krista," he said a few moments later after the intensity of her sobs subsided. "Krista, this is Al, the man I talked with over the phone. He's come to help us."

Krista lifted her head slowly from Alec's chest and looked up into his eyes. He brushed the hair back from her face, smiled at her with understanding, then nodded toward the opposite side of the hall.

Krista took in a deep breath and released it, then turned toward Al, who still stood with his back to her, his hands still covering his face. "I'm . . . I'm so sorry. I didn't know—"

"Come with me." Never looking back in their direction—not giving Krista another chance to see his face—Al motioned for them to follow him as he started toward the back staircase.

Alec traded glances with Krista, nodded and took her hand in his. Together, they followed Al, putting their trust in a man they barely knew.

The steps of the back stairwell were short and narrow, lacking the room and luxury provided by the grand staircase in the main hall. The stairwell's original intent was to provide an unseen access to the second floor for the servants. More recently it had been used as Al's private entranceway to the second floor.

When they reached the lower landing, Al motioned for them to wait while he checked the hall beside the kitchen. Seeing no one, he again motioned for them to follow as he crossed the landing toward a narrow door in the opposite wall.

"Watch your thstep," Al whispered over his shoulder, careful not to turn his head too far so Krista could see his face. "No wighths."

Krista held tightly to a handrail beside her as she followed Al down the unkempt stairs into the basement. Alec followed behind her, and once he'd cleared the door, closed it behind them.

When they reached the basement floor, Al stopped. It was a courtesy on their behalf. Al's eyes could function even in midnight darkness, but he knew their eyes—their *human* eyes—presented a handicap for them. He hoped their vision would adjust quickly to the nearly nonexistent light in the windowless basement and that they could continue on without too many delays. He didn't know how long his diversion would last; he didn't know how soon Graham might return to the house to look for them.

"Where are we going?" Alec asked in a low whisper.

"To the primate houthse."

"Through the basement?" Krista questioned.

"Through the tunnew."

"What tunnel?"

"The one no one uthseths any more."

Al looked around the dark basement, seeing the books and boxes and a host of other abandoned items someone had placed down there years before and had then forgotten even existed. No one used the basement any more, and except for Al, no one ever came down there. Like his various other rooms around the estate, the basement was Al's domain.

Several years ago, he'd straightened up one corner of the basement, found Julia Ann's old rocking chair and placed it there. He'd located an old wooden crate and set it beside the chair; on top of that crate he'd arranged a few of his old toys and several pictures of Julia Ann. Al had spent countless hours sitting in that corner—his own little corner of the world. He'd come there often; he'd come there whenever he wanted to remember the good times . . . the good times with Julia Ann.

Al knew Alec and Krista couldn't see the things around

302

them that were dear to him, but he really didn't care. What concerned him now was that their eyes would adjust well enough for them to be able to follow him safely.

"Can you thsee?"

"I can see a little," Alec answered tentatively, holding a hand up in front of his face and seeing its outline only vaguely.

"Me too . . . a little," Krista added.

"Come thiths way." Alec and Krista followed Al across the basement to a tall stack of boxes, then followed him around them. "The ceiwing'ths wow. Watch your head."

Krista took a few steps to follow Al into the tunnel and immediately bumped into the wall. "I can't see a thing."

"Give me your hand."

Unable to see, Krista extended her hand forward and moved it awkwardly from side to side, trying to locate Al. She came nowhere near him.

Hesitantly, Al reached for her hand; he grasped it loosely. Only after Krista squeezed his hand in a silent communication of trust did Al begin to feel slightly comfortable in her presence. Slowly, he began leading them through the tunnel.

"What was the tunnel used for?" Alec asked, out of both curiosity and a need to fill the silence around them.

"It weadths to the primate houthse. It waths eathsy accethss to the animaws untiw they buiwt the . . . the dairy."

"Why would anyone go to all the trouble to build a tunnel just to be able to get to the animals?" Krista questioned in ignorance of the prime purpose of the dairy—and the original purpose of the primate house.

Al hesitated and thought for a few moments before answering. "Juwia Ann woved her animaws. They were more to her than juthst peths." He didn't offer any more of an explanation; he presumed Alec would inform Krista of everything he'd learned concerning Project GOD whenever the opportunity presented itself. "We're awmothst there."

All along the shaft, Al continued to caution them of the tunnel's low ceiling. When they finally emerged into the basement of the primate house, Alec and Krista were relieved to be able to stand erect again.

The lighting there was a little brighter than it had been in the basement of the house. Still, neither of them could make out any details of the vaguely outlined images around them.

Al led them across the basement to a staircase in the far corner. "Be carefuw on the thstairths. They're owd," he warned as he cautiously led the way ahead of them.

Once they were on the main floor of the primate house, the exit signs at either end of the corridor provided enough light for Alec and Krista to see somewhat clearly. Sensing this, Al again made a point to keep his back turned toward Krista; he still didn't feel *that* comfortable in her presence.

"Where to now?" Alec asked, looking around the interior at the barred, room-size cages that had at one time been filled with a variety of primates.

But Al didn't answer him. Al had disappeared.

"Al?" Alec called softly. "Al, where did you go?"

Alec took a few steps down the hall and stopped in front of an open door. He looked inside the room and saw Al and the technician he'd seen in the dairy's nursery. The technician was lying on a mound of straw, her hands and feet secured with tape and a gag taped over her mouth. Alec continued to watch in silence as Al knelt beside the technician and carefully lifted a pink-blanketed bundle off the straw.

Al stood, turned and walked back toward the door, cradling the bundle tenderly in his powerful arms. He stopped in front of Alec and extended the bundle toward him.

"You were with her when thshe waths born. Thshe bewongths to you." Hesitantly, Alec accepted the bundle into his arm.

"What belongs to you?" Krista asked as she stepped up beside Alec. To avoid Krista's gaze, Al sidestepped around her and walked out into the hall. "What is it?" she questioned as she lifted her hand to touch the pink blanket.

Alec turned toward her and carefully lifted the blanket's corner that had been draped over the infant's head. "Where did she come from?" Krista gasped.

"I'll explain it all later."

"Hurry," Al called to them from where he stood beside the

exit door.

"Where are we going?" Alec asked as he re-covered the infant's head and started walking toward Al.

'We're going to Marian'ths. Thshe'w hewp uths."

A second thunderous rumble echoed across the sky, but the night was clear, and there was no hint of an approaching storm. The ominous sound had come from behind the dairy; it had come from the direction of the red-orange glow that shimmered brightly beyond the milking barn's roofline.

Jameson stopped the car just short of the gravel drive, parking in front of the dairy's offices opposite the equipment barn's large roller-track doors. At almost the same instant the wheels stopped turning, Graham and Jordy exited and continued on toward the burning building on foot.

As they rounded the corner of the offices, they saw, for the first time, the total effects of the fire. Through a hole in the project wing's roof, yellow-orange flames burst skyward like volcanic lava being forced from the bowels of the earth; dark smoke rolled from broken windows like dirty clouds; particles of burning debris rose as sparks on a wave of heated air then fell to the ground as telltale ash.

"Stay here," Jordy said to his father when they reached the corner of the equipment barn.

"I've got to go after the—"

"I said stay here," Jordy countered forcefully, grabbing his father's arm. "There's nothing you can do now, and you'll only get in the way." Jordy glanced at Jameson, who was walking toward them. "Don't let him go near the project wing." Jameson nodded in agreement with Jordy's orders.

Jordy left Graham and Jameson and ran to join Howard and Mike Sellers. They were standing beneath the water tower, working to attach a heavy hose, which they'd taken from the shed, to the faucet connected to a pump line running from the tower.

"Go for it," Jordy called as he picked up the nozzle end of the three-inch hose. He displayed a thumbs-up sign as an additional indication that he was ready for them to turn on

305

the water, then began walking toward the building, approaching as closely as the heat would allow.

Mike nodded, twisted the head of the hose one last time to insure that the threads were set as tightly as he could get them, then reached for the pump lever and pulled it steadily toward him. As the water began to shoot out of the faucet under the pump's pressure, the hose that had been lying flat on the ground fattened to the diameter of a man's wrist. A spray of water shot from the hose's nozzle with such force that Jordy had to hold it firmly with both hands to control its direction. He aimed the powerful stream of water toward the hole in the roof.

"I'll do that," Mike said as he stepped up beside Jordy and placed his hands firmly on the nozzle.

"Did everybody get out?" Jordy asked with concern. Mike shrugged his shoulders, unable to provide an answer. "What about Janet and the unit?" he asked, referring to the technician and the infant. Again, Mike shrugged his shoulders, he had no answer. "What do you mean you don't know? Didn't you see her on the monitors? Couldn't you tell if she was able to make it out or not?"

"The monitors weren't working."

"Weren't working?"

"That's why Howard's down here. He was trying to fix them."

"What happened? Why weren't they working?" Then he added, "Weren't the fire alarms working either?"

"Evidently not," Mike answered, shaking his head. "Al spilled my cup of coffee on the console, and somehow, the whole system must have shorted out."

"Al?"

Mike nodded.

"Al . . ." Jordy said to himself as he focused his attention back on the fire.

If Al *was* responsible for the fire, then Jordy knew why the alarms hadn't worked; he also knew that Janet and the infant were safe somewhere. And *if* Al was responsible for the fire, Jordy knew why Al had done it.

306

A thin smile of understanding pulled at the corners of Jordy's lips. He, too, hoped Alec and Krista had been able to escape.

"What do you want us to do, Mr. Graham?"

Hubert Graham didn't hear the questions of his employees who had come to help fight the fire. He stood at the corner of the equipment barn in numb silence, staring at the fire that was destroying everything he had worked for throughout most of his adult life . . . and now, it was gone . . . gone. He wondered how he was going to tell Julia Ann.

Alec and Krista sat on the sofa in Marian's living room. Krista held the infant girl on her lap, looking at her in awe and cooing occasionally, trying to make her smile. Alec sat close beside her, engrossed as much as Krista by the infant's limited activity.

Al stood beside the front door, his back to the heart of the room, talking with Marian. From the moment she had taken them into her home, Marian had been trying to help Al plan the safest way to get Alec and Krista away from the estate.

"I'w caw when it'ths thsafe for them to weave."

"We'll be ready," Marian responded with a nod. "You be careful," she added, touching his arm lightly. Al nodded and started for the front door.

When Alec saw Al about to leave, he stood from the sofa and walked toward him. "Al," Alec called to gain his attention.

Al stopped, but he didn't turn back toward the room. He didn't want to turn so that Krista might see him.

"Al," Alec repeated as he walked to stand directly in front of Al. "Is there anything I can do?"

"No."

"You're sure?" Al nodded. "Well," Alec said somewhat awkwardly, "I guess all I can do then is thank you for all you've done for us."

Alec extended his hand. Al glanced down at it, then hesitantly extended his own hand to grasp Alec's in a firm shake.

Alec's eyes locked with Al's, and for a brief instant, he felt the kindred of brotherhood. "You be careful, and take care of yourself." Al nodded. "If you ever need anything . . ." The words became choked in his throat. Unable to think of anything else he'd rather do, Alec stretched his arms around Al and hugged him close. He whispered, "Take care . . . my brother." When Alec stepped back, tears were misting in both of their eyes.

"Al."

Krista had left her place on the sofa and was now walking toward Al. When he saw her approach, Al started to turn away, but Krista placed a gentle hand on his arm, urging him to remain where he stood.

"Al," Krista said in a soft voice as she stepped in front of him and looked up into his dark eyes, "thank you." Not hesitating in her actions, Krista rose to her tiptoes, leaned forward and kissed Al tenderly on the cheek. "Be careful."

Tears seeped from Al's eyes as he looked down at her. He'd not known such tenderness since Julia Ann had died. Hesitantly, he lifted a hand and gently touched her cheek. "Good-bye," he said in a soft voice. Al turned abruptly and hurried toward the front door.

Twenty-Seven

"Dan. Dan!"

Dan Myers looked up from the book he was reading when he heard his name being called. Almost immediately, a hard knocking resounded on the door of the front gate's guardhouse.

His eyes instantly sought out the monitor on the console in front of him that was linked to the camera focused on the guardhouse's only door. He saw an unmistakable image being relayed across the eighteen-inch screen.

Dan pressed a button on the lip of the console, activating his microphone and a small outside speaker. "What do you want?"

"Jordy thsent me to get you," Al answered breathlessly. "He needths everybody back at the dairy to hewp with the fire."

"What fire?"

"Didn't you hear the expwothsion?"

"What explosion?"

"The one at the dairy."

Perturbed he'd been interrupted during an exciting part in the book, Dan went to the door and opened it begrudgingly. "What in the hell are you talking about?"

"The fire," Al answered, stepping back and pointing in the direction of the dairy.

Dan took a few steps away from the guardhouse and looked northeast. Over the tops of the trees, he could see a

309

yellow, pulsating glow intruding into the night's dark sky. "Holy shit! What happened?"

"I don't know. Jordy juthst towd me to come get everybody to hewp put out the fire. Come on. We're wathsting time thstanding here."

Al turned and started running up the drive toward the house. After Dan closed the door to the guardhouse and locked it, he hurried to catch up with Al.

"You go on," Al said as they neared the walk leading to the front door. "I'w check the houthse." Dan looked at him for an instant, nodded and continued on, following the lane toward the dairy, alone.

Al stopped on the porch just outside the front door and looked along the house to make sure Dan had passed out of his line of sight. He waited a few moments, to make sure Dan wouldn't return, and then he began retracing his steps back to the guardhouse.

There was no need for Al to go into the main house. He knew no one remained inside; he'd checked when he'd stopped to pick up one of the spare keys to the guardhouse after he left Marian's.

He presumed most of the estate's employees would be at the fire by now. They would have gone out of their own curiosity and with a desire to help—not because Jordy had summoned them. Jordy hadn't summoned anyone, and Jordy hadn't sent Al for Dan.

Al had planned the deception on his own. With no one on duty at the guardhouse, he could open the front gate, and Alec and Krista would be able to go free.

"It's all so hard to believe," Krista said as she looked down at the infant girl who lay sleeping on her lap.

Alec had just finished telling her about watching the baby's delivery and had given her a sketchy synopsis of what he'd learned about Project GOD. He'd purposely avoided mentioning the Delta series, and he doubted if he would ever address the subject unless, sometime, Krista thought to ask. If she did, he wondered what his response might be; he wondered if he would ever tell her they were related by more than just marriage.

"You can believe every word," Marian assured her. "I know it all to be fact. I was keeping house for Miss Julia even before they started working on the project, and she had a lot of confidence in me," she added with a note of pride. "She told me a lot of things about what she wanted to do."

Alec and Krista sat quietly, giving Marian their undivided attention. The older woman seemed to enjoy her moment in the spotlight and continued with the story she had kept to herself for over thirty years.

"I felt sorry for Miss Julia when she found out she couldn't have children. It tore her apart awful bad for a long, long time.

"And then when they tried to adopt, they couldn't find any babies available. I think they were put on every adoption agency's list in the state of Wisconsin, but not one of them could promise them a baby without having to wait for a couple of years. That hurt Miss Julia almost as bad as when she found out she couldn't have any babies of her own."

"I know how she must have felt," Krista interjected sympathetically.

Marian smiled and nodded before continuing. "To keep her mind off her own problems, Miss Julia poured her heart and soul into her work. Then one day when she was showing me three brand new tiger cubs she was so proud of, she asked me what I thought about surrogate motherhood.

"Well, back in the fifties, I sure didn't have no idea what a surrogate mother was, but Miss Julia explained an idea she had to me, and for the life of me, I didn't know why it wouldn't work. But being that I'm no scientist, I don't know why a lot of things might not work.

"Then she asked me that if she was able to accomplish what she was thinking of, would I think it would be morally right. Well, I did have to do some thinking on that one, being I'm a God-fearing woman and all. But you know, the more I thought about it the more I thought it *would* be all right. And I thought if God would give her the skill to do it, then He must think it would be all right, too.

"The procedures Miss Julia and Mr. Graham's friend developed sure have made a lot of people happy over the years. Why, just look at yourselves there with that brand new baby girl of yours." Marian cocked her head to one side so she could see the infant's sleeping face from her chair opposite the sofa. "God wouldn't have let *her* happen if He hadn't thought it was right."

"But what about Al—" Krista's hesitant question was cut short by the phone.

Marian scurried from her chair as quickly as her age would let her and was able to answer the phone before the second ring. Alec and Krista watched her intently, unable to hear the few brief words she spoke into the mouthpiece. After a very short conversation, Marian replaced the receiver, looked at them and smiled.

"Al's taken care of everything," she said as she reached into a basket on the table beside the phone and picked up a set of keys. "He says it's safe for you to leave now, but you've got to hurry." As she walked toward Alec and Krista, they stood. "Here," Marian said, extending the keys toward Alec. "It's an old fifty-nine stick-shift Chevy, but it runs real good and it's got a full tank of gas."

"Aren't you coming with us?" Krista asked.

"My word, no. Lewis is due home at any time now, but I imagine he'll be delayed because of the fire. Anyway, if he were to come home and me not be here, he'd raise a real ruckus trying to find me. No, for your sake, it's best I stay here. Besides, God's used to receiving my prayers from this location, and I don't want to mess Him up by sending them from somewhere else, especially when I have three new souls to add to my list." Marian placed her hand on Alec's arm and turned him toward the door. "Now get on with you. You're wasting time standing here."

Alec and Krista exchanged quick hugs with Marian, then hurried from the house toward the unattached garage. Marian watched as Alec backed the car out, stopped to pick up Krista, then turn onto the drive that would take them to the front gate. When they disappeared from her view, she closed the door and turned to lean against it.

"Dear God, look after them and keep them safe."

*   *   *

312

"Where do you want me, Mr. Graham?" Jordy turned to see Dan Myers standing beside him, his face flushed and his breath coming in short gasps. "I got here as fast as I could. What do you want me to do?"

"There isn't much anybody can do now but watch it burn," Jordy answered, looking back at the fire and shaking his head.

"Then why did you send for me?" Dan asked curtly.

"Send for you?"

"Al told me you told him to tell everybody to come out here to help put out the fire."

"Al?" Jordy looked at Dan, and then his eyes drifted off toward the house. He sensed the motive behind Al's actions, and unconsciously, he nodded in approval.

"Well, do you need me here or not?" Dan asked, his voice still sharp.

"Ah, we could have used you earlier," Jordy answered, carrying on with the deception Al had evidently started. "But I'm afraid everything got away from us. I think we'll be lucky if we can keep it from spreading to the rest of the buildings."

"Then if you don't need me here, I'll get back to my post."

"Dan," Jordy said, trying to delay Dan's departure to assure Al all the time he needed, "since it appears you ran all of the way down here, why don't you sit and rest a spell."

"I should get back to my post."

"Everything was locked up when you left, wasn't it?"

"Of course," Dan retorted, defending his efficiency in doing his job.

"Then what's there to worry about? Nobody's going to be able to get in or out."

Alec had taken the precaution not to turn on the car's headlights, which might have attracted undue attention, but the lack of extra lighting hadn't hampered their progress. The outdoor lights along the drive provided ample illumination for their escape.

As he drove past the front of the house, Krista turned in her seat to look out the side window. She watched the house as they drove past it. All of the grandeur she had imagined to

313

be associated with the house had indeed been there, but that grandeur was now tarnished in her mind by everything else she had learned.

But were the secrets held within those walls—held within the boundaries of the entire Graham estate—so totally wrong and unforgivable? Hadn't Marian been correct in her evaluation of Project GOD? Didn't it provide a special happiness in the lives of everyone it had touched?

She looked down at the infant cradled in her arms and wondered what course Alec would take once they were safely away from Prairie Dells. Did he have a right to expose Project GOD? Did he have the right to shatter the hopes and dreams of childless couples across the country who were waiting . . . waiting for that special child who would fill an emptiness in their lives?

What harm would there be if Project GOD continued—

"There's Al," Alec said, pointing toward a tall, dark figure standing beside the guardhouse. He slowed the car, and Krista rolled down the window. Alec leaned across the seat, looked at Al for a brief silent moment, then spoke the only words that would come to his mind. "Thank you. Thank you for everything you've done to help us."

Al nodded and smiled. "The gate'ths open. Godthspeed."

Krista reached through the open window and placed her hand gently on Al's arm. "God go with you, Al. You're one of His most loved creations."

Al stood motionless for a moment; then he placed his hand on top of Krista's and squeezed it tenderly. He looked at her directly and smiled, tears of joy pooling in his eyes.

"Go on now," he said as he stepped back from the car. "I don't know how wong the fire'w keep everyone occupied. You need to get away whiwe you can. Go on. Get out of here."

"Good-bye, Al, and thank you for everything."

Alec returned his foot to the gas pedal, and the car moved slowly on.

Al visually followed the car's outline until it passed beyond the trees; then he returned to the guardhouse to watch the monitor focused on the front gate. After he saw the car pass through, he pushed down on the lever controlling the electronic mechanism, and the gate began to close. They were gone . . . they were free.

Al continued to watch the monitor even after the gate was fully closed. The vertical steel shafts reminded him of bars on a cage—bars he would have to live behind forever. Forever. What would *forever* hold in store for him now? Forever . . .

Jordy stood beneath the water tower, wet and tired and wondering just how long the fire would continue to burn. His eyes took in the still-bustling activity around him, and he tried to make a mental evaluation of the damage that had been done.

The milking barn was salvageable. Its siding was scorched and blistered, but the fire wall that had been built between it and the project wing had helped to keep the fire contained at its source. The concrete wall at the back of the offices and processing wing was black, but it too could be repaired with a face-lift by a sandblaster and a fresh coat of paint. The only section that couldn't be saved was the project wing itself.

That fact hit Jordy with both despair and relief. Months would pass before they could rebuild and then resume production. And then there were the records . . . All of the records were gone. But along with the records, all of the preserving jars had been destroyed as well. *That* was the element of the tragedy that gave Jordy a hint of relief. He would never have to look at his predecessors again.

"Considering the possibilities, it looks like we came off lucky." Donald had walked up beside Jordy and stopped next to him to watch the fire.

"I guess so," Jordy answered in passing.

"What are we going to do about the units that are due in the next few weeks?"

"We can make some adjustments at the research building and deliver them there . . . or we can go back to the primate house." He paused. "That's where it all started, you know. That's where it all started . . . with my mother."

"How long do you think it'll be before we can start implanting again?" Donald asked, ignoring Jordy's momentary state of melancholy.

"That particular phase of the project hasn't even crossed my mind," Jordy finally answered, returning his thoughts to the matters at hand. He glanced at the people around him. "Have you seen my father?"

"Jameson drove him back up to the house a few minutes ago. He didn't look very good."

"I can understand that." Jordy looked at the burning project wing one last time, then turned toward the gravel drive. "If anybody wants me, I'll be up at the house. I need to go make sure my father's all right."

"I've got my car parked out front by the loading docks. Do you want me to drive you back to the house?"

"No, thanks. I think I could use a solitary walk right about now."

Jameson pulled the car to a stop at the patio's entrance, and Graham got out. "I'll go put the car up, Mr. Graham, and come back to see if you need anything."

Graham nodded half-knowingly as he walked across the patio. He'd just seen the sum of his life's work go up in flames, and now, he wanted to do nothing more than talk to Julia Ann. How was he going to tell her about what had happened?

As he opened the French doors, Graham's eyes were immediately drawn to the portrait above the fireplace. The brass fixture attached to the top of the hand-tooled frame was the only light on in the room; its muted brightness drew him to it like a deprived sapling in search of the sun.

Tears clouded his eyes as he approached the picture, and they ran down across his round cheeks when he stopped and looked up at Julia Ann's smiling face. "It's gone," he said with a break in his voice. "Everything we worked for is gone. It's gone . . . it's gone." That's all he could bear to say.

Graham turned away from the portrait and walked to a chair in the far corner of the room. He slumped down on the plush cushions and looked again toward Julia Ann. One thought kept repeating itself over and over again in his mind. *It's gone.*

Twenty-Eight

"What are you gonna do, Grandpa?" Marvin hadn't said a word since leaving Sheriff Rasdall's house, but the intense expression on his face told Robbie that something of grave importance was on his grandfather's mind. "Grandpa?"

"Not now," Marvin replied curtly; then he immediately regretted his nasty tone. "I'm sorry, Robbie. I didn't mean to yell at you." He glanced at his grandson, who had hung his head in response to Marvin's harsh words and was now lacing his fingers through Amble's wavy fur. "Robbie, I'm sorry."

Robbie looked at Marvin and smiled tentatively. "That's okay. Dad says I'm always sticking my nose in where it doesn't belong, anyway."

"How's a fella ever going to learn anything if he doesn't ask questions?" Marvin said.

Knowing his grandfather was trying to make amends, Robbie's smile broadened. "Then are you gonna tell me what you're planning to do?"

Marvin chuckled at the boy's persistence, then thought it best to tell him of his plan. "I'm going to drop you and the dogs off at the Widow Blessing's up the road here a ways—"

"At this time of night? Won't she be in bed asleep?"

"I doubt it; she's a night owl of sorts. But even if she is in bed, I'd bet she'd do me the favor."

"How can you be so sure?"

Marvin cleared his throat, and if the lighting of the truck's

317

interior had been any brighter, Robbie could have seen his grandfather's face flush. "The . . . the Widow Blessing has a hankering for me—"

"You've got a girlfriend!" Robbie laughed with excitement, then started bouncing up and down on the seat, chanting, "Grandpa's got a girlfriend . . . Grandpa's got a girlfriend—"

"Robert," Marvin said rather brusquely in his embarrassment, "if you want me to tell you what I'm going to do after I drop you off, you need to settle down and listen."

Robbie stopped bouncing immediately and turned in the seat toward his grandfather. "Okay," he said with a giggle, "after you drop me off at the Widow Blessing's," he giggled again, "what are you gonna do then, Grandpa?"

"I'm going to go over to the Grahams' and see if they know where Alec and Krista might be."

"Are you gonna take your shotgun like you said at the sheriff's house? Are you gonna go blast the hell out of them?"

"I might. If that's what it takes, I just might do exactly that."

Alec guided the car through a series of easy turns as the road wound up the gently sloping hills, leading them away from the lake and dairy nestled in the valley below. The night was clear; the moon was almost full. The velvety sky looked as if it had been scattered with a thousand sparkling diamonds. Except for the hum of the car's well-tuned engine, silence surrounded them. Silence . . . awkward silence.

"She's been a good baby," Alec said, attempting to fill the void around them. "I would have thought with as much jostling as she's had tonight, she would have been crying by now."

"I think she already knows we love her," Krista responded as she carefully shifted the corner of the blanket away from the infant's face. "Most living things don't make too much of a fuss as long as they know they're loved."

"Loved or not, I bet she'll make a fuss when she gets hungry," Alec added in a light tone. "With all the reading

318

you've done on babies, do you remember what we're supposed to feed her?"

"Once we get past Prairie Dells, I think it would be a good idea to stop somewhere and pick up some bottles and formula."

"Do you know what kind of formula?"

"No, but I imagine we can find someone who can help us."

Krista continued to study the baby she held on her lap. After all the years of reading—after all the months of waiting—she was finally going to have the chance to be a mother. The thought sent a chill of excitement through her. She *was* a mother.

Even though she harbored ill feelings toward Hubert Graham, she knew he was the one who had given her the opportunity to become a mother. Deep in her heart, Krista wanted to thank him. Maybe when they were safely home, she would call him and express her gratitude for his persistence in developing Project GOD. Project GOD . . . Krista knew the fate of Project GOD rested in the palms of their hands.

"What are you going to do?" Krista asked, directing her attention to Alec.

"Do about what?"

"About . . . about Project GOD?"

"Ah, Project GOD," Alec said with a note of anticipation. He glanced at the birthmark on his hand and thought of everything he'd learned tonight. "It's going to be the best story I've ever done—"

"Story?" Krista stared at him briefly, then looked away, unconsciously focusing on the road ahead. She pondered the situation for several thoughtful moments before asking, "Do you have to?"

"Do I have to what?"

"Do you have to use it as a story?"

"Why not?" Alec asked even though he had a feeling he knew what she was going to say.

"If you broadcast it as a story—if you expose everything they've been doing all of these years—wouldn't the authorities make them stop? Wouldn't that be the end of

319

Project GOD?"

"I would imagine."

"But why should they have to stop? They're not hurting anyone; in fact, they've helped a lot of people. They've helped hundreds . . . maybe even thousands of people in the past, and they could help a lot more in the years to come." Krista paused to get a firm grip on her thoughts. "I'm not saying what they're doing is right, but I don't think it's *wrong* either." She reached a hand across the seat and touched Alec's arm lightly. "Think about it, Alec. If they have to close down Project GOD, can you even begin to imagine all of the unhappy, childless couples there'll be in the country who'll never have even the slightest hope of ever finding a baby to love? . . ."

Alec looked at Krista, then glanced at the infant she held on her lap. He knew she was right, and deep down in his heart, he knew he agreed with her, especially now—now that they were in a position to have the child they'd been wanting for over sixteen months.

Had they not been so closely involved with the situation, maybe Krista's defense of Project GOD wouldn't have touched him—wouldn't have prompted him to change his mind about using the information he'd obtained to score another point for himself in the world of journalism. But they *were* involved—

"And what about Al? If Project GOD is exposed, in all likelihood Jordy and Mr. Graham will be prosecuted and sent away to prison."

Al . . . Al . . .

"The whole farm will probably be closed down. Then, where would he go? That farm's the only place Al's ever known; it's the only place he's ever had to call home—"

"Oh, my God," Alec whispered in exasperation. "Where has my mind been?" He downshifted through the gears and let the car coast as he steered it toward the edge of the blacktop.

"What's the matter?" Krista asked with uncertainty. "Car trouble? Have we run out of gas?" she asked as she leaned closer to him to look at the gauges on the dash. Noting that the gas gauge registered almost full, Krista looked at Alec and emphasized her words sharply in hopes of prompting an immediate response. "Alec, what's wrong?"

"Al." Alec shifted into neutral and pulled on the emergency brake.

"What about Al?"

"I can't just go off and leave him . . . not after everything he's done for us."

Alec turned in the seat and looked out the rear window. In the distance, barely visible above the horizon, he could see a yellowish haze. Had he not known the exact direction in which to look, he probably would have missed it; anyone else traveling along the road at this hour of the night probably wouldn't have noticed it at all.

"I was so obsessed with making sure *we* got away from Graham, I completely forgot the reason behind why I went over to the estate in the first place." He looked at Krista, the lights on the dashboard barely reflecting her face enough for him to make out her features. "I have to go back."

Krista didn't respond verbally. She just stared at Alec, attempting to hold back the tears she felt pooling in her eyes. Her efforts failed; a glistening tear brimmed past her lashes and trickled down her cheek.

"I can't just go off and leave him," Alec said, trying to convince her of his need to return. "Graham already tried to kill him once tonight, and when he finds out Al helped us get away—"

"I know." Krista didn't attempt to fight the tears that skimmed across her cheeks. "I agree with you, we have to help him." She reached for Alec's hand and squeezed it. "Let's go back. Maybe we can find Jordy and—"

"You're not going with me."

"And just why not?"

Alec nodded toward the infant that lay sleeping on Krista's lap. "There's too much at stake now to risk both of us going back."

"But I won't—"

Alec lifted a hand and placed his fingertips lightly against her lips. "You're going to be my insurance policy. I want you to go on to Todd's, just like we planned."

"But—"

"The instant I see Jordy or Graham or Jameson or *anybody,* I'll tell them that if anything happens to me, you'll make sure their operation is exposed even before my body has a chance to get cold."

"Don't say it *that* way."

"Maybe that was the wrong choice of words at the moment, but don't worry about it. Once I tell Graham you and I will agree to keep his secret as long as nothing happens to Al or us, I'm sure he'll see things my way. He thinks too much of Project GOD to let anything happen to it." Alec glanced at his watch. "It'll take you three and a half to four hours to drive to Todd's. I'll call you then—"

"And if you don't call?" Krista asked in hesitation.

"If you haven't heard from me by dawn, then you'll know that . . . you'll know that Graham doesn't care about *anything* any more."

Out of the corner of her eye, Krista saw headlights brighten in the distance. "Someone's coming."

Alec repositioned himself on the seat to face the road. As he focused on the headlights coming toward them, a shiver of apprehension traversed the length of his spine.

Had he been correct that morning in speculating Graham might have connections outside the estate? Had Graham already called in outside help—and was that help now bearing down on them at this very moment? . . .

Al didn't know how long he'd been standing there, staring at the front gate's monitor, but he knew he would be pushing his luck if he stayed any longer. He glanced around the small guardhouse quickly to make sure everything was as he had found it, then left the building and locked the door behind him.

Stopping in the middle of the drive, he looked north and saw the yellow-orange glow of the fire barely brightening the sky. He smiled with satisfaction as he thought about how well his plan had worked. He was happy—probably the

322

happiest he'd been since before Julia Ann had died.

He'd finally done something he felt had real meaning, and he wanted to share his happiness with Julia Ann. Walking with pride, his chin held high in the air, Al started toward the house.

"They're slowing down," Krista said nervously.

"Be ready. Hold on to her tight. If we have to get out of here in a hurry, it probably won't be the smoothest takeoff that's ever been made." Alec released the brake, positioned his feet on the clutch and accelerator and gripped the gearshift knob tightly with a sweaty hand. "I'm out of practice driving a stick shift; I only pray to God I don't kill it."

The truck slowed . . . then stopped with the driver's door opposite Alec's window. "You folks need any help?"

For an instant, Alec and Krista were both speechless. Then, as if cued, they spoke in unison: "Marvin?"

"Alec?" Marvin questioned in his own surprise. "Is that you?"

"Yes."

"And is that Krista with you?"

"Yes," Krista answered for herself. "We're both here."

"Are you two okay?"

"We're fine," Alec answered, relief cascading through him.

"What are you doing out here in that beat-up heap?" Marvin asked, eyeing the old car. "And what in God's name are you doing out here at this time of night in the first place? Robbie and I found Thumper in the van back in town—"

"It's a long story, but I don't have time to go into it now. Will you do me a favor?" Alec didn't wait for Marvin to answer. "Will you take Krista back into town to get the van?"

"I . . . I guess, but what—"

"She'll be with you in a minute." Alec returned his attention to Krista. "Go get the van and take Marvin and Robbie with you to Todd's."

"What am I going to tell them?"

323

"Tell them anything . . . anything but the truth. I won't be able to pull off a deal with Graham unless I can believe in the deal I'm offering."

"But what about . . . her?" Krista asked as she glanced down at the infant. "How am I going to explain her?"

"I don't know, but I have faith in you that you'll come up with something. Now hurry and get Marvin headed back toward town. Every minute we waste sitting here is one more minute I could be using to get back to help Al."

Krista looked at Alec, and tears once again began to swell in her eyes. "I want to talk you out of going back . . . and yet, I don't."

"I know. I don't want to go, but I know I have to. If I don't, I'll never be able to face myself again."

"Be careful."

"You know I will. I have a lot to be careful for." Alec leaned forward and kissed her tenderly on the lips. "I love you. I'll see you soon . . . both of you."

Al paused at the entrance of the patio's low wall to look north. A yellow-orange glow still shimmered above what was left of the project wing, but the flames had ceased to lap skyward like hungry tongues.

He guessed the fire wouldn't last much longer; the building hadn't contained all that much that would burn. It had been constructed of concrete and steel, painted, insulated and paneled with flame-retardant materials. The only things that could fuel the flames were the furniture, the bedding, the employees' personal property they had put in their small rooms, and the equipment that was related in one way or another to the function of the project.

Even though the excitement concerning the fire wouldn't last much longer, it really didn't matter. It had served its purpose; it had destroyed all evidence of Project GOD, and it had provided a diversion so that Alec and Krista could escape. That had been Al's plan, and it had worked without being hampered by any complications. He had come now to share the joy of his success with Julia Ann; he was too happy

324

to even think about Hubert Graham.

Al walked across the patio toward the house. As he approached the French doors, his eyes were drawn to the lighted portrait on the interior wall to his right. A smile brightened his dark face as he entered the room and walked straight toward the fireplace, never taking his eyes from Julia Ann's smiling face. Al felt good about what he had done; he felt good about himself; he felt good about life.

"The fire worked juthst wike we pwanned," he said softly, gazing up into eyes that seemed to sparkle with approval as they reflected the light's gentle rays. "They're gone." Al paused for a few moments as a shudder of happiness tingled through him. "I withsh I could have tawked with them more. They were nice peopwe. I think you would be proud of them." He paused again, his smile growing broader with each passing second. "I . . . I gave them thsomething to remember uths by. I gave them a baby. I thought you would have wanted it that way thsince they coudn't have one of their own . . . after aw, ithsn't that what Project GOD iths reawy aw about—making peopwe happy? And they were thso happy . . ."

Al's solitary conversation with Julia Ann fell on ears other than those covered by the light auburn hair in the portrait. Hubert Graham was still sitting in the chair in the far corner of the room, and he'd heard every word that had been spoken.

Now that he knew that Al was the one who had been responsible for the fire—and for setting Alec and Krista free—Graham's anger teetered on the brink of insanity. He rose slowly—secretively—from the chair and worked silently to remove one of the decorative African spears from the wall beside him.

Holding the spear firmly in his hands, he turned and began taking deliberate, calculated steps toward Al. He stalked as if he were one of the wild cats pictured on the walls around him, and each step Graham took carried him closer . . . and closer to Al.

Al, engrossed in his happiness, was oblivious to all else around him.

325

Twenty-Nine

The tires squealed against the blacktop as Alec rounded the last curve before the turnoff to the bridge. Since parting from Krista, he'd thrown caution aside, pushing the old Chevy for all it was worth. The car had handled beautifully, racing past the speedometer's limit on the straightaways and hugging the curves like an expensive Indy race car rounding the final corner in quest of the checkered flag.

Alec downshifted for the turnoff, but he didn't apply any pressure to the brake. The rear end of the Chevy fishtailed, barely missing the corner of the bridge. He fought for control, regaining it just in time to steer the car into a second turn at the opposite end of the bridge.

Again the rear end fishtailed, but this time the back tires lost their grip on the blacktop. The momentum from the turn carried the car sideways down the drive's sloping shoulder. Gravel pelted the undercarriage briefly; then the car bounced and tilted. Alec feared it was about to roll, but the old Chevy came to an upright stop as its tires slid and then sank into the soft mud at the lake's edge.

Shaken, Alec sat there for a moment, trying to collect his senses. He felt a trickle of warmth seep past the corner of his left eye. Lifting a hand to touch the side of his forehead, he flinched when his fingertips located a cut above the end of his eyebrow. His left shoulder and knee ached; he vaguely remembered being thrown against the door.

"You're all right," he reassured himself. "Let's get on with what you came back here to do."

Alec opened the door and stepped out into ankle-deep water. Using the car for support, he worked his way through the soft mud then climbed the rest of the way up the incline on his hands and knees. When he reached the blacktop drive, he turned toward the estate and began running as fast as his injured left leg would allow.

As he neared the trees, he thought of the gate blocking his way. He hoped someone would be back at the guardhouse by now, monitoring the gate's camera—and he hoped *that* someone would recognize him and let him in. In his current condition, Alec didn't relish the idea of having to climb over the gate.

". . . You thshoud have thseen the wook on Krithsta'ths face when I towd them the baby waths theirths to keep," Al said, his attention focused solely on Julia Ann's portrait. "It brought tearths to my eyeths—"

"You bastard traitor freak!" Graham shouted savagely as he lunged toward Al. "You're finally going to die!"

Taken totally by surprise, Al was only able to make a partial turn to defend himself. The sharp point of the spear entered his back just below his left shoulder blade and penetrated deeply into his left lung, barely missing his heart.

He cried out in agony as he continued to turn, instinctively raising an arm in self-defense. Balling his left hand into a fist, Al swung at Graham . . . and connected, sending him to the floor.

In spite of the pain that intensified with every move, Al was on top of Graham in an instant. "I won't take it any more!" he shouted, reaching for Graham's throat. The instant his hands found their target and held it in a firm grasp, his fingers began to squeeze.

Graham's eyes bulged with terror as he felt Al's muscular fingers tighten around his neck. He tried to roll away, to throw Al off of him, but Al's weight kept him pinned flat against the floor. He clawed at Al's hands with his own, but Al's animal strength didn't falter; he didn't release the pressure but continued to apply more.

In desperation, Graham balled his hands into fists and struck out at Al's head, but the extra length of Al's arms prevented him from making contact. Graham continued to struggle, but eventually, he started to weaken. The cartilage in his throat finally gave way to the pressure, and darkness began to close in around him.

Looking down at Graham's face—his eyelids fluttering, his eyeballs rolled upward in their sockets until only the whites were visible, his swollen tongue beginning to fill the cavity of his gaping mouth—Al suddenly released the pressure. "I . . . I can't," he said in a whisper. "No matter what you've done to me, I can't kiw you. You're my . . . father."

A gunshot pierced the silence following Al's words. The bullet struck Al just to the left of his spine, ripped through the bottom of his heart and exploded from his chest with a spray of blood and tissue.

Al cried out. His shrill scream was the scream of his jungle ancestors.

Ravaged with pain, he turned toward the fireplace and the portrait of Julia Ann. Looking up at her . . . reaching up for her, Al fell forward onto the floor.

"Mr. Graham!" Jameson shouted as he ran across the room. "Mr. Graham!" he called again as he knelt down on the floor.

Hubert Graham didn't respond. A few tiny bubbles of blood escaped the corner of his mouth with his last desperate breath.

No one had been monitoring the gate's camera to answer Alec's summons. Fighting the pain searing through his left knee and shoulder, he'd climbed the gate and was just cresting its top when he'd heard what he feared to be a gunshot. Swinging his legs over the top of the gate, he'd dangled for a moment then released his grip, taking too much of the drop's shock on his left leg. Now, he hobbled along the drive, making his way toward the house as quickly as his injuries allowed.

He feared he'd arrived too late to be of any help to Al. Alec's gut instinct continued to confirm his speculation, and for the first time in his life, he prayed his instinct was wrong.

"What's going on?" Jordy demanded as he ran in through the French doors. "I heard a gunshot."

"Al was attacking Mr. Graham," Jameson said in explanation. "I did the only thing I could to stop him, but," he looked down at Graham's body, "but I . . . I don't think I got here in time. I think he's dead."

Jordy glanced at his father, not surprised by his lack of feeling. He didn't feel any pain of loss. Then he looked at the blood-covered form lying on the floor in front of the fireplace, and his heart immediately felt heavy.

"Oh, Al . . ." Jordy said as he walked toward Al and knelt down beside him.

"Aren't you going to help your father?" Jameson asked, his voice revealing both his surprise and anger. "He's your father. He's the one who gave you life."

"He's also the one who made Al's and my lives a living hell." Jordy hadn't thought about his reply; the words had left his lips spontaneously.

"But he's your father, for God's sake."

"Yes . . . yes, that he was." To appease Jameson's persistence, Jordy felt along his father's neck in search of a pulse. When he found none, he looked at Jameson and shook his head. "You were right. He's dead. Would you call Dr. Ford and tell him?"

Jordy didn't hesitate any longer to return his attention to Al. Carefully, gently, he rolled Al over, lifting him slightly to support his head and shoulders.

Bright red blood oozed from Al's nostrils; a mass of crimson ran out the corner of his mouth and seeped down the side of his face. His chest rose and fell laboriously beneath his blood-drenched shirt as his only functioning lung strained to make a brief exchange of air.

"Can you hear me, Al?"

329

In response to Jordy's soft-spoken words, Al's eyelids fluttered briefly, and then for a moment, he was able to keep them open. "Jor . . . dy," he said in a forced whisper.

"I'm here, Al," Jordy answered, taking Al's hand into his own. "It's okay now, I'm here."

Al coughed weakly. A light spray of blood and saliva speckled the front of Jordy's shirt. "Keep . . . keep Awec and Krithsta . . . thsafe."

"I will, Al." Jordy fought against the tremble that came to his voice, but he couldn't control the tears crowding his eyes—tears he couldn't shed for his father. "I promise you, they'll always be safe."

A thin smile came to Al's lips. He squeezed Jordy's hand with the last ounce of strength to pass from his body . . . then, he was gone.

Alec followed the lane around the corner of the house. He'd been drawn there by the sound of the gunshot, and apparently, others on the estate had heard it as well; a small group was already gathering on the patio, clustering at the French doors.

As he approached the patio's wall, Alec heard his name called out. He turned to see Marian walking toward him from the opposite side of the drive.

"What are you doing here?" Marian asked with concern. "What happened?" she queried, after noticing the cut on his forehead. "Couldn't you get away? Where's Krista and—"

"It's all right," he said, laying a reassuring hand on Marian's arm. "Krista's gone. A friend of ours is driving out of town with her."

"Then why—"

"I came back for Al. I couldn't just go off and leave him here, knowing Graham would take our escape out on him. Do you know where he is?"

"No."

Alec looked toward the house and the group on the patio. "Do you know what's going on in there?"

"No, I heard something that sounded like a gunshot

330

and . . ." Marian looked fearfully into Alec's eyes. "You don't think . . ." Her words trailed off in a tremble.

"I don't know."

"Al," Marian said with a quick intake of air. "You don't think Mr. Graham—"

"Stay here."

Alec took a step toward the house, and Marian grabbed his arm. "You can't go in there. If Mr. Graham sees you, he might—"

"I'll be all right. Graham won't dare do anything to me once I tell him Krista's prepared to expose his whole operation if I don't call her by a certain time."

Alec hobbled across the patio, excused himself as he nudged his way through the group, and stopped just inside the French doors. The fixture above Julia Ann's portrait was still the only source of light in the room, but even through the dim illumination, he could see Jordy sitting in front of the fireplace. He also saw Graham . . . and Al.

"Jordy," Alec said as he approached him.

Jordy looked up; the trails from his tears glistened across his cheeks. "He's gone, Alec. Our . . . our brother's gone."

"I'm sorry," Alec said, placing a hand on Jordy's shoulder. "I came back to try to—"

"You!" Jameson's voice ripped through the room.

Alec turned with a start toward the hall door, the door Jameson had just entered. Alec stood as if frozen, watching Jameson draw his revolver from the holster beneath his arm.

"No!" Jordy shouted. He stood quickly and positioned himself between Alec and Jameson. "There won't be any more killing. No more! Too many people have already died because of my father, and now that he's gone, all of the killing is going to stop!"

"But *he's* the reason your father's dead," Jameson said, gesturing with the gun toward Alec.

"No. My father's to blame for his own death. Years ago, his greed overcame his compassion for life, and it finally caught up with him." Jordy stared directly into Jameson's dark eyes. "You should know that better than anyone. You were his right-hand man in that area. You were the one he

331

always turned to when he felt someone was about to . . . to *betray* him."

"I owed him whatever he asked of me," Jameson said as he let the weight of the revolver carry his arm down to his side. "He gave me back my life."

"Oh, no!" Marian had been hesitant to follow Alec through the crowd, but she'd finally found the courage to enter the room. Now, she stood at Al's feet, looking down at the man she'd helped raise from a boy.

"Marian, you shouldn't be here," Alec said as he stepped toward her and slipped an arm around her shoulders.

"Would you take her out of here?"

Alec looked at Jordy and nodded. "Is there anything else I can help you do?"

Jordy hesitated for a moment, then said, "After I've taken care of my father, I could use your help to bury Al." Alec nodded; he wouldn't have wanted it any other way.

After seeing that Marian was settled comfortably in the kitchen, Alec had called Todd to leave a message for Krista. He now stood at the kitchen window, watching as Graham's body was loaded into an ambulance.

Alec wondered how Jordy had explained his father's death to the coroner; he wondered how Jordy was going to get around having the incident investigated as a homicide. He also wondered how Jordy had explained Al. Alec's investigative mind had emerged to the forefront, and he was curious as to the answers for all of the things taking place around him.

"Dr. Ford knows about everything." Marian spoke up as if she'd been able to read the questions crossing Alec's mind.

"Dr. Ford?" Alec questioned, moving away from the window to join her at the small table in the kitchen's corner.

Marian nodded. "He's known about Al ever since Al was little, and he's been the main supplier of eggs and sperm for the project. Being he's the county coroner, he's had access to almost an endless supply of donors." She took in a deep breath and let it out slowly. "Over the years, he's done a lot of

332

other favors for Mr. Graham. He's helped cover up—" Marian stopped short in her sentence and stared at Alec, wondering if she was overstepping her bounds by confiding in him.

Noting the look of uncertainty in Marian's eyes, Alec attempted to calm her apprehensions of betrayal. "You know Jordy's already told me about Project GOD." Marian nodded. "Then knowing he trusts me with something as important as the project, won't you trust me enough to tell me about the . . . the coverups Dr. Ford did for Mr. Graham?" Alec paused. "Were the coverups for the killings Jordy mentioned a little while ago?" he prompted.

Marian shifted her eyes away from Alec to stare at the small bouquet of flowers she'd set on the table that afternoon. She'd placed them there to help brighten the table for Al's dinner, but he hadn't seen them; Al hadn't come to the house for supper, and he would never come to the house again.

She knew Hubert Graham had been the cause of Al's death, and in her own small way, she wanted to avenge Al's death; in her own small way, she wanted to get back at Hubert Graham. Marian decided to tell Alec everything she knew.

"Outsiders," she began, "people who didn't owe their lives to Mr. Graham or those not connected directly with the project who were paid outrageous sums for their loyalty, they . . . they just didn't seem to last too long around the estate. I know every big business must have their share of accidents, but . . . but I don't think they have near as many as we've had.

"Not too many of the accidents happened in relationship to the research complex. There were too many *legitimate* big bucks to be lost if there were some kind of misgivings connected with it. But the dairy and the workings of the farm associated with it—" Marian shook her head.

"And Jameson always seemed to be there when something happened to one of the new workers. We all had our suspicions about him, but none of us knew for sure.

"Then Dr. Ford would come in and file the death as an

333

accident. He couldn't afford to let the project be exposed any more than Mr. Graham."

"Can you remember how many accidents have happened over the years?"

"It'd be a guess, but I'd say somewhere between fifty and sixty."

"Fifty or sixty?" Alec questioned in amazement. "You mean that after fifty or sixty *accidental* deaths happened here on the estate, the authorities never came to investigate?"

"Some of the accidents were varied enough not to make them look suspicious." Marian looked away from Alec as if to hide her face in shame.

"And?" Alec prompted, knowing there was more. "You said *some* of the accidents. What about the others?"

"Some of the workers," she continued hesitantly, "the ones Mr. Graham researched and found to have no close friends or relatives . . . their deaths went by unreported. I doubt if Dr. Ford even knew about most of them."

"But what happened to—"

"To their bodies—to the evidence of the *accidents?*" Marian swallowed hard and glanced at Alec briefly. "The incinerator behind the dairy was used for more than just disposing of trash and old cows."

Alec sat in silence. He was numbed—paralyzed by the fact that alongside the secret project to create life had also been a plan to deliberately destroy life.

"Fresh sperm was much harder to come by than the eggs," Marian added as an explanation for the accidents, "and so were body parts."

"But I don't understand," Alec said, not hearing the last few words she'd added in a whisper. "I don't understand why someone on the estate didn't . . . wasn't bothered enough by their conscience to—"

"To turn Mr. Graham in to the police?" Marian turned in her seat to again look squarely at Alec. "You have to consider the fact that those of us who work for Mr. Graham have been bought . . . body and soul. Some of us owe our lives to him." She hesitated briefly before continuing. "Making babies wasn't the only thing he'd become good at. I

334

would have been dead over fifteen years ago if he hadn't seen to it that I got a new heart. And Lewis, well, he had emphysema so bad a few years back, he would have died too if Mr. Graham hadn't given him a new lung. There are others around the estate, the ones who worked closest with him like Jameson, they owe him their lives just like Lewis and me. Owing someone your life brings out the strongest sort of loyalty anyone can imagine . . . even if we didn't always agree with what he did."

She looked away from Alec to gaze upon the bouquet on the table. "If it hadn't been for Al, I'm ashamed to say that I doubt if I'd opened my door to help you tonight. And if Lewis would have been home instead of out playing poker over at Calvin Ream's cabin, I doubt if he would have let me, even with Al being with you. He didn't hold any special feelings for Al like I did."

Alec watched Marian attentively. He sensed by the expression on her face that she still had more to tell.

"But the bonds of loyalty can be broken. The presence of respect can be erased. The link between father and son can be shattered. I saw that happen a few years back."

"Did Mr. Graham do something to Jordy?"

"Not *to* him . . . well, I suppose you could say he did do something to him . . . indirectly.

"Her name was Gloria. She was going to be Jordy's wife, but she died six weeks before they were to be married. She died the day after he told her all about Project GOD."

Marian's face contorted with sadness. "When . . . when I told Lewis I'd overheard Jordy and Gloria arguing about the morality of the project, I . . . I never knew—I didn't know she'd be dead by the next afternoon."

"What happened?" Alec asked barely louder than a whisper.

"Jordy left that morning for a meeting in Madison. After lunch, Gloria asked if she could go riding. She told me she needed to think about everything Jordy had told her. She said she didn't know if she could live with the burden of keeping Project GOD a secret for the rest of her life.

"Jameson accompanied her to the stables and saddled

Prince Gallishean for her. He knew that was Mr. Graham's horse—he knew nobody else could handle him, but he did it anyway; he said Gloria asked him to." Marian released a heavy sigh. "Gloria took off riding alone and didn't come back.

"They found Prince Gallishean at the stable a couple of hours later, and they found poor Gloria at the north end of the meadow, impaled on a metal fence post.

"And no, I don't think it was an accident . . . and neither did Jordy. For all practical purposes, Mr. Graham lost his son that day, and try as he would, he was never able to win him back."

The phone rang, interrupting their conversation. Marian started to go answer it, but Alec motioned for her to remain seated as he stood and walked across the kitchen to the wall phone.

"This is the Graham residence," Alec said. "The Grahams are unable to come to the phone at the moment. May I take a message?"

"Alec?" the caller questioned in surprise. "Alec, is that you?"

"Krista?"

"Oh, Alec, it's so good to hear your voice."

Alec glanced at his watch. "Where are you? You can't be at Todd's yet."

"I'm in a phone booth just outside Madison. I called Todd to tell him I was coming, and he told me you'd called him. Is everything all right there?"

Alec hesitated before answering. "Yes, everything's okay." He knew the tone in his voice might make Krista wonder what was actually happening on the estate, and to keep her from inquiring about the situation, he countered with a question of his own. "How are things going with you?"

"Fine."

"What did you tell Marvin . . . about the baby?"

"I think I pulled it off. I told him the real reason I went to New York was to finalize our adoption. Then I told him they brought the baby to Prairie Dells tonight and called me to come get her, but I had to go in alone because you were out

336

doing something with Jordy and couldn't be reached. I told him I had to leave Thumper in the van in town because they brought me back to the cabin in their small, overpacked car, and that we were on our way back to get her when we came across him on the road."

"I had faith you'd come up with a good story," Alec said with approval. He expected Krista to thank him for his compliment, but instead, she said nothing. "What's the matter?" he asked, suspecting her silence was an indication that something was on her mind.

"I had to do something you may not agree with."

"What was that?"

"When Marvin asked me what we'd named the baby, I had to tell him something . . . I had to give her a name."

"So what was it?"

"There was only one name for a little girl I could think of on the spur of the moment."

"And what was it?"

Krista hesitated. "Julia Ann." She hesitated again before asking, "Is that all right?"

A smile tugged at the corners of Alec's lips, and he answered, "I think that name will be just fine."

Thirty

Alec and Jordy stood beneath the branches of the maple tree that kept watch over Al's favorite place in the woods. Bathed in the dappled light of morning, they looked down on two mounds of dirt. One mound was a few days old; the other mound had been there less than an hour.

Marian stood between the two graves, her head still bowed. She had just finished leading them in a prayer, asking God to accept Al's soul into His kingdom.

When she finished an additional silent prayer of her own, she stooped to lay a bouquet of wildflowers on top of Al's grave. "At last he's found peace," she said with relief. She straightened and turned to face Jordy. "He loved you, you know."

"I know," Jordy responded softly.

Marian's eyes shifted to Alec. "He loved you and Krista, too." Alec nodded, assuring her that he had known. "None of you must ever forget him. He was more than just your brother."

She turned away from them and started walking toward the cow path that led down to the pasture behind the research complex. Lewis joined her, leading the horse that had pulled the litter bearing Al's body.

"She loved him like a son," Jordy said, looking after her. "Al deserved that much out of life; he deserved for someone to love him . . . really love him." Jordy shifted in his stance to look out over the estate. "God knows he didn't get anything else he deserved—he didn't get anything else that was rightfully his."

Alec stepped up beside Jordy and looked out over the panorama before him. His eyes moved slowly, sweeping across the lake, the house, the stable, the research complex, acres of rolling pasture, and off in the distance, the dairy . . . the dairy and the destroyed project wing.

He glanced at Jordy and noticed that his attention had been drawn to the project wing as well. "Have you thought about what you're going to do?" Alec asked.

Jordy was silent for several moments; then he looked down at the mark on his hand and turned to face Alec. "Do you know what I'd like to do? Do you know what I'd *really* like to do?" Alec shook his head. "I'd like to find the other three members of the Delta series. I'd like to find our other three . . . sisters." Again, he glanced at the triangular marking on his hand, then returned his attention to Alec. "That's what I'd really like to do, but I can't. I can't chance trying to find them."

"Why not?"

"Because that might lead to the project being exposed." He turned to look back at the burned project wing and stared at it for several moments, shaking his head. "Maybe it would be best if it was exposed; maybe it would be best to put an end to Project GOD."

"Why do you say that?"

"You have your gut instinct when it comes to investigating cases, and I have an itch in the back of my mind when it comes to questioning science. Unlike you, I haven't had an opportunity to verify my itch one way or another." Alec looked at Jordy in silence, waiting for him to continue.

"Even after all these years, the project hasn't been tested and proven to be one hundred percent . . ." He hesitated, searching for the right word. ". . . one hundred percent *safe,* and that kind of bothers me." Alec still didn't comment, but his interest in Jordy's "mental itch" was beginning to intensify.

"According to the records, there were problems in the beginning, and . . . and who's to say there still might not be a

339

few problems happening today we just don't know about. I'm the only product of Project GOD who's ever been tested from infancy through adulthood."

"You're healthy, aren't you?" Alec asked, a seed of concern having been planted in his mind.

"For the most part. I've had a few allergies over the years, but—I'm the one who should be asking you the questions."

"I think your father did a pretty good job of interrogating both Krista and me last night."

"Yes, and by the answers you gave, we couldn't detect anything being wrong with either of you. You both seem to be perfectly healthy. But . . . but he couldn't ask the one question both of us were curious to know the answer to, even though we thought it might be irrelevant." Jordy looked directly into Alec's eyes. "Have you ever been tested for . . . are . . . are you sterile by any chance?"

Alec turned away, somewhat embarrassed . . . and depressed to be reminded of the fact that he was unable to father a child. Jordy immediately interpreted Alec's reaction as a positive response to his question.

"Just because we can't produce children of our own," Jordy said as he laid a hand on Alec's shoulder, "doesn't mean it was caused by something related to the project . . ."

Alec's audiographic memory tugged at him. It tried to lead him to concentrate on something he'd heard not too long ago, but Alec ignored it. He was too wrapped up listening to Jordy—he wanted desperately to believe he was normal . . . no matter what his origin had been.

". . . There are thousands—possibly even hundreds of thousands—of men across the country who are sterile, and I'm sure there are hundreds of different reasons for it. It's probably just a coincidence with us. I can think of nothing related to the project that might have caused it."

"So you think the . . . the *products* of Project GOD are really *safe*? They're . . . *we're* all right?"

"We have to be. There's no evidence to prove otherwise. For as many years as all three farms have been producing, I've never known of even one unit being returned because it was defective. That's around thirty thousand babies.

340

Everyone *has* to be all right."

Wanting desperately to believe in Jordy's reassurance, Alec forced himself to repress his fears; he also overlooked Jordy's unanswered "mental itch."

Jordy looked at Alec and smiled with satisfaction. "Thirty thousand . . . thirty thousand childless couples have been given the opportunity to know happiness. Our mother would be very proud to know that; she would be very proud to know her efforts allowed it to happen."

Thinking now of Julia Ann—thinking of the dream she'd had to provide every childless couple with a baby—Alec felt a warmth spread through him. He glanced at the distant project wing, then looked back at Jordy. "Are you going to continue? Are you going to try to make our mother's dream come true?"

"I would like to, but that really depends upon you and Krista."

"Why do you say that?"

"Because you two know about Project GOD, and you're in a position to tell the whole country about it if you decide to." Jordy looked directly into Alec's eyes. "The decision to continue with Project GOD rests with you."

As Alec returned Jordy's gaze, segments of various conversations he'd shared in the previous evening flashed across his mind:

. . . surrogate mothers . . .

. . . some of the most brilliant breakthroughs in science have been scrapped because they didn't meet with society's Puritanical attitudes and judgments . . .

. . . made a lot of people happy over the years . . .

. . . look at yourselves with that brand new baby . . .

. . . God wouldn't have let her happen if He hadn't thought it was right . . .

. . . brother . . . my brother . . .

Alec glanced down at the birthmark on his hand. "Krista and I believe in Project GOD . . . we're both a part of it." He looked at Jordy. "But we won't condone any more killing."

"There won't be any more," Jordy assured him. "I'm not like my father, and I never will be. I value life too much to

341

sacrifice it. Dr. Ford can continue to supply us with what we need, and if we have an order to fill that we can't match perfectly, we'll just make do with what we have. I promise you, Alec, no one else will ever die because of Project GOD." Alec looked deeply into Jordy's eyes and saw no lie there; he knew Jordy was a man of his word.

Alec looked out across the estate. His eyes shifted from one location to another, then finally came to rest on the primate house. The primate house, the place where it had all begun—the place where the Delta series had been conceived . . . and then born.

"I think Marian was right when she said that owing someone your life brings out the strongest sort of loyalty anyone can imagine. We all owe our lives to Project GOD," Alec said as he turned toward Jordy and extended his hand to shake in agreement, "and I can't think of any reason why it shouldn't continue. Your secret's safe with us."

Epilogue

Nine years later

Alec and Krista stood patiently in line, waiting for the gate to open. Ahead of them, six nine-year-old girls huddled in excitement, giggling and chattering like magpies.

Today was Julia Ann's birthday. Instead of requesting a party, she had asked to go to the zoo—to the St. Louis zoo—and had asked if a few of her friends could go as well. Neither Alec nor Krista had ever denied a reasonable request by their daughter, and even though the trip from Louisville to St. Louis would require a five-hour drive, they'd consented.

"Can we go see the big cats first?" Julia Ann asked as she turned and looked up at her parents. Her eyes were as large and round as sable buttons and were fringed by long, dark lashes. Her chocolate-brown hair was held back from her face in a French braid that reached to the base of her shoulder blades. Her skin had darkened in the summer sun and glowed with the health of youth. She was a pretty little girl, and someday, she would be a beautiful woman.

"We'll see, honey," Krista said, looking up from the zoo's map she'd been studying. "Remember, even though it's your birthday, you need to be considerate of what your friends want to do, too."

"Oh, please," Julia Ann said, batting her long lashes in a manner that usually led to her having her way. "You know the reason I wanted to come here was because it's the closest zoo that has white tigers." Julia Ann was an animal lover, but she especially adored cats. The walls of her room were covered with picture posters ranging from the domestic tabby to the majestic king of beasts. She also had two yellow cats, named Penny and Ring, which she'd obtained from the Humane Society. Julia Ann took the responsibility of caring for her pets, and in turn, they always slept on her bed.

Thumper had tolerated the felines' invasion into her domain a few years ago and had gradually learned to accept them. Even though her age prevented strenuous play, she now engaged in an occasional frolic with the cats and could oftentimes be found being used as their pillow. Thumper accepted the cats' companionship as compensation for the attention she'd had to share since Julia Ann had joined their family.

"You heard what your mother said," Alec stated as reinforcement. "We'll just have to wait and see."

Julia Ann's full lips puckered into a soft pout. She batted her eyelashes a few more times before turning around to rejoin her friends. Within a matter of moments, she was once again engrossed in preadolescent chatter.

As Alec watched Julia Ann, questions he'd considered hundreds of times before—questions he was sure crossed every parent's mind—surfaced. Was he too strict with her? Was he strict enough? Was he teaching her the things that would make her a happy and productive adult? Would she understand that everything he tried to do for her was in her best interest—even if she wasn't always happy with his decisions? Would she—

"Here they come to open the gate!" one of Julia Ann's friends shouted.

The words worked like a magnet. Everyone who had been waiting patiently suddenly squeezed in tightly around them. People bumped, pushed and shoved as they crowded toward the entrance. A young woman, pushing a baby stroller, rammed it into the back of Alec's legs, then maneuvered it on around him without so much as an apology.

Alec had seen similar situations before, and it always amazed him that some people were so rude and inconsiderate toward others when a few moments' wait would provide the same opportunity to all comers. What was it about the human species that prompted everyone to want to be the first out of the gate?

"Daddy."

Alec heard Julia Ann call for him. He looked around quickly, unable to locate her, then finally spotted her at the turnstile. The attendant was detaining her and her friends.

"Daddy," she called, stretching to look around the half-dozen people who had pushed their way in between them, "show him our tickets so he'll let us in."

Alec pulled out the tickets from his shirt pocket and held them up for the attendant to see. "Six of them," he said to verify that their admissions had indeed been paid. "Julia Ann, you wait for us just inside."

"We will." But when the attendant finally let them through, all six girls took off running.

"Julia—"

"Hey buddy, move along," a gruff voice snapped from behind. Alec looked over his shoulder to see an obese man in cutoff jeans and a dirty undershirt holding two small children who looked as if they'd just been playing in the mud. "My kids wanna see the seal show. It starts in ten minutes, and it's clear on the other side o' this damn place. Now shit or get off the pot. Quit holdin' up the line."

Alec's eyes opened wide, and he took in a deep breath, preparing to respond, but Krista grabbed his arm and said, "This way, Alec." He looked at her, shook his head in disgust at the man's rudeness, then followed her silently through the turnstile.

When Alec and Krista walked out into the spacious welcoming area, they immediately saw Julia Ann and her friends standing directly ahead of them. The girls were clustered in front of a large weatherized map of the zoo that had been mounted on a board in plain view of the entrance.

Julia Ann pointed to an area on the map's left side, then turned to her friends and appeared to ask a question. Two of the girls nodded enthusiastically; the other three merely shrugged their shoulders.

345

"Have you girls figured out our plan of attack?" Krista asked as she and Alec stepped up behind them.

Julia Ann turned and looked up at her parents, her face beaming with delight. "Terri and Brenda like cats almost as much as I do, and Connie, Wendy and JoAnne said they don't care where we start. So can we go see the big cats first? Please!" She turned back toward the map and pointed again toward the area indicating the cats' location. "It's not very far, and if we go this way," she said, pointing to the path to the left of the map, "all we have to do is go up to the central plaza and turn left, and we'll be there in no time."

"All right," Krista said with a laugh, "we'll head in the direction of the cat house, but I want to take the time to look at the other animals between here and there. By the looks of the map, this is a pretty big place, and I don't want to have to backtrack to see something we were in too big of a hurry to catch the first time. Is that a deal?"

"I suppose."

The group of eight began walking along the path toward the central plaza. They stopped at each viewing area to watch the animals eat, swim, play or just lie sleeping in the morning sun. Occasionally, an exhibit's information sign contained a picture of an antelope's skull on a red background and the words *Vanishing Animals*.

As they progressed from one exhibit to the next, Alec's mind wandered back through time. He hadn't thought about Jordy or Al or Hubert Graham or Project GOD in a long time; in fact, he'd made a point, several years ago, to try to block them from his mind. But now, as he walked among the animals—and especially when he saw the emblems denoting an endangered species—his mind suddenly flooded with the knowledge he and Krista held in secret.

A beading of nervous perspiration developed along his upper lip. A feeling, deep in the pit of his stomach, began to gnaw at him.

He looked at Krista, and then at Julia Ann. They were both happy and healthy—all three of them were happy and healthy. They were a close and loving family, and what difference could it make how they'd been conceived and

346

born? Nothing was wrong with any of them. Nothing was wrong! So why was his gut instinct trying to tell him otherwise?

"Alec."

Alec had been walking with the group, but since his thoughts had drifted elsewhere, he hadn't been paying attention to their location. He didn't know they had come to the central plaza and that they'd turned onto the main path that led straight to the cat house. He wasn't aware that the rest of the group had stopped at the entrance of a building while he had continued to walk on.

"Alec?" Krista called again.

"What?" he answered, startled. When Alec finally found the presence of mind to stop walking, he had to turn completely around in order to look at her.

"Aren't you going in here with us?"

Alec looked from Krista to the large sign at the right of the building's entrance: *Ape House.* Written beneath the bold print was a list of the various animals that could be found within: chimps, orangutans, gorillas . . . gorillas. . . .

"You . . . you go ahead. I'll wait out here."

"Suit yourself."

Alec's eyes remained fixed on the sign. Had he not been thinking of Al just a few moments before, he would have probably gone into the building. But he *had* been thinking of Al, and his present state of mind wouldn't allow him to go stare at a creature, imprisoned behind bars, that would have reminded him of someone he had once loved—

"Daddy!" Julia Ann ran toward him, her face beaming as happily as if she'd just received her most cherished birthday wish. "The Ape House is closed for remodeling, and it was the last stop we had to make on the way to see the cats. Come on. I can't wait any longer!" She grabbed Alec's hand and began tugging for him to walk with her.

"I guess that's that," Krista said as she and the girls walked up to join them. "Lead the way."

Julia Ann indeed led the way. She walked quickly . . . skipped . . . almost ran along the path ahead of them. Everyone had to quicken her pace in order to even attempt to

347

keep up. Alec walked briskly beside her, laughing, happy his thoughts had been channeled toward a more pleasant subject.

As they rounded a gentle curve in the path, Julia Ann stopped abruptly. Directly ahead of her was one of the side entrances to the cat house; sitting in a spacious cage beside the entrance was a magnificent full-grown white tiger.

"Isn't he beautiful!" she gasped. Julia Ann released Alec's hand and began walking slowly toward the cage, her eyes never wavering from the animal she had come to see.

"I guess this makes her birthday complete," Krista said as she stepped up beside Alec. "We might as well have a look around and then find somewhere to sit down. I have a feeling we're going to be here quite a while."

After touring the cages inside the cat house and walking completely around the building to see the animals that were outside, Alec and Krista sat down on a bench near the main entrance to wait for Julia Ann and her friends. It was a beautiful midsummer day. The sky was a brilliant blue; cottony white clouds drifted lazily overhead, and a gentle westerly breeze coaxed the leaves into subtle dances. The crowd that had jammed in through the main entrance had dispersed, spreading throughout the zoo until there no longer seemed to be a crowd at all. Everything was peaceful, calm, and serene.

"Excuse me, sir."

Alec squinted against the sun as he looked up at a man who had stopped beside their bench. The man looked to be in his mid-60s, and since he wore a safari hat, shirt and shorts, Alec assumed he was one of the zoo's volunteer hosts.

"I don't mean to bother you," the man said, "but I noticed you in the cat house and thought you looked familiar. By any chance, do you happen to be that special reporter from that TV station in Louisville?"

"I'm Alec Crispen," Alec answered with a smile, "and I do work at WBDC in Louisville." He'd grown accustomed to being recognized by people on the street, but he was a little surprised to be recognized by someone so far away from home.

"I thought so. I'd like to shake your hand." Alec stood in order to accommodate the man's request. "I'm Verne Samuelson. You helped my sister out a few months back when she got taken by some phony financial advisor. Her name's Dianne Webb."

"Yes, I remember."

"I sure would like to thank you personally for what you did for her. That conniving rascal talked her out of almost all her life's savings, and you were able to get at least part of it back for her."

"I was just doing my job," Alec commented modestly.

"Job nothing. I'd call you a real humanitarian—" The beeper on the man's belt sounded. "Excuse me a minute." He walked to a phone box, hidden in a mock tree trunk, and dialed a three-digit number. As he listened to the person he'd called, a broad smile spread across his face. After returning the phone and closing the box's door, he rejoined Alec. "Well, I'll be darned. I've been a volunteer here for over three years and it finally looks like I'm going to have a chance to see something being born." He paused for a moment, and then asked, "Would you folks be interested in coming along? It's Sinna, our white tiger female, and it's her first litter."

"Our little girl would love to see it," Krista said as she stood.

"Don't you think she's a little young for that?" Alec asked.

"At her age, she already knows more about sex than I did when I was in high school," Krista informed him. "But there're more than just our daughter," she said, looking at Verne Samuelson. "Today's Julia Ann's birthday, and she brought five of her friends with us."

"That shouldn't be any problem," he assured her. "The observation room is fairly big, and I can't think of a better birthday present than being able to see a new life come into the world."

Alec, Krista and the girls squeezed into the corner of the observation room. The birth appeared to be a major event for the zoo personnel; nearly forty people were jam-packed into the room, vying for a spot at the observation window that overlooked the spacious cage confining the female white tiger.

In spite of the eagerness consuming everyone, three of the zoo's hostesses stepped back from the window to allow the girls to squeeze in in front of them. This would be a day Julia Ann would remember for the rest of her life.

Everyone watched as the large female paced back and forth across her cage. Occasionally, she would stop and turn her head as if to sniff at her belly that hung low and heavy; then she'd continue to pace back and forth . . . back and forth. Her time was near, and she knew it—everyone watching knew it; that was why they were there.

"Isn't this exciting?" Krista whispered. "Imagine being able to watch tiger cubs being born. Brand new tiger cubs that . . ."

. . . brand new tiger cubs . . . Alec didn't hear the rest of Krista's sentence; his thoughts were focused on the four words he knew he'd heard in the same sequence before. *. . . brand new tiger cubs . . . brand new—*

Marian! Marian had used those exact words nine years ago when she had spoken of Julia Ann—when she had spoken of . . . Alec's mother.

But why had the words' sequence come back to haunt him now? What was it that was unleashing all those memories he'd tried so hard to repress? And why had his gut instinct been gnawing at him so furiously—as furiously as it had attacked him nine years ago—

"Alec!" Krista grabbed his arm in excitement. "They're coming!"

The tiger had lain down in the corner of her cage. She was stretching, rolling, her muscles rippling. Coming to rest on her side, she craned her massive head toward her hindquarters, all of her attention directed toward her own birth canal.

Alec's attention remained elsewhere.

. . . brand new tiger cubs . . .

. . . the procedures Miss Julia and Mr. Graham's friend developed . . .

350

An agonized roar filled the observation room.

There was a major flaw with Schmidt's animals. The males were sterile and about half the females produced deformed offspring. The words Todd had spoken nine years ago emerged from Alec's memory as clearly as if they'd just been uttered.

Someone screamed. Someone gagged. Someone pushed his way through the crowd toward the door. Two of Julia Ann's friends began to cry.

"Alec, we've got to get the girls out of here!"

. . . we still use the same formulas my mother and Dr. Schmidt developed years ago . . . Jordy's ominous revelation came to Alec's mind as well. *. . . the formulas are exactly the same . . .*

"Alec!" Krista screamed. "Help me get the girls out of here!"

Ignoring her pleas, Alec turned his head slowly toward the observation window. His eyes settled on the grossly deformed cub that lay by the tiger's side.

. . . the formulas are exactly the same . . .

. . . why, just look at yourselves there with that brand new baby girl of yours . . .

. . . brand new baby girl . . .

Alec's gaze shifted from the deformed cub to the uncomprehending expression on Julia Ann's face that was reflected in the observation window.

. . . the formulas are exactly the same . . .

. . . brand new baby girl . . .

. . . females produced deformed offspring . . .

Alec's gut instinct ripped deep into his core.

"No!" he shouted. "No!" he screamed.

Alec leaned back against the wall and closed his eyes in despair. His head began to spin; all color drained from his face. His legs buckled beneath him, and he slid down the wall to sit on the floor.

He'd known about it all along; he'd known there had been a flaw in Schmidt's formula, but until that very moment, he hadn't made the connection—even though he should have. That day on the hill—the day he helped Jordy bury Al—

Jordy had expressed his own concern about the safety of project GOD. But Alec hadn't let Jordy's doubts enter his mind; Alec had been more concerned about hearing that he and Krista were indeed all right. He hadn't *let* himself—he wouldn't even consider the possibility that something *could* be wrong.

But something *had* been wrong. Something was *still* wrong—terribly wrong. And it had been wrong for over forty years. Forty years . . .

"Daddy? Daddy, are you all right?" Alec opened his eyes slowly and tried to focus on Julia Ann's face, but it was distorted in a blur. "Daddy—"

Alec grabbed her and pulled her close to him. "I'm sorry," he whispered coarsely. "Oh, God, I'm sorry."

God . . . Project GOD . . . An idea that had been conceived out of hope and love had been tarnished by horror.

How many deformed babies could have been born over the years? How many deformed babies could yet be born in the future to infant girls who might have been adopted as recently as today?

Nine years ago, Jordy had boasted of having produced around 30,000 babies. With updated technology and automation, that number could have easily doubled. And how many of them would have been female? Alec guessed that at least half the number would have been girls.

And what of his own little Julia Ann? What did the future hold in store for her . . . and for Alec's grandchildren? Would they be safe from the horrors of Project GOD . . . or would they be branded by the flaw in Edgar Schmidt's formula?

Alec closed his eyes tightly to hold back his tears of fear. He whispered a short prayer for every child of Project GOD, and for an instant—for the first time in his life—he wished there had never been any children of *GOD*.